Meg stopped and watched her dog. "It's a person out there, that's what you're telling me, Erda." She hesitated while she decided what to do then opened the heavy door carefully, letting the dog out ahead of her. Once she slipped outside herself, she stood close to the door, feeling its solidness at her back and the reassurance of the slab of stone under her bare feet. The two of them waited, the woman and the dog both searching the road.

The man walking up the road was caught in the giant sweep of colors from the sunset. In fact, he looked like he had walked straight out of it: walking, stopping, turning around and looking back at the sky, then turning and walking a littlc ncarcr, then turning around again and standing looking back at the sky. As the man made his way toward her, Meg watched him quietly, with her hand on the dog's neck, and her whole body gripped in that prophetic anticipation again. When she saw his face, she knew.

She said, "How did you find me?"

First Edition
Published by Blue Raven Press, January 2010
ISBN 978-0-615-34360-0

Illustrations by Trudi Carleton Peek
Author's Photograph by Lisa Kirkemo
Cover & Book Design by LLPrindle Design

Printed in the United States of America

BLUE RAVEN PRESS
P.O. Box 882
Port Orchard, WA 98366
USA

Publisher's Note: This is a work of fiction. Names, characters, places and incidents either are the product of the author's imagination or are used fictitiously, and any resemblance to actual persons, living or dead, business establishments, events, or locales is entirely coincidental.

TOUCHING EARTH TOUCHING SKY

TRUDI CARLETON PEEK

ACKNOWLEDGEMENTS

My parents, Linus and Cecile Carleton, in their love for each other and where they lived, showed me the land called Montana, walked me over it, pointed out its beauty, taught me its history, sang around its campfires, cooked its bounty, fed me its tastes, and advised me—by their example—how to honor it.

And the land of Montana…ah, the land itself… Its breezes whispered to me, its winds bent me, its coulees offered me flowers, its clouds pelted my face with raindrops and snowflakes, and its vistas lifted my spirits. And inside its blue mountains, lying so splendid under its cobalt sky, it showed me its secret springs, its slim minks, its heavy bears, its questioning deer, its creeks that smell of fish and mint… And the sky itself… One can touch the sky in Montana.

Kristi and Larry Roy—who are my models for successful country living—encouraged me with their interest and support, as did Kay and Lee Drew and my parents. Gennie Nord, teacher, believed from the first that this was a story worth telling. Janet Trefts offered her invaluable counsel through the book's many phases. Lynn Lever, Barbara Weingard, Rich Nelson, and the Gordon Webbs read it and said, "Yes!" Laurie Prindle designed it, Rosemary Carstens edited it, and the Maureen and Mike Mansfield library, on the campus of the University of Montana, offered me its endless resources. To all of you I say thank you.

To Kristi and Kay,
Mom and Dad

...That which is boundless in you, abides in the mansion of the sky, whose door is the morning mist, and whose windows are the songs and the silence of night...

– KAHLIL GIBRAN

Part One

1

MEG

Meg Halverson would remember that she hesitated before leaving. In those few cautious seconds before she opened the door she knew that leaving would change everything. She analyzed the sounds behind her—rather, the lack of them, the deadly quiet. The women would be half-smiling, half-looking at each other as they waited for the sound of the door closing and her footsteps running down the porch steps. Once they caught their collective breaths someone would break the silence. It would be Evelyn Stone's breathy, little-girl voice that would say, "Meg was always marginal—just a farm girl who got in because she married Ed."

Meg shook her head. Those women didn't matter, because the real war was between her and Ed. But to be the cause of his disappointment—she didn't want that. She honestly wanted to help him.

Well, hang the consequences, she thought. Hang them all! I've already left! She closed the heavy ornate door firmly behind her and walked, head high, across the veranda and down the broad steps. At the landing she said an encouraging "yes" to herself and kept repeating it as she worked her way around the cars parked in the long driveway. Jill Handley's green Jaguar, the car that had brought her, elicited another "yes," even as it reminded her that she would now have to walk home. There was no one she could call to pick her up, or would call. She flinched at the prospect of three miles, possibly four, in these new, medium-heeled pumps and her suit skirt. But she'd do it if for no other reason than it would give her time to think up her reason for leaving—if not the real reason, then something pretty darn close to it.

By the time Ed came home for dinner he'd know, because one of the women would have phoned him about it.

. . .

As she widened her pace to test the walking limit of her skirt, she felt an ominous give to some threads near its hem. But she only said "yes" a little louder. Her skirt and shoes didn't matter, but getting away with her dignity did. For the benefit of those women undoubtedly watching her from the window, she slowed to appear nonchalant. Stopping at the sidewalk she looked leisurely to her left up Halverson Avenue—named for her husband's family—and let her eyes linger on the imposing red brick house in the next block up, the "Halverson House" of Ed's childhood, and of her bridehood (that's how she referred to the eleven years she'd lived there too).

The Halverson House: tall windows, cold rooms, ancient plumbing, an impossible kitchen, and all those Halverson ghosts she couldn't argue with. She'd loved its huge circular driveway though, as had Kurt and Sara—their baby legs powering their tricycles around and around it, safe from the university traffic passing the house. Yet, even with those happy memories of her children, it was the wrong day to be reminded of that historic monstrosity and be forced to give credence to the ghosts that still directed her every step. Undoubtedly those ghosts had been at the meeting just now, as appalled at the manner of her leave-taking as the women were.

Shrugging off thinking about it, she looked beyond the house to where the street ended and the University Campus began. The clock in Central Hall's steeple, which appeared to float upon a sea of pale-green maple trees, had just chimed a single tone to mark the half hour. She could just make out its white face and ornate black hands: 3:30 P.M. She checked her watch. If she kept an even pace she'd get home in time to put the potatoes in to bake. Resisting a final glance behind her, she turned right onto the sidewalk following Halverson Avenue, and began the long walk west through town to her home.

She had a determined walk, taking long strides and moving like a woman who enjoyed her body and was proud of its fitness and energy.

She hadn't always felt this way. When she was in middle school, a wild spurt of growth left her a full six inches taller than both her mother and Tolly, her only, eight-years-older sister. Hoping she could reverse the process she began slumping forward. Once her mother understood what she was doing, she'd commanded her to "Stand up, throw back those shoulders, and enjoy your height!" Now, in her thirty-eighth year, Meg still thought herself overly tall at five feet ten inches, but she always presented herself proudly.

Whether others considered her attractive or not, she didn't know. Whenever Ed made any comment about how she looked, saying, "Yes, that's nice," he was referring to what she wore, concerned that her clothes were up to the current fashion and looked expensive enough (which, of course, they did). It would be nice to hear him comment on her face and the care she took of herself; but if he noticed that at all, giving her compliments wasn't his style. Privately, she liked her face, proud that she resembled her Irish mother, who'd also had dark wavy hair and fair skin with a few freckles here and there. She thought her mouth was a bit too big, but it smiled easily. Her eyes, large and grey, were her best feature. Her three children teased her about giving them "the big look" (their term for it); but that look still brought them to a standstill when their behavior needed restraining.

The length of her hair was a problem between her and Ed: she wanted it short so it would curl on its own, but he demanded that it remain midway down her back in length. With all his demands that she look the very model of fashion, she thought he was inconsistent in refusing to allow her to cut it. But, with no choice in that, she caught it back with a silver clip in front, and twisted and pinned it in back in as elegant a knot as she could manage. Around home and in the garden she wore it in a single braid and tried not to wish it was conveniently shoulder length.

On the few occasions when she really studied her reflection, she saw strength in her face, an underlying softness around her eyes, and a willingness to get along. She hoped that was what others saw in her too, but she wasn't sure. Today she had shown another side of herself: a frustrated and angry person at the absolute end of her patience.

Before today she'd kept all that in check.

Aware that her face still wore its "I am Mrs. Edward Halverson" mask—which pulled her features into horizontal layers of calmness, objected to nothing, and was so easy to hide behind—she decided to wear it a little longer, at least until she got away from the part of town where she might be recognized. Anyone who knew her might think she was just taking a lovely afternoon stroll through this old, still-elegant part of town. Or perhaps they'd think she was on her way to another meeting. She began to sing to herself softly and deliberately off key, in rhythm to her steps: "...luncheons, meetings, parties, teas, luncheons, meetings, parties, teas...." When she tried to find some kind of meter in the words "committees and organizations" she began to giggle and got quite out of step. She caught herself just in time when she saw two young women walking toward her. Even though she didn't know them, she assumed a grave, dignified expression and nodded as she passed. Mrs. Edward Halverson must never, never be observed as...as what? Most certainly not as *herself*. Who in this name-dropping part of town knew *that* Meg Halverson? Who indeed? And that included her husband and, perhaps, even herself.

Looking around, she was grateful she wouldn't have to *pretend* to enjoy this beautiful early May afternoon, at least what was left of it. There were too few spring days in this part of Montana. Between winter loosening its grip and summer's abrupt arrival, spring days like this were already numbered.

As unsettled as she was, walking through this splendid part of town and along this lovely old university street calmed her. It never seemed to change. How many times had she walked here—as a student, as a bride, as a young mother? On her first walk here it had been late summer; she was fresh from the farm and twenty-one years old (old for a new student). The trees were what impressed her. She'd never seen large maple trees before, and couldn't believe the grace and beauty of their branches meeting and arching above the whole street. And under the trees were the enormous Victorian houses—looking like so many overly fat Easter hats—sitting so smug and comfy amid their manicured lawns and broad sidewalks and boulevards. And today, just as before, their antique look was enhanced by a lacework of tiny shadows cast by the sunlight through the tree leaves above them. She held out her fingers to let the bits of sun land on them, too. As though the sunlight had weight and substance, she wanted to scoop it up and pour it over her, in the hope that it might make her feel all right again.

Halverson Avenue. Old lumber money—Halverson money—had built this street. In spite of the expectations the Halverson ghosts placed on her, she never discounted the importance—to the town and to this part of the state—of that historic name. As she walked along, she tried to imagine what Ed had felt growing up in a house and on a street named for his predecessors. Now, as a man, in the telling ways he often acted, his Halverson name seemed more like a burden to him, with those Halverson ghosts having assigned him the task of keeping their past relevant.

A person's legacy was something she could understand, for she had her own. Her roots were sunk deep in a humble central Montana wheat farm, far from here. Despite the eighteen years since she'd lived there, she was still connected to the land surrounding it and to the ideals of her long-dead parents who had cared for it.

Their life had been a simple one, directed by the weather gods and the price of wheat, and it was in their home and family where their comfort and safety lay. How many times had she heard Papa say, "Things will turn out right if you aren't afraid of hard work, if you take care of your land, and be respectful to all creatures." He might have been talking about things that pertained to the farm, but his words spoke of personal responsibility, and she had used them as rules to live by.

Meg had come to the University primed for the rest of her life. Her goal seemed simple enough: after acquiring a vocation (whatever that would be), she'd meet a good man, get married, raise a nice family, and "things would turn out right"—wasn't that what Papa said?

Being three years older than the other freshmen girls had given her no advantage; in fact, she felt far behind them socially—they appeared to know exactly what they wanted and how to get it. She'd been so eager for her adult life to begin, but the most enduring lesson she'd gained from her short stay on campus was that poor choices often came in attractive wrappings. Now, walking along this beautiful old street, she wondered, as she had wondered so many times before, how she could have quit school and agreed to marry Edward Halverson.

Her face clouded as she thought about that. On this mutinous day, instead of *her* trying to gucss thc answers to those questions, she wished Ed were here to answer for himself. She slowed her pace and spoke the troublesome words into the air. "Why, with your opportunities, did you ever, ever choose me to be your wife? Was it because I was so obviously naïve? Was finding me akin to finding a slate with nothing yet written upon it? After your flattery was over and the seduction made, after you plucked me from this campus and installed me in your bed, why did our marriage seem more like an ending than a beginning? Why do I always feel alone, Ed?"

In silence, she walked on.

Once the University District was behind her, her attention turned to the less grand part of town she was now passing through. Here the trees were not so imposing, the houses were small and close together, garages opened onto the narrow streets, children and dogs tumbled in play, and mothers like herself basked on porch steps or lawn chairs, reading or talking or laughing at their kids. The beginning smells of dinner drifted on the air—roasting beef, onions, fresh coffee, cookies fresh from the oven. Glancing now and then at the women, she sighed with envy at the simplicity of their lives—so far from the complications of her own. The word "complications" hardly described her predicament. The women in the grand house behind her must even now be clucking like hens over her departure and deciding her fate.

There were fewer than seventy thousand people in Clark Fork, but she supposed it to be as socially stratified as any mid-sized Montana town. Without her being aware of it—or wanting it—her marriage to Edward Halverson had separated her from people like herself, even as it took her from being "an outsider" to being at the very center of the highest social level of the town, where everyone seemed to be connected to each other through business or their history. People at that social level made a grand display of being friendly to outsiders; but unless there was a good reason for an outsider to be asked to join in, that person remained an outsider.

Ed had just become a partner in Art Stroud's bank when he introduced her, his bride, to his social group. The women were mainly wives of Ed and Art's downtown cronies, the movers and shakers of the business community who had known Ed all his life. Being a Halverson, and being handsome and charming too, Ed had long since been awarded "favorite son" status by that group. Of course, she went along with it.

From the start she found most of the women superficial. Their main concerns were protecting their precious dynasties from all those "outsiders" they deemed eager to gain a foothold into their world. Even though they were nice enough to her, Meg felt like a curiosity—Ed having married an outsider and a farm girl to boot. When she first expressed her anxiety over this, Ed advised her to keep quiet about her background and listen and learn about the other women instead. She felt like an orphan doing this: never talking about her parents and the beloved life they had created for her and her sister.

She and Ed entertained these people, but they never seemed like friends—at least as Meg understood the word. When Meg asked about this, Ed said he didn't need personal friends. Meg kept in contact with some of her college friends, but Ed wasn't interested in including any of them at their parties, so, other than exchanging cards at Christmas, they drifted away.

All events concerning their present neighborhood and the kids' school fell to Meg, so any social contacts she made there went nowhere. Her only real friends now were Marc and Doris Webster—a sixtyish couple living in her present neighborhood. Ed viewed the Websters as nothing more than dependable folks who looked after his children when he and his wife were otherwise engaged; but Meg and the children loved them, and the feeling was returned. When she was with the Websters, who had no part whatsoever in the social group she and Ed were caught up in, Meg was free to express herself as she really was, rather than as others expected her to be.

Over the eighteen years of her marriage, however tightly she clung to the hope that she was not nor ever could be like those other women, the social page of the town's only newspaper told her otherwise. Whenever it lovingly recorded the Edward Halversons' most insignificant comings and goings (which was often), describing in detail the clothes she'd worn to such and such an event, Ed read it aloud to her as though it were his reward. If it were up to her, she'd like to complain to the newspaper that the wrong news was being published; that (as happened today) it should publish the cruel comments the women had bandied around, along with the names of who said what about whom. And tomorrow, if the paper *were* to report that Mrs. Edward Halverson left the meeting early (which it wouldn't, but if it did) it should be honest enough to print that she left in a huff after having told everyone, in exquisite detail, exactly what she felt, and that she had slammed the door on her way out.

As she thought back to those moments, self-doubt crept into her mind. If only she hadn't left like that. In those few precious seconds when she'd hesitated at the door, if only she could have treated it like a joke and rejoined the women. Surely she could have thought up some kind of excuse. But, no, like a freight train without brakes, she couldn't stop herself. However trifling this might appear, something important had happened that was going to hurt her very much—that much she knew. She had openly scorned the very people she was expected to get along with, over nothing more serious than their petty gossip; then she'd left with no explanation or apology. It had caught them all off guard, but her even more. She hadn't planned it—nothing like that—it had just happened.

Wanting to leave that group was nothing new to her; she had wanted to do it a hundred times before, just leave them, call out, "That's enough! This is stupid. Don't think I'm part of this!" How she'd managed to hold her tongue all these years she couldn't say. Well, yes, she could; she'd done it because Ed expected her to do it. But why blow up today?

Her day had started poorly. Ed had been so distant at breakfast—more distant than usual. When she'd told him what Kurt's teacher had said about Kurt's excellent math skills, Ed hadn't reacted in the slightest—and Kurt was sitting just across the table from him, his face eager for his dad's praise. She hadn't told Ed that the teacher had pointedly asked why Ed never attended such important conferences, or that his excuse of having to work every evening wasn't cutting it anymore with *any* of the kids' teachers.

After breakfast Ed had left the house without saying goodbye. She was busy making the kid's lunches and hadn't heard the front door closing. In fact, the only way she'd known he'd left was when she heard the garage door close—and even that was softer than usual. She'd wondered briefly if he'd deliberately muffled its usual bang so he could escape without notice.

As for today's meeting, she had intended (for once) to play hooky and stay home and work in her garden. But Jill Handley had already offered to pick her up so they could talk about the party they were co-hosting later in the month.

Now, having compounded that poor start to her day, she was faced with explaining her actions to Ed. She simply had to make him understand that she could no longer sit in stuffy houses full of even stuffier women with their swirl of perfume—each scent canceling out the others until all that was left was something metallic-smelling.

Earlier, it was that metallic smell she was reacting to when the lace curtain near her had made that tiniest beckoning curl, and the tiniest whiff of fresh spring air had managed to locate her nose. As much as she might wish to use that image in her defense to Ed, she knew it wouldn't work. Tonight, after dinner (or worse, during it, with the children listening), Ed would tell her what he'd heard about her leaving early. She wondered which lecture she would hear: the one about "The Givers and The Takers" or the one titled "You Don't Seem To Understand My Job, Meg"—she'd heard them often enough, in all their variations.

Early in their marriage she'd challenged him on how she spent her time. They'd been living in the Halverson House for two years by then and were still trying to get pregnant. (There'd been an earlier miscarriage, but it was a full five years before Kurt was conceived.)

That day she'd told Ed she felt at loose ends, that, with the housekeeper and gardener to help with the place, she'd decided to return to the university and finish the degree she'd only begun before their marriage. To her everlasting regret, she'd also told him that although she'd tried, she didn't have much in common with the women of their social set, and felt the endless entertaining was a meaningless waste of time.

She was hardly prepared for the intensity of his "Givers and Takers" speech, intoning it as if talking to someone less than bright, someone who, having come from a different social level, wouldn't naturally know what he was talking about. As he went on and on, she'd stood looking at the floor, humiliated, and willing herself not to cry.

The Halversons (she was to learn) had long since attained the "Giver" status; and the town was their grateful heir. In the next day's mail she'd received a typed list (on Ed's official bank stationery, no less) of all the things their name would be connected with and the events she or he or they together would sponsor. To make sure she had no choice in the matter, next to his signature he'd hand-inked, "Business being business and our security being our security, Meg, Art and I are confident that you'll want to do your part."

All that mattered was that a Halverson be seen out front, be listed first, and be the first to volunteer. It was only about business and money—getting it and keeping it. It didn't matter that anything beneficial was accomplished. It was just meaningless talk, showing off something, dressing up to be admired, trying to outdo each other. And that applied to today's party: the real reason for it was that the hostess, Cora Lee, wanted to show off the antique loveseat she'd just had recovered in blue Italian velvet. A perfect waste of a day!

Meg heaved a discouraged sigh. Despite all her attempts at justification, she longed for Ed's appreciation and counted a day as good when he smiled at her in gratitude over any tiny thing. Thinking that, her eyes filled and she pushed at the tears with her fingers. What words could she use to make him understand that what he wanted her to be was no longer bearable?

She looked at her watch and shook her head; she was still a long way from her house.

2

AN EARLIER TIME

As Meg continued walking her grumbling stomach reminded her that she'd missed lunch all together. At Cora Lee's, right after the business meeting, Meg had looked at the table wistfully, wishing for *real* food, even though she knew that such afternoon spreads were more decoration than nutrition. In spite of her hunger, Meg chuckled remembering the difficulty she'd had juggling a napkin, a spoon, and a precious porcelain plate, on which were two half-dollar-sized sandwiches, a diminutive pink cookie, and a thin violet-colored teacup. Despite her years of practice she'd always had trouble managing such things. And was that coffee or tea in the cup? As she'd peered at the pale liquid, then tasted it, an ancient picture of her mother pouring steaming coffee and real cream into the farm's massive crockery mugs camc to mind. Ma said that a cup should bc a comfort to thc hands and its aroma should make folks lower their noses to it in anticipation of its contents. Such pictures of her mother's sturdy figure and face still brought Meg pain, reminding her of Ma's early death. She wondered what Ma would think about the way she'd left the meeting today. Would she have applauded her courage for having finally left, or shaken an admonishing finger at her? It was a moot point, but she yearned for her mother's advice, on more occasions than this one.

She turned her attention to the beauty around her. In this newer part of town the mountains encircling the valley were clearly visible. The higher peaks, still white, stood aloof behind the many layers of lower mountains. Their colors went from a dark bluish-green in the foreground to the palest blue layer in the distance, and all were patterned with snow. The grassy foothills on the town's edges showed the greatest effects of the warming season. Last week they had been a drab, dormant tan, but today their soft green assured her that the long winter was truly over.

Each season laid its own brand of beauty on this high Western Montana country. When winter cast its brooding light over the frosted mountains, tingeing their edges with pink, she declared that winter was the prettiest. But with spring bestowing its hope on every blade and leaf and promising quiet days in her garden, she declared spring her favorite. Yet how could she not choose summer, with its distant slanting storms and cloudbanks removing whole mountain ranges in one swipe, then, with mist still clinging to their tops and hiding their feet, slowly giving them back? She guessed she'd have to love them equally.

The flat country of her birth had a different beauty, with its huge cobalt sky vaulting above the strips and squares of grain fields running to the horizon. But however beautiful that land was, she could never separate it from its affect on the people who farmed it. Her parents had spent their lives hoping that abundance would come from all those beautiful green fields, that enough rain would fall (but not too much and not at the wrong time), and that the labor they put into their crops would somehow be commensurate with the price they'd be paid for its grain. But what they learned was that hope was only hope and never a promise. With no irrigation, a dry-land farmer had to depend on the grace of the weather gods, and they were fickle.

When conjuring up the picture of her long-gone parents, they stood in bas-relief before giant fields of greening wheat flowing past their sheds, barn, and windmill, and on over the hill. And, like all dry-land wheat farmers, their faces were scarred with their disappointments. And now it was her sister Tolly, with husband Charlie, who she worried about, as they scratched their living out of that very same farm.

Eighteen years ago she'd decided that dry-land wheat farming was for the brave, and that it was cowards like her who left it and moved to the safer ground of the mountains—at her very first glimpse of this mountain country she'd determined that.

She'd been banished from the farm by her parents (that's the way she laughingly told it). But, really, it had been a tradeoff. Her parents had decided that she needed more options—options meaning something other than Tommy Southers. Her parents delivered her sentence (her banishment) in the kitchen just after breakfast one morning. Papa had put off doing chores and her mother was standing beside him, worried and chewing on her lip. Once Meg had taken in the scene she knew it was important and suspected it was about her and Tommy. She had managed to suppress her ire and stayed to listen.

Before Papa spoke he picked up her hand, stroking it with his thumbs and examining it gravely, as though he could divine its destiny from its bones and skin. His thick hands had felt strange around hers, but good, too, in the rareness of their touch. Those clever hands of his held the entire farm together—the animals, the buildings, the equipment, and the people. And now, in his fifties, they were as scuffed as old shoes and were no longer able to appear clean. In the odd intimacy of the moment she'd noticed, almost for the first time, the harsh imprint of farming upon his face—his eyes, a crackling blue, set deep in their protective caverns, and his skin, mahogany colored between the stark white of his hat-shielded forehead and his shirt-covered neck. But however climate-marked his face was, it was a dear, dear face, as was Ma's. It was in that instant that Meg fully imagined how Tommy's careless beauty would be erased by the discipline farming demanded, and how it would erase her youth and beauty as well.

Papa, having finally decided what he would say, had loosened his hold on her hand and given it one of his familiar pats before carefully returning it to her side, as one lays down something cherished. He said, "Meggie, when your Ma and I met, it didn't take but a few weeks before we both knew there was a good reason for us to be together. We wanted to farm together and live together." He looped his arm around her mother's shoulder and tugged her closer. "It's been my pride that that's never changed. And it appears that your sister Tolly has found the same thing. I'm proud to call her Charlie my son-in-law. He's a good man. But I'm proudest that he knew a good woman when he found our Tolly. Now with their baby Johnny, and their being nearby and willing to help us, your Ma and I are happy they're here."

He had shifted uncomfortably, looking at Ma for backup before he continued. "Now we don't want to interfere, Meggie, but about the Southers boy... He's young, but you know yourself that there's more to farming than roaring around in a truck all hours. More important, we see him putting off deciding about you. What's worse is we see what his indecision is doing to you. There's a question on your face, like you're thinking there's something wrong with *you*. Well, your mother and I think the fault lies in him. Before you decide if he's worth spending your time waiting for, we want you to leave here for a while, see new country. But not just anywhere, we want you to go to the University in Clark Fork. All we ask is that you *try* it for two semesters. Just try it. Then, if Tommy decides to grow up...or not...well, neither of us will interfere after that."

She'd felt it her right to wail in protest, but Papa's next words calmed her. He said, "Meggie, I predict that you, of all people, will end up wanting more from life than Tommy Southers' procrastination."

It was prophetic. Tommy was sorry enough to see her leave and made all kinds of plans to come and visit her when he could get away, but the fact was he didn't even see her off. As the train took her away she was still caught up in her emotions at having said goodbye to her parents and at leaving all her treasured life on the farm behind her, even for a year. For a long time, she'd watched herself crying in the reflection of the train window—her puffy eyes and screwed-up face getting all mixed up with the rush of empty country outside the glass.

Eventually she began noticing the country she was traveling through. Her tears were replaced by wonder, then a prickling down her neck. By the time the flat land changed into the steep grade of a mountain pass, dipped into a cliff-edged valley, and skimmed alongside a wild, tumbling river, she had very simply fallen in love with Western Montana. When the train left her and her little pile of possessions in Clark Fork, and she stood looking around her, she would have told anyone who'd listen, "I've been here before," even though she'd never seen the place.

. . .

Still in the grip of that memory, Meg paused for a moment on the sidewalk, then made her way to a nearby rock retaining wall that was low enough to sit down on and rest her feet. She was removing her shoes when an older woman—obviously the rock wall's owner—came over and asked if she was all right. Meg laughingly held up her feet and waggled her toes. She said, "I've had to walk farther in these darned shoes than I intended to. Is it okay if I rest here a bit?" The woman gave her a pleasant, "Of course!" Meg swept her hand admiringly to the scene in front of them, saying, "You have a stunning view of the mountains." The woman agreed and they talked a few moments more before the woman returned to her house.

As Meg rubbed her feet she looked at the mountains and imagined herself surveying all the land around her from the very top of the highest peak. She knew that this Western land was old, but not old in the Southern or Eastern sense, where time and gravity had smoothed it and men had combed and tidied it with their plows for three hundred years. The land here was still a jagged original. From up there, she would see that the lower blue mountains were not blue at all, but were endless seas of green trees that extended for hundreds of miles in any direction. She'd see that that ocean of green was punctured with valleys—like this valley holding the town of Clark Fork. And she'd see lakes and the trailing of rivers and creeks and occasional clearings, and a myriad of logging roads going up and down and around—leading nowhere, leading somewhere.

Up there, if she were viewing this huge valley, the town of Clark Fork would appear as a cluster of buildings huddled against the valley's eastern and gentlest side, as if to escape the dangerous geology to its west. Cutting through the town would be the river, with its four bridges. The pioneers who possessed the river for its commerce, had named their town after it; and even though they loved the river for its beauty, they'd positioned their buildings so as to hang over its pristine waters, turning it into an ever-moving cesspool. That practice was changed with the amenities of a modern sewage plant, and the river's water was cleaner, but it was still far from what it had been in the millennia before. She supposed that its riverbanks now had more grace than in the town's beginning, having been shaped and smoothed into parks to walk in, furnished with tiny shops for browsing and the ever-present espresso bars. After all, wasn't that what progress was all about?

She tried to imagine what this valley had looked like a thousand years ago and wished she'd been there when the earliest Indians had first entered the valley and seen the beautiful river winding through it. In the practical part of her mind she could justify man's adapting something so it could be made useful, but, in another part of her mind, she felt grief and mourned those things that were being irrevocably changed.

A melancholy mood settled over her. She attributed it to the concrete she was walking on and the asphalt streets with their endless lines of houses. These things seemed close to burying the earth now. Even though she knew land had to be made more accessible, that roads and houses had to be built, rivers had to be harnessed, and forest products were vital to all those things, she struggled with depressing thoughts of how recklessly and heedlessly these things were done to the land.

She shook her head. Why should she even worry about such things? Shouldn't she only feel gratitude? She and her family had every advantage, living so well in their big, efficient house, located on its own handsome square of this vast valley floor. But she felt sad for what was being lost by such extravagant and ruthless development. Her grief extended beyond this valley, to all the land being grabbed up and transformed, with so little thought given to the future.

Those who lusted after the land, to change it and profit from it, earned her special wrath. Unfortunately, that included land developers like Art Stroud and her husband. A memory jarred her: right after she and Ed returned from their honeymoon, Ed announced that he had accepted Art Stroud's offer to become a partner in his banking and land development business.

She'd stood there blinking at his words, trying not to show her disappointment. Collecting herself, she'd said, rather timidly, "But the university has offered you a position in the Physics Department. You told me you wanted to teach."

He'd laughed and answered, "What prestige is in *that*, compared to the bank?"

She'd thought, Prestige? Prestige? She knew the word, of course, but she hadn't heard it used in that context before and, somehow, it changed everything.

· · ·

After looking at her watch, she'd begun walking faster, when, without warning, she heard a man's voice say, "*Meg, it's your turn now.*" It was whispered from a distance, watery and filled with dread, and it stopped her, startled her. She looked around alert to where the words might have come from. Again she heard the words, fainter this time, but just as distinct, "*Meg, it's your turn now.*"

Inexplicably, she answered, "*My turn for what?*" And stood there stupidly, waiting for an answer. Hearing nothing more, she walked on. Although fearing to look back, she was compelled to. But there was nothing there, other than a bedraggled tree and a toddler's pink plastic tricycle lying on its side. She scolded herself and then laughed. Was she going mad? Or was it a phenomenon of her need for food after a stressful day and a long, strenuous walk? Whatever it was had frightened her, and she picked up her pace. She was almost home.

3

HOME

Her house was new seven years ago, and Meg took full credit for their living here instead of the Halverson House. Doing so had cost her dearly, but in the end, with the impending birth of her third child, Ed had been overruled.

The house occupied the choicest lot of the subdivision; Ed had seen to that, what with Art Stroud's bank having developed the land. All its houses were low-slung, aglitter with glass, and self-consciously expensive, even though the streets here were narrow and without boulevards. Considering the grace and beauty of the older districts she'd walked through earlier, she couldn't help noticing how frail the trees were here—some were smaller in girth than the stakes holding them upright. Overall, they hardly seemed up to the task of framing and shading the giant architecture they guarded.

The very last house on their block was almost finished, and it was huge. Each house had gotten a little bigger as the subdivision grew, as though an owner's only hope for recognition was in the size of his house. Meg's tendency toward thrift made her shudder at this newest monster, forcing her to wonder what it would cost to heat it, decorate it, furnish it, insure it, and clean it. But then, she had always resented it. The ground it sat on had been the neighborhood children's playground. Her daughter, Callie, had come into the house, sobbing, "The digging machine is eating up our fort! It just ran over our kitchen! And the driver told us, 'Get out of here!' Oh, Ma, make him stop! Come out and stop him!"

It was a mournful group she'd joined, as her three children and their friends watched the metal jaws of the shovel chewing through the assortment of trails and holes and lean-tos that made up their kingdom. But it destroyed more than that. Parks had not been included in the subdivision, so the children had to leave the neighborhood to find open ground. She would have gladly transported them to the farm and the freedom she and her sister Tolly had as kids. Having loving parents during their formative years was important, but so, too, was having land to explore, and unplanned time to do it.

The sight of her own house cheered her. She had managed to soften its entry with her choice of shrubs and flowers; and the front garden was at its most appealing stage, with more earth showing than plants. Indeed it was a paradox: after all the work of gardening, by late summer the flowerbeds would be too extravagant in their jumble of colors. With a wry smile, she thought back to the excitement of finding a single yellow-bell or rooster-head in the coulee near the farm as a child.

The new growth from around the dry stalks of last year's chrysanthemums drew her. She stooped and brushed them with her fingers, itching to feel the warm earth crumble and respond. A new regret for this waste of a day poked at her mind. If only she'd stayed home and gardened this afternoon, instead of making that fuss. Well, maybe tomorrow.

She hurried into the foyer of the house, footsore and hungry. She kicked off her shoes, walked gingerly into the kitchen, grabbed a piece of cheese to quiet her stomach, and put the potatoes and meatloaf into the oven. Ed would be home in less than an hour, and the kids would come home once she called Doris to let her know she was back. After inspecting the ruined shoes, she threw them into the trash. Then she went down the long hall to the bedroom, where she hastily and gratefully removed her clothes, including her bra, and donned the softest pair of jeans she owned and a faded pink sweater, satisfied that nothing confined her body in the least.

On her way back to the kitchen she stopped in the family room and turned on the stereo. With her arms held high she did a little waltz around the coffee table in rhythm to the music, finally stopping to sweep the ashes from the fireplace. Using the kindling and logs her son Kurt had brought in before he left for school, she started a fire, then knelt before it to watch the flames leap quickly from the kindling and start licking at the dry logs. Sitting back on her heels and holding out her hands to feel the new heat, she marveled at the comfort a fire gave her. With their large furnace needing only the flick of a finger to turn it on, the heat from a fireplace wasn't that necessary. She decided that building a fire fulfilled some primitive need; and providing a proper setting for the gathering of her family was part of that.

The family room was something her mother would have liked: its warm earth tones, the comfort of its furniture, its display of art done by her and the kids, and the music that so often filled it. And Papa would definitely have approved of the bookcase she and the kids had built. Its homely workmanship still gave her a chuckle. It had been a long ambitious project, exacting more patience than she thought she possessed. Its boards came precut to her specifications and while she and Kurt assembled them, they had much prompting from the two girls. Once it was together, sanded and stained, the kids were beyond themselves with pride that they could build something that important and display it for all to see. It took an inordinately long time before they allowed anything to be laid on it—having nearly forgotten the reason for making it in the first place. But in the end they had relented, and in no time it took on the jumble it now was.

She ran her eyes lovingly over the boxed games and puzzles, the stacks of school papers, the jars of pencils and paintbrushes, the trays and tubes of paint, and the reams of paper awaiting their handiwork. Their books looked a little shabby and a little too used, but they sat there anyway like friends in need of yet another reading.

Ed had removed his expensive leather-covered books, with their gold titles, to the glass-shelved case in the grand room through the arched French doors. His other books, which in the past had interested him, were now in his office at the bank—as was he most of the time.

Standing now with her back to the fire, Meg looked through the French doors across from her into Ed's grand room, where they entertained. "The Edward Halverson Specialties Room" was how she thought of it. Its corniced windows and brocade furniture commanded a sophisticated style she was sometimes hard-pressed to match. Yet, when she had to, she did. Gliding around with her Halverson face on, silver-voiced and chatty, she attended to their guests' every need and fulfilled Ed's every expectation. She was glad her Ma and Papa had never seen her in that room, or had to wonder what their younger daughter was up to. But then her parents hadn't lived to see her in either of her homes, or known her children, let alone had to wonder where her choices had taken her. What should she feel about that: sorrow or relief?

Meg pulled away from those bitter thoughts and went to the phone to call Doris. On the fourth ring, Doris's low voice greeted her and assured her that the two girls had arrived after school, had been given milk and cookies, and were happily playing with paper dolls. She said that Callie had fallen down on the way there, but the scrape was minor and Marc put an oversized bandage on it because it was the only size he could find, and not to worry. Kurt, too, had dropped in on his way to meet his friend Chip for their scheduled bike ride, and been fed. Doris then asked about Meg's meeting.

Meg hesitated before telling her about walking out of it and walking home.

Doris said, "You *walked* from Cora Lee Jensen's? That's miles away!"

"Yep, all the way. Jill Handley drove me there, and I realized too late that I'd walked away from my ride, too. My feet might never be the same. I had to throw away my shoes. Poor things, they were new, and the hem in my suit skirt, well..." Before Doris replied, Meg added, "Why I chose today to jump ship I can't say. I'll plead insanity when Ed quizzes me about it at dinner. On the way home I thought I'd place the blame on a little come-hither signal from the window curtains I was sitting by. It reminded me that my lifespan is just so long, and being trapped inside by useless meetings wasn't making me younger. But I know Ed won't buy that excuse."

Doris laughed, "Is this really Mrs. Edward Halverson I'm talking to? The woman who never rocks the boat?"

"Yep, the one who finally got smart. Well, actually, who finally got stupid. What I did was unforgivable, Doris."

"Tell me what happened, besides the come-hither curtain."

"Oh, I don't know. I thought about it all the way home—you know, two miles of the reasons for doing it, then two miles of the regrets."

"Then you *must* tell me."

Meg spoke seriously. "I shouldn't have been there. I was critical of everything. I couldn't keep my judgment in check. As I listened to Jill read the minutes from the last meeting—and that was after she'd held a long discussion on the difference between *new* business and *old* business—I started thinking of all the wonderful things I love to do, and how I'm wasting my life." She groaned. "Maybe all this happened because I was so hungry. Jill picked me up a little early, so I left home without lunch. After the meeting was adjourned I set upon those tiny things you eat at parties, except I forgot my tweezers. I wouldn't even classify those things as food. After the tea—or was it coffee—I was trying to keep track of who brought what and whom to compliment. I smiled so much my face felt like it was in a vise. Just listen to me, Doris. You'd think I'd never done any entertaining. But these meetings are just so damned endless and stupid."

Doris said, "Come on, Meg. What really made you walk out."

Meg didn't answer for a moment, then said, "The last straw was delivered by Evelyn Stone. She'd been waiting to drop a little bombshell about her friend. God save us from *friends* like Evelyn Stone! I wondered why her face had been twitching during the meeting. She was waiting for an opportunity to give an account of this poor woman. Evelyn has such a fascination with lurid details that cut down a person. After she had her say, everyone there—not everyone, but those who *should* know better—started agreeing with her like robots. That's when I had to leave. I'd had enough. I exploded and said that just this once it would be damned nice to hear words of understanding, even kindness, instead of the cruel remarks they routinely make about people less fortunate than themselves. I might have said it a little stronger than that...yes I did. I'm afraid I used one of those big, bad words. I ended by saying the whole damned meeting was, as usual, a total waste of time. Now it's Ed's reaction I'm dreading."

"If I were you I'd stick to the excuse about the curtain."

"He will already know, Doris. I don't know who reports these things to Ed and Art, but he will already know. I should have just smiled and nodded and kept my opinions about their...their intolerance of other people to myself. My Papa used to say, 'Meggie, you can't fight others' intolerance by being intolerant toward them yourself.' He said that, but he never told me exactly what to say instead of what I'd just said."

Doris's commiserating chuckle helped Meg feel better, but not by much. She sighed and said, "I'm getting pretty good about thinking up excuses. The truth is the last thing Ed ever wants to hear from me." She stopped talking for a moment, then said, "Doris, on my way home the strangest thing happened, something really weird."

Doris waited. "Tell me."

After another pause, Meg spoke, "Is hearing voices a symptom of something? If it is, I hope gardening in the sun for one full day is the only cure. Really, Doris, it's nothing. I'm sorry I mentioned it."

"You sounded serious, dear, like something really happened. And now you try to make a joke out of it."

"I don't mean to. But you've got to promise to laugh when I tell you. I was just about home when out of a clear blue sky I heard a man's voice say, 'It's your turn, Meg.' Then I actually asked out loud, 'My turn for what?' as though there was someone to say it to." She tried to laugh.

Concerned, Doris said, "I'm not laughing, Meg. I think you're under more strain than you let on. It's times like this that I'm happy my Marc doesn't have any expectations as to how I spend my time. It's a cliché, dear, but that saying about a square peg in a round hole applies, especially today. When you go to one of those *do's* of yours, I want to ask if you're going as Edward Halverson's wife or as the Meg I'm acquainted with—the one who potters around in the garden, growing lovely chrysanthemums and huge armfuls of beans and squash, and even lovelier kids. I'm talking about the Meg who can tell Mozart from Liszt, and a Rembrandt from a Vermeer, and who makes the most wonderful crusty bread I've ever tasted. And we can't forget the woman who rattles around in comfortable old clothes—mostly without a bra on. Need I say more?"

"Gosh, that was wonderful!" Meg laughed. "I take it that I've just been flattered, but I'm sure only you and I would consider it that."

"I don't much like the word 'flattery,' Meg. Can't you take what I say as an honest compliment, one woman to another? And by the way that's Marc's opinion, too."

"The braless part?"

"Especially the braless part."

The two women laughed companionably. Then Doris said, "Well, I hope you can get out in your garden soon, dear. As for what happened today, your nice walk probably did you good. And saying what you said to those biddies, I can only say it's a bit overdue."

"Right. Whatever the risks." Meg's laugh was short and brittle. Taking the opportunity to confide in her friend, she continued in a somber tone. "Doris, Ed's been in one of those unbearable moods of his for what seems like a month or more. The kids and I are all tiptoeing around him again. I've been trained to not ask what's going on. I want to help him, but..." She paused. "I should have controlled myself today. When he finds out... I don't like to complain, but..." She caught herself, then stopped and, sounding a little too upbeat, said, "Could you tell the Littles that their Ma is home after a big day in society? And, Doris, thank you for being so good to them. What would I ever do without you and that lovely husband of yours? And I mean that in more ways than you two riding herd on my crew when I need help."

· · ·

Meg glanced at the clock as she put the carrots on to steam. If Ed were on time for dinner, it would be the first time this week. On the other hand, the kids wouldn't miss the sacred dinner hour for any reason—the words "6:00 P.M." must be permanently tattooed on their stomachs. No sooner had she thought this than she heard the rattle and bump of Kurt putting his bicycle into the garage, then his loud teasing greeting to his sisters and their shrill giggles. The door banged open and the three of them trooped into the house.

Meg met them in the family room by the hearth, shushing them and laughing at their noise. She hugged and touched each one, patting them and inspecting them proudly, and all the while marveling at the similarity of their faces. The taller girl, eight-year-old Sara, thrust a drawing into her hand, while the youngest, six-year-old Callie, pushed against her to show the over-sized bandage Marc had put over a scrape on her knee. Kurt, her eleven-year-old son, somewhat generously held back while the girls talked, then took his turn to tell her about the bike ride he and his friend had taken to the mouth of the canyon.

She heard it all in bits and pieces then shooed them down the hall to wash up before they set the table, calling out to Kurt that he could help make the salad after he washed up. Once they had all left the room she stirred the fire and added more wood, and thought of her children's beauty and newness and vigor.

When they were away from her she saw the three of them as individuals; and when they were with her, with all their noise and demands, she saw them as a clump. Maybe this was the way any mother coped with three energetic children close in age. She knew that they also played the group part to the hilt, catching excitement from each other and moving happily together like a gang of noisy puppies.

Kurt was the easiest to see as himself. As the first child and only son, his unique position was sealed. He was tall for his age and already handsome like his father, with the same hazel eyes and abundant sandy hair. He was serious, bright, thoughtful, and a good student. His teachers often mentioned his leadership. Meg thought him too solemn and was overjoyed when his humor burst out, infecting everyone around him. On the rare weekends when his father chose to stay home, Kurt dogged his footsteps, asking him questions, aligning himself with the few jobs his father had around the house. Meg knew Kurt needed those moments when his life was neither dominated nor controlled by women.

Sara and Callie had early become known as the "Littles." Kurt had disdainfully invented it when explaining the family structure to his friend Chip. The label had stuck.

Meg thought that Sara, the older girl, already showed a singular beauty, not of a cute female child, but of an interesting small person. She was fine boned and hazel eyed, and had straight silky blond hair.

Her eyes had Meg's directness and held a curious wisdom. She was as quiet and serious as Kurt, choosing her words carefully, but could burst into laughter easily. Even so, Meg felt she was the shyest and most delicate of the three children, and Meg was more protective of her.

Where both Kurt and Sara had inherited their father's coloring, Callie, the baby, was an Irish brunette like Meg, with short dark curls around her pert face. Long dark lashes framed the startling blue of her eyes, which Meg felt would someday turn grey like her own. Her face and body still had a baby's roundness. Both her laughter and her tears were nearer at hand than her siblings. It was only recently that Meg had observed both a restlessness and stubborn determination in her. Although Callie resented her position as the baby of the family, she used that position expertly.

Callie and Sara were best friends and they looked up to Kurt. He was a tease, but a kindly one. Yes, Meg thought, they are quite a clump—a peace-loving clump—and in this she was pleased.

When Kurt came into the kitchen, his hands were clean only to mid-arm, but Meg let it go. He began chopping the greens laid out for him with more vigor than finesse and ate everything that fell off the cutting board. He stopped cutting and said, "Say, where's Dad? I didn't see his car in the garage."

"He's where he always is, at the bank."

"But I heard he was sick today."

"No, Kurt, he's not sick, or if he is I don't know about it. He's not here."

"Didn't the bank call back, Ma? When I came home to get my bike after school, the phone was ringing. This guy—I think it was Mr. Stroud—asked if Dad was feeling better. I told him, 'Gee, I suppose so, but I really don't know for sure. He isn't here.' Then he asked for you. When I said you weren't here either, he said he'd call back later. I didn't know what else to say, Ma. I didn't know Dad was sick."

As Kurt spoke Meg felt a clutching feeling around her stomach. She set the salad bowl down carefully, and without looking at Kurt, said, "No, dear, you did just right. Perhaps your father wasn't feeling well today. Maybe he just took the day off." She looked at the clock and noted that Ed was already late. "Tell you what, dear, when he comes in for dinner we'll ask him. Until then, could you get the Littles to the table? I'll put the food on and maybe you could dish things up for them and start eating. I'm going into the bedroom and make a couple calls—you know, just in case. Okay?" Without waiting for his answer, she quickly took the potatoes from the oven and sliced the meat loaf, then left the kitchen and walked rapidly down the hall, instructing the Littles to get to the table, as they clattered past.

She closed the bedroom door and sat on the bed, wrapping her arms around her in an attempt to dispel her fear. Was Ed sick this morning? She tried to remember if he'd looked sick. His leaving quietly without saying goodbye was what she remembered. But why would he leave without telling her he was feeling sick? And if he planned on leaving for the day—for whatever reason—why wouldn't he inform her about what he was doing, or leave her a phone message? Then again, maybe Kurt had heard it all wrong. She couldn't imagine Ed taking the day off and telling Art he was ill, and putting her in the position of having no explanation for his actions. If Kurt was home after school Art must have called sometime around 3:30. How did Art find out that Ed was sick? Ed must have told Art this morning—but why not her? There had to be an answer.

First she called Ed's personal office phone. It rang a long time without an answer, and she sat there, impotently, holding the phone and wondering what other calls she should make. If she called Art... but she didn't trust herself speaking to him; she'd say too much. She'd tell him, "You should know better than I why he's not here. You see him more than anyone around here does." No, she better avoid that conversation. Was she overreacting? No, she wasn't. Ed had been distant and uncommunicative for a long time.

She finally called the hospital, embarrassed to admit to a stranger that she didn't know where he was. The woman's voice said, "There's no one here by that name. I'd call the sheriff."

Meg thanked her and hung up. There was no way she'd call the sheriff, but without an answer the anxiety quickly settled over her again. But why did she feel this fear? Ed took his car and got away for a day. By getting away he would feel more like himself. He worked too hard and had for years. When Art called, she'd be light and happy, and teasingly accuse him of overworking the mainstay of his bank.

Having made up her mind to all that, she went to the table and sat down. The children were eating quietly, and the clink of silver on dishes was a comfort to her. Kurt's eyes asked a momentary question above the girl's heads. Meg shrugged and gave a small negative shake of her head. She then looked at the food on the table and felt a quivering nausea in her throat, when earlier she'd felt a throbbing hunger.

. . .

When the phone rang, at eight P.M. sharp, Meg, thinking it was Ed, had fairly flown to it, saying, "I'll get it, I'll get it, I'll get it!" She put her impatience aside when it was Art's voice on the line. Then thinking he had news about Ed, she braced herself for the flattering words that loaded Art's every conversation…and consistently raised flags of caution in her mind.

He said, "And how is our lovely lady on this beautiful evening?"

She was out of breath but managed, "Our lovely lady is great! And you?"

"Tip Top. And how could one not be fine on such a splendid day, eh? It looks like we've got winter on the run. But, of course you already know that, Meg." He paused then spoke each word slowly. "I understand you were at Cora Lee's this afternoon…and left earlier than planned? Are we still keeping in mind our duties to the community, Meg?"

She cowered at his words, furious that he dared say that, but not surprised that he knew. Making her voice as light as she could, she cooed a saucy, "Like you said, on a *splendid* day like this, I just couldn't resist a walk, Art."

Changing the subject, he said, "Did that fine son of yours tell you that I called earlier?" When she said yes he went on, "I hope Edward is feeling better. There's something we need to discuss. Be so kind and ask him to step to the phone."

"But Ed's not here, Art. Kurt said you mentioned about Ed being sick." She gave a short laugh. "I'm afraid that was news to me. He's missed dinner and hasn't called. I have no idea where he is. My guess is he's taking a vacation day from everyone." Her laugh hadn't rung true; she'd seen the children's heads turn from the board game they were playing, and were now watching her.

Art sputtered "A *vacation* day? That's absurd!" His voice calmed. "I don't mean to imply that Edward has to get my permission. We all need a day off. But there was an important meeting I'd set up that he needed to be in on. Quite frankly, I called because I was curious to know just how sick he could be to have missed it. When he called in sick this morning he sounded preoccupied." He paused. "It isn't like him. Edward is most attentive to the programs we've laid out here. Perhaps I've asked too much of him."

The uncertainty in Art's voice gave Meg a perverse joy. She said, "Well, anyway, I hope this can wait until tomorrow."

"Yes, yes, of course, of course. When he gets home, tell him I called. Tell him I said for him to take a few days off and rest up, if that's what he needs. But I still need to talk to him. Tell him I'll call him in the morning. I'll let you go now, Meg. You and those youngsters have a nice evening."

. . .

It was later, while Meg lay alone in bed, that Art's words started running around in her mind—the part about "when Edward called in this morning he sounded preoccupied." Funny how the exact sound of a phrase could keep nudging one's mind before its significance was caught. It was as though her brain cells knew it was important right from the first, but it was easier to be rankled by Ed calling Art, rather than her, and the fact that he'd made the call from an outside phone. Even so, it took a while for her to think about what all that might mean.

4

EDWARD

It was the clock striking three that roused Meg: three sharp chimes cast into the stillness and dark, leaving widening circles of sound, then retreating into a silence so absolute she shuddered. Even though she'd dozed off she knew some part of her brain had been alert to any sound or sign of Ed's return—the car's engine, the swing of headlights turning into the driveway, the garage door opening. His homecomings had trained her ears for his footsteps along the breezeway and up the three outside steps, the slight squeak of the door's hinges, the thump of it closing, then the hangers rattling in the coat closet. And, yes, even the distant tired way he had of saying he was home.

But all these things were only in her memory, for he was not home and had not been home for three days. The portent of that fact chilled her more than the cold room and the dying fire at her feet. She sat measuring her need for sleep against the thought of walking down the dark hall and climbing into their huge bed with its cold, expensive sheets. No, this high-backed chair and fireplace were what she needed most.

She left the chair long enough to lift a new log onto the healthy bed of coals in the bottom of the grate, then scuttled back into the softness of the chair, curling her feet under her, gathering her heavy robe closer, and tugging and tucking it to cover her knees and toes until it was again holding all the parts of her together. Before she settled down completely, she studied the telephone on the table beside her—that link to the outside world and to disappeared husbands. Freeing a hand, she gave the phone cord a vicious tug—as if it were her tether—then lifted the receiver to her ear. Hearing again the never-changing hum she replaced the receiver and pushed the phone away angrily, then thrust each hand into her robe's opposing sleeve and stared into the fire.

. . .

The morning after Ed disappeared, Art, true to his word, had called asking for Ed. It took courage to tell him that Ed had not returned and that she still had not heard anything from him. Art was silent for a long time—Meg could hear him breathing heavily. Finally, he said, "Can you wait another day before notifying the sheriff? Let's give Edward a little longer to come back. After tomorrow, well, if he's not back, then we'll call. No need to stir up any bees. I'd like to keep this whole thing quiet for as long as possible." She agreed, even though she felt a lot of apprehension about waiting.

Today being that day, she'd gone to Sheriff Gray's office. He'd been upset that she'd waited this long to tell him. He talked about the trail getting cold (Meg pictured a hound dog sniffing one of Ed's silk ties or his hair brush). Gray asked questions about the days prior to Ed's disappearance, then asked about how he and Meg were getting along (he'd dropped his eyes to some papers on his desk as he'd asked that). Inwardly, she had bristled at his audacity then recovered by assuming her sweetest Mrs. Edward Halverson face and sketching a portrait of a happy family man in a demanding job. To her ears her answers sounded vague; but then, that was what hers and Ed's life together was: indistinguishable from that of two strangers. The sheriff asked for the make of Ed's car and about his credit cards, explaining that the receipts could help trace his movements. The interview ended with the sheriff putting out a missing-person report, explaining that it would extend far beyond Montana's borders. Meg had come home shaken, understanding that it wasn't just that her husband hadn't come home, but that he was now the object of a large search that a lot of people would be interested in.

Nothing about his disappearance had yet appeared in the newspaper. Then again, she might easily have missed something on the social page, something stating that Edward Halverson, banker, had been called away unexpectedly. She wondered if it would also report that, due to the press of committee work, his wife was unable to go with him.

But what the town's gossips (Art Stroud's "bees") were saying, she could only guess. In a town the size of Clark Fork, the way news got around was something akin to jungle drums, especially in the particular social layer where all the Evelyn Stones resided. Speculation like this was just too juicy not to have an opinion on it. Wouldn't Evelyn's mouth twitch if she knew all there was to know about the Halversons? My-my-my-twitch-twitch-twitch. Whenever the phone rang, Meg answered it with a sense of dread, wondering if the person on the line would be a do-gooder or a do-badder.

The day after Ed disappeared, Meg told Doris and Marc before they might hear it from someone else. Once the children were asleep, they'd hurried over. Doris understood immediately and put her arms around Meg to comfort her; but Marc laughed at the two of them and suggested all kinds of easy, bawdy, masculine explanations, ending with a kind of nervous laughter that was meant to quell further serious concern on the subject. Meg knew it was his way of helping and she loved him for trying.

She told them that all she needed was their company for a while, that waiting alone was getting to her. Of course they understood. She made a pot of spiced tea and the three of them sat by the fire without expressing their similar thoughts. She put some music on the stereo—a disk of Aaron Copeland's *Appalachian Spring*, which she called "hopeful music." Now, if she ever played that stirring music again, she knew she would recall that circle of firelight and the feeling of love from those two friends. She'd slept better that night.

. . .

Seeing that the fire was burning low again, Meg got up wearily from her chair and replenished it. Then she stood in the hall listening for any sounds coming from the sleeping children. Hearing nothing she tucked herself back into the chair, wondering sadly what this was doing to them. Tonight when she put the Littles to bed in the room they shared, it was obvious that Sara had been assigned to ask, point-blank, where Daddy was.

While she sorted through the jumble in her mind, Meg stood

there blinking and voiceless, rubbing Sara's buttery-smooth cheek with her hand and avoiding looking at either girl. She wondered if mothers were ever allowed to say, "I don't know."

It was Callie who smoothed the embarrassing silence and announced, "Daddy's on a trip. I think he went to see Uncle Charlie and Auntie Tolly in Wyler." She said it with the assurance of a six-year-old, but her voice still held a question. When Meg left them and went across the hall to Kurt's room, the girls made no noise, and she knew they were listening for what Kurt would ask when she kissed him goodnight.

Kurt said, "Why can't Dad call and tell us where he is, Ma?"

Meg's mumbled response hardly pertained to his question; and, after tucking him in listlessly, she wandered into her own bedroom, seeking out the comfort of her robe—needing to lash its old blue cloth up tight around her skin.

. . .

Long tongues of orange flame now wobbled up the curve of the new log, gathering everything around her into its soft possessive glow; and for a moment she was cheered. She had to keep positive for everyone's sake. There was a logical answer to Ed's absence—there was always a logical answer to such things, if you could just live long enough to find it. The waiting was what was killing her. Waiting was the hardest thing she ever did. This stupid vigil! She spoke aloud, "Where are you, Ed? If something has happened to you, why can't they find you?" The words having been said so many times inside her head came out unevenly, in an agonized litany; and once spoken simply hung there, as unanswered aloud as they were in the hideouts of her mind.

In the silence she tried to remember Ed's face, his smile, something cheering, anything positive about him, maybe a joke he'd recently said… But there was nothing, and in the blankness of that, the unwelcome and unbidden strands of her resentment toward him came into her mind—resentment, like the tangle in her sewing box, that over the years had turned the spools and twists of good intentions into matted webs of bright colored ends and knots and the treachery of hidden needles.

It was the way he came home and turned down the hall, without coming in to where she was, without needing to touch her, that brought the bitterness to her mind. It was she who ran to him, like an eager puppy—something low and wiggly with an ever-present willingness to do her master's bidding. In that foolish puppy way she would follow him and stand by the bedroom door while he changed from his office clothes. Encased at last in the soft clothes that she'd washed and ironed and hung on the hangers just for that moment, he would put his body away, tucking, buttoning, zipping.

When she inquired about his day, he'd say, "Busy" or "Fine." Just that. Occasionally, courteously, he'd ask about her day and about their children, even as his eyes were wandering to the evening paper he'd laid upon the dresser. It had to be read, after all, before he went back to the office.

"You must have things to do in the kitchen, Meg." (It wasn't a question.) After saying that, he'd leave the bedroom, striding quickly past her, sometimes brushing against her in the bedroom doorway. Had he ever said, "Excuse me, Meg." No, it was she who would have said it, and added, "What am I doing, standing here like a lump?" Then she'd become the eager puppy again, trailing behind him down the hall, her mind still bursting with the thousand unsaid things he had no time to hear: about the kids, the garden, her baking his favorite chocolate cake, the look of the mountains this morning, the letter from Tolly, that wonderful interview she'd heard on public radio, a joke Sara had played on Kurt, the concern Doris and Marc had for a grandchild's illness—all those little parts of her day that evaporated in his heedless rush to his silken chair by the corniced window in his grand living room. Thus rebuffed, she'd return to the safe recesses of her kitchen, all of her unspoken words bottled inside.

She examined another image, the one she called "H.U.," for Halverson Uprightness. When she was "H.U." she stood very straight, her Halverson mouth arranged in a gracious smile, her body elegantly dressed, her makeup and hair just so. Halverson Uprightness was donned as one draws on a silk dress, lifting it over one's head and shoulders, fitting it down the hips, settling it, smoothing it, patting it, then walking slowly and carefully correct around the obstacles she encountered in that uniform. There was no puppy in "H.U." Well, if the truth were known, the puppy was there, but no one could see it.

With a deep sigh she discarded both pictures and wondered if perhaps that was the trouble. Who exactly was she if who she appeared to be had to be endlessly created? And Ed, who was he, now that he'd added *absentee banker* to his other labels of *absentee husband* and *absentee father*? As concerned and frightened as she had been these last three days, it wasn't a matter of where Ed was right now, but where he'd been for a long time.

She'd long given up any thought of his being interested in her life. And watching the kids' attempts at trying to make him a part of their lives made her ache. What they thought a father was supposed to be was hard to imagine—something untouchable, no doubt.

How tidy his excuse of having to be at work all the time! Working an eight-hour day wasn't enough, so he made it twelve or fourteen hours every day, including weekends; vacations were out of the question. Regardless of the financial demands put on him by their growing family, she knew they were in good shape financially, with his inheritance, investments, their savings, and the house paid off. How much money could one family use? Why was being together as a family secondary to his work? One day she'd said, "All right, Ed, think of this family as *money*, as an *investment* that's going sour." He'd turned and left the house without answering her. But then, he left, not from her remark, but because it was after dinner, the time he usually went back to the office.

Many times during their marriage—because she simply had to find out—she'd made a point of calling him at his office at night, just to check if he were actually there. And he had been. It was obvious that she was checking up on him, and he had been impatient at her interruption. She didn't interrupt him anymore—in the past year or so there'd been no good excuse to call him.

Now she wondered if his disappearance was somehow connected with last October, when in a fit of loneliness and lack of direction in her life, she'd called him at the office during lunch. She'd told him she couldn't get along this way, that there had to be more. Perhaps they could get away for a while, maybe take a trip together. Her vehemence and desperation and the ragged touch of tears in her voice seemed to embarrass him. He'd told her that a meeting was about to begin and they'd have to talk about this later. She already knew what "later" meant. She hung up and cried bitterly.

When he got home she hoped he'd notice her distress and voluntarily take her aside and listen to her ideas. But he went into the bedroom and closed the door. She supposed he slept until dinnertime. At her instructions the children walked around quietly and played in their rooms (they could be so quiet at those times, as if they, too, were waiting for some kind of change). When she finally called him to dinner, he ate without meeting her eyes, and left for the office right afterwards. He came home after she was asleep.

How long had she felt this overwhelming aloneness and this anger: One year? Two? Three? Five years? She searched for a date. No, make it seventeen of their eighteen years. She'd had only that brief half year of delight. The blatant truth of that made her feel sick.

As a university student, before she met Ed, she had enjoyed an occasional date, always with a classmate and always just for fun. After escaping that doubt-filled time with Tommy Southers, she wasn't ready for anything serious. Her classes had become so exciting. She had always loved writing and art and music, and from the response of her professors she discovered that she had enough talent in any of those areas to pursue a career.

As she'd done before, she wondered sourly what wondrous quality Ed had seen in her during their first dance the night they met. That confident, sophisticated, handsome man, four years her senior, and so at ease in his clothes, which hinted of wealth. And she, just a happy twenty-one-year-old coed, there at the mixer with a bunch of noisy, giggling girls who were there because they all loved to flirt and dance and have fun.

They had noticed Ed come into the ballroom, watched him standing by the door surveying all the possibilities, and even joked among themselves over the thought that he would come over and dance with one of them. Meg was surprised, almost shocked, when he came up behind her and put his arms around her, pulling her onto the dance floor before he'd even asked her for a dance. He held her close as he guided her expertly around the floor, and his effortless, flattering conversation was all directed at her. How could a girl resist?

Cooling off with cups of punch, he told her he had just graduated from Yale, in Physics, and had recently returned home to Clark Fork, where he expected to remain. He spoke enthusiastically of his plans to teach and of applying for a position in the Physics Department on her campus. When a fellow from her art class came over and asked her for a dance, Ed put his arm around her and told him she had promised him the next dance (which wasn't true). Turning back to Meg, Ed praised her for her interest and began talking about the town and what he planned to get from it.

After their second dance, just for something to say, she asked if he was connected in any way to Halverson Avenue, at the entrance to the campus? He said he was, and said that the big, red brick antique of a house, which was practically sitting on campus, was where he lived. He invited her to come and tour it the following day. He told her that he lived in it alone except for an older couple serving as housekeeper and gardener. He added, almost in passing, that both his parents had "unfortunately died" a year earlier at a railroad crossing east of town. Meg was amazed at how calmly he said that and thought how differently she would have told it, had it been her parents who had died.

He met her the next day in the elegant foyer of his Halverson House. As he took her from room to room he told her of his recollections about growing up there, and spoke of the many interesting stories of its history. The early Halversons, all lumbermen, were among those who settled Clark Fork; and they had built the house and named the street. Ed had also made a joke about his father telling him that the house was still full of Halverson ghosts. His father had said that in deference to those ghosts and what they represented, Ed was obliged to return to Clark Fork once he'd gotten his Yale education. A curious, sad expression had moved across Ed's face when he'd said that. On seeing it, Meg knew that he had just told her something significant, and she had never forgotten it.

That evening, as she walked back to her dorm, alone, she felt overwhelmed by the day and everything he'd told her; but she was disappointed, too. With all his excitement over his plans to become a professor, he hadn't picked up on the few things she'd said about her own education. And, after all his stories of living in that huge house—with its ghosts still dictating to him—it would have been nice if he could have been interested in where she had come from, or about her parents, or about her life on the farm. But, after telling him about her background, she'd been silent and had let him do all the talking.

Later that evening, her roommate had asked about her day with the "big shot." Meg had snapped, "I don't like him, and you wouldn't either. He's arrogant!" And she meant it. Was she supposed to be impressed by his being a Halverson? She resented his implication that she was fortunate he had chosen her to tour his precious house.

While she was annoyed at him, much of her anger was directed at herself. She had disregarded her negative impressions of him and had let him talk her into going out to dinner the following Saturday. When he'd asked her, she'd felt backed into a corner, feeling grateful for the tour and the attention, but feeling confused, too. Moments before, he had reached out and touched her hair. It wasn't like the tugs on her ponytail while walking to class with her friends—not one of those little flirting moments, which she clearly understood—but he had caressed it, then brought it to his lips, his eyes seeing something else. She was too polite and shy to call him on it. But his touch intrigued her, sending a shiver down her spine and weakness to her legs, along with a sense of wanting more.

Edward Halverson harbored no idle thoughts or whims; everything he did was for a purpose. Showing her his house, presenting her with lavish gifts, escorting her to dining rooms that she wouldn't otherwise have gone to, was part of a plan he already knew the ending to. Wasting no time, after their first dinner date—as though the good dinner had given him every right—he reached out and caressed her long, dark hair, after asking her to free it from its clips. She had agreed; and, in that strange hypnotic way, as before, he drew its strands to his lips and kissed it then brushed his hands against her breasts, his finger shaking and urgent now...to get inside...to get inside. That was how it always started, and in that gesture her life changed.

He said he would call her; and not wanting to miss it, she stayed in the dorm to be near the phone. He began calling her every evening, but his calls were just late enough that she stayed back and canceled everything else with her friends, just to be there to answer the phone. By the time he called she was at her wits' end and angry. But by the time he arrived to pick her up she was trembling with an anticipation that she was hardly able to contain; and she forgave him his tardiness; she always forgave him. She was learning the steps to obsession—the obsession being hers.

Because of the live-in caretakers at his mansion, he suggested they go to a motel on the town's western edge. She laughed and said she didn't care, although she really did. He parked his sporty car out of sight, behind the motel. And soon those parts of her she had kept safe, that no one else had been allowed to know, she had not so much given him as he had taken.

She had never been singled out as someone special before, or knew how sexually desirable she might be to a man. "Desire" was only a vague notion before Ed. Nothing had prepared her for the feelings he engendered in her, with his almost greedy possession of her body, and her willingness to submit. He didn't like kissing or soft words; it was her long, dark hair that turned him on. After that prelude, with every nerve in her body screaming for relief, the sex was quick and violent before he turned away. She was left panting and oddly puzzled. Was that all? With no opportunity to talk about it, or even know what to ask, she assumed that not being satisfied was a defect in her.

When her judgment finally warned her that the waters she had willingly strayed into were too deep for escape, there was no one to help her, no time to think objectively, and less inclination to do so. One month after she met Ed, Papa had a stroke and died. Then Ma had simply stopped wanting to go on without Papa; and, despite the efforts of her daughters, she had joined him.

After each funeral, Meg trooped back to campus, as alone as she had ever imaged the word meant—deserted, adrift, rootless, and unable to feel or cry or ask for help. With the two people she loved most gone forever, and with Tolly and Charlie busy with their son, the farm, and their own lives, who was there but Edward Halverson—the man who didn't speak of feelings, but, because he came from an important, well-known family and was going to be a professor, seemed safe and sane and rooted.

Two months after Ma died, Ed carried Meg over the threshold of the Halverson House. He wanted a big wedding and, because her parents were gone, he'd paid for it—the only exceptions being Tolly's matron of honor dress and Charlie's rented tux (he had given Meg away). The ceremony was held in the chapel by the river. She, in her gorgeous white wedding dress, trimmed in seed pearls, carried white orchids tucked among white roses. Her attendants—none of whom she'd known before—were dressed in shades of green. Their wedding was featured on the society page of the town's newspaper.

What a hopeful person she'd been when she was a new bride: eager and optimistic, with everything good ahead of her. Ma had once told her that marriage was a doorway through which a woman and her husband stepped into a broader life; and what had been impossible to accomplish alone was now possible, for there were two to accomplish it. Ma had never spoken to her on the subject of sex. Meg, having seen her parents so content with each other, working so happily around the farm, and solving their problems so reasonably, had come to feel that marriage simply launched a person into a satisfying life, that all a reasonably intelligent girl had to do was find a suitable man and get married. In fact, if there were any problems, marriage would solve them.

They had honeymooned in San Francisco. The luxury of their suite, the food, the wine, the boutiques, and the clothing stores were beyond anything she had imagined. It was there that he bought her all new expensive clothing, after insisting that she give away *all* her other clothes: everything she had brought with her and, when they got home, everything there—her underwear, shoes, stockings, nightgowns, dresses, skirts, slacks, blouses, sweaters, coats—everything she had worn before their wedding; everything except her wedding dress and veil, which he helped her pack away. The only thing that escaped being razed, that she'd thought to push to the very back of the closet, was the blue robe that Papa and Ma had given her their last family Christmas.

Her lessons had started in San Francisco. At dinner one night in the hotel dining room, she'd spoken to their waiter—a delightful man with dark humorous eyes. He had attended them closely, anticipating what they might need before being asked. His presentation of the wine bottles and the proud, almost loving way he filled their glasses completely charmed her.

She told him, laughing as she spoke, that she was from a farm in Montana. She said, "Before I came to California, with all its lovely wines, I thought that wine was something one kept in a gallon jug on the bottom shelf of the refrigerator." She had meant it as a joke on herself, and a compliment to the waiter. But Ed was furious and excused the waiter, just as he was about to make a funny comment back to her.

Back in their room, Ed told her to keep her great ignorance and her offhand remarks about the farm to herself. And, further, she was never to speak to waiters in that familiar way again, that things like that weren't done or said by the people they would be with in Clark Fork. He added that when they drank wine she was to remember what kind it was and what food it went with. He said he would help her with that; but she was to remember. "For our future," he'd said.

She paid attention and learned many things in San Francisco. She went there an eager girl, wanting only to please. She came back fully-fledged.

In eighteen years things change. Once Ed had added her to his bed, installed her in his kitchen, and delivered her into the hands of his Halverson ghosts, he was free to go about his business. He turned down the position in the university's Physics Department. Art Stroud, in need of the entrée the Halverson name would bring him, persuaded Ed to join his banking and land development business. Ed rarely referred to his early life in the Halverson House, or to the years they'd lived in it together. But all that didn't matter. Shortly after they moved from it, Ed donated it, with much fanfare, to the university, to be used for a faculty center.

As to their love life: when they made love, it felt—at least, to her—as though it was only two bodies getting something over with. Without words and kisses, without looking into each other's eyes, it was a violation. What he was doing inside her had no connection to anything else, not even the past. During those times, when she was bound in the powerful grip of his passion, she felt absolutely alone, the words of love like ashes in her mouth, and her mind hidden somewhere by the light fixture above their bed—a tiny figure sitting on the rim of the etched glass, weeping and rocking back and forth in the rhythm of the moment.

Afterwards, exhausted, when the requirement of being with him was over and she was once more banished to the twenty acres that was her side of the bed, she would hug herself, enraged that what she hungered for had not been released. Later still, she covered her ears with her pillow to drown out the sounds of his sleeping, hating his sleeping, hating him for not missing what she missed—for not mourning, along with her, those things that were not so much gone, as never discovered.

. . .

At the sound of the alarm Meg struggled out of bed the next morning. After splashing water on her face and brushing her teeth, she went into Kurt's room and called his name. His eyes opened quickly.

She said, "No, dear, he's not home yet. I wish I could tell you otherwise." She felt the tears building above the tightening in her throat and turned from her son, looking out the window until she mastered her voice. She came and sat on the edge of his bed and said, "Last night I made a decision. I'm going to call your Aunt Tolly in Wyler later this morning. Maybe she can come here for a while and help us get through this. It's a busy time on the farm at this time of year, but maybe Uncle Charlie and the new man they hired could handle things by themselves for a while. Wouldn't it be nice to have her here again?"

"Yeah, Ma. But, since she always takes the bus, it'll take time for her to get here. Will you be okay until then?" He looked steadily into her eyes while he asked this.

Meg felt almost undone by his concern. Feeling another wave of tears coming on, she again turned her head away. Finally, she rested her hand on his forehead, smoothing back his hair and stroking his cheek. "I'll be fine, dear, as long as I have my three little chicks. So, come on, little chick, get up. School awaits. Time's a-wastin', as they say."

5

TOLLY

Tolly and Charlie were early risers, but Meg felt it was way too early to phone them. While she waited, she made herself a pot of coffee, then paced around the family room, coffee cup in hand, plumping the pillows on the sofa and doing a one-handed sort of the hodgepodge of art supplies on the children's bookshelf. Deciding it was hopeless; she sat down and thought about her sister.

When they were children living on the farm, even though Tolly was eight years older, they'd been inseparable. At times Meg struggled with Tolly's bossiness and her tendency to shepherd her, but now that they were older Meg accepted both traits with understanding and good humor.

With Ma's death coming so soon after Papa's, there'd been no will, so they'd decided between themselves that Tolly should inherit the farm. That had always felt natural and right, since Tolly and Charlie had been helping Ma and Papa work the farm ever since Meg was in middle school.

At the time, Tolly and Charlie were living in a small house in nearby Wyler, so it wasn't a chore moving their things into the old place. Carrying on Papa and Ma's work like that had helped both women deal with their grief. In fact, it was like the kitchen stove had hardly cooled from Ma's last fire; and like Ma's breadboard, which still held flecks of flour from her last batch of bread, released those flecks to be kneaded into Tolly's cinnamon rolls. And Papa's old abandoned pail, that still bore his fingerprints, was used by Charlie to feed the chickens.

As though Papa's death wasn't hard enough, Ma dying just a few weeks after him was devastating. Ma's efforts to keep her mourning for

Papa private had been short-lived. Looking pale and drawn and walking carefully, she'd nevertheless tried to appear bright and optimistic at the meals her daughters prepared for her. She'd said she was doing just fine, instructing them that a person should limit the grieving period and get on with life.

But those were just words. Ma's leave taking began when she no longer looked at the land she loved so well. Then she confessed that without Papa her life had no point. Even the antics of Tolly's son, Johnny, couldn't rouse her interest. As her health gave way, the sisters despaired at seeing her gathering reasons to leave, much as she'd once collected firewood and kindling for the kitchen range, and they were horrified that they had no way to stop her. It was in anguish that they listened to her rocker's "creak-creak, creak-creak" slow then stop altogether. Early one morning Tolly found her dead, lying on her side of the bed, with Papa's side just as neat and undisturbed as it had been for weeks. When they buried her beside Papa in the little family plot in the wheat field east of the house, both sisters admitted to feeling a kind of relief that Ma was again with Papa.

It took a while before the sisters could speak of their mother in any way but hushed tones; and even then their words came out crooked and oddly obscure. During one of Tolly's phone calls, months after Ma's death, they were talking about this and that when Tolly blurted out, totally out of context, "She never showed me how to make that taffy." Both women had cried then, knowing full well that a recipe for taffy wasn't the reason they cried; they cried because they wanted it all back. They wanted Ma back, wanted Papa back, wanted back those simple days on the farm where everything revolved around Ma—the kitchen table, the wood range, the clotheslines, the smell of ironing, the old songs played on the piano, the blue spaghetti bowl, the Dutch oven, her roughened hands braiding and tying ribbons in their hair, their little-girl dresses she'd sewn and starched for them, her red hands on the pump handle or dipping hot water from the range's reservoir into the round tin tub for their baths, her smiles and kisses. They missed, too, the look she gave Papa that showed her daughters, more than words, what loving a man was all about. A recipe for making taffy was just easier to talk about.

Meg hunched forward in pain, remembering. At least she and Tolly still had each other, even though their lives seemed farther apart than the three hundred miles that separated them. On one of Tolly's annual visits, Tolly had examined Meg's closet, running her hand thoughtfully over the silk fabric of the many dresses hanging there. When Tolly held one of Meg's fine leather pumps against her own practical shoe, Meg went over to the closet, blocking it, feeling something like shame at its contents, and looking like she'd been caught in a clandestine act.

Tolly dropped the shoe, but stood looking in the mirror and shaking her head. "My lands, Meggie, are we even related? Next to all that elegance I feel like a—a loaf of bread!" She chuckled, "I'm even shaped like one—short and round and compact like a proper loaf should be. And I have golden brown skin, thanks to the life I live."

Meg had put her arms around her sister, drawing her close. Looking down at her she said wistfully, "Oh, Tolly, you know those clothes aren't real. I'm made of wheat, too, because that's how Ma and Papa made us." They'd laughed together.

Thinking of the farmhouse and Tolly's kitchen brought to mind the phone Tolly would speak into once Meg called her. She could almost hear the odd gargle of the phone ringing across the miles to the Jefferson household; almost see Tolly scuttling across the big old kitchen, through bacon and coffee and fried potato smells to the ancient relic hanging on the kitchen wall. While Meg curled up around her own little ivory-colored phone as she talked, Tolly's phone remained as thrifty and utilitarian as the people who used it now and in the past.

That phone, long since updated for this modern age, hadn't moved a smidgen from its original location—between the tall single-paned kitchen window and the stairs going down to the cellar. And it still looked the same: a varnished oak box housing its collection of parts, the silver bells on top, the neck still swooping and proffering its guileless black daffodil of a mouthpiece, the stubby cone-shaped earpiece dangling from a cord, and that funny little crank on the side—now just a decoration.

When she and Tolly were little they had considered that particular corner of the kitchen as the source of all things new and noteworthy. At any interesting sound coming from outside the house, the girls raced to that corner and waited by the window's low sill. The dirt path leading to the house ran close to that window, and anyone entering the house walked by it, sometimes even brushed against it. To their delight, Papa made as if to tweak the girls' noses through the window glass when he came in to wash up for meals.

Meg remembered that it was the phone and the window that brought most of the news to the farm—the good news and the bad. In times of storms the window and the phone worked together. Because the window faced west—the direction the wind and most weather came from—it was there they got their first real glimpse of what was headed toward the farm. And it was from that phone they'd usually received the official weather alarm (in the form of four short rings) issued by Mrs. Thompson, Wyler's one phone operator. She'd send this alarm all at once to all thirty-five telephones in the general area, in the unlikely case that the farmers hadn't already noticed a storm's looming presence.

Meg clearly remembered her mother surveying their wheat fields in those times of imminent weather: standing straight-backed, her chapped hands making fist-sized lumps in her apron pockets, and her eyes gauging and assessing the where and the when and the how-bad of the approaching storm. At those times her eyes held a wariness that put both girls on alert. But it was when Ma clamped her lips together a certain way—and the sky was getting dark—that Meg knew it wouldn't be long until Ma would say, "Tolly, why don't you take little Meggie down into the cellar." Then she'd lighten up her voice and add, "Looks like we're going to have a little spell of weather, girls. I'll be along as soon as I see where your Papa is." And to Meg (who feared the crash of lightning and racket of hail against the house even more than the dreaded mourn of wind winding around the chimney at night), Ma would say, "Now Meggie, you just remember, if it hails and the hailstones are big enough, we'll gather them and use them to freeze some ice cream. And, Tolly dear, while you're down there in the cellar, why don't you and Meggie get our old ice cream grinder from under the stairs, and decide what flavor you'd like me to make." It was usually chocolate or burnt-sugar, but even the anticipation of that didn't lessen Meg's fear of the storm.

. . .

Meg picked up the phone and dialed. While she waited for someone to pick up, she pictured Tolly—all five foot four inches of her—standing on her toes to reach the phone's mouthpiece. The picture almost brought Meg to tears as she anticipated the comfort she knew she'd find from speaking to her sister.

"Hello? Hello?" Tolly's voice was always loud at first, not often trusting that the phone was working.

"Hi, Tolly. It's me."

"Meggie? Why, for land's sakes! How nice to hear you. I was just tellin' Charlie and Old Flint that when we hear the phone ring at this time of day, it's got to be Meggie callin'. And here you are. Is everthin' all right with the babies and all?"

"They're fine, they're great, and me too, only—"

Meg heard her sister cover the mouthpiece and say a muffled, "Yes, yes, Charlie, it's Meggie, and she says everthin's all right. Could you switch down the radio a bit?" Then she again spoke loudly to Meg, "You say all three of those babies are okay? Did I hear that right?"

"Yes, they're fine, they're fine. It's all right, Tolly, I can hear you just fine." She lowered her voice in the hope that her sister would take the hint, but just in case held the phone away from her ear. "The kids had a good winter, but they're looking forward to having school over for the summer in a few weeks. You know how that goes. Kurt is enjoying his new bike. He's getting so handsome. And the Littles are growing so fast. Callie was just able to squeeze into Sara's last year's jeans. And poor Sara always needs something new. Even her socks are too small. They're both such tomboys and would be happy if they could live in jeans all the time. How about you and Charlie?" She plunged on, hating to move on from these small inconsequential words of everyday life, words no one else would think important. "And what about that new man you wrote about that you've hired? Is he working out for you? Will Johnny have to take leave from college to help with the heavy fieldwork coming up? You mentioned you'd like to come here for a visit. Are you thinking that you can get away any sooner?"

When Tolly answered, her voice was quieter and confiding. "We're just fine as can be, Meggie. As for Johnny, no, he won't be back for a spell. Charlie and I, we decided it's no good to lean on Johnny bein' here to help us, what with his college and all. I'd forgotten I'd written you about our fancy new help, about how Old Flint just walked off a bus and there he was, almost before we knew we needed him." After that Tolly's voice raised again and Meg heard low laughter in the background, like Charlie and the old man were nearby and listening, and what she was saying was more for their benefit.

Tolly continued, "My-oh-my, Old Flint's workin' out real fine. Been as big a help as Charlie was when Papa and Ma were alive and we were able to take some of the load off their shoulders. Old Flint and Charlie get on real well. They're cut out of the same piece of cloth, if you know what I mean. I tell you, a body better watch out when those two get goin'. I've heard so many tall tales here lately that I'm beginnin' to wonder just what the straight of a story really is." Again Meg heard the men laughing.

Tolly's voice turned fully back to the phone, and she spoke softly into it. "Old Flint's real quiet like Charlie, and his humor runs slow, then just kinda leaps out at you. We really lucked out with him." She laughed contentedly. "Hold on a minute, Meggie." Her voice again turned away from the phone. "Now what?" then came back "Charlie wants me to tell you we've had plenty of moisture this year and it looks like it's gonna be a good wheat year." She paused. "He says, 'Of course, that's if the hail don't get us or the heat or the wind or the grasshoppers or...'" she broke off, laughing. "You of all people know there's always somethin' waitin'. But we'll do just fine, long as Hope don't let us down and we forget to laugh!"

Meg closed her eyes and felt comforted by that last statement. Tolly's words were a lesson on just how contagious Charlie's way of speaking could be. His soft, slow talk, with all its shortcuts and

Southern expressions, was by now almost perfectly mirrored in Tolly's speech, and Meg had no doubt it was there permanently. It didn't take Meg more than a day's visit in the Jefferson household to find she'd started dropping her "g's," too. Weeks afterwards she'd hear herself calling the kids "Babe" or "Sugar"—which always tickled them.

Charlie was born and raised in southwestern Montana, in country that had been settled by Missourians after the Civil War. Even though his Missouri twang was many, many generations removed from its origins, it had changed little. Montana's size and geographical barriers had a way of isolating people in out-of-the-way pockets for decades, thus keeping their idiosyncrasies of speech and culture free from contamination.

Those sweet words and sounds were only part of Charlie's influence. Tolly's whole way of looking at things, her stoicism, was now like his. Of course, just being farmers made for a different viewpoint. To any *non*-farmer, what looked like a late spring dip of the thermometer, or a mere cloudburst, or a lifting of the wind, was something that had already gotten a *real* farmer's full attention. Any one of these things could spell disaster to a whole year's growing season, heralding a lean year, and possibly prompting a hurried trip to the local bank for a loan—just to survive another year. Yet somehow Charlie and Tolly Jefferson took it in stride, with their soft slurring of forgiveness laden with the hope that they would fare better next time.

Papa had reacted differently, been less accepting. To the weather gods that ruled his little kingdom, he'd shake his fist and roar a healthy "Damnation!" for what they'd just dealt him. Those reactions of her father, as he'd looked at a disaster that had befallen him, caused Meg to wonder about her own response. In her years of discontent with Ed, she'd never raised her fist to the gods; but like someone doing penance, she had accepted his neglect, and blamed *herself* for having made such a poor choice of mate. Even now, she couldn't shake her fist about that; reaching out to her sister for help was the only thing she could think of to do.

Longing to hear Tolly speak more about hope for a while longer Meg pushed her ear tightly against the phone. But finally she just had to tell her. "Tolly dear, I hate to interrupt, but there's something else. We've run into a situation here. Ed left four days ago right after breakfast, and he hasn't returned. No one knows where he went. Even though he took his car there haven't been any new credit card receipts—you know, for gas or food, which might indicate where he went. He's just gone. He left us without a goodbye."

"Oh, Meggie!"

"Yes. I don't know how a person as well-known as Ed can get lost, but he has. He didn't leave any notes saying where he was going, and his doctor doesn't know anything. He just disappeared."

There was silence on Tolly's end, so Meg asked softly, "Did you hear me?"

"Of course, Meggie, every word. Excuse me, dear, Charlie will want to know."

Meg closed her eyes and leaned her head back against the loveseat's cushion, while Tolly's muffled voice explained about Ed. When she came back on line, she said, "Our hearts just pain for you. You should have called sooner, but we're grateful you did now. What can we do to help? Do the babies know what's goin' on?"

"It's hard to say anything because I don't know anything." Her voice broke for a moment then continued, "They're wonderful, but I can tell they're afraid, too. Ed's been in such a weird mood lately. We've been walking on eggs for months in hopes he'd snap out of it. But I wasn't prepared for this." She paused, "If only he'd said something. But he never did. What's wrong with me that he couldn't tell me?"

"There, there, Meggie, don't you go puttin' the blame on yourself. I won't hear of it. With all you're called on to do, and that big house to care for, and those babies and all. If I recall right, you've never had someone around like Charlie here. A body can only do so much, you know. Would it help if I come there to be with you and the babies 'til Ed comes back? Would that help? Of course, it would. Charlie's standin' here waggin' his head up and down at what I'm sayin'. Here, Charlie, you tell her."

Charlie's kind voice came on the line and Meg could almost see his pale blue eyes and his sandy mustache moving up and down as he said the very same things Tolly had said. "...So if my little bride can anywheres near help you, I can get her on the bus tonight around midnight. That's when it comes by the feed store in Wyler. Let's see now...it'll take about eight hours, so, if I 'member right, that'll put her into Clark Fork tomorra' morning around eight. I'd be pleased if you'd call up the bus people and make sure of the time, so you can collect her without her worryin'. I'll do fine here. I'm tellin' Toll this along with you, Meggie. Old Flint and me'll be jest fine as rain here. He keeps tellin' me he was a hell of a better cook than any of his wives were. He tells how he kin even arn a shirt. So, hell, I reckon I'll jest find out if he's tellin' the truth. 'Course, I'll more'n likely find out jest why all his wives left 'im! But don't you worry, gal. Toll'll be there to hep ya. And if I was at all able to leave the farm, I'd be there, too." His soft feathery voice turned away from the phone and Meg heard him say, "Toll-babe, you wanta add anythin' else? This here is runnin' into a pricey call fer yer sister."

Tolly came back on the line and said, "There's nothin' more to say, just that I'll be there tomorrow morning and we can get all caught up on the news then. Now, Meggie, you just keep rememberin' that things just can't get any worse."

. . .

But, things *did* get worse.

Ma used to say, "Things just couldn't get worse." Meg could see her good face looking out that window at the black-bottomed clouds with their giant jags of lightning scuttling toward them and their wheat. When her mother said that things couldn't get worse, Meg knew that things were about to get worse; that the tall perfect greening wheat that the wind was presently stroking, that was yielding softly like hair under a hairbrush, was in for it. When Ma made that statement, the words were said, not as a fact of law, but as a prayer, a forlorn hope.

. . .

The kids were up by the time she finished talking to Tolly, and she fed them breakfast and got them off to school. Her initial excitement about Tolly's impending visit was replaced by inertia. She was trying not to go back to bed when the doorbell punctured the silence. She moved sluggishly toward it—not thinking of Ed being there anymore and too tired to be wary of whom it might be.

It was Art Stroud. Once she noted the look in his eyes, she knew for a fact that the forlorn hope of Tolly and Ma was about to go down in flames. She wondered if she should chant the words to the old ritual, saying, "Come on now, Art, you know very well that things can't get any worse." But all she managed to say was, "Tell me!"

He said, "I waited until the children were in school. I know you have a lot on your mind, but—" He put his hand on her arm, gripping it hard. "It's not what you think, Meg. I haven't heard from Edward."

As he said this, she looked down at his hand on her sleeve. It was an old, rich-man's hand, and she didn't want it touching her. A blue vein in his white skin moved in little tics, and the curved nails at the ends of his fingers showed a perfect patina of clear lacquer. As she lifted her eyes and looked at him, she drew her arm away and shifted her position slightly, to block him from entering—to make him have to stand outside.

Something far back in his eyes registered her gesture and his voice became sharp-edged. "I've been going over things at the bank, Meg, and I'm concerned that something's missing. At first glance I think there might be some irregularities with something Edward was working on. I won't know for sure until we have an audit. I called the Feds. Understand, Meg, I had to call them, in light of Ed's association with the bank. Someone will speak to you about his leaving, particularly that last morning. And they'll undoubtedly be inquiring about your and Edward's finances. You need to be aware of all this. They're flying in tomorrow and you'll have to come down to the office and tell them what you know. But now it's time that you tell me what's been going on. Tell me about his last morning, the day he left."

Stunned, Meg tried to think of the morning Ed left, but it was only the little inconsequential things she remembered: Ed's last breakfast, his wiping his mouth on the corner of the napkin as he left the table, his hand flicking at a crumb on his striped blue tie, his brushing his teeth while letting the water run full blast—and her critically thinking that, because he'd been raised in Western Montana, he wasn't aware of such things as wasting water.Then there was his closing the garage door so quietly.

While she stood, stricken, by the door, she began to answer Art's questions. She told him that Ed had appeared distant and depressed, but he was often like that. She said they weren't in need of anyone else's money—if that was what he was talking about. She reminded Art of what he already knew, about Ed being an only child and his parents leaving him considerable wealth.

As she faced him, she felt a terrible anger rising inside her, mixed with bitter tears. But she held them off by looking calmly at him as she spoke. And all the while she thought of her mother—of her back so straight, of the composure on her face, of the defiance in her eyes as she looked out that window by the phone. She'd never seen her mother cry in despair at the destruction coming straight for them and their crops. Even when the roof's shingles flew through the air; and the window glass splintered; and balls of lightning rolled down the fence, spinning off somewhere; and the roaring wind tore at the wheat, flailing it about, snapping off the precious heads of grain and grinding them into the mud, her mother had never cried.

6

THE MOUNTAIN

She couldn't believe how methodically she did everything. After the door closed behind Art, she calmly went into the bedroom and changed into her old wool pants and heavy walking shoes, and pulled a wool cardigan over her shirt. In the kitchen, as though someone other than she were doing it, she went to the refrigerator and took out cheese and lettuce and mayo, found bread, and watched her hands make a sandwich, saw them write "lettuce" on the grocery list clamped to the refrigerator, saw them open its door again and reach for an apple, then grapple for a bottle of water on its lower shelf. The hands with the square fingers then stuffed the food into the pockets of her sweater and she left the house.

She didn't have a plan when she got into her car. Go some place where she could think of what to do and what to tell the children. Go to the mountains maybe. It was not bearable to wait at the house and defend a man she no longer knew. Art's questions had disparaged everything she and Ed had worked for. As she got in the car she went over those things she knew for sure, that Ed had been depressed and he had disappeared. The rest was just Art's insane imaginings—she had to remember that.

Had anything she'd said helped Ed any? She tried to recall. She spoke aloud, "Ed, you've got to come back. I can't answer Art's questions. Come back and tell Art he's wrong. And when those friends of yours find out, you've got to tell them, too. You've got to explain for the kids' sakes." It was that litany she repeated as she sped away, away from her futile vigil, away from the front door bell, the phone, and even away from the stricken faces of her children as they left for school in the morning.

Once she left the town's eastern edge, she turned onto the familiar road leading into the deep canyon separating two steep-sided mountains. There was a picnic ground several miles farther up this road where she and the kids had often gone. If she could get there she'd park back in the trees, get out and walk a while, and think about what to do. After passing the last few homes along the canyon road she changed her mind: someone she knew might be at the campground. Instead, she'd find a road to take her up into the mountains. That's where she needed to go. Wasn't that what Papa said, that a person can always find refuge in the mountains? It was an early lesson and she could hear his voice saying it.

When the canyon road narrowed she slowed the car and began searching for a turnoff of some kind. Within a mile she noticed a dirt road cutting off to her right and took it. For a while the road followed a creek, swollen with the melt water of the May thaw, and then it turned, losing the creek, and the car was at once climbing the north slope of the mountain, just as she had hoped it would.

She saw the road only as a means of escape—where the road went she would go. She thought of nothing but to drive higher and leave all that was familiar as far behind her as she could. When the road split into two roads she hesitated. The fork to the left was bigger and in better condition, but it looked like it might eventually flatten out and leave the mountain; the other smaller fork was headed up the mountain. She turned onto it.

The road would be designated a road on a map, but, in fact, it was only two narrow ruts winding up the steep grades and switchbacks through the dense stands of trees anchored to the mountainside. In places it was only a narrow shelf carved into the side of the mountain. Yet, despite the road's condition, driving on it satisfied her. It reminded her of the roads they had encountered long ago on her family's camping trips. She and Tolly called them "Papa's roads."

On one of the switchbacks she caught her reflection in the car's mirror and was appalled at how haggard she looked. In that second of inattention, a deer bounded across the roadway in front of the car, scraping the bumper. Meg twisted the steering wheel and stomped on the brakes as the deer slid down the slope and out of sight. From the tilt of the car Meg knew the front wheel was nearly hanging off the road. She steadied herself, eased the car into reverse and backed carefully away. Once she was safe, she set the brake and just sat there.

The shock had cleared her mind, and she realized she was humming an old tune from her childhood, one she and Tolly had sung so they wouldn't have to think about Papa's roads. The memory made her laugh and she started driving again. The road was awful: rivulets of water from the sun-tattered snow banks ran down the ruts and splashed under the tires, and she had to maneuver around rocks and little mudslides. Even so, it didn't faze her, and she kept on humming. When her grip on the steering wheel finally began to relax she felt her past and present dip toward each other and meet—and all the while she remembered Papa's roads.

. . .

It was the quality of a fishing stream that determined where they camped, and it was Papa who was in charge of getting the family there. The problem was that sometimes the road connecting the two didn't actually exist.

Papa's sturdy two-wheeled trailer—stuffed with camping gear and wrapped in mud-splashed canvas and rope—bumped obediently along behind the car. But in the worst parts of their route it began a cowardly sliding and tugging at the car like a great unwilling fish. And although Papa's hand was gripping the steering wheel and maneuvering the little caravan along an ancient roadbed—around washouts, rocks, landslides, and sudden peril—his head and elbow and shoulder were outside the window, assessing a creek somewhere far below them.

Every so often Ma would pat Papa's arm worriedly and ask in a squeezed-down voice, "Now, James, do you really think the car can drive over that?" To which he would answer, "Tess, I always get you there, don't I?" Papa's words squeezed out around the pipe stem clamped between his teeth as he leaned further out the car window. "I can see the crik down there, and it's a beauty! Would you three stop just sitting there and look at that water. Those trout are just waiting for us. Can't you imagine how they'll taste in the morning with coffee and bacon? Now, if I can just get over this damned thing—" One of the car's wheels, that had crept onto a large rock, came to the end of it and dropped off; and the thud was followed by a sickening metallic grind of the trailer's hitch and chain being dragged over the same rock. Miraculously the car kept going (having given up on Papa and found surer footing on its own, it would seem).

But if the fishing holes below them were all that wonderful, Papa had to look at them all by himself—no female in the car could bring herself to peer out the window. Tolly, beside Meg in the back seat, had given her a terrified look after that last thud, and was now twisting a piece of her hair, pulling it way out in the air above her head and squinting up at its ends. She did that hair thing when she was scared. But she wasn't half as scared as Ma was, sitting in the front seat by Papa—her body all angles and corners, her feet jammed against the floor boards, her arms braced against the door and the dashboard—but still managing to turn around and give those in the back seat her white-lipped report on their situation. As if the girls hadn't heard, she'd assure them about the trout before again turning back and confronting her family's possible demise.

Meg and Tolly had learned to hum songs during these occasions. If one word of doubt was uttered, Papa would stop the car, draw his head back inside, and inform them that he was a mountain man at heart and a flat-land farmer only by trade, and after this past year of farming he really needed their encouragement.

In all ways Papa was a careful and considerate man. He was a loving husband and a thoughtful and just father. He asked little for himself, other than peace and respect, good food, Irish tobacco for his pipe, and the chance, at least once a year, to leave the farm and go into the mountains in search of the wily trout.

A week or so before the trip a kind of pioneering madness fell over him. He stood taller, took longer steps, swore more often, and made many references to the side of his family that had come west on the Oregon Trail. In anticipation of the upcoming vacation he also exchanged his farm cap for his felt fishing hat. Somehow this proper headgear lent an official stamp to his going over every inch of his fishing equipment: checking his rod, analyzing the contents of his fishing box, buying new snelled hooks, a bigger spool of leader and sinkers enough to hold down the hooks in the tearing waters of whatever "crik" they would camp by.

The family's three females felt a great pride in his ability as a fisherman, and were confident that they would be well supplied with delectable fish on their vacation.After a satisfying day along a mountain creek, Papa would come back to camp and present them with a creel full of shimmering rainbow trout—in fact, he flung the creel down before the women in much the same way as his ancestor would have unslung a dead deer from his shoulder and thrown it onto the cabin floor. Somehow Papa's gesture with the fish said that he'd kept the wolves from their door a while longer.

It was with that same pioneering zeal that he prepared the hapless car for its mountain journey. Where his predecessors would have fattened up the oxen, bought a new whip, and thrown in a spare axle or two, Papa went over the car meticulously and lovingly, testing pressures and fluids, and making sure the two extra wheels and tires were among the emergency equipment laid out for their adventure. In a final gesture of readiness, he removed the big red car jack from its burlap bag and greased it up, as though the trip's success relied upon it, so it had better not fail.

It was where he placed the jack in the car that terrorized the women. It didn't get buried in the car's trunk, or put alongside the other tools in the two-wheeled trailer, but was laid naked on the floor behind the front seat—and anything that handy reminded the women that their camping experience could only be reached by roads that were too often figments of Papa's imagination. That jack was used more often than Meg liked to remember; and when it was used, she always had the feeling that it made Papa's fishing trips that much richer, a fact not particularly shared by the females of the family.

Without fail, they went camping every spring for two full weeks—"Long enough to know where you're at," Papa said of it. They named it a fishing trip, but it was more accurately a pilgrimage to the offerings of the mountains, the family's annual reward for surviving the austere wheat country they lived in. According to Papa, camping at established campsites that were overrun with other people wasn't camping. It was a wilderness experience he was after, a chance to live in the wild, as far from civilization as he could get.

Although Papa *said* he valued their opinions, picking out the actual campsite was entirely up to him. Ma called him, "Our benevolent dictator." Even when he announced, "We're here!" the clump of females could only wait silently for him to decide if the campsite was adequate. Even though everyone knew right off it would be perfect, customs were followed.

The big wall tent determined the size of the site, and there must also be room for the fire pit, Ma's wooden kitchen boxes, and the table Papa would nail together. As Papa paced off the site, he was thinking of such things as drainage and levelness, overhanging trees above the fire pit, and if the "crik" was close enough to be heard from the tent. All these considerations were critical, and no commitments could be made should his measurements, through some tragic error on his part, fall short. It was only after hearing his, "Yep, it'll do," that they could take possession of the chunk of land, "move into it" as it were, and start arranging the elements of their housekeeping as though they would be there forever—"forever" being a smaller measure then.

Each had his or her job. Ma had to settle the kitchen so she could cook supper, and it was up to the girls to gather enough wood to last until the next morning. The driest wood came from small, dead, standing trees that were easy to push down and drag back to camp.

The tent was not an aluminum/nylon quick-to-assemble thing, but a giant canvas and log structure, and it required the whole family to assemble it. Papa had to locate no less than seven thin trees to serve as the tent frame. These he cut down, trimmed, and dragged to the campsite. It also took yards and yards of rope to lash them together, but, in the end, with everyone near exhaustion, they had a crude, lumpy edifice that was not pretty or neat, but was sound enough to protect them and their gear from the weather for the next two weeks.

For a refrigerator a wooden box with shelves to hold the

perishables was placed into the water's edge. Holes had been bored into its side so the icy water could flow through it. A heavy rock was placed on its lid to discourage anything from getting at the food. Even so, wild minks were slim enough to swim through the holes, lured in by Papa's just-caught trout, or bacon. But it hardly mattered, surplus food was packed away in watertight cans; and watching the minks' efforts—often in full daylight—was part of the adventure.

By the time the camp was set up and their first meal eaten, the sun had set. In the fading light the camp looked tucked down and snug, as if it were an old Indian encampment on the bank of an ever-prattling creek. The tent's squatting form, with its giant poles rearing uneven and pointed above its swaddle of grey canvas, looked right at home among the willows, white-barked aspen, and green conifers that surrounded it.

As night came on, the chill of evening pushed the family ever closer to the fire. Meg loved the crackling fire with its sweet smoke and dancing sparks tunneling into the darkening sky. It was then that a sober quietness would overtake her, a feeling of being small against the wilderness. The campfire's glow marked a line beyond which safety seemed uncertain. In those long ago camps, even with the light of the big gas lantern hanging on a tree branch in the middle of their camp, and a flashlight clutched in her hand, Meg thought that the pain of a full bladder was easier to endure than the trek alone to the log designated as the toilet.

She had never conquered her fear of night in the mountains, thinking it a flaw in her character. In camp, when those unidentified night sounds poked at her, it was as if an unknown ancestral past sent a shiver down her spine. It made her think about how a dog must feel as it lifts its head and listens with its wolf brain and wonders what it once was.

In thinking of those campfires, Meg could finally summon up her parents' faces, their whole young faces—content and strong and funny and safe. And it was then that she could feel their arms around her, and clearly hear their voices, too. She saw Papa holding out his cup and heard him asking Ma if she could squeeze another cup of coffee out of those coffee grounds. Meg heard her Ma reply, "Yes, James, but you'll have to chew it." Meg held onto their words as long as she could, marveling that, despite the years, a whole scene could reappear like that.

. . .

Driving slowly, Meg wondered how old she'd been when she first felt the difference between living exposed on the austere landscape of the farm and being enclosed in a comforting forest. As a child, having lived nowhere else but Wyler, she'd thought the whole earth was accompanied by that lonely monotone of wind pouring unimpeded over the fields and into her ears, inflaming them and making them ache and drain. But inside one of Papa's forests, the trees' tiny sighs only tickled her ears.

There were no trees on the farm or any in the whole town of Wyler. In that country, what trees there were cowered in little sheltered breaks where water might chance to collect and where the wind couldn't reach them. So the mountains' trees were a major part of the magic of camping, as were the creeks.

On the farm, water was pitifully scarce and, because it had to be pumped by hand or by windmill, it was never used lavishly. Water meant effort, a bargain to be struck. Their well, reaching deep beneath the farm, filled to brimming in the spring, but by August it had dwindled. In especially drought-ridden years, the well produced a brownish sludge only fit for livestock. Potable water had to be hauled by tanker-truck from an artesian well twenty miles from the farm. Often water was used twice or more. Bath water, from the round tin tub that she and Tolly shared, was collected and saved, then reheated for laundry or general cleaning. One year, their "recycled" water ended up in the parched garden. When they dug up the potatoes they smelled a little like soap. Ma joked, "If they don't lather up when I boil them, they'll be okay to eat."

Having to work for every drop of water on the farm, it was hard to forgive a mountain creek's wastefulness, allowing all that water—its taste so sweet, with its hint of mint and fish—to rumble by so carelessly, pouring itself into a cupped hand or bucket while hardly stopping on its race to—where? When Meg asked Papa how that pretty water stayed on top of the ground, he shrugged and said,"So we can see it, Meggie. Isn't that why we're here, to see it? Maybe we wouldn't care about it otherwise." In her heart Meg knew she'd always care about it.

Papa identified the little darts in the pools as trout. Sometimes he took Ma and them fishing, and they took turns using Papa's one fishing rod. When it was Meg's turn, Papa would put his big hand over hers on the rod's handle, then help her flip out the line, with its little weighted hook and worm, so that it would land just above the riffle and drift into the trout's unsuspecting world. When a trout grabbed it, the electric chill of its terror traveled up through the line and into her hand. She would shriek with delight and jerk it out of the water—the fish flying through the air. She felt remorse at ending its silver wriggling life, with its solemn eyes, but her sorrow was short lived. Tasting the sweetness of the fish after Ma had rolled it in flour and fried it golden crisp in bacon fat, was...well, so good that eating a trout made the water running so freely seem okay.

. . .

An overwhelming yearning for those cherished times with her parents filled Meg. The losses that time imposed were so absolute: Tolly grew up and got married; she herself left the farm and got married; Papa died so young, and Ma soon after. What had been their family and those wilderness experiences now seemed like an empty hole, filled with remembered joy, yes, but full of loss, too.

And now there was this terrible thing with Ed. There were maps and rules for any number of things, but for surviving something like this there was nothing—no advice, no how-to manual and, outside a movie theater, no real success stories that she knew of. Over time she had found ways to make her Halverson life tolerable—with her children, her garden, painting, and music, her pride in her cooking, her secret pride in herself—but if Art Stroud was right and there was the possibility of public scorn, she would be forced to go it alone.

The laboring of her car's engine cut into her thoughts. Finding herself in a fairly flat recess of the forest, she parked the car, set the brake, and got out. Walking slowly, she stopped in a grove of large trees. Lying in its center was all that remained of a huge old fallen tree. It had lost its bark eons ago and now was silver with age. She was drawn to it and looked around in wonder.

The colors and smells and sounds of the forest leaped vividly into her senses, as though just created. The air was pungent and she wanted to put her nose against the earth to discover the source of each smell. She brushed her hand over the moss growing on the log's silvery wood, then leaned down and touched the buds swelling along a twig of huckleberry, marveling at its perfection. By July it would be bent under the weight of luscious berries. Although there were still traces of snow around, fragile stems and tiny shoots of plants were already poking out from the forest floor, demanding their small share of the light falling through the forest's thick canopy.

In the quiet and darkness the very essence of the old forest started to become clear to her. She thought of her problems in relation to all these things. Everything around her had existed without her awareness: the ancient log lying so peacefully in this beautiful grove of trees, the dense shrubbery around it, the unknown succession of big and little plants at her feet. She thought, all these things are part of a continuum, of things living their lives, facing what they must, and dying quietly as the next generation takes over. Surely this is what life on this earth is, and I am only one small part of it. She was filled with a sense of the rightness of things and a feeling that everything would be all right.

At last she could put her face in her hands and weep—weep for the love that had been lost, weep for her children, and weep for what would be asked of her.

When the tears were gone she understood she had been comforted. Still she lingered in the quiet light, listening to the distant "groak, groak, groak" of a raven, the odd questioning of a bird, and then the perfect silence.

7

THE FORTRESS

Calmed at last, Meg arranged her lunch on the mossy top of the log and began to eat. It had been days since she'd enjoyed eating and her body ached for the nourishment. Sipping the last of her water and picking the crumbs of her sandwich off the paper, she marveled at her luck in choosing this beautiful place. But coming up here without telling Doris or the children wasn't like her. It was wrong to have taken any risks, considering her responsibilities. And that dicey road and the near accident with the deer, she shuddered. But the thought of going back right away was unbearable. It was three hours until she had to be home.

She gave the log a companionable pat and wondered what she should do next. She could go back to the car and drive farther up the road, in the hope of getting a really grand view of the country from there. Or she could walk east for a ways under these beautiful old trees; maybe there was a view that way, too. She left the log and headed east.

It didn't take long to question her choice, for she was soon in a jumble of underbrush and downed trees. It was slow going and she was about to turn back when she glimpsed a road skirting the far edge of the tangle. She worked her way over to it and found that the road was in far better condition than the one she had driven up on; perhaps it led to a Forest Service lookout. She began to follow it, but only after getting her bearings—she certainly didn't want to get lost.

She hadn't walked far when she saw a short path and a cabin tucked under some immense fir trees. It looked so perfect there! She stood back utterly charmed. Judging from the amount of forest debris littering its roof and front step no one had been in it for a while. With that assurance, she walked up to it.

The cabin's lower half was built of beautiful stones. The craftsman who'd done the work had an eye for beauty and proportion, having combined the diverse gold and blue-green stones so artfully. With that same attention to detail the upper half of the cabin was built of logs, laid horizontally onto the stonework. Its windows were set into deep window wells.

The cabin's door, opening onto a single low step, was wide and substantial, and had black hand-forged iron hinges extending across its entire width. Had it not been locked she couldn't have resisted going inside.

Through a window, she got a clear view of its one large room. There were no cupboards or table and, most remarkably, there was no stove, even though there was a rock chimney to accommodate one. In the far corner she saw a narrow cot with metal springs and a mattress. Beside it was a dilapidated upholstered chair that mice had been working over—pulling out its stuffing for nests, she supposed. Other than a scattering of beer bottles, there was nothing else. Before leaving the cabin, she walked around it. This darling cabin, what a shame it wasn't being used. And why was it even here?

Spurred on to see what more she could find, she again followed the road. Rounding a bend she saw a massive three-story house sitting high and alone on the top edge of a large clearing. The road ended abruptly at a garage built into the lower part of the house. Power lines, coming from a swath cut through the trees, were connected to it. There were no tire tracks crossing the remains of a large snow bank lying in front of the garage doors. Undoubtedly its owners were gone for the winter and would be back any day now that spring was here. In spite of that, Meg kept back in the trees as she tried to comprehend what she was seeing. A cabin at this altitude was imaginable—as a hunter's cabin or a hiker's getaway—but a house up here on the side of a mountain, miles from town?

She was struck by the building's ugliness. Quite frankly, it looked more like a fortress than a dwelling, with its dark brown siding and blocky shape. All it lacked were battlements around its roof to complete the picture. An extraordinarily heavy hand had designed it, but the word "designed" was too charitable for its uninspired appearance. Its numerous windows were big equal-sized squares of glass, and none of them appeared to open. Their very spacing hinted of a modular likeness to the rooms inside.

But it was the overall look of the place that Meg found so perplexing. Where the cabin had been tucked into a cozy space under the trees, this building stood alone on the barest part of the slope, and was completely devoid of shrubs or trees—as though it didn't need coddling. But considering the buffeting the house undoubtedly took up here, it looked like it could withstand anything the elements could throw at it. The patches of snow that still lay around it attested to the severity of winter at this altitude. For all that, it was in remarkable condition.

Curious, but aware of her trespass, Meg moved out of the trees and went up to it. The house had two outstanding features: its immense stone chimney of the same beautiful rockwork used on the cabin, and a very large slab of blue-green stone serving as the front doorstep. The stone was so perfect in size and so remarkably smooth and beautiful that Meg concluded that it was there first and the house built beside it.

The view from the house would be to the north and the west; and when she looked to see what the owners would see from their windows, she was awestruck. From this highest point of the clearing was a magnificent view of the town, the entire valley, and the distant mountains beyond it. She shook her head in disbelief: up here, a person had the earth and the sky all to one's self!

The huge clearing below the house was remarkable. It was dotted with shrubs and small trees, and it still had snow in spots, but she could imagine what a few weeks of spring warmth could do to its large lush meadow. From the lower edge of the clearing, the thick forest hung like a great green blanket slung between two mountains—one edge caught on this side, and the other edge held firmly by the feet of the impassive mountain directly across from the house.

Turning from the view and looking at the house, Meg noticed that the remnants of snow hardly hid the fact that the soil around the house was lying in the same heaps pushed aside for the foundations years ago. A few ragged clumps of grass still clung to the old mounds of dirt. As a gardener she was puzzled. Why had the owners not restored the beautiful flow of the slope after the house was built, then planted shrubs and grass and made any attempt at a garden? Not doing that gave the land a violated look. What kind of uncaring people lived here? She shrugged and went over to the rock doorstep and ran her hand over its smooth warm surface before sitting down on it. She would bask in the sun and enjoy having this strange place all to herself.

A Red-tailed Hawk was soaring high above the meadow. As Meg watched it circle and glide above the mountainside—its wings a dark silhouette against the sky one moment then lost in the brilliance the next—it seemed the very symbol of the magnificent isolation of this place. For a long time she watched it; and as she did, she had the impression that the sky itself must begin right here. Looking up at the cloudless blue, she lifted her hands as if to touch the sky's border, and laughed at the thought. Sighing, she closed her eyes to absorb those things around her—the clean smell of the air, the feel of the sun on her shoulders, the tiniest thread of breeze lifting the curls on her neck. When she opened her eyes a feeling of tenderness came over her.

Bending down she laid her hand flat on the ground in front of her, to feel the earth's warmth. *This beautiful earth...* She wondered how long it had been since she had consciously reached out and felt the earth—not as a gardener, sifting soil purposely through her fingers, but as a person tries to ascertain what the earth itself is, what the earth as a separate entity is. The last time she'd done that was as a child on the farm. Had it really been that long ago? It brought to mind that old game with Tolly, "Touching Earth and Touching Sky." What the game's rules were she couldn't remember. Oh, yes, because Tolly was always the *sky-toucher*, she could only be the *earth-toucher*. She laughed. Up here she could be both the *earth-toucher* and the *sky-toucher*. Tomorrow she'd have to remember to tell Tolly that.

At her feet, a few grass spikes leaned toward the warmth of the rock. She watched an ant emerge from the grass and climb the toe of her boot, his antenna waving a brief hello before he descended her sole and disappeared. Her eyes moved from his tiny world to the trees moving gently in the same breeze that furled her hair.

It was fascinating to see the town from this height. She could spot its tiny landmarks, could guess where the Stroud bank was, the university, and her house. Distance subdued the town, turning it into a handful of toys strewn around on one side of the valley. Beyond the town and past the airport, a thick white plume identified the Kladstone Paper and Plywood Plant—another of Art Stroud's holdings. Seen from here the cloud was singularly beautiful. Its top, having hit some kind of ceiling, flattened out and was creeping slowly across the valley, as if searching for an opening through which to escape. Looks were so deceiving. That innocent cloud laid an all-pervasive stink across the whole valley and, with the jobs it created and the endless wood from these mountains being readied for its giant appetite, it most certainly wouldn't be allowed to escape.

Seeing it, she was reminded of the one argument worth having with Ed; the one she called "overharvesting" and Ed called "progress." Meg wished that he were here beside her to see what was happening, see the ugly denuded squares of clear cuts on many of the mountain slopes. From the valley floor a person could disregard it, but not from here. But thinking Ed would see the land as she did was silly. Any time she used the words "wood industry" and "environment" in the same sentence she could expect a fight. Ed viewed these things in purely economic terms, and wanted no check on the industry. He said that this was the kind of progress his predecessors (his ghosts) had only dreamed of. To Meg, his response never recognized what would happen to that industry when the forests were depleted and the environment changed—if not within his and her lifetimes, then certainly during those of the kids.

It was because of the kids that she wanted to openly state her views. As they grew and became more aware of the world, she wanted them to understand how human's very survival was dependent on nature. She wanted them to think of the consequences of overuse of resources. Otherwise they would grow up as just three more people who were oblivious to the effect they were having on the beautiful land around them.

As she got up from the rock to leave, she wondered if she would ever see Ed again. And if he had done what Art said, she just hoped that no scandal would touch the kids and hurt their Halverson name. But, if the last eighteen years had taught her anything, it was to fear the judgment of those friends and colleagues of Ed and Art Stroud. As she looked bleakly at the town below her, that old chant of her mother's came back, that things couldn't get worse. If only the worst was over... There was just enough time to explore the clearing before she went back home.

. . .

Clues of the clearing's history were still visible. The ruts of an old wagon road led to a gnarled apple tree, more prone than vertical, leaning against the remains of a fallen rock wall. There was a spring there, too, and Meg drank from it. Near it were the scattered stones of a crude fireplace, and, protruding from the soil, were two startling white pieces of broken pottery. When she picked them up and rubbed away the dirt, she saw they were not pottery, but of the most delicate paper-thin Irish porcelain, on which a fine border of tiny blue flowers were painted—the kind of porcelain that only a woman would bring up here. Meg was deeply moved by her discovery. Long ago, here on this mountainside, far from any amenities, a woman had lived. Perhaps it was she who had planted the apple tree, drunk from the spring, and cooked in the fireplace. Thinking that, Meg tucked the porcelain chips carefully back into the soil, then stood by the old wall a few moments longer, looking out over the meadow at the valley, seeing it as the woman must have seen it. Perhaps the woman's spirit was still here.

8

THE GATHERING STORM

Meg made a bet with herself that Tolly would be the first passenger off the bus. Tolly would have taken a front seat to be closer to the driver, or, more precisely, to be closer to his speedometer. Not that she would have said anything if he'd gone over the speed limit. She wouldn't have to. Long ago Tolly had perfected "the short sniff" as a deterrent to unlawfulness of any kind. Tolly was a formidable woman, who made up in determination for what she lacked in height, and her critical sniff really meant something.

Meg smiled in recalling one of Charlie's good-natured stories about Tolly. They'd been sitting around the farm's kitchen table when he'd said, "That sister of yours made my gettin' to know her pure hell before we were hitched. She could read my thoughts—that is, my *hand's* thoughts—and with just one sniff she could clear my thinkin' quicker than a whole raft of Baptist preachers could on a Sunday mornin'. Fact is, she has the makin's of a hell of a good huntin' dog. Even if a critter had only *thought* of crossin' under the fence and chewin' on a piece of our wheat, with one sniff she could blast it at twenty paces, and if that critter weren't dead, it was nigh on to wounded."

Before Charlie quit laughing, Tolly, with her eyes screwed up and twinkling, had waved a big wooden spoon at her husband, saying, "It's gettin' almighty treacherous in this kitchen today. Just remember, Charlie, you haven't eaten yet, and the cook has the last word around here."

. . .

Meg checked her watch. Even though the schedule board listed the westbound bus as on time, the bus was already twelve minutes late. The thought that the driver might have intended to make up time in the long stretches, and Tolly might be keeping him in line, gave Meg her first laugh of the day—and it might be her only one. She drained the last dregs of coffee from the heavy mug and took it back to the station counter for a refill. Its acrid taste didn't matter; it was hot and it was coffee, and she hadn't found time to brew any before she left the house. Just getting through these days and keeping things together was taking all of her energy.

Last night's dinner was a sorry affair of canned soup and peanut butter sandwiches. Cooking had become such an effort, and meals were more a matter of necessity than pleasure. But last night's upset was no one's fault but hers. Her return from the mountain took more time than she'd thought. When she'd arrived home, a whole hour after the kids' homecoming, both Callie and Sara were crying miserably. They'd thrown themselves angrily against her in a punishing gesture. Even Kurt was so resentful he hardly looked at her. Poor boy; for that whole frantic hour he'd dealt with the Littles' fears, and most likely his own. While that was going on, Doris had called, worried sick and sounding angry; the kids had called her and she didn't know what to tell them.

Meg lied to them all, saying that she had taken a drive and encountered some car trouble. None of them knew about Art Stroud's suspicions or why she felt she had to get away, not even Doris. And she certainly couldn't tell them of the wonderful afternoon she'd experienced up on the mountain; by that time she hardly remembered it herself.

Once the kids were in bed, instead of cleaning up the kitchen, she lay down on the sofa with a headache. It was way past midnight when she woke up, every lamp blazing, the fire long since dead, and the cold room feeling so alien. The walk to her bedroom seemed unbearably lonely. Even so, she had slept.

But this morning, Callie, dressed in her school clothes, threw her arms around her mother; and with her eyes brimming with tears, asked her in a quavering voice, "Are you sure you'll be here when we get back?" Meg promised her over and over she wouldn't go for any more drives alone. All the time she was reassuring Callie she was searching in vain for the tranquility and perspective she had gained on the mountain. But to no avail.

From the kid's actions Meg knew that there was talk about Ed at school. She could only imagine what cruel things were being said. Before this had happened going to school was fun, with Kurt joining a group of his raucous buddies, and Sara and Callie following in their group of girlfriends—the sidewalk was hardly wide enough to accommodate them all. But now all three of them dawdled over breakfast, then lingered around the front door, or looked for nonexistent books, or, at the last minute, decided to exchange something in their lunch boxes—an apple for an orange, or an orange for an apple. Their anxiety was almost more than she could bear. She kissed them, touched their faces to reassure them, tried to make a joke, then hugged them again. When they finally ran out of excuses, the three left together, running in a tight bunch, with just enough time to get to school before the tardy bell rang. She decided that the kids were the brave ones; their mother could hide in the house.

But she was hardly safe from the phone. Of the few calls she'd received, the one that upset her was from Evelyn Stone two days after Ed left, when, supposedly, no one knew he was gone.

Evelyn had actually sounded sympathetic, calling her "Hon" and making little cooing sounds. But after the "Hon" was over, Evelyn got into character. "We've wondered how your walk was, Hon, from Cora Lee's? Did Ed have anything to say about it? Art keeps him pretty busy, and I suppose his being gone that much is hard on a marriage." A few questions later, Meg had the strange impression that someone besides Evelyn was listening. She'd even imagined Evelyn's eyes widening and her mouthing the words, "What did I tell you?" Evelyn went on. "From what I hear, your children are pretty tense. And that business of Kurt hitting Ray Snyder's boy... Really, Meg, Kathy Snyder said that her Bobby was only asking Kurt how his daddy was." It was the first Meg had heard about a fight. She decided to take the coward's way out and not ask unless Kurt brought up the subject himself.

Meg made a few noncommittal replies, but with Evelyn so

obviously in search of something to report back to the girls, Meg remembered just why she'd left Cora Lee's that day, and she hung up. Then she kicked herself for not having the imagination to sidestep the woman—Evelyn Stone wasn't a good friend, but she was a very good enemy, and her tongue held a lot of power over women less inclined to give Meg a break.

That conversation was enough to make Meg hesitate every time the phone rang. And now, when the news about the audit got out... She didn't even want to think about it.

· · ·

Coming to the bus station was the first time she'd been in public since Ed left, other than a few quick grocery runs and her furtive trip to the mountain. Chiding herself for her cowardice, she had driven by the bus terminal twice before summoning the nerve to go inside. From the doorway she'd checked for familiar faces in the overflowing waiting room. There was no one she knew. Even so, when she went over to ask the attendant about the arrival of Tolly's bus, she agonized over how she must appear to everyone there. With her feelings of paranoia in full bloom, she even imagined that every eye was turned on her, expecting her to board the next bus and, without a backward glance, leave her family just as Ed had. She gripped her elbows hard enough to hurt and deepened her breathing. What was wrong with her? Who of these people knew what was going on with the Halversons, or for that matter cared? Thank heavens Tolly was coming. The whole family needed a protective fence around them, and tough little Tolly was the best person in the world to be that fence.

Meg sipped her coffee and gratefully turned her attention to the other people waiting for the bus. She felt at once drawn to, then repelled by, a young couple leaning against the wall, whispering quietly and unable to keep from touching each other. Whether it was love or just lust, seeing them only sharpened her feelings of loss and anger.

Opposite her, an American Indian woman, with whom she'd exchanged a smiling nod, drew her attention and her empathy. The woman, fighting her own need to sleep, crooned an odd little song in a minor key to her baby, bundled in an old quilt and sleeping beside her on the bench. All the while the woman made the gentlest rocking motions with her big hand on the baby's stomach. Just watching the woman's struggle to stay awake made Meg's eyes sag. It was all she could do to concentrate on the others.

Further on, two thin middle-aged men caught her attention. Both had big sweat-stained western hats pushed back on their heads, and wore frayed denim jackets and rumpled jeans. Their scuffed cowboy boots vied for the same floor space their luggage occupied—a dilapidated saddle and a box tied with rope. Each man held a little stub of hand-rolled cigarette between his nicotine-yellowed thumb and finger. Hunkering forward they talked without looking at each other, but looked up in unison each time a blonde girl dressed in pink jeans, with a long purple-fringed purse swinging from her shoulder, moved in the space she had staked out at the front of the waiting room. As the two men swung their heads up toward the girl, Meg was reminded of Papa's old geldings, Jake and Jess. They'd looked just like that whenever Tolly's little filly swished by them—running sideways, neck arched, tail up, and making snooty comments to them in that hard to define but easy to interpret language of horses.

Papa had loved those two old plow horses. Because the tractor was so much faster, those horses were "bygones" even when Papa used them. When the last one finally died, something happened to Papa's face. He looked peeved every time he started up the tractor, and at the end of the day, too, when he climbed down off it. He acted like he'd spent the day all by himself. And he had.

. . .

The hiss of air brakes, like punctuation at the end of a long sentence, heralded the arrival of the bus. It was followed by an official teeth-grinding intercom announcement that hurt the ears. And just as Meg had surmised, Tolly—that little general—was the first one off. The driver had a guarded look on his face as he steadied Tolly down the steps, and he looked positively unburdened when Tolly turned from him and called out, "Meggie!"

Meg suppressed a giggle as she pushed to the edge of the crowd and gathered her sister's tidy little figure in her arms. By the time all the "How-was-your-trip?" and "How-long-have-you-been-waiting?" questions were answered, Tolly, along with her bag and box, were being tucked into the car.

As Meg turned the car into the morning traffic and was nervously going on and on about how clean the streets looked,Tolly put her hand on her arm and said, "Now that's enough of that. Those circles and puffiness around your eyes are what I want to know about. I gather Ed's not back yet."

Meg shrugged and gave her a bleak look."No and I haven't heard a word from him. But it's worse than that,Tolly. Worse than I thought, and so damned stupid—"

"Of course it's stupid. It's idiotic, leavin' you like this. Charlie said—"

"No,Tolly, listen," Meg interrupted "it's not just Ed that's gone. Right after I called you, Art Stroud came to the house to tell me he's calling for a bank audit, implying that Ed might have made off with something. I told Stroud it's got to be a coincidence that Ed is missing too."

"Oh, Meggie!" Tolly steadied herself on the dashboard.

Meg continued."Stroud warned me that the auditors would want to question me, too. I wouldn't know what to tell them—"

"You tell them what you think, that's all."

Meg turned her face away."I'm the wrong one to do that—"

"Of course you can."

"No, I really can't,Tolly. I wouldn't know how to defend him. I've begun to question everything about him and us and whatever it is that he does at the damned bank." She gave up trying to drive and pulled into a space along the curb. Once the motor was off the two women looked silently at each other, their faces reflecting the same pain.

Tolly finally spoke,"Why in heaven's name would a man like Ed do that? All his talk about shoppin' centers and housin' developments and lumber mills and money, why would he risk doin' that? How could he ever come home to you again? People go to prison for doin' that."

The word "prison" sent a shiver down Meg's spine."That's too big and scary a word. Let's not talk about that. Okay?"

Tolly nodded and went on, "Sometimes I just hate money, and with Ed, it's like there's nothin' else to talk about. Charlie and I would have just fainted away if he ever asked us about the farm. Oh, he's asked us, polite like, but he's never been interested in what we answer; he never draws us out about it. The only reason we ever visited here was to see you and the babies."

Meg shrugged, and her words, "I know," were almost whispered. After a moment she said, "I keep wondering what my part is in all this. If only—"

"Now Meggie, like I said yesterday, I won't stand for that kind of talk—"

"But as his wife, they might think I had a part in this."

"Meggie, it wasn't you who left and is bein' accused."

Meg took up her sister's smaller hand and rubbed it with her thumb, taking comfort in it. She finally said, "He's really changed in these last couple months, he's—"

Tolly interrupted, "*Changed*? Changed from what? You mean he miraculously changed from what he always is?"

"You have to understand the demands on him, his deadlines—"

"Listen to yourself, Meggie. That's absurd! You're still makin' excuses for him."

"I guess I do."

"Even as a little tyke you always had a lot of hope, like you knew in your heart that good things would happen in the end, that all you had to do was wait." She looked over at Meg and laughed. "You thought Tommy Southers would change, as I recall. But I don't ever want you to change. Thinkin' the best and bein' optimistic was the way Ma and Papa raised us."

Meg smiled and nodded.

Tolly raised her voice, "What galls me is that none of you expect anything from Ed. You're his wife and those children are his babies, but he only claims you when he wants to brag about something, like it's *his* accomplishment. Land sakes, he doesn't know what a marriage is all about or what a husband and father is supposed to—" She stopped her tirade and looked sharply at Meg, who was leaning her face against her hands on the steering wheel. "Are you cryin', Meggie? Sounds more like you're laughin'."

Meg turned up her face and showed she was laughing, in fact was laughing so hard she had tears running down her face. When she was able to speak, she said, "You sniffed! You just did that famous Tolly Jefferson sniff!" She laughed into her hands again and finally looked over at her sister. "Oh, Tolly, I think I'm laughing, but I don't know why. There's not much to laugh about. But one thing I do know is I love you."

She dug a tissue from her purse and wiped her eyes and blew her nose. With a tentative smile, she said, "I've done a lot of thinking these last few days. Everything you've said is right. Just a little while ago, when I was waiting for your bus, there was a couple that reminded me of how it could be between a man and a woman—you know, *together* and everyone else nonexistent. But watching them got to me: while the woman talked, the man really listened to her, with the sweetest smile on his face. And when he answered her, he touched her cheek in the most solicitous way.

"I resented them and tried to pretend they had just met and the woman was saying something suggestive about sex, and he was agreeing and maybe wondering where the nearest bed was. But in my heart I knew by the look of them that they knew each other well and that that was the way they talked abut things: I didn't hear them, but it was husband and wife talk. I knew it was wrong to begrudge them that—I was just jealous."

She bit her lip at the sadness of her confession. "That time of intimacy between Ed and me...well, I don't know if it ever existed. We still sleep together and...have sex..." She gave a short laugh. "I was going to say 'make love,' but we only have a kind of mucky sex." She hesitated then gave Tolly an odd look. "I don't want to ask anything you aren't comfortable answering... But, does that happen to everyone's marriage? Lose its flavor? What about you and Charlie?"

Tolly swallowed and looked down at her lap for a moment. Then making up her mind, she spoke shyly, a little breathlessly. "With men and women bein' so different and all, and with Charlie and me doin' different things around the farm, I often wonder just how Charlie does it—keepin' me feelin' so special. But it's the little things he does, things like—in the spring, I can always plan on him pickin' me a bunch of those purple rooster heads and yellow bells and crocus in the coulee, like you and I picked as kids. He brings them to me with the strangest look in those pale blue eyes of his, like he's almost afraid to show me how deep he feels. He fusses around with them, puttin' them in the little glass basket we always use for wildflowers, tryin' to decide if there's enough flowers to fill the space, and offerin' to go get more, fussin' and wonderin' if the water in the vase might be too cold for them, and *always* askin' me if they're as pretty as last year's." She laughed as she looked over at Meg.

"Sometimes, when I'm at the stove or doin' dishes, he comes up behind me and puts his arms around me and kisses the top of my head. When he starts tellin' me somethin' about the tractor or the combine I know he's just usin' those big machines as an excuse to come in and touch me. While he's there behind me, tellin' me these things, I'm glad he doesn't see my smile, or sometimes my tears. I think I'd ruin it by tellin' him just how much I'm on to that old boy."

Her voice broke but then she continued, "You spoke of 'havin' sex.' I've heard that term of course, but I don't ever want to know what 'havin' sex' is—like it's a choice similar to havin' measles or not havin' them. Come October, we'll have been married twenty-four years, but bein' together in that way is still a special part of our lives, Meggie. Afterwards, we lie in each other's arms for the longest time...talkin' or quiet, but knowin' we've been blessed. I love that man and he loves me. Oh, we might never say it like that to each other, but that's what it is. Papa told me that Charlie had his full approval—and that was even before Charlie proposed! Maybe Papa saw in Charlie and me what he and Ma had: the possibility of a real love affair."

Tolly looked over at Meg apologetically. "I don't know if you wanted to hear all that, but you asked. When Ed comes back—if this ends up in any kind of manageable way—maybe you two can figure out somethin'." Her look wasn't hopeful.

Meg reached over and brushed Tolly's cheek, but her voice was sad. "Gee, Sis, where were you when I was picking out a husband? When Papa was in the hospital I told him about my doubts about Ed, but it was too late for him to advise me.

"About Ed and me getting together again, I don't know... Being his wife is demeaning. I need credit for who I am and I can't see him ever giving me that." Looking straight ahead, she continued, her voice bitter and sad. "I think back on that last morning I saw him—it's more like four years ago than four days. I try to remember if there was something I should have picked up on, some signal he was sending, a cry for help—but I can't remember any. What I remember are the negatives: he left as quietly as possible and he never said goodbye. He didn't praise Kurt when I told him how Kurt's teacher had praised him. It's absurd to say this, but his jaw tightened when he looked down at his plate—like eating the food was repulsive beyond description, and was something he just had to get through. I take a lot of pride in what I do and the kids are so good and so helpful." Her voice wavered, then started to rise. "He shouldn't look at me and our kids that way. He's my husband and their father. If he left voluntarily—and I have to believe that he did—why couldn't he say goodbye to us?"

Tolly nodded and spoke softly, "Yes, dear. I know."

"Oh, Tolly, how will we get beyond this thing? It's like he erased all the good things of our life together. He has to stand in front of me and tell me *why* he left. Then I've got to figure out how to live in this town—he's the fair-haired Halverson, not me! What's going to happen to the kids and me? We deserve better than this. Please help me, Tolly."

This time there was no mistaking it, Meg was crying. Tolly reached across the seat and pulled her sister into her arms. "I'm here, Meggie, I'm here. You can depend on me. I'll take care of you, just like Ma and Papa always asked me to do."

9

THE TOLL

The ring, the ring...he was giving her Sara's ring. The two of them were rolling over and over in the car, their legs intertwined, and her long dark hair wrapping around them, binding him to her. They were frantically trying to get free of the hair, their arms flailing, their eyes bugging out, looking at the rocks along the bottom of the river, their faces screaming. But every time they screamed the water flooded into their mouths.... Meg awoke with a jerk, soundlessly mouthing, "Noooo, that's Sara's ring, not hers!" Before she could open her eyes, she drifted down into another fold of sleep, thinking ...it's only a dream...only a dream...a dream...a dream...a dream.... But no more pills...No more... No more... I've got to get out...

. . .

Tolly opened the door quietly and tiptoed in to see if Meg was still sleeping quietly. She was, but even as Tolly watched, Meg jerked and started making those disheartening little sounds she'd made off and on last night. The sounds stopped as she stroked Meg's forehead and her face became peaceful. The sedative must be taking hold, or was it that with Tolly's touch Meg sensed she wasn't alone in this?

Tolly began moving quietly around the room, straightening this up, pushing that back, and generally restoring order to a room already in order. As she worked she looked around critically and shook her head. This once lovely room was as removed from the goodness and blessings of life as anything could be. She longed to fling open the windows. Surely the sunshine and cool spring air would cleanse away the sadness that now defiled it. But she had only to remember the look of fear on Meggie's face as she'd pleaded that they be kept closed and the drapes drawn at all times.

With a sigh, Tolly moved tiredly to the bedside chair she'd occupied most of the previous night. Picking up her book, she found the page she'd fallen asleep over and began to read. But like the night before, her concerns kept her from comprehending the words. Finally she closed the book and sat watching her sister as she slept. When some unknown demon pulled at Meggie's face, she had only to touch her hand to sooth her. Why wouldn't Meggie have bad dreams, after all she'd been through?

. . .

It was a truck driver who spotted it—that's what they'd heard. He had driven that stretch along the Clearwater River twice that week, but the second time more slowly: he wanted to see if that big shadow was still in the water. It was. When he got to the cafe in Kamiah he asked the waitress if anyone had reported anything in the water where Telephone Creek dumped into the river. That particular stretch of highway, skirting that deep eddy in the river, was notorious for the toll it had taken over the years, especially when high speed was involved. The waitress said, no, she hadn't heard anything, but she'd ask the Idaho State Patrol officer when he came in for coffee that afternoon. She thanked the driver when he left.

The Clark Fork *Daily News* reported:

> On the east side of Telephone Creek, an officer found a trace of skid marks at the edge of the pavement. From there, he could see a large dark shadow down in the river. A diver found it was the car that had been reported missing, and it was Edward L. Halverson's body inside it. Halverson had been missing for twelve days. The other passenger in the car, a female, has not yet been identified. The coroner stated that both Halverson and the passenger had been in the water for some time.
>
> Halverson's wife, Margaret, identified his body, along with his briefcase and wallet, in which was an

antique diamond ring. She told the authorities that it was of sentimental and great actual value, having belonged to the Halverson estate.

An intensive search is being made to identify the woman passenger. The body had no I.D. or major dental work that might identify her. If the woman had a purse with identifying cards, it has not been found, having possibly been swept out of the broken window by the river's strong current. The woman was Caucasian, slim, of medium height, in her late twenties, and had extraordinarily long brunette hair—a fact that might help identify her. She was dressed in a navy blue skirt, white blouse, and low-heeled red shoes. Her only jewelry—two small gold studs in her pierced ears, and a fine gold chain around her neck—could have been purchased anywhere. She wore no rings. The public is being asked to contact the authorities if they know anything about a missing woman fitting that description. As yet, no one has been reported missing in this area or the surrounding states.

Divers, making a search of the Clearwater River, found a lightweight jacket, matching the skirt the woman was wearing, caught on a tree root some two hundred feet downstream from the accident. Fifty yards farther down from that, a small zippered overnight bag was found jammed between some large rocks. It held makeup, a blouse, a nightgown, and some underwear. Neither the clothes she was wearing nor the overnight bag contained anything the authorities could identify as belonging to a particular woman. Nothing had been found since.

The incident is listed as an accident: Halverson, a family man, and an unidentified woman (thought to be a hitchhiker), had the bad luck to skid into the Clearwater River. Because autopsies had been

> performed on both victims, and there was no indication of either alcohol or drug use, the accident was put down to the driver's misjudgment of a bad curve and, possibly, excessive speed.

After Meg identified Ed's body, she and Art Stroud went through the sodden briefcase together. They found nothing of personal value and nothing of interest to the bank. Both she and Art were shown photos of the young woman in the car. They had never seen her before or knew of anyone fitting her description. When Meg came back to the house, she threw up and went to bed crying.

The bank audit was concluded the next day. Art phoned Meg to say that everything was in order, and there was no reason to question anything regarding Ed's disappearance. Tolly overheard Meg demanding an apology from him, her voice shaking with rage. She asked Art, "Why did you come over that day and say that? If you couldn't be specific, why did you even *think* he could have taken something? After all these years that Ed *slaved* for you and was so loyal, how could you even think he was a thief? Have you any idea what that did to the kids and me? You and your outrageous suspicions and damned audit; wasn't it enough that I was worried about where Ed was?" When Tolly got to her she was shaking uncontrollably. She slammed down the receiver without his answer, and the call became just one more thing she refused to talk about. A memorial service was held three days after Ed's body was found. He was buried in the old Halverson mausoleum in the Clark Fork cemetery. Less than thirty people attended.

. . .

Tolly's distaste for those thoughts brought a shiver. Poor Meggie! Finding Ed had solved nothing. With Ed beyond all explaining, the questions of why he'd left and what he'd intended were as unanswered as ever. And the still unexplained presence of the woman in the car had made everything even worse for Meggie. Tolly was pondering that when she heard the phone in the family room. Closing the door as quietly as possible, she hurried down the hall, glad she'd had the foresight to unplug the phone next to Meg's bed.

"Tolly, it's Doris. How's everything going there?"

"Oh, Doris. I'm glad it's you. I'm gettin' as bad as Meggie, not knowin' if it'll be a reporter or a curiosity seeker. Meggie's no worse, but no better either. Doc Attix is goin' to change one of her prescriptions and will drop in later with it. I told him she wouldn't eat or hardly take any water. He said if she keeps that up he's goin' to have to admit her to the hospital and give her an IV. Soon as she wakes up I'm to instruct her she better make that choice herself. But, for now, at least, she's sleepin'."

Doris began cautiously, "I suppose those pills help her, but if you would only get her up, Tolly. Put her into her robe and have her sit on the patio. It's such a beautiful day."

"No, she's not ready for that yet. She looks terrible, looks peaked and sick. And, oh, Doris, last night she cut off her hair! I was outside the bathroom smoothing up her bed sheet when I heard the scissors. I don't mean she chopped it off close to her head, but just took a big handful of it and hacked it off at her shoulders, without sayin' anything. It shocked me seein' her do that then gathering it up and flinging it into the wastebasket with such an awful look on her face. Afterwards I trimmed it up, you know, just neatened it up. It makes her looks younger."

"I bet it does. She's such a beautiful woman, beautiful in every way."

Tolly said, "She's talkin' in her sleep so I know what she's worryin' about. Last night she was askin' Ed why he left without a note of some kind; and this morning it was about him and that young woman drowning in the river. Meggie sounds so sad and I hate to hear her."

"I'm so sorry for her. Marc and I have gone over this again and again. If they identify the woman and she's *not* a hitchhiker, what are we left to think? Whatever was Ed thinking, having her in the car with him? It's crazy. This morning's paper said, among other things, that conjecture goes on about Edward Halverson."

"I've stopped the paper here. Did the kids see it?"

"No, Marc threw it in the garbage as soon as he read it. Does Meg ask about the kids?"

"Of course she does. She thinks they're quiet because they're outside playin'. Then she goes back to sleep."

In a patient voice Doris said, "You've done such a good job of taking care of her, but we need to get her off those drugs and outside in her garden. If the kids were over there they'd cheer her up in a minute."

"I'm not goin' to second guess Doc Attix."

"But I'm just saying that if she could be with her kids again... Your Doc Attix has a reputation for being too eager with his prescription pad. Being drugged like that is just delaying her recovery. Meg is as tough and resilient as you are. Don't baby her."

Tolly's words were unyielding, "My job is to spare my sister everythin' I can. Before our mother died she made me promise to look after Meggie, and I'm not about to let her down. She's not up to being disturbed by the babies. They can get awful rowdy." Doris's sigh was too loud to ignore and Tolly faltered before saying, "Well, Meggie *is* better, a whole lot better than she was after the memorial service. You and Marc saw her. Instead of cryin', her face was set in that smile that means nothing, and she was pushin' herself to shake hands with each one of the few folks who did come to the service, like she was at a weddin' reception or somethin'. I could see people lookin' at her strange. I'd have liked to ask 'em just how they would have handled it, especially with the Strouds leavin' like that. When Charlie and I got her home from the service, we couldn't get her out of the car. She just sat there her eyes glassy and not blinkin', and Charlie had to practically carry her into the house, beggin' her to lift this foot for this step, and that foot for the other. When we finally got her into bed, I'll tell you, we were plenty thankful then for those pills Doc Attix left for her."

Doris had to agree, "Yes, that service was pretty awful. And Art and Elaine Stroud, honestly."

After a silence Tolly said, "Charlie left for Wyler last night. I hated to see him go, but you can't leave the farm for long, even though Old Flint's there and he's real dependable. I better go now, Doris. It's about time for Meggie's pill."

Doris was happy to end it. She was frustrated with Tolly's lack of understanding about Meg, as well as upset at herself for failing to say how unhappy the kids were and how difficult it was handling them. Kurt was too quiet and inscrutable; and the Littles cried miserably for their mother. They needed to go back home. This morning, Marc got them to go outside to play, but a few minutes later he found them sitting in a line on the back step, their shoulders together as if glued. Marc finally cajoled Kurt into tossing the old baseball back and forth, while the Littles watched listlessly. But it was a pretty somber affair. Callie began to suck her fingers, and Sara never laughed once.

. . .

Doris walked wearily down the stairs, holding tight to the banister. After sitting with two girls on her lap, her legs weren't working as well as they might. She moved toward the light in the living room where Marc worked at his desk. She leaned against him and kissed the bald spot on his head.

Marc said, "I was just about to check on you, but I didn't know if my coming up might upset things."

"Thanks for the thought, dear. Poor little kids. They're asleep now. I'd forgotten how taxing kids are. How did we ever handle our two?"

"I seem to remember that we were just out of kindergarten ourselves then."

She chuckled as she sat heavily into the chair nearest him. "Darling man, do we deserve a nightcap? A good strong one?"

"I'm on my way."

She watched him at the sideboard and was once again aware of how pleasurable the clink of ice and splash of Scotch going into a glass could be. Marc smiled his most endearing smile as he handed her the drink and again took his seat. In an old ceremony, they raised their glasses in a silent toast and took their first drinks in tandem, nodding conspiratorially at each other.

Doris held the liquor in her mouth before letting it slide down and warm her throat. "We need to talk about returning the kids to their home. We're not doing *anyone* a favor by keeping them away from Meg. But Tolly isn't about to hear that. Poor kids. Their world is upside down and now they're banned from home and can't be consoled in the least. What do you think, Marc? Are we allowed to cry uncle?"

"Of course we are. Tolly's trying to do the right thing—letting that pill-pushing doctor keep Meg in oblivion and sheltering the kids from it all; but for all her fussing, she doesn't know Meg." He leaned over and gave her a kiss. "You've been a real trooper to do this. Call Tolly tomorrow and... Better yet, we'll just take the kids there. If she can see how sad they are, maybe she'll loosen her grip on Meg. We'll offer to ride herd on them if they get too frisky, but they have to be home."

Doris laughed, "You're braver than I am. Tolly is about as determined a woman as I've ever met."

Marc laughed with her. "She's a tiger, but she'll back down. We'll tell her we're betting on Meg."

Doris said, "I haven't had a chance to tell you something. Tolly said that last night Meg cut off her hair. She assured me she didn't chop it off close to her scalp or anything, just cut it shorter. Tolly made it sound pretty dramatic. I think she was scared hearing the scissors, and ran into the bathroom to see what was happening."

Marc rolled his eyes at her words. "I hope you're not expecting something intelligent from me. Meg isn't the type to take her life with scissors, if that's what Tolly was worried about." He shook his head. "Jesus, I hate to talk about things like that."

Doris was still chuckling when Marc stood and helped her to her feet. He walked her over to the couch, settled her into one corner, and, after adjusting a pillow, sat down himself. Grinning down at her he said, "How's my favorite girl? I've missed you. I might even be a little bit jealous. How do you like that?" He gave her a peck on her nose and, seeing her glass was empty, got up once again and replenished both their drinks.

Sitting down, he said, "While you were upstairs I was thinking again how finding Ed didn't solve a damn thing. His phoning Art that day and saying he was sick only adds to the puzzle. Where the hell was he and where was he going? And nothing explains the woman who with him. We don't know why the car went off the road. We don't know if Stroud is telling the truth about everything being just dandy at the bank. The only thing we know for sure is Ed is dead. And what was Stroud trying to prove at Ed's memorial service, shunning Meg and leaving like that? It was the perfect occasion to put all the questions away, but, with everyone watching, Art and his wife snubbed her then scuttled out before the sounds of the organ had died. Damn Art anyway! After all the years his bank benefited from the Halverson name, couldn't he and Elaine have stood beside Meg and been supportive for a few seconds? They surely knew how the town would interpret that."

Doris shook her head. "Meg was bearing up pretty well before that service, which cut the legs out from under her. Now she has to suffer from the very gossip she abhorred. I think I'd have a breakdown, too. Over the years we've known her and the kids I've come to hate the very name 'Edward Halverson.' How could Meg have married him? She and I have talked about a lot of things, but never about that. A couple years ago she told me that she had burned her wedding dress. I was stunned over her remark, feeling that she was telling me something personal. She didn't elaborate and I was too damned chicken to ask her if she meant just 'burned a hole in it.' Knowing her, she'd have said, 'Of course I mean a hole, silly.' That's pretty typical of her: turning back the comment in some way, to keep the appearance that everything's wonderful. Maybe that's her way of telling me how she feels, without stooping to the ugly details."

Marc nodded thoughtfully. "Ed was a complex character, the town's favorite son, the boy who does everything that's expected of him. Think of it: after graduating from Yale—in *Physics*, no less—he became a banker. Was becoming Stroud's flunky what he had in mind for himself? He must have had more options back east. But no, he trotted back to Clark Fork and started working at the bank."

Marc continued, "He and I never had much to say to each other, but he always impressed me as someone who never realized what he was meant to do. His eyes never leveled with mine. I doubt he was happy. Perhaps he was tired of doing what others wanted—and by 'others' I'm talking about Stroud and his cronies. I bet his Halverson label was a damned bore." Marc stopped talking and they finished their drinks.

Doris said, "You're more generous than I could be about him."

She picked at a thread in her skirt. "I doubted he liked Meg's and my friendship. If he suspected I encouraged her rebellion, he was right. Ed never laughed at himself or talked without making sure people knew he was someone to be reckoned with. I despise that kind of person."

Marc shook his head. "That's pretty strong coming from you."

Doris considered his comment thoughtfully. "What was Meg thinking marrying someone like him? She didn't *have* to...I mean, they'd been married more than five years before Kurt was born." Her voice softened, "If she married him and then... How can a smart woman get it so wrong when making such a profound choice as picking a husband? When a woman is attracted to a man, and vice versa, luck better be there, because it's certain that calm and reason won't be! I see a woman's plight in her. We are so driven by our biology. Think of what happens when a woman doesn't have luck when her biology catches up with her, when her empty places are screaming to be filled? And I'm not talking about her heart! Solving that situation is so fraught with danger. Luck was on my side when I met you." She reached over and rubbed her hand lightly on her husband's leg, letting her fingers linger on the familiar bulge lying beneath the cloth. Searching his eyes for understanding she went on. "What does a woman do when the man behind this wonderful organ isn't the person she had hoped he would be? Suppose...well, what if the man just wanted to-to—"

"By any chance are you trying to say 'screw around'? And if that's not the word, I can think of another."

"You know I hate that word. But '*play around*' will do beautifully, thank you."

Marc chuckled, "I just want you to know I'm all for it—"

"Old man, you've never let me forget *that* all these years. You better behave yourself."

"You're the one who just...got my attention—and very provocatively at that—and now you're instructing me to behave myself?"

Doris began to laugh, resting her head against his shoulder as she did. "You're really impossible." She raised her hand to pat his knee then thinking better of it, made a face at him. Her voice became solemn. "Seriously, though, why Ed picked Meg is easy to understand. Call me cynical, but can't you see him planning how to bend and shape that gorgeous, talented, ready-for-love woman to *his* plans? All he'd have to do was tell her he loved her, tell her he couldn't fulfill his dreams without her, and then just install her into his life like—like a person installs a carpet. Then he's free to go about his business. Oh, he'd give her a little encouragement every so often, a little fluffing up. But not too much, understand. He wouldn't want her to get used to being praised."

He looked at her in surprise. "You amaze me. That *was* cynical. Is that how women think? Did I 'install' you like a carpet when we eloped?"

"Hardly. I'm just sorry that Meg didn't have my kind of luck when she chose."

"What do you call having three handsome kids, a large house, and all that Halverson security?"

"Oh, sure, that looks good. But she was always alone. What woman wants to spend her life without companionship? Not me. I couldn't live with an Ed Halverson!"

Marc laughed and hugged her. "You're cute when you get pissed."

"I'm serious, Marc."

"I know that, baby."

"I couldn't live with someone I couldn't talk to. And I've found myself cheering on every last little rebellious thought Meg ever shared with me. You'd be surprised."

"They weren't the greatest couple. But they shared one thing—neither of them had much of a chance to make an independent choice. Ed was being a dutiful Halverson and Meg was being his ever-dutiful hostess."

Doris nodded.

Marc was thoughtful for a long time then said, "You know, pet, something's bugging me. What if Ed *was* making a choice in this? Meg spoke of Ed being withdrawn, that she and the kids had to tiptoe around when he was home. What if the word was depressed, sad, discouraged, overwhelmed? The investigating officer said that there was just a trace of skid marks where Ed's car went off the pavement. That doesn't sound like a car avoiding trouble. And this happened on that *renowned* bad curve where a number of people have died over the years. Ed knew that road and that river. He must have traveled that road many, many times. Wouldn't he have known about that deep eddy and that curve being so deadly?

"What if it wasn't an accident at all? What if he was having second thoughts about everything, including the woman in his car? He knew things would be all right with the family, with Meg in charge. He had insurance. If it *looked* like an accident his family would be okay. Perhaps driving into the river was his choice. Maybe he gave Meg her due after all. Maybe just before he made that sudden right turn into the river he thought something like, 'Okay, Meg, you do it!'" Marc looked down at Doris. "So, how about us leaving it there? We can't prove it, but we can't disprove it either. Poor guy. Let's not judge him further. Let's leave the poor sap in peace. Maybe that's all he wanted. What do you say?"

Doris sat quietly thinking about it. "Oh, Marc, that makes me feel so sad. But if he did give Meg her due I could forgive him. I don't want to think of him doing that, destroying his and the woman's lives, but it's a thought to end on."

Marc was silent as he brushed his lips back and forth against Doris's hair, smelling the good familiar smell of her and the perfume he faithfully got her every Christmas. Gratitude and love for his luck gripped his throat. When he got his voice under control he said, "Now, my little chick-a-dee-dee-dee, before we trundle our way to our boudoir and correct this little situation you so kindly started on this dangerous organ of mine…" He turned and gave his wife a wicked smile. "Want to know a secret?"

Doris blinked at him and said, "Looking at that grin, I'm not sure I do. You look as though you're going to tell me something I might not want to know. It's not going to make me mad, is it?"

Marc chuckled and tweaked her nose. "Maybe. But maybe you already know."

"Do I have to guess?"

"No, no. But there's an old saying, probably from my Army barrack days, that goes something like, 'A woman who ain't gettin' any, shows it' and I happen to think Meg wasn't."

"You really think that?" Then she nodded, "Yes, actually I've thought that, too. I should have known that a sly old fox like you would have picked up on that."

"Picked up on that? Jesus, woman! I might be sixty-two and married—happily married and well taken care of, thank you—but when I see a body like Meg's, barefoot, with those breasts of hers moving free under her shirt, working in her garden... Well, let me tell you that my nineteen-year-old mind makes my decrepit old body wonder if that tidy little ass of hers is also unencumbered. From what I hear, when she gardens she's a hell of a complication to the male contingent of her neighborhood. And I'll be damned if she has any idea just how good she is to look at. I can't imagine what Ed was thinking about...I mean not thinking about with Meg. She could be pretty vulnerable now."

"Darn you, Marc. You did tell me more than I wanted to know." She laughed. "I'm not angry, but you did rather give me a new insight into you, you devil." She jabbed him hard with her elbow, then leaned over and kissed him on the lips, in what she intended as a quick peck, but ended with the tip of her tongue lingering invitingly on his lips.

Marc made a little humming sound and gestured toward the stairs. "Do I take it I'm forgiven? Isn't this our bedtime?"

"It looks like it. Decrepit or not, I'm glad we're not beyond those thoughts entirely—"

"It's not the thoughts I want, *entirely*."

"You!"

As they started walking up the stairs Doris asked, "So you think Meg is really vulnerable?"

Marc turned on the step and looked at her. "I think she's in an unsympathetic position. That former crowd of Ed's probably suspects the worst about her. Why did Ed leave? Why, he was obviously getting away from Meg. And the woman in the car? Hell, she was no itinerant hitchhiker! If a married man wanders into another woman's arms, whose fault is that? It's the wife's, of course, for giving him the cold shoulder."

Doris said, "Meg's too strong for people to sympathize with. Not that she ever tried to gain people's sympathy. I wonder how many times she's made a joke of the fact that she always wished she could be the helpless blond type. She told me that the nearest compliment she gets is when someone tells her how capable she is. One day when she was joking about this, she said, that in a clinch a man would probably whisper in her ear, 'How's your pot roast, sweetheart?'"

Marc shook his head, laughing.

Doris continued, "But it's not fair. Now that she's a widow and deserves respect and support from the community, except for Tolly and the two of us, she's alone. In the town's silence I feel their judgment. That silence is the loudest comment the town could make."

"So, now what?"

"So, now what, indeed."

10

THE CHILDREN

Meg thought it was Tolly's hand resting on the blanket. Before opening her heavy eyelids, she reached out for her sister's hand, but felt instead something rough and heavy. She raised herself up on her elbow and turned on the light. It was something lumpy wrapped inside a piece of drawing paper and fastened with a rubber band. It had to be a rock. When she loosened the paper it was Callie's special magic rock, with its diagonal stripe of white quartz. The paper was from Sara. It was a drawing of a woman, with her long arms around three children—a tall boy and two little girls. Everybody was crying, even the woman, their mouths open, wailing, and their eyes forlorn. Great blue tears dripped from their faces and flew through the air like in a rainstorm. Meg studied the picture then held the gifts to her breast, puzzled and wondering just how long it had been since she'd seen her children.

She called out to Tolly, "Where are my kids? Are they all right?" But her voice never rose above a whisper, so she held the rock and the paper even closer, smiled contentedly, and went back to sleep.

. . .

She smelled them before she heard their whispers. Their smell was of wind and sun absorbed by their skin and wild flopping hair, the sweet delicate smell of child sweat, the clean smell of garden dirt around their wrists and under their nails, and the smell of the soft downy hair on their necks. With great effort Meg opened her heavy eyelids and turned to look toward the murmurs coming from the bedside chair. There they all were: Sara and Callie sitting in the chair—

all knees and eyes—and Kurt beside them on the floor, looking at her. There was fear in their eyes and restraint, as though they had been told they could watch, but not disturb her.

It was a low guttural sound that came out of her throat as she held out her arms. They came flying into them, hurting her body as they landed, and crying like things wounded. Then the four of them lay on the bed rocking each other. They spoke no words; there was no need. The tears that Meg had not yet cried fell from her eyes. "Oh, my kids! My Kurt and Sara and Callie. It'll be okay now. It's okay now. I don't know where you've been or where I've been either, but it's going to be all right now. Do you believe that?" She put her hand beneath each chin in turn and tilted their faces to her and asked each one that same question. "Do you believe that, Sara? Do you know that, Callie? Do you know that it's going to be all right, Kurt? Daddy's gone, and we're all we have now. But it will be all right. I'm so sorry all this happened, but we'll be fine."

She took her fingers and wiped the tears from their eyes as they lay there, going from one to the other and wiping her hand on the sheet. Then she had to start all over again, running her hand over their wet faces, wiping her eyes, and mopping their noses on the sheet. She said, "We're just like Sara's picture, aren't we?" They agreed.

As they quieted, she laughed to see them all tucked into the bumps and folds of the bed around her. When she played the old finger games down their noses, even though they were far too old to play that game, they squealed. And then she sang the old *Mrs. Mouse Song* to them. Kurt groaned appropriately, but joined in with Sara and Callie on the second repeat…

"Do you have a little house, Mrs. Mouse, Mrs. Mouse?
Do you have a family, Mrs. Mouse?
Yes, I have a little nest,
Where my little children rest.
It's the place we love the best.
That's the song of Mrs. Mouse."

When everyone was singing loudly enough for Tolly to hear, she came in and stood by the bedroom door, a wooden spoon stained with spaghetti sauce in one hand and the other hand holding her apron to her eyes.

At last Meg said, "I don't even know what time it is. Could someone open up the drapes and windows?"

The light seemed to have built up behind the drapes, and now it poured into the room, driving out the fear. With it came the lilac-pungent air, clean and damp, announcing a spring shower.

Beyond that, in the far, far distance, Meg imagined she heard a faint "groak, groak" of a raven—and she remembered.

PART TWO

11

RECOVERY

"What you need is joy, Meggie, and that's spelled J-O-Y in case you've forgotten. 'Course, that'll have to come after food, unless we're fortunate and they both come in the same pot."

Meg laughed, not so much at Tolly's words, but because they were spoken in perfect cadence to the blows Tolly's broom was delivering to the corners of the pantry. After three weeks of this, the presence of any dirt existed solely in her sister's imagination.

Meg turned away and spooned a bite of oatmeal from under the pool of melted butter in her bowl, determined not to disappoint Tolly with her slow progress on it. Yesterday it had been pancakes and ham, and the day before that it was fried potatoes and red-eye gravy (a specialty learned from Charlie). Looking at the oatmeal intently, she wondered if she could actually see the calories lining up for their one-way trip to her thighs. Today she was wearing her old blue robe *by choice*, but in a few more days of this she wouldn't be able to fit into anything else.

From her vantage point on the kitchen stool, she idly wondered where Tolly had put her recipe file and if the red-veined plant she'd babied for a year had been thrown out. Whatever its fate, it was no longer a resident of the kitchen window. The whole house looked different. The children now placed their shoes on a sheet of newspaper by the front door; and towels were neatly laid along the backs of the sofa and loveseat where any unclean head might rest. And the children's shelf full of books and supplies… How was it that arranging those things in descending order of size made them so unapproachable? Meg heaved a sigh as she regarded her houseplants. Tolly tended to over water everything, while Meg believed in benign neglect, at least for plants. Still, even though she hadn't thought so previously, maybe that went for the whole house, too.

Tolly was saying, "—and to let that food do its work, after your bath, I want you to go into your bedroom and take a nap. And don't forget your vitamins, dear, we don't want you to—" Tolly stopped mid-sentence, "You just dripped some butter. I'll get it." Tolly grabbed a sponge and wiped up the tiny dot of butter with the same gesture one would use in netting a giant butterfly. As she washed out the sponge, she eyed Meg, making sure her latest orders had been understood. Figuring that they were, she explained that after Meg's nap, a deck chair would be waiting in the sun for her, and she could read out there for an hour or so.

Meg, after mulling over her chances of escape, nodded obediently. The schedule Tolly was outlining sounded very much like yesterday's, and the day before that, and all the days coming up, if she couldn't stop her. But resistance to her edicts only brought guilt—and Meg didn't need any more of that. The trouble was Tolly was enjoying this, every morning sounding like a sergeant creating a soldier from a rag-tag wastrel. How could she have forgotten Tolly's propensity to manage? Once Tolly got a toehold...and this was definitely a toehold situation. Her gratitude toward Tolly knew no bounds; even so, the words "wrest control" came to mind as she sat as a guest in her own kitchen.

She gratefully turned to the sounds of the kids in the family room and thought, yes, we all need J-O-Y, and especially the kids. But that was hard to sustain in the kids' present circumstances, where they had to wonder which woman would be at the head of their household on any given day: Tolly had replaced Meg; Doris had replaced Tolly; then it was back to Tolly, who was not quite willing to allow Meg her turn. That had better change soon. Only this morning, Kurt, behind his Aunt's back, had silently mouthed something inappropriate to the Littles, which they'd answered in kind. Their behavior seemed to be asking when they'd get their regular life back.

Meg knew she'd made great progress after her breakdown: she'd gotten off those pills and was facing things on her own. Occasionally she had a back slide, but not often. Yesterday afternoon, as she and Callie lay contentedly in a square of sunshine falling on the couch, listening to Beethoven's Pastoral symphony, Meg had suffered a sudden malaise, with its rush of despair and sadness. Was it the music touching those still-raw places in her mind, she wondered? Whatever its cause, the peacefulness of the moment was whisked away as though a cloud had passed over the sun.

Callie had sensed the change in her and asked if something was wrong. But Meg tweaked Callie's nose and said, "Just an attack of the ghosties, dear. Let's listen to the French horns and the flutes of this particular passage." As they listened, Callie reached up and, with a soul-shaking gesture, simply laid the flat of her small hand on Meg's cheek. Meg's fear disappeared as quickly as it had come, leaving her weak with love for her daughter and strengthened against the bout of sadness.

Until recently her nights were a problem. As she lay alone in that big bed, specters she had no defense against trailed into the darkness above her, triggering the white static of her panic. One night she summoned up the serene picture of the mountain—the silver log lying majestically in the grove of trees, with the shafts of light falling all around it. In her mind she walked around that mountain scene—smelling it, feeling it, and remembering the comfort it had given her. As she did, sleep simply opened its arms to her.

Although she laid much of her peace of mind to remembering that forest scene, she believed that her recovery lay in confronting the hard truths of Ed's death and meeting head on the alternatives left to her.

With a pang of guilt, Meg realized that Tolly was looking at her and waiting for an answer. Meg said, "Forgive me, sis. I've only been half listening. What did you say? Oh, I remember. You were telling me what Charlie said when he called this morning."

Sounding hurt, Tolly said, "What I said was, he's mighty glad you've turned the corner and are gettin' better. And he's happy hearin' that the babies are back under their own roof again. Oh, you know, Meggie, Charlie said all those little things that don't mean much, but are so good to hear. He talked about the meadowlarks fairly shoutin' from the fence posts. He knows I love those birds so. When I hear 'em I just know everythin' is right with the world."

Meg looked encouragingly at her sister. "I bet Charlie wants to know when you're coming back. Now that I'm okay, I think you should start planning your return home."

"Now, Meggie, you're not to worry about that. Just for once Charlie can get along without me. Of course he always asks when I'll be home; but he asks that no matter what's happenin'." She looked at Meg, concerned. "I'm not leavin' 'til I know you're fine and we get a chance to sit down and make our plans for what comes next. I've got some ideas of my own about that."

Meg looked at her worriedly. "Make our plans? I don't know if I like the sound of that."

Tolly laughed. "Never mind about that now. Isn't it nice to hear the babies gigglin' in there?" Both women smiled at the sounds of the game in progress. Judging from the moans of the other two, Callie was winning. Tolly said, "Now if only their friends would come by to play with them. Do you suppose there's a mark on the outside of the house that warns folks to stay away?"

Meg shrugged and spoke bitterly, "Or published in the paper, something like, 'Watch out for the Halversons, you might get contaminated!' I'm getting used to getting the big eye at the store or Post Office, but why anyone would hold this against kids is beyond me. Will we ever feel part of the town again? I worry about the kids when school starts up next fall."

"Don't upset yourself, Meggie. You know what Doc Attix says. While I scrub this floor, you stay here and talk to me; then I'll run your bath." As she talked, she exchanged the broom for the mop and pail.

Watching her, Meg barely suppressed a yawn. As Tolly suggested, after a bath she'd go to bed and sink into blissful sleep. From there, she wouldn't have to see Tolly working.

She picked up her bowl and wandered aimlessly to the sink, rinsed the bowl, and put it in the dishwasher. Jamming her hands into her robe's deep pockets, she stood looking bleakly out the window, giving a listless look to her garden with its untouched flowerbeds. Beyond them were the mountains, made of a smooth blue fabric today, and looking as lazy as the perfect cloudless sky above them. There was hardly a patch of snow anywhere on them now. After studying them a minute more, she pulled her hands out of her pockets and slapped her palms on the kitchen counter. "No! No more!"

Tolly dropped the mop and asked, "What is it?"

Meg said, "We're going to get out of this house! We're going to go to the mountains! There's something I want you and the kids to see. And after we hike around there, we'll drive down to the campground in the canyon and cook our dinner."

"Now, Meggie, you can't even think of doing that!"

"Oh, yes, I can! Put away that damned mop and pail and come over here and see what I'm looking at. This day is just begging us to be out in it! I'm not spending the rest of my life being waited on. Look at me, Tolly—clear eyes, steady hands, big smile. I'm getting out before I stop believing that I can!"

Tolly looked angry. "You might tell me who I should believe, you or Doc Attix?"

"Believe *me*, for God's sake! For your information, for a week I've been tossing those pills of his down the toilet. I don't need pills anymore; I need my life back. I'm fine."

Tolly sniffed. "Well then, tell me just who's goin' to drive us up to those mountains? Don't tell me you're up to doin' that."

"I wouldn't think of doing it if I didn't *feel* like it. Please understand, I have to start doing things again." She softened her voice. "Look, sis, the day before you came out to help us, I drove up into the mountains. Come here, let me show you." She pulled Tolly to the window and pointed. "See that biggest mountain, the one with the rocky ridge running along its top? Yes, there. That's where we're going. I found the most beautiful place about half way up where there's a wonderful view of this whole valley. And there's a little cabin and a great big house there, if you can imagine. The cabin is the dearest thing, and the house is…a bit odd, except it has a big rock for a doorstep. You'll just have to see it for yourself." She laughed. "Unfortunately, the road to it is…well, it's passable, like those roads of Papa's." Remembering Tolly's fears, she joked, "We won't need to take along a car jack or anything."

With no reaction from Tolly, she hurried on, "I learned something the day I was there. I thought that the Forest Service owned all these big stretches of forest. I know they lease land for logging and grazing and such, but the piece of land the house sits on looks privately owned. The trees are still big and there weren't any stumps indicating past logging. I found an old wagon road and the remains of an old cabin. I'd so like to show all that to you and the kids. No one was home that day; but they should be there now. Maybe they'll tell us why on earth they built their house up there. We'll ask for permission to walk out into the clearing and see the view of the valley. Come on, let's tell the kids and get ready."

Tolly shrugged. "Well, why not? But once we get to that campground you're goin' to sit down and rest. I've got a chicken and I'll cook it in Ma's Dutch oven like in the old days."

. . .

The car fairly sagged under its load. In a wild burst of excitement everyone had pitched in to the preparations, and right after lunch they climbed into the car, gassed it up at their usual station, and set off.

With the steering wheel under her hands and her car full of excited and noisy kids, Meg felt stronger than she had in weeks. For Tolly's sake, she resolved to make a show of driving carefully on the switchbacks. Sitting in the back seat with the Littles would keep her mind busy.

She found all the right roads and started up the mountain like she'd driven there a dozen times before. It soon became apparent that the farther the kids got from town the better they felt, and the better they felt the noisier they became. The air flowing into the open car windows tossed their hair and teased their noses with its fresh, half-remembered woody smell, and it reminded them all of past camping trips.

On her previous trip, Meg's impression had been of a sleeping land half out of the snow. But now, all around them was the industry of early summer, with every plant bright green and leaning toward the light, and the very air filled with the sounds of squirrels and birds. Even though they saw no large animals, Meg felt they were there, hidden in some stop-action frame until their droning car passed. Kurt spotted a grouse sitting on a log right next to the road. It blended perfectly into the log's bark and remained sitting, unflinchingly, as the car ground noisily by.

From the corner of her eye, Meg looked at Kurt sitting next to her, serious and protective of his right to be there. Besides pointing out something, Kurt was cautioning her of obstacles on the road, just in case she hadn't seen them. And when she responded by slowing the car and crawling even more carefully around those things, she made a point of thanking him. He nodded with a smile, more confident than before. He was obviously enjoying this, as any eleven-year-old boy would, but especially a boy who had been confined to a house full of hand-wringing women for an interminable time. Her heart caught at the thought of this sensitive, uncomplaining child caught up in that dreadful happenstance. In profile, he reminded her of his father in his younger days; and that similarity caught her somewhere between the pain Ed had inflicted on her and a memory of an earlier happiness she'd long forgotten. But despite their resemblance, Kurt's patience and kindness were traits Ed never had.

The road was better than she remembered, but only a little. Even though the kids peered trustfully out the windows and urged the car on when she slowed to crawl around something, she felt their apprehension. She said to Kurt. "There has to be an easier road than this. Remember that fork we took at the beginning? I'll bet it goes to the house. But today wasn't the day to have tried it."

Kurt said, "Don't worry, Ma. It's okay. It's great doing this."

It was Tolly who reminded Meg of the danger she was placing them in; and this she did without saying a word. From the rearview mirror, Meg saw her sitting grim-eyed between the girls. First Sara would pull Tolly over to one side to look *down* at something. Then it was Callie's turn to pull her over to look *up* at something. In spite of the girls' excitement, it was evident that neither view brought Tolly any enjoyment. Finally, as they were passing around a particularly nasty spot, Tolly scooted forward and asked Meg how the driving was going, in a manner usually directed at a helmsman manning the only lifeboat. When everyone laughed, the tension was gone, at least for a while.

When at last Meg began to recognize the landmarks near the

place she'd parked before, she slowed to a crawl. Turning a corner, they were there. She *had* remembered. Everyone climbed out, happy to leave the car's cramped interior and walk on solid ground again.

The log was an instant hit. Kurt climbed up on its roots sticking up in the air, while Sara and Callie straddled it and took turns lying down on the moss growing all along its length, pretending it was a giant's bed.

While the women leaned against it, Meg told Tolly, "This is the place I told you about. And this log, well, there's something so enduring about it: dead but not gone. It's the way I think of Ma and Papa—that they aren't ever really gone." She looked at Tolly hopefully. "Maybe they're here, too." Without any acknowledgment, she added, more to herself, "Well I think so."

Tolly shrugged, "With these trees growin' so thick and these woods so dark and spooky, and everythin' under snow and ice for half the year, and that road. No, I don't think Ma and Papa would be up here, and neither should—"

Tolly stopped, but Meg could have completed her sentence. Dejected that she'd even mentioned it, she rounded up the kids and pointed them toward the jumble that would bring them to the road. Kurt stayed with the women, while the two girls scrambled deftly through it, hiding and shrieking as they jumped out from behind a tree and chided them for being so slow.

The cabin charmed everyone, as Meg knew it would. They walked around it and peeked in its windows, eager to go inside and sorry they couldn't. Back on the road again, Callie was first to see the power lines. Then Kurt and Sara spotted the roof of the big house. They were silent as they looked at it, astonished at its size and very presence on the mountainside.

Meg said, "It's not pretty, but isn't it fascinating?" She hesitated. "Why, it's empty. I thought the people were gone for the winter or something, but now it looks empty; I can *feel* it, can't you?" Still they approached the house cautiously. Meg said, "I think it's all right to look around; we're not going to hurt anything."

The kids let out a pent up chorus of cheers and begged to run down into the meadow. Meg cautioned them to stay within view of the house and to come back immediately when she whistled. With that assurance, she shooed them away, saying, "Have fun!"

With Kurt in the lead, they whooped and laughed and scattered away. With a catch in her throat and a gathering of tears, Meg watched them race down into the clearing, disappearing into the dips and folds of the meadow, then reappearing below where they were last seen—all the time leaving echoes of rapture in the crystalline air. To Meg, it sounded like music. With their blowing hair and loose billowing shirts catching the light, and their voices calling back and forth, they were as much a part of the mountain as the birds and ground squirrels and the ever-restless wind breathing through the trees. As never before, she saw her children as part of the land; and that felt right to her.

With a great pulse of relief at their happiness, she spread her arms and threw back her head and let out a cry of her own. It was wild and edged with a strange ring of sorrow at first, but then it rose into a sound of absolute joy; and it echoed against the rocky ridge above them—first touching the earth then touching the sky.

Meg's ecstasy frightened Tolly, and she turned and started toward the house. When Meg caught up to her, Tolly was shaking her head at its starkness. Meg suppressed a giggle as Tolly squinted up at the bleak brown walls and modular windows; she could almost hear her sister's famous sniff. Tolly sat down on the slab of stone and declared, "Well, this is nice."

Meg laughed as she joined her and they sat looking at the town below them, pointing at parts of it they recognized. Meg finally stood up and pulled Tolly to her feet. "Come on, we'll explore the bench above the house. I didn't get up there before."

Stopping to catch their breath, they looked back at the house. Tolly sniffed and said, "It's easy to understand why no one's living in it."

Meg shrugged to placate Tolly, but seeing it there affected her deeply: it looked like a huge brooding animal sitting motionless on its haunches while contemplating the valley below. It seemed trapped inside itself somehow, neither like houses in town nor part of the land it was built upon—and now it was abandoned.

12

SECRETS

Tolly, walking on ahead of Meg, called out excitedly, "Look, Meggie, here's a spring!" The large natural catch basin of glistening rocks was almost hidden in the low-hanging bushes. Fascinated, the two women watched its water well up strong enough to send ripples over its surface then disappear. Meg finally spoke, "In the meadow where the kids are, there's another spring. They must be connected." She moved her hands through the icy water, scooping up a handful and tasting it. Satisfied, she lay on her belly to drink from it, and was heartened when Tolly laughed and lay down beside her.

When they got up, Meg lifted the wet front of her shirt away from her skin, giggling. "Isn't this wonderful? Feeling the coolness and listening to the sound of the water and the trees? Let's sit here a while. The kids aren't going to wander away. Trust me." She patted a rock next to her and Tolly sat down.

Tolly said with concern, "Really, Meggie, you're overdoin' it."

"No, I'm really not. Right this minute I'm feeling better than I have for months, maybe years." With her arms around her knees, she sat back, her whole manner that of a happy, relaxed woman. "I'm free, Tolly. I don't need to feel guilty. I always had to deal with Ed's disapproval when the kids and I kicked up our heels too high. Now that's over." She picked up a twig near her feet and placed it carefully on the surface of the water, pushing it around with her finger, as one would a little canoe. As they watched, it hit the main flow of the spring and whirled around in the tiny vortex.

Meg sighed deeply before she continued speaking. "I have to remind myself that I'm in mourning. I lie in bed and try to grieve for Ed, trying to remember the good times; I really try. But I think my grief dribbled out of me a long time before he died. Over the years the kids and I have become a team. What else do you do when you're neglected? You get stronger."

She scooped up the twig and snapped it into little bits and threw the pieces angrily into the bushes. "Do you know how lucky you and Charlie are? You know exactly where you fit into life on your farm. I never knew what Ed wanted of me. It was like playing a game without knowing the rules. But now I'm free to find my own life. Saying this should make me feel guilty—poor Ed died, and poor Meg's a widow. But the truth is I feel wonderful. I feel alive and strong and rich in kids. This morning you used the word 'joy.' Well, that's what I feel. And I see my life as heading toward something glorious. I feel— "

"Meggie, that's enough!" Tolly laid her hand hard against her sister's lips, cutting off her words. Then she softened her action by saying, "I know. I know, Meggie."

Meg sat up straight, angry. "How can you say you know while you stop me from saying how I feel? What does 'I know, I know' mean?' "

"There are some things you shouldn't say out loud, is all."

"Not say to my *sister*?"

"But you *are* a widow, and you're vulnerable. I look at you and wonder just how to advise you. Seein' you, right this minute, against this wild backdrop, I'm afraid. You've been so safe, but now you seem in danger. I keep tryin' to think what Ma would have me do. And right this minute, I'm thinkin' that when I go back to Wyler, you and the babies should come with me—maybe for a visit at first, but then to stay. We could find you a place in Wyler, or maybe you'd want to move into a bigger place in Lewistown or Great Falls. You need to be near people who love you after all this mess."

Meg didn't say anything. Instead she watched the water rise from the bottom of the spring and spread out free and glorious upon the surface. It was there for only a moment before it disappeared, as though with only one glimpse of the sky it could be content to resume its subterranean journey.

In a soft voice she finally said, "I couldn't have gotten through any of this without you, sis; none of us could. I will be eternally thankful that you came when I needed you." She looked through her unexpected tears at the woman who had always been a part of her life. Tears were also rolling down Tolly's face. Almost at the same time they reached out their arms and drew together. They sat there quietly, grateful for the feelings between them.

Meg continued. "I know you worry, but I'm going to be okay. Surely you can see I'm better."

Tolly squeezed Meg's hand hard. "Better, yes, but you were real sick, you know. I want you to think real hard about comin' home with me. You don't have to answer me now."

Meg thought about it a while, then, even more softly, and picking her words carefully, she said, "No, dear, I'll answer now. Thank you, but my life is here. I've been in love with this country from the moment I saw it, and Ed's death didn't change that. We need to move forward, not backward. You saw the kids running into the meadow. They're the fifth generation of Halversons, so they need to be here, too." She reached over and tucked an errant strand of her sister's hair behind her ear, all the while searching her eyes for understanding.

Tolly's eyes clouded up again. "Oh, Meggie, I feel like I'm losin' you."

"No such luck, sis. I think it's more like you saved me for something." Meg sighed, then determining something, raised her head and listened for the children. Hearing their laughter in the distance, she said, "There's something I want to share with you. I think I'll feel better if I tell you. But it has to be a secret just between us. Not even Charlie should know. Will you promise never to tell anyone?"

Tolly looked worried, but said, "Well, yes, I promise. It will be just our secret."

"It's about that woman in the car with Ed." Seeing that she had Tolly's full attention, she went on. "They called her 'an itinerant', a 'hitchhiker.' You remember. But she wasn't; she couldn't have been. To my knowledge, Ed never picked up a hitchhiker in his whole life. Never! He scoffed at every hitchhiker he ever saw, calling them lazy and no-count, using another's vehicle for their own benefit.

"But even more important was the ring in Ed's wallet. I was shocked when I saw it in there—no one knew just how shocked I was; I could hardly breathe! I thought how the hell did that ring get into his wallet. I identified it as coming from the Halverson estate, but it was his grandmother's ring. What no one else knew is that Ed presented that ring to *Sara* when she was born, because she's named for his grandmother and was his first daughter. I was quite touched at his symbolic gesture. It's a beautiful old thing and quite precious, with its large white, flawless diamond. Ed thought of it as part of his Halverson heritage and was very attached to it. Theoretically, it could have been mine, but he didn't give it to me—it was pure Halverson, and I've certainly never been that. Anyway, I was glad he saw Sara as a Halverson who deserved it.

"But all this time since Sara was born that ring has been in our safety-deposit box in a vault at the bank. And in all these years *it has never been taken out*."

Tolly said, "Why didn't you tell me this sooner?"

Meg said, "I guess I needed to think about it for a while. When I was sick I mulled these things over and over, asking myself what Sara's ring was doing in Ed's wallet. Did he habitually carry sentimental things around with him? No, he didn't. Were there pictures of the kids in his wallet? No!" She gave a short laugh. "In my wallet I carry so many pictures I can hardly bend it. And I carried Kurt's first baby tooth there until it practically crumbled. But, no, there weren't things like that in Ed's wallet. In that sodden mess were his driver's license, a number of credit cards, over one thousand dollars in brand new hundred-dollar bills, and that damned bulky ring. And the ring wasn't tucked away in some safe corner of his wallet, with the leather all scuffed and dented from being carried there for a long time; the ring was on top of the money. Do you hear what I'm saying, Tolly? Seeing it there, I have to wonder if the ring was about to leave his possession! And, say he hadn't died, and somewhere down the line, when Sara was grown up and was ready for the ring, would Ed have tried pretending it was lost, thinking I'd forgotten all about it? What I'm saying is, if he *had given it to... to someone else*, and I ever asked about it, would he say, 'Oh, my, I wonder where that ring went?'

"It's my opinion that he was carrying that ring to give to that woman. Why else was it in there? And there's something else. From her description she was slim, pretty, young, and had long dark hair. She had *long, dark hair*. What you don't know is that long, dark hair was a real sexual turn-on to Ed. When we first started going together he'd undo my hair with his hands shaking, and... Well, you don't need the details, but, trust me, it was always a real turn-on, and, frankly, a little kinky. I came to accept it, but I really didn't like it. When I heard that that woman had extraordinarily long dark hair I felt like I'd been hit with a truck.

"I believe that woman was someone special to him. I don't understand why she hasn't been identified, but she's no itinerant hitchhiker. They were together for a reason. I have reason to believe that Ed took that ring out of the deposit box and intended to give to her—a precious, precious gift from him, a token of his feelings, and maybe a promise of...well, who knows what? I've wondered if he was taking her somewhere and the ring was the very best memento he could think of. I've wondered if the money might also have been for her...a sweet good-bye maybe, or to help finance a new start for her.

"Ed was in agony for months, Tolly. Could that agony have come from frustrated love? There were so many other frustrations in his life. I know that I was one of them, but so were people like Art Stroud. I don't know why Ed and the woman died in the car like that." She paused and her face got sad before she continued. "Tolly, I even wonder if it was an accident. With no answers yet, and the time passing, I have to wonder if we'll ever know. But whatever happens, it doesn't matter to me anymore."

Tolly asked hesitantly, "But wouldn't your tellin' the officials this help them identify her?"

Meg looked at her sister intently. "I have no proof of this; it's only my guess. Think about how intensive their investigation of her has been. What would my guess add? She was officially spoken of as an itinerant stranger, and there's nothing connecting her to Ed. I owe it to the kids to not add any more fuel to that fire. Think of what the paper would say if it ever got wind that I was wondering these things. My God, we've suffered enough!

"Anyway, I put the ring back into the vault at the bank and Sara will get it when she's old enough to take responsibility for it. I'll always hate to look at it, knowing where it's been and what my suspicions are about it. But Sara must never know that. Hopefully, by the time she gets it, this scandal will be long forgotten, and we'll cross our fingers that that's the way it ends." Meg looked at Tolly. "You're awfully quiet. Do you think I'm wrong?"

Tolly mulled that over. "No, not wrong. But I'm amazed about the ring. I see your point. There's nothing clear about this, and there never has been. I've always wanted the woman to be just a hitchhiker. While you were laid up you mentioned the ring a few times. I wondered if more was botherin' you than you let on."

"From start to finish, Ed hurt me so. It's going to take me a while to feel good about myself again—if I ever do."

"But that's why I wanted you to come to Wyler."

"It's not going to happen, Tolly. And please get that look of sympathy off your face. Frankly, I can't stand sympathy."

At that Meg stood up and dusted off her jeans. "Let's walk down into the clearing and find the kids." She reached down and helped her sister up, then slipped her arm through Tolly's, and the two of them walked away from the spring.

When the kids heard her whistle they ran up the slope toward them, breathless with excitement and discovery. Sara ran up to her mother and aunt, with something in her hand to show them. She was holding a piece of white porcelain, on which were painted tiny blue flowers. She said, "I think a mother lived down there."

Meg knelt beside her and said, "Yes, I think you're right." She rubbed the chip and said, "Know what? I found this exact piece when I was here before. Wasn't it on the floor of that old fallen-down cabin by the apple tree?"

Sara shook her head vigorously, "Yes!"

Meg went on, "Well, what do you think about putting it back where you found it, like I did? It will only get lost, and then no one will ever know she lived here. Do you think you can put it back right where you found it, Sara? Maybe we can come back and see it again someday."

"Oh, yes!"

"Now, you show us what else you found down there, then we'll show you the big spring we found. It's wonderful water. Only you have to drink it like an Indian, flat on your stomachs."

At that, the children raced down the slope ahead of them.

13

LONG NIGHT

In the veil of smoke twisting up through the layers of branches above their camp, the pungent smell of burning pine was joined by the luscious smell of chicken frying in butter. When Meg raised the lid of the big Dutch oven and rearranged the browning chicken, her empty stomach complained loudly. Closing the heavy lid with a clang, she darted beneath the smoke and helped Callie put the opened cans of green beans in a pan and place it on the back of the grate. After they put their pared potatoes, one at a time, into a kettle of hot water, Meg asked Callie to shake a little salt in before Meg lifted it onto the fire. As they retreated, the ever-changing smoke wrapped itself around the two of them, moving as they moved, until they ducked beneath it and sat down on a chunk of wood they had dragged there just for that purpose.

While Meg dabbed at the smoke-tears running down Callie's cheeks, then at her own, she said, "That smoke wouldn't dare come and get us here," and gave her youngest child a kiss. Then, with Callie watching, she pushed the unburned end of a piece of wood directly under the kettle of potatoes. It took only a moment for the water to break into a furious bubble. Callie squeaked in laughter. Meg handed Callie a stick and instructed her to do the same. With one hand shielding her face from the heat, Callie squatted down and carefully thrust the stick into the fire, then pushed in the cold ends of other burning sticks, and watched expectantly.

Resuming her seat beside her mother she smiled proudly. "This is the funnest. Am I a camp cook now, like Kurt and Sara?"

Meg said, "Just about. There's much to learn here. All three of you kids are good learners. I only wish your grandmother were here to see this. She was my teacher." Callie, who last year had been too young to be anything but underfoot, had volunteered to be a camp cook. Meg welcomed the opportunity to introduce yet another child to some of the outdoors cooking techniques she had learned from her mother.

She gave their little campsite a satisfied grin. If Kurt hadn't found the new spring on the way back to the log, they would have driven down and cooked dinner at the canyon campground. With the kids begging, she had agreed to make camp here, but only on the condition that they help restore the campsite to its former natural state as soon as dinner was over. If there was anything that irritated her it was finding an old camp with refuse left scattered around—and that included smoke-stained rocks and half-burned sticks strewn on the ground. So, with those rules agreed upon, she felt this old place might even welcome a change—including frisky children and the smell of wholesome food.

From the moment she had stood by the kitchen window and declared her independence she could feel her strength coming back. And she had even gotten her way about being the cook. Surprisingly, Tolly had backed away from arguing about cooking and declared she'd rather just 'poke around,' as she called it. Sara had been last year's cooking helper, but she'd announced she also wanted to poke around and had joined her aunt. Kurt, after digging the fire pit to accept the large grate and finding rocks to encircle it, had taken off with the axe. Even though she couldn't see him, the hollow pound of his axe on wood announced his location. Tolly and Sara had spread the red-checked tablecloth on the old log then laid out the dishes and silverware and other odds and ends. From where Meg sat, the very dimensions of the giant banquet table made the cloth look like a doily and everything on it like mere doll offerings for a summer's tea.

When everything was cooked and ready, it was a feast, no doubt about that: the dented black kettle held a huge amount of mashed potatoes, and beside it was the container of thick cream gravy. Another pan held the golden chicken, soft and glazed with butter. There were hot green beans, pickles, sliced tomatoes, veggies and a dip, apples, brownies, Tolly's soft ginger cookies with a large dollop of white frosting centered on each one, and marshmallows to toast later. After piling their plates with food they found a seat near the fire, and were soon reveling in the civilized tastes eaten in an uncivilized setting.

As they ate, Meg realized that none of the sun's rays were hitting the camp. Their exploring had set back their dinner preparations. It was June, but at this altitude she already felt chilly. She hoped she hadn't been too optimistic in allowing sweaters to be packed instead of something warmer. Without appearing to, she would hurry along the evening activities. She longed to sit around the fire as they usually did, but she certainly wanted to get down that miserable road before it got dark—and dark it would be, with clouds now moving into the sky.

While she and Tolly hurried about the camp, washing the dishes and packing things up, the kids toasted marshmallows, occasionally popping those rare perfectly browned ones, teetering dangerously on the end of the stick, into the opened mouths of their aunt and mother. They all lingered, hating to leave.

A long howl from a coyote, followed by a series of short yips, cut through their serenity. The sound, originating from the trees just above them, was so immediate and taunting that the group instinctively drew closer to the fire. While they listened, more coyote howls joined in to make a joyous chorus. Before anyone could say anything, another group of coyotes, not to be outdone, answered from lower down the slope, their thrilling cries echoing across the mountains.

As captivated as the family was by the eerie sounds, they felt no fear, for they had heard and been thrilled by coyotes' howls many times before, although never this close. During a break in the sound, Meg said, "I think they're reminding us that we're just visitors here. Imagine, we're only a few miles from town, but we're probably feeling the same things people who lived here a thousand years ago felt."

In a voice smaller and less sure than it had been just a while ago, Callie asked, "Are there any bears here, Ma?"

Meg hastened to reassure her, "There are no bears here; we're too close to town! I suppose there might be a few somewhere in these mountains, but they're very smart and stay away from people. And aren't we glad about that!" She picked up Callie in a big swoop that ended with giggles from everyone.

Seeing the beginnings of a sunset, Meg said, "I hate to be the one who ends this, but we've got to clean up the camp, lug this stuff to the car, and start down that road." Everyone groaned, but with the message from the coyotes lingering in their memories, and the sky losing its light fast, they hurried. Meg put out the fire by pouring the dishwater on the coals. Kurt and Sara took turns lugging even more spring water to drown it until every trace of smoke and steam was gone. They pushed the rocks and the soggy burnt ends of the wood into the fire pit, took the shovel and placed soil over the hole and smoothed it. Lastly, they scattered twigs and needles and small pebbles over it all. Only they would know where their campfire had been. By the time they left for the car the sun was disappearing over the horizon.

. . .

"Oh, damn!" The word gave Meg a brief feeling of power over the helplessness she felt. The car wouldn't start no matter how she tried, and she'd been trying for the last ten minutes. She and Kurt found the flashlight and peered under the hood hopefully. Unfortunately, the belts and plugs and wires and black lumps of things made as much sense to Meg as a dish of dirty spaghetti. She asked Kurt, "Have you any ideas?"

"Gosh, no, Ma. I wish I did."

The bleak sound of his response matched her thoughts exactly. She gave him a hug and giggled inanely as she stared into the mysterious mess of parts in total frustration. She finally said, "When we got here and I turned off the key it was fine. But, come to think of it, the car was struggling the last mile or two. I blamed it on the steep climb."

Still peering hopelessly into the motor, Kurt mumbled, "I spose."

Meg said, "Well, let's try it once more. Maybe it's flooded. You turn the key while I see what happens here." She rolled her eyes.

Kurt climbed into the car and did what she asked. After a little metallic click, there was nothing. He came back out to stand beside his mother.

Tolly and the Littles had been standing behind them, watching, but because the girls started to shiver, the three of them were now sitting in the back seat awaiting Meg's verdict. Meg could almost feel Tolly's eyes on the back of her neck when the coyotes started howling again, a little farther away, but just as jarring. Meg spoke quietly to Kurt, "I really love to hear them howl, but they aren't helping much right now."

Kurt laughed softly, "Yeah, I was thinking the same thing."

With darkness descending, Meg checked her watch: it was almost eight o'clock. "Darn it all, Kurt, we don't have more than a few minutes of any kind of light left." In a low voice she continued, "Looks like we're in a fix for sure. Somehow, I doubt that we're going to experience a miracle and have someone drive up this road and offer to help us. Looks like we're going to have to spend the night up here, then walk down tomorrow and get help. I don't see any other way. Do you?"

"No, I don't, but I've been thinking, why don't we have Aunt Tolly and the Littles sleep in the car tonight, and you and I can go back to the camp and build a fire and stay there. We can keep the fire going all night."

"It's a great idea, dear...but building a fire?" With an ironic laugh, she added, "Wasn't that a great idea I had about totally putting out the fire and drowning every darn stick in sight?" She sighed. "I'm not keen about searching for a lot of wood in the dark."

Kurt laughed sympathetically, "Yeah, it might be hard."

"About Tolly and the girls in the car... A car really gets cold during the night, and I'm afraid for the Littles. Since we only brought sweaters and we have only two small blankets...and a tablecloth, of course, for five people... For a while it would be okay." She stopped and considered, then added, "With no lights, and it's already chilly, it would be an awfully long night around the fire, Kurt. There isn't enough daylight to do something more heroic, like build a little shelter for all of us around the campfire. It would be a great adventure for a while, but I'm afraid that later, everyone would be miserable. But we really need to be inside something."

Kurt said, "There's that little cabin, Ma. We could figure out how to get inside it." He thought for a moment then added, "But it doesn't have a stove and we probably couldn't get inside, with those little windows."

His voice brightened, "But the big house has a fireplace, Ma."

Meg looked at him intently. "I'm thinking that, too. We could break one of its back windows. I hate the thought of that, but we can worry about that later. We've got to get inside and keep everyone warm. But, my gosh, what a tangle we have to go through to get to that road, and in the dark." She chewed her lip while she thought. "Okay, Kurt, let's decide right now that we'll get to the house just as fast as we can and get inside it and build a fire in the fireplace. We'll take the leftover food with us for tomorrow." At Kurt's nod they both laughed shakily. Meg went on, "Tolly hasn't been very happy today, and I don't want the Littles to get worried, so let's make it as fun as possible. But we have to do it fast, because every minute we're talking it's getting darker."

"The lantern's full of gas and I still remember how to light it."

"Thanks, Kurt, and don't forget to bring the matches with you for the fireplace. I'm really depending on you. Now let's tell Tolly and the Littles what we're going to do."

Once the lantern was lit, and they all knew the plan, everybody pitched in, as enthusiastic as ever. As chilly and dark as it was, it was just another part of their adventure to have to unpack their car and sort through things. While Kurt helped his mother and aunt put the leftover food and cups into a small kettle, the girls got the sweaters, both blankets, and the tablecloth.

Meg had completely misjudged the amount of light left in the sky. In the short time it took to walk back and gather by the old log it was pitch dark. A cloud cover had moved in fast and there wasn't a trace of light in the sky. Under her breath she swore to herself. Being alone in the dark had been her nemesis from the very beginning of her life. Papa had teased her about it, praising her on camping trips on those few times she was able to leave the circle of the campfire without someone holding her hand. But now…

She looked at the people around her. The hiss of the lantern and its cold, unfriendly light turned their faces into those of strangers and threw huge shadows into an already alien world of hidden branches and unseen barriers. She made her voice cheerful and said, "Before we move from this log we need to talk. I'm a little concerned about finding the road in the dark. I don't want to get turned around while we clamber over all those trees and things—you remember how tough it was earlier. We'll make it, but we need to keep in mind what we're doing." She thought a moment. "As long as I'm by this log here I have the picture of the road in my mind, but with all of us trying to get through it, I'm concerned we might lose track of where we are." She thought to herself, *wouldn't that be a mess, wandering though the night, going farther and farther from the car into god knows what?*

She considered the possibilities, then said to the family, "New plan. This is how I think we should do it. I'll take the flashlight and go on ahead and find the road. You stay here with the lantern, and don't move. The lantern throws a lot of light and I'll use your light to keep my bearings, so I don't wander off. Once I'm on the road I'll whistle and waggle the flashlight; and I'll keep doing that. That's your cue to come toward me. But, just remember, don't come until you hear me whistle like this (she demonstrated), and pretty soon you'll see my light.

Once they assured her that this was the only reasonable plan, she started walking in the direction her mind told her to follow. She'd gone only a short distance when she turned around and was comforted by seeing the little group standing around the lantern. She called out jauntily, "This won't take any time at all. Just wait there until I whistle." Then, with all her old fears of the dark coming back to her, she struck out into the blackness again. She determined she'd fix her mind's eye on the location of the road and the little cabin to its right.

It was slow going. The puny beam of her flashlight reflected off the bigger obstacles, but was useless in announcing holes and rocks and branches suddenly looming at eye level. While she pushed her way through, she thought of the ancients living in such unrelieved darkness, with only the stars and the moon. What a blessing firelight must have been to them, along with its warmth and safety, and the feelings of community it lent them. Coming from the constant light of her modern life in town, it was hard to even imagine life without light: indoors, outdoors, street lights, yard lights, headlights, lights from signs, store lights, lights from windows, light globes, lamps, and, she added, of course, lanterns and flashlights. What it all added up to—though she hadn't thought of it before now—was that there was so much light available that a person considered it his right not to think of darkness at all. Well, she would value light after this.

After staring so hard into the darkness, to catch sight of anything vaguely familiar, she looked back over her right shoulder to get her bearings on the lantern, but saw nothing. However, when she looked to her left she was shocked to see a dim glow. Just as she'd feared, clambering over the obstacles that lay all around her, she had gone in a circle. She leaned against a tree trunk to gather her wits and think about where she was. If only she had asked the family to keep whistling or calling out to her, so she could keep their position in mind. She struggled to quell her panicky fears as she started out again.

She sensed the animal's presence before she heard it moving to her left, with a snap of a twig breaking under its foot and a slight swish against the bushes. It moved heavily through its familiar environment, pausing once to listen. Again she heard the whisper of brush against its coat that signaled its retreat—at least she hoped it was retreating, and not just taking a position of ambush further ahead.

Once she had felt its presence, she, too, had stopped—her hand refusing to shine the flashlight at the sound, for fear of seeing what it was. And while she listened to this unseen thing, she felt more frightened than she had ever been in her life. With her instincts on alert, her reason hovered somewhere between covering her head and throwing herself on the ground, to screaming and running away to anywhere but where she stood frozen. But with her family waiting behind her and the house somewhere out in front, her mind drew away from the implications of the sound, and she deliberately created a milder animal than she feared it was.

A deer, she thought, it's a deer. She swallowed rapidly as she pictured a deer's kind eyes and its protectiveness toward its young. Somehow it cleared her mind of lurking possibilities and she again walked forward, clearly picturing where the road was and where she might be in relation to it.

In moments, her thin beam of light struck the ruts of the road and she knew exactly where she was, where the cabin was, and where the house would be. She whistled with all her might and waved her flashlight for everyone to follow. She heard whistles and shouts coming toward her now. When she finally saw the little troop, led by Kurt and his lantern, moving slowly toward her through the intervening darkness, she moved to them, sure of her position now and feeling braver. While she whistled, and they whistled back, she thought: those coyotes had a heck of a good idea.

It was 10:15 by the time they reached the back porch of the house. And it was Meg who threw a rock through the window—she certainly didn't want anyone else to do it. Once she'd removed the glass from around the window, she boosted Kurt inside and handed him the flashlight with instructions to go to the front door, where they would all be waiting. They arrived at the front of the house just as Kurt unbarred the door and, with a great creaking of its hinges, opened it. They stepped up the stone doorstep and went inside.

With more hope than reason Meg tried a light switch by the door, but there was no electricity. The room was empty, dusty, and cold. Holding the lantern up high and turning slowly, she was able to see the interior for the first time. Even in that poor light some of the details of the huge room had interesting details: stone steps leading up to a balcony and, on another wall, she got an impression of bookcases. Kurt pointed out the outlines of at least five doors opening onto the balcony, and told them it was the far door, at the very end of the balcony, that he had come through. As tempting as it was to look around the place, Meg would not allow it. Regardless of the good reasons for their being there, they were worse than trespassers; they had broken in.

Thankfully there was wood in a storage area built into the rock wall that held the fireplace, and it had more than enough wood to get them through the night. Kurt pointed the now fitful flashlight beam up inside the fireplace, found the draft lever and pushed it open. With everyone pitching in, finding small bits and scraps for kindling, then larger wood, they soon had a fire flickering behind the heavy andirons, and filling the room with a delicious coziness. They grouped in front of the fire and held their hands out to its warmth.

Sitting back and looking at her ragtag band kneeling expectantly in front of the fire, Meg was satisfied that everyone had come through the adventure well. And it was an adventure, every minute of it, first to last. She watched the children stare into the mesmerizing flames, with their great tired eyes and barely stifled yawns, as though their eyes were unaware of what their gaping mouths were doing.

Tolly smiled over their heads at her. It was a proud smile. She hadn't let go of her "babies"—at least the female ones—all day.

As the big room warmed, first the Littles, then Kurt, sagged down, curled their bodies trustfully into the heat and slept. Tolly and Meg slid them gently between them, covering them with the blankets and tablecloth. After refilling the hearth with wood, the two women lay down too. When Tolly joked, "Are you sure you're not overdoing it, Meggie?" the two women laughed softly together.

Just before Meg dropped off to sleep she looked around happily, grateful that this house was here, and grateful that never once had anyone questioned or objected to her plan for getting here. It was a day and a night they would always remember, this stalwart group.

14

THE ROAD DOWN

"Meg . . . Meg . . ."

Meg awoke to her name and opened her eyes grudgingly, then lay wondering what had awakened her. It had been someone calling her, a man's voice; she must have been dreaming...

It was early and only beginning to lighten. Remembering where she was, she rose up painfully on one elbow and looked around. Callie, lying next to her, turned with a sigh and threw her arm around Sara. The two girls nestled closer, then lay still and slept on like contented puppies. She envied them their resiliency, lying half on the hard stones of the hearth and half on the hardwood floor, while her body felt permanently dented. As she massaged her shoulders and stretched to relieve a kink, she gave up further sleep. She reached over and adjusted the blanket around the girls, and drew the other blanket higher up on Kurt and Tolly. No one moved.

The fire she had tended once, maybe twice, during the night was all but gone. As quietly as possible she pulled out some small sticks and chunks from the wood storage area and laid them on the ash-covered coals, which, judging from the hint of warmth coming from them, still had the ability to ignite the new wood. Pressing her face close to the hearth, she blew a steady stream of air onto the coals, loosening tiny peelings of ash from the red-centered coals. When a tiny flame sprang to life she sat back on her heels and felt extraordinarily pleased with herself. And why shouldn't she? Once the floor and the stones of the hearth had warmed, the room had stayed comfortable.

In less than twenty-four hours she'd been forced to think about more basic necessities than she'd thought of for years and years. To her mental list she added the words "shelter" and "warmth" to the word "light" from last night's scramble. Then, as she thought of the lovely spring above the house that brought water from who knows where, she added "water" to the list In town, as water thundered from a faucet at the flip of a wrist, whoever thought about its origin, or imagined its beauty bubbling from the bottom of a gravelly basin? With a rueful smile, she added the word "luck" to her inventory—more appropriately, "blind-ass luck"—for that's what brought them to this moment (she now understood what that particular expression meant).

Yet, even in her gratitude, she shuddered at the events that had led her and her little band to be inside someone else's house on this isolated mountainside. She could hardly forgive herself for the situation she had gotten them into—pushing the car beyond its ability and her total lack of knowledge about its working parts. They were lucky to have reached this house unscathed. They could still be shivering in a cold car, or worse, be roaming the mountainside, lost and exposed and hurt. Her eyes caressed the tousled lumps breathing rhythmically around her on this foreign floor. Grand adventure or not, these were her charges and she felt a sobering responsibility for them.

Still, each one had held steady, and they were safe. Tolly had been wonderful, having dropped her grudging attitude and taken full charge of the Littles. And Kurt was so everlastingly dependable. She wondered, as she had so many times, if it was excusable to lean upon that trait in him? Would he be an adult without ever being a child? That thought had nagged at her even before Ed had died. She would have to be extra vigilant about that. But overall the three kids, for all their youth, had been quiet and trustful and had enjoyed themselves immensely, as though receiving an unexpected gift. But the adventure was hardly over. She had a big day ahead of her, with a long walk down the mountain to get help, and get everyone back home.

Home, she grimaced at the word. What and where was "home" now? It used to be the place where she waited for Ed's daily return, where the children drifted back from school, where she tended her lovely gardens with her children playing around her, where she spent hours cooking what her family loved to eat, where her family assembled around the table, where they found comfort in the house's beautiful rooms and furniture, where she filled her heart and mind with music and the sounds of children's laughter and even their spats… Less than a day had passed since they left town, and already their house seemed as distant as the moon—not in miles, but in this feeling of separation from all it had meant before. Something had shifted—the very definition of home had changed; perhaps because the future had altered so radically. Always before it was fun to go back home; in fact, a trip always had a double benefit: of getting away and of coming back. But now, it was different.

She rose quietly and assessed their strange oasis. Last night, in their rush to get settled, the hissing light from the lantern had done little more than give her a tantalizing hint. But in the new morning light, the room's details were emerging, and she was fascinated.

On the north wall, the massive stonework containing the fireplace soared two stories up to the beamed ceiling. The huge room had two levels: the living room, where she stood, and the second level—resembling a large L-shaped balcony—built along its eastern and southern walls. Located on this balcony level was the large dining area and, beyond the dining area, a kitchen could be seen through a doorway.

Six stone steps connected the balcony level with the living room level; and there was a beautiful iron railing on the steps as well as along the entire length of the second level balcony overhanging the living room. Along the south side of the balcony, Meg counted the five doors Kurt mentioned. Beneath this part of the balcony, and facing the fireplace, an immense walnut bookcase ran along the entire length of this wall. Meg could imagine the elegance it would give the room when filled with colorful books and art objects.

There was also a staircase leading down from the living room to a door below her. It must lead to the garages—and thus was another entrance to the house.

The details of the huge room were intriguing. Where the exterior of the house was rough, the interior was paneled in dark wood, which would counter the amount of light flooding through the windows during the day. From the outside, the large windows that she had assessed as modular and uninteresting, were, inside, spaced perfectly. On each side of the fireplace the giant windows provided a view of the clearing and across to the mountains. Through the large window on the west-facing wall, she could see the road, a tiny corner of the cabin, and the grand view of the valley and town. There were no shades or draperies on the windows, probably because they were located so high from the ground and no one could look inside.

The fireplace was the room's focal point. Its stony texture against the wide plank floors and the wood-paneled walls made it even more spectacular. She imagined looking down from the balcony level to a fire burning behind the great black andirons. During the day the room would be filled with light coming from the huge windows, then, at night, it would change. Last night, just before she fell asleep, the room's walls had seemed to draw down around her—as the fire itself drew down in size—holding her family in a most comforting flickering light, until that light was all there was.

Meg longed to climb the stone stairs and explore the entire house. But beyond this room she would not go, as she was here under the most illegal terms. Of her many questions about it, one had been answered: the owners had chosen this site for a view that was beyond belief. Last night, looking at it as she replenished the fire, the town, with its lights sparkling and twinkling, looked for all the world like a diamond and ruby bracelet thrown carelessly across the valley floor.

Curiosity pulled her to the north window to look at the meadow. Somber and grey, the meadow still slept. But as she watched, the sun lifted over the trees, and sent light flying across the clearing, like a major chord drawn from an orchestra by a conductor's quivering fingers. Before her, the interplay of light and color, as clear as flutes and as bright as brass and violins, pushed away the monotone of bass and cello shadows. In the new brightness she saw a deer browsing near the lower spring. It looked up, alert to the change in light, then continued eating. When it moved away it was unhurried, then disappeared into the trees. It was hard to believe this was the same place she had stumbled through so fearfully last night. She was pondering her fear of the dark when Sara woke up…

. . .

Breakfast—if it could be called that—was eaten outside on the stone doorstep. Kurt and Callie brought water from the spring above the house, using the same kettle they'd hastily stuffed with fruit and cookies last night. Wishing the water were something other than what it was became a game. Callie wished for orange juice, Kurt for hot cocoa, Sara wished for milk, and both Meg and Tolly described, in exaggerated tones, their missing mugs of coffee.

While they ate, the two women discussed the day's plans for getting help. Rather than having everyone walk down, Meg would go. She said, "It probably won't take me more than a couple hours to reach the bottom of the canyon, where I'll phone for help from one of the homes there. I'm going to follow this better road here. It has to be more direct."

A chorus of "I want to come, too," interrupted her.

She said, "Now wait a minute—"

Kurt said emphatically, "But you shouldn't go by yourself. Aunt Tolly can stay with the Littles, so I'll come with you."

Seeing Tolly's face she said, "Kurt honey, if you could stay up here I wouldn't worry."

Kurt shook his head defiantly. "If I have to stay here, take Sara with you."

Tolly said, "That's out of the question, she's just a baby. She can't walk miles and miles."

Meg said, "It's downhill and it's only to the bottom of the canyon—"

"Now, Meggie, you can't mean you're even thinkin' about taking Sara."

"Sara's an old toughie. Aren't you, Sara? Do you think you could walk down with me?"

Sara was already jumping up and down and beaming. "Yes! I'd like to go, Ma." When Callie buried her head in Meg's lap and started to wail, Sara put her hands on her hips and said to her. "Be a good sport, Cal. I get to go 'cuz I'm older."

Callie raised her head and sobbed, "You're always older!"

Meg gave her a big consoling squeeze. "Your turn will come, Callie."

Tolly sniffed and again protested, "Sara has little legs—"

Meg laughed and put her arm around her sister. "Of course she has, but we'll take it easy. And it's such a wonderful day. I just know that this road is shorter. If Sara gets tired, I promise I'll let her ride piggyback. Come on now, Tolly, I want Sara's company."

Somewhat mollified, Tolly shrugged, then shook her head yes.

Meg said, "Then it's decided. Now listen, everybody. Sara and I will hurry as fast as we can, but I can't really say what time we'll be back. Kurt has the matches and you can build up the fire if you get cold, and there's plenty of food left and there's water. Sara and I will take along some food and have a picnic. And as soon as we get down to the canyon road, we'll phone a mechanic to drive us back up here and fix the car. I promise we'll all be back home before dinner. There's one more thing, though. This isn't our house and it wouldn't be right to go exploring inside it. Every room but the living room is off limits. And I mean it."

Tolly pulled Callie up on her lap and dried her tears and told her, "We'll visit that spring in a little while."

. . .

Tolly and Kurt and Callie followed them as far as the cabin. In a quavering voice, Tolly called out to them as she waved, "Watch where you put your feet! You don't want to break a leg or twist your ankles. I packed a little extra food for you, seein' as how you're the ones goin' to save us. And watch out for those coyotes. You can never tell, sometimes they get rabid."

When they were out of sight of the house, Sara started giggling. "Aunt Tolly thinks everyone is a baby. Kurt said he was going to lie down and suck his thumb if she called him a baby one more time. And doesn't Aunt Tolly know coyotes are little and scared of us? Don't they have coyotes there on their farm?"

"I'm sure they do, honey. But your Aunt loves us all very much and she means well. Sometimes she needs to warn people about things. She feels a little bit uneasy up here because these mountains are so different from the farm. Uncle Charlie will be glad to get her back. But it's been nice having her here, hasn't it?

"Uh huh. We like her spaghetti, but you cook best, Ma."

"Thank you. We're a regular cookin' and eatin' family, aren't we?"

Sara giggled. Patting her pocket she said, "I like what Kurt did."

Meg smiled down at her. "He's a neat brother. I used to wish I had one just like him. He's pretty nice." At the last minute Kurt had handed Sara his precious pocketknife to take along. Sara took it gingerly, not believing she was to be the keeper of anything so precious. Then, something like alarm came over her face, thinking he was expecting her to use it in ways she didn't understand. But he only pounded her on the back and grinned and threatened her with absolute death if she lost it. Considering his disappointment in not accompanying her, his generosity grabbed Meg's heart again. He could tolerate just so many words of praise, but she resolved to tell him how much she appreciated him.

Sara's silky blonde hair, swinging above the blue pack Kurt had fashioned from a sweater, reminded Meg of the inventiveness and imagination all three kids had. They also had stamina and were gong to be tall. Kurt was already enjoying his size and strength—she'd seen him before the bathroom mirror, flexing his arms and inhaling grandly. She hoped both girls would never regret their size, as she had. Just as her own mother had helped her, she would see that they were proud of their bodies.

Meg figured they had walked almost two miles when they came to a tiny stream trickling from a spring half hidden in a tunnel of overhanging shrubs. White trilliums, growing in the shady edges of the spring, drew them as much as the water. They were thirsty and it was cool and shadowy, and sitting down felt good to both of them. Sara found a place where the water was deep enough to flow into the cup. As the official water gatherer, she solemnly brought the brimming cupful to her mother, watched her drink then drank some herself. They ate their cookies while letting the sound of the tiny water and the calls of the unseen birds filter into their consciousness. When an occasional current of warm air drifted into the coolness, they lifted their faces to it.

Sara squatted down to examine one of the trilliums, cupping its blossom in her two hands and touching its petals gently with her thumbs. Smiling back at her mother, she let it spring back as crisp and saucy as before. Judging from the game trails coursing out of the forest and converging here, this was a watering spot for animals, too. They identified the tiny scrambling of mice and rabbits and squirrels and birds, and the pointy tracks of deer. They decided it was like reading a book about who lived in this forest. Sara was moving further up the draw when she said, "Look, Ma. What's this track?"

When Meg saw the imprint of furry toe pads in the mud, she answered, "I'm not sure, but it looks like some kind of wild cat. I wouldn't be at all surprised if such animals live here."

She had no sooner said that than Sara said very quietly, "Ma, look, there it is. It *is* a cat!" At the very back of the spring, a Canada lynx was sitting on its haunches, emotionless and still, watching them. With its great yellow unblinking eyes, and without the slightest twitch of its whiskers or black-tipped ears, it sat as though it would be there forever. But then, with both Meg and Sara looking at it intently, it got up, almost leisurely, and vanished into the greenery without so much as a whisper of sound. It was as though it was made of something transparent and only the light had changed.

They were stunned, breathing in unison. On Sara's face was a look of pride at having spotted it. She whispered, "Oh, Ma, I still see him, even though he left."

"So can I, Sara. He'll always be there in our brains. In fact, I think our brains take permanent pictures of some things—"

"So we never forget?"

"That's right, honey. When you're a mother and you're telling your children about this day, I bet you'll be able to tell them how the air felt and smelled and about each leaf and stick and trickle around that exquisite lynx."

Sara patted Meg's arm. "I'll tell them you were with me, too, Ma."

At hearing that, Meg's eyes immediately filled with tears. "Oh, yes, do that." This child, she thought, she dispenses immortality with a word.

Sara said, "We better not tell Aunt Tolly about the lynx though."

"Why not?"

"She's scared up here. And she'll never want to come up here and visit us."

"Come up here?"

"Can't we live here, Ma? Can't we live in that house?"

"Oh, Sara—"

"But Callie and Kurt and I talked about it this morning. No one's living in it."

"Just because it's empty doesn't mean we can. The owners are just away for a while. Anyway, how could we ever live up here? You three kids have to go to school, you know. It's not always summer up here, Sara. Remember how white these mountains look in winter? Think of how much snow falls on these roads." Meg shook her head. "Can you imagine three little kids living here with a woman who doesn't even know one end of a car from another? No, Sara, this isn't any place for us. I'll admit it's an interesting house—what I've seen of it—and the land is beautiful, but it's a place that needs a—a daddy to help."

Sara said, "But can't you get us one?"

"Oh Sara—" Meg laughed and looked down at her "you don't get one like that."

"Can't Kurt be our daddy?"

"No, he's little like you, even if he looks big. A daddy is..." When Meg started describing what a daddy was, it didn't take her long to realize that she wasn't talking about Ed, but about her own father; and she had difficulty tying her words to anything Sara had ever experienced.

Sara's definition was a little different. "Once Daddy swung me around and around, but that's when I was little. He didn't look at the pictures we drew. My friend Marcie's daddy comes home and takes her to shows and reads her stories and cooks breakfast sometimes. Why didn't Daddy do that, Ma?"

"Well, he got awfully busy at the bank. You remember that, Sara."

"Yeah, but Marcie's daddy goes to work and is busy, but he comes home and plays. Callie and I want our daddy to do that."

"Yes, I know." Every word Sara said revealed the loose connection

Ed had with his children. In contrast, Meg felt the familiar ache of how much she had loved her Papa, and the pain his death still caused her.

Sara kept on talking, "Daddy told us to stand up straight and breathe with our mouths closed, even when we had runny noses. He said we always left our bikes in his way, and he didn't want us to play on the grass. And he didn't give me big hugs like you do, Ma. He didn't hug you either." An uncertain sadness crept into her voice. "Was it our fault, Ma? One time Kurt said if we all acted better maybe Daddy would stay home with us. But even when we were good he didn't stay home. We had to be quiet or he'd get mad at us. And he got mad at you, too." She stopped then asked, "Ma, if we'd all been better, would he have stayed home and not died?"

"Oh, Sara, no! His dying wasn't your fault or anyone's fault, not even mine. I don't want you to ever think that again."

Sara was quiet as she thought that over, then said, "Callie and I know something that we haven't even told Kurt. Wanna know it?"

Warily Meg said, "Well . . . yes."

"Remember when our goldfish died and we picked him out of the water and put him in a box? Callie heard Aunt Tolly and Uncle Charlie talking about Daddy in the river. Is that how Daddy was? Did they have to pick him up and put—"

"Sara! No!" Meg sat there, shaken at the totally dispassionate way Sara had asked such a horrid question. She had to fight her emotions just to keep from getting up and walking away. She snapped, "You shouldn't listen to other people's conversations."

Sara's eyes started to fill with tears. "But nobody would tell us about Daddy or about you, Ma. What made you sick after Daddy was dead?"

"I guess I was feeling sorry for myself, and—and I was angry at him." Hearing her own lack of concern, she softened her voice and added, "I was so sad about what had happened."

Sara's eyes got big and she started to cry. "But why did we have to go to Doris and Marc's all the time? Callie and I and Kurt thought you didn't want to see us any more. And we thought you were going to die, too." She started to wail.

"Oh, Sara!" Meg pulled her into her arms and rocked her back and forth. She kissed the top of her dusty head and felt Sara's hands gripping her as she sobbed.

Meg thought: I failed them. When I couldn't come up with the words they needed to hear, I was failing them. While I was lost in a world of pills and self-pity, my children were shuffled back and forth without any explanation. She was almost overcome with rage at herself. She had a picture of her children staring into an abyss of fear that she could have helped them through, if she had only taken the time to imagine their despair. She had neglected the three people she loved the most. And she had thought she was sparing them!

While she rocked and sang to her precious middle child, she realized that their conversation had helped her. At least Sara's condemnation of Ed hadn't extended to her. While she felt sorry for Ed, she was glad for her own motherhood. A fierce swell of pride filled her. She had always cared for her children, loving them every minute. She had earned those tears now spilling onto her arm. These kids no longer had to be shared with a man who used them as mere ornaments and then, without a word or a backward look, casually walked away.

She was happy Sara had reminded her of the very legitimate benchmarks of a child's judgment. By not allowing a child to play on the grass, by not taking the time to read to them or examine their drawings that illustrated their world, by not understanding the difficulty of breathing with a runny nose, by not being an understanding father, Ed had earned the enmity of his children; and they would have adored him, if only he had tried.

She crooned into her daughter's hair, "You mustn't worry about me dying. Someday, well…you know everyone dies sometime. But I'm not going to die for a long, long time. I'm so sorry I didn't know how worried you were. Your Aunt Tolly thought I needed the rest. And I guess I did; I wasn't myself. But while I was in bed I didn't know how you all felt. Everything's fine now, isn't it?" She put her hand under Sara's chin, smiled down at her, and joked, "Ya got that, kid?" She watched Sara intently until the anxiety was gone from her face and only an occasional hiccup of a sob came out. She repeated, "Ya got that kid?"

Sara finally smiled and gulped and said, "Yeah, Ma, I got that. But you gotta promise me you won't die. You gotta say it. You gotta cross your heart and say, 'I-cross-my-heart-and-hope-to-die-I won't.'"

Restraining her laughter, Meg pulled her mouth into a serious line and made a big "X" on her shirt over her heart, and said, "Okay, I-cross-my-heart," leaving off the last part. Then she stood up and dusted off her bottom. "Come on now, partner. Let's have another drink, and then we better get going. We're on a mission!" She felt relieved to see Sara smiling again as she sorted through her little pack.

· · ·

They hadn't gone fifty yards when they heard the grind of a truck motor approaching. But it was a while before they saw the green and grey pickup truck that Meg immediately identified as belonging to the Forest Service. She waved at the driver to stop, and the blond, tanned-faced man inside braked and leaned his elbow on the open window. He looked first at Meg and then at Sara, to whom he gave a big wink, asking, "Are you ladies lost?"

Meg pointed up the mountain. "I don't think we are, but we've had a bit of trouble up there with our car. My daughter and I are walking down to get help."

His face became serious and he asked, "Is this an emergency?"

"Well, no, not exactly, but, yes, sort of. You see, I drove my family up there yesterday and we cooked our dinner out and were ready to start for home, but the car wouldn't start. I had to break into a house up there, where we spent the night. Now we're walking down to get a mechanic. The rest of the family is still up there waiting—"

"At the Turner place? That's the only house up there. You say you broke in?" he asked.

Nodding her head, she said, "I'm afraid so. I broke out a back window with a rock." She thought for a moment, then said, "The Turner place. I've heard that name before, but I couldn't say where. I don't know any Turners. But, even if I did, I didn't think I had another choice. My other daughter is young, and it was cold, and we'd only brought sweaters. We built a fire in the fireplace to keep warm. I certainly intend to tell the owners and pay for all the costs for fixing the window and any damage we might have caused—and we'll replace the wood we used."

He put back his head and laughed. "You forgot to breathe! Come on, get in." He leaned over to the opposite door to open it and said, "This sounds like an emergency to me and, as long as it is one, I'll take you to wherever you need to go. But first I'll radio in to get clearance to transport you in this government car. You know how that is."

Meg nodded and quickly gave Sara a boost up the big step into the cab, where the man grabbed Sara's hand, saying, "In you go, Punkin." When he'd helped Meg in, too, he unhooked the microphone hanging from the dashboard and spoke into it. Meg and Sara heard the crackle of the men's voices talking back and forth.

Sara, having watched all this intently, looked up at her mother and whispered, "Won't Callie just kill me when I tell her?" She put her hand over her mouth and giggled into it.

The man said, "I got permission, but that's because I didn't tell them how pretty my two passengers are. Now, let's talk about this. Is your family all right up there? I mean, should we get them first and all go to town, or shall we go to town and get the mechanic and then go get them? I gather your car isn't wrecked."

"No, not wrecked." Meg pondered her choices for a moment. "Well, given a choice, I'd feel a lot better if we could get everyone from the house first. It might take a while to find a mechanic with a tow truck in town. Could we all fit in this truck? There's my sister and my son and other daughter, but none of them are giants. Could we all squish in here?"

"We'll make them fit. This is a big truck." He extended his hand, "By the way, my name is Brodie, Ellis Brodie."

Meg took his hand and said, "This is Sara and I'm Meg Halverson." She caught his look when she said her name.

Sara waited for her turn, then shook his hand, too. Looking up at him, and speaking in a soft voice, she said, "You can call me 'Punkin' if you want."

He smiled and said, "Punkin it is." Then he shifted the truck into a lower gear and they were again going back up the mountain. He looked over at Meg and asked, "You said Halverson? Any relation to— "

"Yes, if you mean— "

"It's a familiar name. I'm sorry about— "

"Yes, yes, thank you…but now…this is a nice vehicle. I don't think I was ever in anything like this. Well, I come from a farm, but that was a long time ago. Trucks keep getting bigger."

When they passed the spring, both Meg and Sara craned their necks looking at it—just in case the lynx was there, but they said nothing.

Meg turned to the man and said, "About the Turner place? Would you by any chance know how to get in touch with them? Not only do I have to give them my grand confession, but they need to get someone up there fast, to fix that window before the whole forest walks in. That's really been bothering me. When I threw that rock and broke the window, I knew I was being pretty blasé in making a choice between that and my family's well-being."

He looked over at her and nodded, "I can certainly understand that. But it's just Mrs. Turner now. Her husband, Al—Albert—died very suddenly this past winter. They built the place about fifteen years ago and have lived there rather sporadically. I hear Mrs. Turner is in Clark Fork now; she moved out right after he died. I only know her as "Mrs. Turner"—that's what Al called her—but maybe Albert is still listed in the phone directory. I've been to their place a number of times. It's a mighty nice piece of land up there and unique, with its thousand or so acres surrounded by federal lands on all sides. Al Turner really liked it and had about a million plans for it. He was always talking of fencing it and moving cattle onto it or turning it into a sheep operation, maybe doing some logging on the side. Mrs. Turner pretty much hated it."

All the while he talked, Sara watched him intently. When he finished she said, "I bet their kids were sorry to leave it. Ma didn't let us go up the stairs or open any of the doors, but we had fun running around in their big yard. We found two springs—no, three, counting the picnic place—and there's an old house that fell down. I found some broken dish pieces but I put them back where we found them. We had so much fun."

He laughed. "Well, Punkin, that puts you in a pretty special category. The Turners never had any kids or grandchildren; so, as far as I know, no one at all has ever had any fun playing up there except you." To Meg he said, "Without any kids, I never could figure out why they built that big house. It seemed like Al just had a building bug pushing at him and he never found a logical place to stop. I swear to god he mentioned putting on another floor. Maybe he thought he could see over the next mountain from there." While he laughed he pounded the steering wheel with his free hand. "By the way, where's your car?"

"It's not on this road. It's on another road near the house. I know where to walk to get to it."

He looked at her with a teasing smile. "Ahh, so you came up by way of the I-Want-To-Live-Dangerously road."

Meg smiled at his good-natured ribbing, and said, "I admit it's not the best road I've ever driven on, but you can't beat the scenery. We live in town and I don't know these mountain roads at all."

He leaned back comfortably, "There are only two roads into this country here. Remember where the road forks down in the canyon? That's both of them. The fork straight ahead, that looks passable, is the one we're on, and the other fork—that obstacle course—is the one you took."

"Is the one my car's on a logging road?"

"On that poor road? No way. For a century or more there's been no logging up there. Haven't you noticed?"

"Actually, I have." She laughed down at Sara. "We're learning something today, aren't we?"

He said, "Tell you what, I'd like to look at your car myself. Maybe it's something I can fix. There's a shortcut close by that joins that other road. I'm sure this truck of mine can get to it, but you'll have to hang on. It'll be a little rough and I might have to make up the road as I go."

Meg laughed, "My Papa used to say that. Believe me I've had that kind of experience before. Tell me you have a big jack to get us out of a bad spot. My Papa always did!"

Sara looked at him and said, "Is this going to be an adventure, too?"

Ellis gave her a big wink. "Punkin, it sounds to me like you thrive on them. You must like it up here."

Sara's expression turned serious when she looked up at him and said, "My brother Kurt and my little sister Callie and I would like to live here, but Ma said she has to find a new daddy for us, first. Have you got any kids?"

Before he answered he looked at Meg's red face and saw her shaking her head helplessly behind Sara. "Nope, no kids, Punkin. Now you hold on." He shifted into a lower gear and turned off the road, and soon they were bumping their way around trees and underbrush. He smiled at Meg and said, "I'm not sure this is legal, so don't report me."

Sara's eyes grew fearful when the truck tipped slightly, righted, then tipped the other way. She held onto the material of Meg's jeans with one hand and steadied herself against his leg with the other. But it didn't take long to intersect the other road and, in no time, they saw the car.

· · ·

Sara's nose just cleared the rim of the motor as she, too, peered under the hood. Ellis jiggled wires and pulled belts and unscrewed this and that while Meg explained what happened and admitted having a total lack of knowledge of cars. Finally, he said, "Okay, if you could give that key a little spin when I say to."

On the first try nothing happened. After making another adjustment, he was going to call out to try starting it again, but Sara asked, "Can I tell Ma?" When he nodded, she yelled out, "Ma, give that key a little spin!" All three of them were laughing when the car started up with a flourish.

Ellis picked up Sara and deposited her in the truck, "Okay, Punkin, now let's go get your family and bring them here, and then I'll follow you down to town to make sure everything keeps on working until you get there."

It was Kurt who first heard the motor and alerted everyone, and they were waiting as the truck drove into sight. After Ellis Brodie was introduced, Tolly, beaming, said, "My lands, I think I can believe in knights in shining armor all over again."

15

DREAMS

There was no Albert Turner listed in the phone book and, of the twenty-four Turners listed, none had a canyon route address. Faced with that daunting number, Meg decided she'd have to ask each one, "By any chance are you the Turner who lived up on the mountain east of town?" Settling herself into one corner of the sofa and starting at the very first listing—an Alice Turner—she was hardly prepared for the answer, "Yes."

"Yes? You're Mrs. Albert Turner?"

"Alice. Alice Turner. Albert Turner died."

"Yes, I heard. I'm sorry."

"And he did it just when we were about to move to Arizona."

"He did it? You mean, he—"

"He up and died, and I'd done all that work convincing him it was the right place to go."

"I'm sorry. But, Mrs. Turner, there's someth—"

"I told him I was done putting up with it, and he'd finally agreed. But a week later he up and died. You can imagine who had to do all the packing. Oh, I had help, but it couldn't have been a worse time, with the snow and all. I was looking forward to Sun City, you know, and I—"

Throwing politeness to the wind, Meg plunged in. "Mrs. Turner, my name is Mrs. Hal—ah, that is, Meg, and I have to explain what's happened." She hadn't thought out what she'd say about their night in the house, but once she began describing the fix they had been in, using words that were guaranteed to have more impact than those she would normally use—"three little children and an older lady marooned and shivering in the cold and the dark"—the fact that she'd thrown a rock through the window and broken into the house sounded far more legitimate than it actually might be. She ended her account with her sincerest expressions of apology and gratitude, and assured Mrs. Turner that she would pay whatever it cost to replace the window and clean up the glass, and that she'd send her a check as soon as she knew what it cost.

During her emotional story, she heard occasional bursts of exasperated breathing and an irritating tapping sound coming from the other end of the phone; but she'd soldiered on. When she finished there was a long silence; in fact, it was so long she reasoned she was in real trouble and should consider contacting a lawyer. She was hardly prepared for Mrs. Turner's peevish reply, "I hate that place!"

"You what?"

"I hate it. You saw it! I don't want to go up there. I'd appreciate it if you'd do the calling and make the arrangements with the window man. You can pick up the key here and go with him and see to it that the window gets fixed."

Meg stammered, "Yes. Yes, of course I will. And I'll do it right away. Please tell me where you live so I can pick up the k—"

Mrs. Turner's strange rasping voice interrupted her, "I always hated it!"

"But, it's—"

"From day one. But Albert, he insisted. That place...."

While her voice droned on, Meg took the phone from her ear and looked at it with distaste before propping it up to her ear again. The direction the conversation had taken was surprising, to say the least. Clearly, the woman was in need of an audience—any audience—and she'd chosen Meg to be the listener. With a sigh, Meg leaned back and examined her nails.

"...like now, I live in town where it doesn't take an expedition to buy a loaf of bread! I'm near Sadie, of course. We're going to Vegas. It didn't take more than a wink to forget that place. And now I'm getting rid of it."

Meg sat up straight, "You mean you're selling it, Mrs. Turner?"

"You heard right. Do you know anyone who might want it?"

"I don't, but—"

"Well, like I told the realty people, anyone can see how impractical it is. *Impractical!* With that house, it's just one pain after another. I told Albert, when he was building it—and he was always building it—I'd tell him, 'Why would anyone sensible ever want to live up here? When you get through playing around with this place, how'll you ever get rid of it?' And now, just like what you was telling me about with the window, it's a pain chasing off just to check it out."

Meg said, "But the house is so interesting, and the land, why, it's beautiful land to hike around on and see and—"

"You'd never catch me walkin' around on it. Things watch you there. Albert, he said my imagination was doing double duty. I'd watch him through the window, walkin' around, walkin' around, and always planning something else, like a garden. I told him that a garden would be like flypaper, drawing in those things, and all that work would be going down their gullets. I told him, I'm not one to put my precious time into something with no guarantees. He came around and gave up thinking about a garden."

"But, Mrs. Turner—"

"Yes, he *finally* took my advice on that. But do you think that stopped him? Not for a minute! He was always planning things. When he'd come in to eat he'd talk on and on about what the land wanted. Yes, you heard me, *what the land wanted*! To hear him talk, you'd think the land had a mouth and a brain. What the land wanted! I told him those rocks and piles of dirt were telling him to get rid of it! That's what! And get this: he said, 'you have to listen to the land's natural rhythms and study where the light hits the land first thing in the spring.' As if anyone with eyes and ears couldn't tell right off where it lands. A few years back he built a cabin up there beyond the house—you might have seen it—"

"Yes, I did, and it's beaut—"

"Albert, he called it his 'hide-e-hole.' Sometimes, right in the middle of lunch, why, he'd pick up his sandwich and say, 'If anyone wants to know, tell em I'm in my hide-e-hole.' I'd say, 'Albert, this is craziness!' I told him he could stop going to his hide-e-hole and listen to me for a change. But then, if he stayed, he'd just stand there by the window looking down into that big empty clearing, or looking off toward town, dreaming his dreams and not paying the least attention to me. I used to—"

"Mrs.Turner, about the key? If you could just give me your address, I really must go—"

Mrs.Turner went on."I used to tell him he was a man practiced in not paying the least attention to his wife. Let me tell you—God rest his soul—his dreams were about as practical as the house. I told him he had delusions of grandeur. Especially when I saw what he was planning on building next. But I put a stop to that.The house was big enough. Place gave me the crawling creeps.The crawling creeps! Why, Mrs.—what did you say your name was?"

"Meg Hal—"

"You know, he never could see how the sun coming into the windows used to practically blind me, and made me want to hide from it, and all the time giving me headaches. And when I had one of them, I could almost draw a line from my skull down behind my right ear and into my shoulder blade.When I'd get that pain, I used to come down in town here and visit Sadie, and we'd sit around and drink tea and knit and have a cozy time of it—"

"Mrs.Turner, I'm so sorry about your headaches, but I really have to go—"

"I'd tell Sadie that I had to practically learn how to speak all over again after a month of being up there.The walls of that place would start closing in on me and I'd start to get my heart problems. It would start beating fast-like and I couldn't breathe. No particular pain, just a gallop-a-trot, gallop-a-trot. Scared me half to death. My doctor said it wasn't anything to worry about, just a little cabin fever. I told him, 'You call that cabin fever? Ha! You come up and see the size of the cabin I live in!' I told him my symptoms should be called,'castle-in-the-sky fever, pie-in-the-sky fever.' That's what it was. Place just gave me the crawlin' creeps. All those rooms. Of course I shut off those upper rooms. Al liked to brag about that fancy furnace of his, but no reason to heat those upper rooms.

"I had fifteen years of that place, off and on, when I wasn't off visiting my brother and his family in Boise. 'Course I couldn't stay long with them, their being so busy and all, or their being called away suddenly. Then I'd come into town here with Sadie.

"It was last fall when I finally wrung it out of him and he agreed to spend the winter in Sun City, Arizona, where we could be with people. I told him it would be his little retirement place. I told him that it even came with people who could actually *talk*. Praise the Lord! I told him, if he couldn't go with me to Sun City, I'd just go by myself or move into town here permanent. Then he up and died.

"Well, anyway, that's what happens to my best-laid plans. A week or so ago I decided it was long past time to sell that place. I signed it up with those Rainbow Realty people. Anyway. Now if you know anybody who wants it, Mrs.—what did you say your name was? Meg Hal?"

Meg decided to let it go at that: "Yes, Meg Hal." While she wrote down the address, she thought sadly, Yes, God, please rest Albert Turner's soul. No one else ever had.

She was rubbing her ear when she saw Kurt standing in the doorway. He asked, "Who was that? You just kept shaking your head."

"I was talking—no, I was listening—to the woman who owns that house on the mountain." She grinned. "She is some strange kind of woman. Now I've got to meet her and pick up the key. She wants me to go up and help get her darned window fixed. I have no problem with that, but, please do me a favor and come along and give me an excuse to *not* stay one second longer than I need to."

"Yeah, sure. I'd like to go."

Meg called down the hall, "Tolly, Kurt and I are going to run an errand. And you two Littles, stay here with Tolly." She heard a muffled "Okay, Ma." from the girls' room.

While she was backing the car out of the garage, she said, "I was wondering if this car would even start up again, after its workout yesterday."

"It sounds okay."

"Hummmm, I remember thinking that yesterday, too." They both laughed.

Kurt said,"We should get a truck like the man had."

"Ah, Mr. Ellis Brodie. He really did us a favor, didn't he?"

"That was neat. He sure likes driving his truck. We should get a truck like that."

"A new car maybe, but not a truck, Kurt."

"But we'd have the same problem with a car, Ma, if we ever wanted to go up there again."

Meg laughed. "I'd veto a truck, dear, but sometime, maybe, we could look into something like a Jeep."

"Yeah, Ma. That would be neat. A Jeep is great on mountain roads."

Meg looked over at him, saying, "Hummm. Mountain roads, eh?" She reached over and gave him a little poke. "I don't know whose idea it was, but on the walk down yesterday, Sara told me that you three kids had it all decided that since the house is empty we should live up there. I told her, just because it was empty didn't mean anything. And even if it were...you know...for sale, it would be out of the question. A woman with three little kids living in a place like that?" Seeing his reaction, she said, "I mean two little girls and one big, almost twelve-year-old boy. If you've got any ideas about that, forget them."

They traveled on in silence. Then Meg made a quick turn and pulled into the drive-up lane of a root beer stand. "Any one besides me interested in a float?"

"Yeah. Neat. You can make that a large one for me."

Meg laughed. "I could have almost guessed that, dear." She placed their order while Kurt dug in her purse for her wallet.

When they got their drinks, she parked and turned off the car. After a while she said, "I was so proud of you yesterday. I liked your ideas, and letting Sara carry your knife was really a nice thing to do. All the way down the mountain she about wore out her pocket making sure it was still there. I knew you wanted to go with me, Kurt, but it was a bigger help that you did what I asked and did it so nicely. We were quite a team." She reached over and patted his shoulder. "Where'd you learn how to be so nice? You're a terrible tease, but awfully good to your two little imps of sisters...and to me. Where'd you learn that?"

Kurt's cheeks flamed red and he looked awkwardly into his root beer container. After an enormous gulp, he shrugged and said, "I dunno."

"Well, I think you're a neat guy. We've gone through some bad times this last month. I have to think we have better days ahead us. Don't you?"

Kurt shrugged, "Geez, I hope so. But I hate those people who don't like us."

"What about your friend Skip?"

"Geez, I don't know. I thought we were buddies. He was kind of okay about things the last part of school, but he was going to visit his grandparents for two weeks. He should be home by now, but he didn't call me back." He didn't look up while he said that.

Meg shook her head sadly, "Oh, honey." She thought for a moment. "I know it's frustrating for you. But people will eventually forget this. Your father was an important man. After he disappeared there were things said in the newspapers and speculation over his death. And even though he was found, there was no explanation for why he left like he did. Some people have nothing better to do than say nasty things. Even so, Kurt, I'd like it if you wouldn't use the word 'hate' any more when you talk about people. My Papa—your grandpa—never used that word for any reason. He said that word only made a problem worse. He made a point of being respectful toward all creatures, and that included people. If one of the horses acted up, all he did to calm it down was put his hand on it and tell it a story. If he told it the kind of stories he told me, I bet that horse just giggled. I think the only things Papa got really mad at were windstorms. He was pretty good at chewing out one of those, especially when it blew down his crops. So, if you could save your biggest, baddest words for a windstorm, I think he'd be happy." She put her hand on him. "We can't do anything about other people's opinions, dear. All we can do is live our lives as well as we can, and not hurt other people. We know how that feels, don't we?"

"Yeah, we do."

Meg smiled at him, then gathered her courage and said, "And speaking of that, Sara told me how bad you three felt when Daddy died and I was sick, and you kids were sent to stay at Marc and Doris's house. Sara said you all thought I didn't want to see you anymore.

Nothing could be further from the truth, dear. I love you guys with every fiber of my being. And my love for you won't change or ever stop. After they found your father, I was so sad that I got sick, and Aunt Tolly and Doris and Marc were just trying to protect us. I was given medicine that made me relax and not be so sad, and it made me sleep. I knew you were safe, because Tolly was here, but I—I kind of lost track of you. It's a whole blank area in my mind."

She went on, "I feel so badly about that, Kurt. It was hard for Sara to tell me how you all felt, and awfully hard for me to hear it. A mother doesn't like to hear that she's neglected her kids, especially when she had no idea she was doing it. I want you to know how sorry I am. I just assumed that you three knew what I was feeling."

Kurt frowned as he looked at her. "Yeah, I guess. Aunt Tolly didn't want us to go in and see you, because...geez, I don't know. And why does she always call us 'The babies'? Geez, I can't stand that! And why didn't anyone tell us anything? It was like that with Dad, too, like everyone thought we didn't know things because we were little kids."

Meg took hold of his hand and looked steadily at him. "Some things are just about impossible to explain. I couldn't even explain them to myself. But I have always thought that you knew what was going on. I don't think of you as a little kid. I think of you as a young, intelligent growing person who is my son. I am very proud of you, and I trust you."

Kurt's eyes held hers for a long time, and he looked relieved and gave her a shy smile.

Meg took her courage in hand and said, "Well, then, I need to ask you something else, Kurt. Your Aunt Tolly thinks we should pull up stakes here and move closer to her and Charlie and the farm. What do you think about that?"

Kurt's reaction was immediate. "No, Ma! Please don't say yes. I like visiting the farm, but I don't want to live there. Geez."

Meg studied his face for a long moment then patted his arm. "I told Tolly I didn't think it would be the right thing. I said we would be happier in this country, but her offer is still there and I wanted to ask you for sure. I'd say we four Halversons have some big decisions to make this summer, about where we're going to live, here or somewhere else. I needed to hear what you felt about what Tolly asked, and you told me, didn't you?"

Kurt nodded his head and smiled back at her. Almost at a signal they both drew air noisily through the straws in their empty cups. Meg looked at him admiringly and said proudly, "Just look at this lovely boy growing up so fast. Will you do me a favor, dear? Will you tell me when you don't understand something? Will you make me explain things better? I promise to try to explain things. Is that a bargain?"

Kurt nodded his head and smiled so hard that his right dimple showed. "If you're done, Ma, I'll put our cups in the trash."

With a bemused look, Meg watched him lean out the window and, with his best one-handed basketball shot, toss them toward the can. He missed, but he shrugged and got out of the car and picked them up and tried again, this time successfully.

With a playful shake of her head, and using one hand, Meg backed out of the space expertly. She said, "About that 'babies' label. Technically you're a little kid, but, appetite-wise, you're a giant. I guess we can say that, on balance, you are somewhere in the middle. Right?"

"You mean I'm not one of Tolly's babies?"

"Nope, I've just graduated you. Now, let's see if we can find this Alice Turner's place; and remember, we have a million appointments and can only stay a second."

· · ·

A half-hour later they were driving home. Meeting Alice Turner was just as difficult as speaking with her. The woman's mouth was drawn into a permanent "no," and her body had a sparse and grudging look—her thin chest seemed to have no space for a heart inside, nor room for the large pendulous breasts fastened to its outside. The whole encounter had disheartened her; she had certainly pictured different people living on that gorgeous mountain.

It was strange to have the key to the mountain house in her hand, and she fingered the funny little wooden bear hanging from its ring before handing it to Kurt for safekeeping. Dreams, she thought, dreams.

What were the dreams of that faceless Albert Turner at the bitter end of his frustrated life? And that huge puzzle of a house sitting amid its piles of dirt? No wonder it had confused her. Was there anything significant about the key in her possession and her knowledge that the mountain place was for sale? At the moment it appeared to her like someone was saying, "The ball's in your court." No, she thought, that's not the phrase. What was that phrase that kept drifting into her mind? Oh, yes, "It's your turn now, Meg." The moment she remembered it she felt the dregs of the past evolve into something tantalizing. After she drove the car into the garage and brought the door down, with its usual bang, she put her arm around her son and they walked together into the house.

When Kurt had gone back to his room, Tolly came up to Meg and whispered, "There's an important looking letter for you on the dining room table. I had to sign for it, swearing I was your sister. It's from an insurance company." The two women stood together as Meg opened it with shaking fingers, then moved the letter so that Tolly could read it too. When Tolly saw the check she dropped into the nearest chair as though someone had hit her behind her knees. She said, "I've never seen that many zeros on one check. You better get that into the bank right now. Don't stop for anything. You never can tell, sometimes these things can be taken back."

"Oh, I doubt it's going to be taken back, sis." Still studying the letter, she had pulled out a chair and was sitting on the edge of the seat. She looked numb and a little bit sad. "Yes, of course, I'll deposit it in a few minutes. But first I have to get used to it. I knew Ed had insurance, but it says here that he had some kind of double indemnity, in case of accidental death. It *is* a lot of money, Tolly, but I have a lot of mixed feelings about it. I don't want to feel happy about it, as though this is some kind of final payment for Ed's not being here anymore. On the other hand, I'm thinking of it as a wonderful gift. And having it arrive at this particular time, it's really fantastic." Her face had brightened along with her words.

Tolly got up from her chair and spoke sternly, "Well, you have a lot of thinkin' to do, Meggie, and lots of time to do it. It's best that you get that into the bank as fast as you can and let it start to draw interest.

With the future and all, you don't want to think about spendin' it."

Meg said,"You and I have never talked about financial things,Tolly, but the kids and I are really well taken care of.We have the money from Ed's investments, his family's money, and our savings.And this house is all paid for.I put my part of my inheritance from Ma and Papa into small trusts for the kids that have drawn interest over the years, and I'll add more. If I manage things carefully we won't have to worry.And now there's this. Good Lord!" She stopped talking and looked thoughtful. "Sis, let's invite Marc and Doris over for dinner tonight. I really need to talk to them. Could you see what we have for a nice dinner while I call them? It doesn't need to be fancy, just a family dinner."

Tolly was already on her way to the kitchen when Meg heard Doris's cool voice over the phone,"Meg, you must have read my mind. How are you?"

"I'm up and at 'em again and feeling great. Look, I know this is short notice, but are you and Marc free this evening? Could you come over for dinner? Say, yes. I need to talk to you two about something."

Doris laughed and said,"Of course, yes. I have some apples and can make a pie."

"No, no, but thank you.Tolly loves any excuse to make something spectacular for dessert. Just bring yourselves. Dinner at 7:00 will give us a nice cocktail hour. Okay?"

Doris said,"Okay! Is this a fancy occasion?"

Meg laughed. "Yeah, your fanciest, most comfortable jeans. Oh, Doris, come sooner. Come just as early as you can. We have so much to talk about." She was about to hang up, then added, "Doris, do you believe in dreams?"

"Dreams? In what sense?"

"The kind of dreams that are wishes. People have so many kinds of dreams. Some never come true, and others seem half formed for the longest time. But after a while, the most impractical ones that your heart makes can come true, too. I was thinking that Ed must have had dreams...although he never told me about them.And I have dreams, too." She stopped, even though she knew Doris was waiting for her to say something more."Oh, Doris, who knows what I mean.We'll talk tonight."

16

DINNER AT SEVEN

The Websters did arrive early, and the greeting they received was, as usual, effusive and warm. While they were still in the foyer, Marc inspected them through the bottom half of his eyeglasses and hummed a little tune as he did so. With a special look over to Meg, he said, "You look just as good as my wife said you *sounded*. And you've all put a little meat on your bones. I think we have Tolly to thank for that. Eh?" As they seated themselves in the family room, he added, "Yes, indeed, you look in fine shape. I believe this occasion calls for a toast."

Meg agreed heartily and put him in charge of drinks. He appointed Kurt to assist him, saying, "If you can get something for the Littles and yourself, I'll find something a bit stronger for the elder segment of this group." Kurt ducked jauntily into the kitchen, grateful to be included.

Once everyone was seated and had glasses in hand, Marc walked to the fireplace and, striking the appropriate pose, said, "I'd like to propose a toast." Everyone nodded expectantly and he looked slowly and kindly around the group. "The people in this room—Meg, Kurt, Sara, Callie, Tolly—have endured some difficult days of late. I'll include Doris and myself in that, for what affects you most assuredly affects us as well." He paused and, raising his glass, said, "There is a lot of strength in this room and a lot of love. I make this toast to strength and love."

Sighing and smiling, they all took a sip of their drinks.

Meg went over to stand by Mark and said, "That was beautiful, Marc. Thank you," and kissed his cheek. "Now it's my turn to toast you." She cleared her throat. "Some people go through their entire lives without knowing true friendship. On behalf of my children and myself, I want to thank you, Tolly Jefferson, and you, Marc and Doris Webster, for all you have given us. We're doing okay now because of you three. Thank you!" Her voice caught for a moment, then she raised her glass. "Let us drink a toast to true friends." And everyone drank to that.

Callie said, "Is there more toast or can I finish this, now?" And everyone laughed and the glasses were drained and the room grew noisy again.

Marc said to no one in particular, "It's been a while since we've seen you, so what have you all been up to?"

In answer, all three kids spoke at once, then laughed, then became silent to let someone else do the talking, and then all three talked at once again.

Marc held up his hand and said, "Is there a spokesman for this group? How about you, Kurt? It sounds like you've all done something special, but I can't hear what."

Looking pleased, Kurt said, "The day before yesterday we went on a picnic way up in the mountains, you know, the ones up from the canyon road. When we were ready to go home, Ma and I couldn't start the car, so we had to stay there all night. There's a neat house up there and Ma and I led everyone to it in the dark, and Ma broke the window and boosted me in so I could unlock the door and let everyone in. We slept there—"

Callie interrupted, "Let me tell the part about how we slept in front of the fire like dogs and cats. Ma built a fire in the fireplace. It's bigger than ours and—"

Doris said, "You've got to be kidding! An abandoned house, up there?" She looked at Meg for verification.

Meg nodded her head and said, "Yes, it's true."

Sara said, "And it was dark and spooky, but Kurt had our gas lantern and, the next day, when Ma and I walked down the road to get help, we saw...we saw a..." Biting her lower lip, she stopped and looked at Tolly.

Callie piped up, "They saw a lynx! A cantata lynx with fierce yellow eyes and huge feet and he was going to attack them. He growled at them until they ran away!"

Meg groaned and looked at Callie reprovingly. "Now, Callie, it didn't growl. Sara, did you tell Callie it growled? It just disappeared into the brush. And, Callie, that's '*Canada* lynx.'"

Sara spoke, "And then a man of the forest picked us up in his truck and we went through the trees instead of on the road and he fixed our car and he had a radio that talked back to him. You tell them his name, Ma."

"Ellis Brodie, dear. And he was very nice and very helpful, wasn't he? He packed us in—"

Sara interrupted, "I get to tell the part about him always calling me Punkin!" She turned to Doris and said, "He always called me Punkin. He's really, really nice and he's got curly, red hair on his arms, but his hair, you know, on his head, is the same color as mine. Blonde."

Doris's eyes widened as she took this in. "Punkin. That's nice." She looked past Sara at Meg and raised her eyebrows. "Ellis Brodie, eh? That's a nice name."

Meg put her arm around Sara and smiled knowingly at Doris. "Yes, Doris, the *young* Ellis Brodie. Like Sara said, he really was quite the *young*, hasn't-yet-seen-thirty, strong, outdoorsman type." She then mouthed the words, "gorgeous" to Doris and, seeing that Doris had gotten her message, she continued, "I forget now what he said was wrong with our car, but he fixed it and it's running fine. He insisted on packing Kurt and Tolly into the front seat of his truck and, with Sara and Callie with me in my car, he followed us all the way back to the house. He was really very kind, going out of his way to be helpful." Looking at Doris and Marc she added, "For just an old run-of-the-mill picnic it turned into quite an adventure, and we had the most wonderful time up there, even though it sounds kind of, well—"

Tolly broke in, "It sounds kind of dicey, that's what you mean, isn't it, Meggie?" She turned to Marc and Doris, saying, "Now it's my turn. Let me tell you about the house, that terrible house—"

Her words were immediately drowned out by a chorus of kids' voices, "It's not terrible!"

Meg shushed them and looked apologetically at her sister and was going to say something, when Sara pursed her mouth and spoke directly to her aunt, "It's a wonderful house, Aunt Tolly. It has a big yard and some really pretty springs where we can get drinks."

With a distressed look, Meg said, "Now, Sara, Aunt Tolly didn't mean anything by that. She has a right to her own opinion. Anyway, we have to admit that the house is pretty unique."

Tolly sniffed and said, "Unique? I call it weird? It's the weirdest house I've ever seen. And it's clingin' to a cliff. Up there, the land's so tippy you can hardly find a flat place to put your feet without fallin' down. And the road going up to the place is unsettlin', to say the least." She looked at Meg accusingly. "And what's all this about a wildcat lynx? You never told me about that." Turning to Marc and Doris, she said, "It's a wild place. I've heard a coyote or two in my life, but there must have been twenty of 'em howlin' around us during our picnic. And they were really close by. You should have heard them. And there we were, the car wouldn't start, and it was pitch dark and we had no place to sleep but that big creepy house that was somewhere off in the night. We're lucky we survived, with just sweaters, two thin blankets, and a tablecloth to keep us warm. And these tykes just babies."

Almost in unison, all three kids burst out, "We're not babies!"

Meg, feeling her party teetering dangerously on the edge of a free-for-all, clapped her hands sharply together once and gave them the big look, "Kids, be respectful!"

Tolly, after looking like she was going to say something back, just frowned and put her hands over her ears. Then she got up, said, "Our dinner—" and headed for the kitchen.

Meg watched her go and said, with her best hostess smile, "I don't know about you, but I'm starving. Doris, let's go and see what Tolly has been cooking for us all afternoon. It smells so delicious." The two of them followed in the wake of the small square-shouldered, stiff-backed Tolly.

Once the women left the room Marc began asking more questions of the three kids. They were enthusiastically filling him in when Meg stuck her head back into the room and said, "Kurt, dear, please put on some music, something soothing, maybe a little Ralph Vaughan Williams?"

. . .

Dinner was delicious, if a bit tense. The music helped, and so did the wine. Marc, having been thrust into the role as head of the Halverson's table, found that there wasn't much conversational value in talking about the weather. Neither did he want to risk delving further into what the children had been doing this summer. He plunged, instead, into the possible ramifications of an oil spill and his opinions on the German economy. However, as much as he tried, it was pretty evident that there was a division of thought between the four Halversons and Tolly Jefferson, and it couldn't be mended with food or lofty opinions.

Dinner was eaten a little faster than usual, with Meg giving the children quick warning looks. They were answered by barely contained intransigence—if not a threat of mutiny—on their faces. Tolly's chocolate cake was barely touched by the adults and everyone got up and helped clear the table. Then Meg directed them all to the family room—even the children—and set a tray of coffee and a decanter of brandy on the coffee table in front of the sofa.

As she finished pouring coffee and sat down, she said to the children, "You can go outside in a minute, but for now, sit down and get comfortable. There's something I want to say." Her eyes went over to Tolly and she added, a bit worryingly, "I want you to hear this, too, Tolly dear, and after our conversation before dinner, I'm afraid you're not going to like it. Forgive me, but this is something I can't put off talking about until some time in the future."

With that caveat, she sat forward in her chair, took a swallow of coffee and withdrew from her pocket the key ring hung with a single brass key and a little wooden bear. She held it up in the air and jingled it provocatively, then said, "This key belongs to that house on the mountain, and today I found out it's for sale. I guess what I'm saying is I'm thinking of buying it."

There was a collective gasp from the group, but of the various reactions none was louder than Tolly's. She said not a word, but got up and walked out of the room, thump-thump-thumping down the hall, and closing the guest room door firmly behind her.

In the silence that followed Meg looked around and, with a dispirited shrug of her shoulders, said, "Any more comments?"

Callie asked in a whisper, "Can we laugh?"

Meg gave her a brief smile and gestured to keep it low, and all three children got up and started dancing silently around for a brief moment, then sat back down on the couch and looked anxiously over at their mother.

Kurt grinned at her. "Sounds like we'll be getting a Jeep."

Sara said with a big smile, "Oh, Ma, you said you didn't think we could do that."

"I changed my mind, dear. Today I just plain changed my mind. But I'm only thinking about doing it. It's not for sure yet. I'm telling you this because I have to know how you kids feel about it before I decide anything. It would be a huge step for us to take. There are more than a thousand acres of land in that piece of property. There's so much I need to find out about schools and who plows the roads up there in winter and all that. I want you three to think about it. Whatever we do, it'll be all four of us in on it, not just me. Your money will go into it as well as mine. Remember, it's just a *maybe*; I have no idea how much it will cost or if we can afford it. For now, could you kids go outside and let me talk with Marc and Doris? We can talk more about this later. Okay?"

When they had gone, Meg said, "Well, there you have it. I apologize for setting off the bomb." She lowered her voice. "I thought Tolly would be unhappy, but I didn't know how much. Somehow, I thought this was going to be a joyous occasion."

She stopped and looked at the two of them, noticing for the first time that they hadn't said anything. Marc was polishing his eyeglasses on his handkerchief and Doris was staring into her empty cup; neither face indicated what they might be thinking. Meg spoke anxiously, "Tolly will come back here in a minute, just wait. She never stays mad at me very long." After a few more moments of silence, she added, "This is just her little way. Perhaps she's tired. Will you have a little more coffee?"

Marc shook his head and leaned forward and said, "Actually, I think I need something a bit stronger, if you don't mind. Can I interest either of you in something of the same? I assume those nods give me permission to fix each of us a stiff jolt." He went to the sideboard and splashed unadorned whisky in some glasses and came back, placing one in front of each woman. When he sat down he took his drink all in one gulp. Wiping his mouth, he said: "As your friend, I don't want to butt in or anything— "

Meg interrupted him, "No, Marc, say what you feel. I need your advice."

"Well then, Meg, let me see if I have the whole picture here. I gather you haven't been acquainted with this house for long? Did I hear right that you first saw it just two days ago?"

"I'd been up there once before. But, yes, I guess it's kind of sudden."

"Please understand, my dear, Tolly's description wasn't very comforting. A weird house on a…what did Tolly call it, on a cliff, for God's sake?" He laughed then said, "And was that twenty wildcats howling around you?"

"No, they were just coyotes during our picnic, and probably no more than five or ten at a distance. And there was just one lynx minding his own wildcat business way back in the bushes near a spring. And look, we're not talking about a place in the Bitterroot Wilderness. The house is on a mountainside up from the canyon. I checked the odometer on the way down yesterday; it's only a little more than fourteen miles from the outskirts of town. Granted, even being that close to town it's in remarkably wild country."

Marc said, "Well, I assumed there was some exaggeration going on…nevertheless… If I have this straight, you were stranded up there and, after breaking and entering into this house, you five spent the night sleeping in front of the fire *like dogs and cats*? Then you were rescued by a Forest Ranger? And it is your intention to go back to that again? Do I have that right?" He leaned weakly against the back of the loveseat, trying to keep from laughing.

Doris shot him a warning look and said, "Marc, don't make light of something this serious. My goodness." She reached over and put her hand on Meg's arm. "If we can get this comic to get himself under control for a minute, I'd like to hear why you're considering this." She shot Marc another warning look.

Meg played dejectedly with the key ring. She had been feeling so positive about this idea, and now she just wanted to take back her words and hide. If only Tolly had said something kinder about the house and the land, it wouldn't have sounded so bizarre. It wasn't fair. It was a wonderful place. She said, "Pardon me just a minute. I've got to go get Tolly."

She threw the key ring on the coffee table and walked rapidly down the hall and knocked at the guest room door. When Tolly didn't answer she put her mouth close to the door and said, "Tolly, don't be mad. I need you to tell Marc and Doris something nice about the mountain place. Come on, Tolly, please come out." She knocked softly again, put her cheek against the door, then let herself in.

Tolly's suitcase was open on the floor, her clothes were in it, and Tolly was already in bed. She drew up the covers and said, "I'm stayin' right here. You do what you want about that place. You obviously don't need any advice from me. I'm leavin' on the bus in the mornin'. I just called Charlie and he'll pick me up there in Wyler tomorrow night. You can either drive me to the station or let me call a taxi. You decide. But goin' home now is best. I'm only in the way here."

She continued, "You are just as impulsive as you ever were, Meggie. I thought you'd change as you got older, but I see you haven't. If you won't listen to reason and come back with me to Wyler, if you've made up your mind to take your children, leave all civilization behind, and live in that wild place, well, that's your decision. I can only hope you won't regret this—or forget that I warned you.

"Ma asked me to take care of you, Meggie, and I'm sure she said that because of your impulsiveness. Well, I've tried. God knows I've tried! But just you remember, both Ma and Papa would be shocked at what you're plannin' to do! Now you and your friends go ahead and make your plans. And you don't need to whisper. Quiet or not, I probably won't sleep a wink. Not a wink. Goodnight!"

All through Tolly's speech Meg was silent. When Tolly finally finished, she gave a stubborn toss of her head and said, not too quietly, "I can't believe this, Tolly! But, okay! Fine! Good night!" She shut the door and headed back to the family room, Tolly's unsettling indictment and that terrible word "impulsive" ringing in her ears. Was she impulsive? Was the joy she'd felt up there on the mountain even real?

Regaining her seat in the family room, she said, "Tolly's gone to bed and won't come out, and there's nothing I can do about it. She's not going to support me in this, and she's going home tomorrow morning. She's been holding on to a hope that we would move back to the farm with her. I thought she knew we wouldn't, but I guess I was wrong." Seeing the disbelief still flitting over their faces, she said. "Please, don't look like that. I need some trust and understanding on this."

Leaning back into the cushion, she searched for the right words. "That was an eloquent toast you made, Marc. I especially liked the part where you said we had love and strength in this family. I hope you truly meant what you said because I believe the kids and I do have those qualities. If I didn't think that I'd never even consider moving us up there."

She looked intently at her two dearest friends and continued, "I can't tell you how alive I felt when I was up there. It's like something just let loose in me. With the kind of kids I have, I know it would be a wonderful place for them to live, too. It was strange, but today I received the check from Ed's insurance company, and it's a large one, with almost too many zeros for Tolly to count. It made me think that I might never have another chance to do something big like this. Let me tell you what I'm thinking. That's really why I wanted you over tonight."

She continued, "So much has changed for us. So many of the folks I used to know seem to want to treat Ed's disappearance and death as their chance to be nasty. It's not the whole town, of course; but enough who can make the very word 'Halverson' poison. I have no idea what people are saying, but something's going on. I didn't make any friends leaving like I did that day, and then everything else happened. Even the kids feel it, and they resent it terribly. I've told them that we've done nothing to deserve it and to be patient. But they have just so few years at home, and I want them to grow up proud and not worrying about what others think of them just because they happen to have the name Halverson."

She looked at Doris. "You know, I look back, almost with longing, at that day when I had my little snit and walked home from that meeting. You remember. Ed left the house in the morning and by evening he was gone; in fact, by evening he was probably dead." She shivered. "I remember the carelessness of that day, being so unaware of what was happening. As I walked down the sidewalk, worrying how my actions would fall back on me, thinking that kind of nonsense, I didn't know that my world, as I'd known it, was already gone. There's nothing of that simple world left now. Oh, sure, same people, same town, but it's changed for the kids and me in ways I could never have predicted." Looking at Doris, she added, "And after enduring all those damned meetings!"

Doris nodded.

Meg continued. "Sara and I had an interesting talk when we were walking down the mountain. Of the many things she revealed to me, in her wonderful eight-year-old way, the most curious was her asking me if it was our fault that Ed died. I told her, no. But then, last night in bed, I wondered if maybe it was *my* fault as much as Ed's.

"I've been trying to keep the damned peace in this household all these years, and now I think I was wrong to do that. I've always cherished my parent's marriage, but the memory of that wonderful communication between them has always caused me a lot of pain, too, probably because it was something I've never had myself. I keep wondering why I allowed Ed to walk through that door night after night and go about his business. Why didn't I grab his arm and say, 'You can't leave! Don't you dare abandon us again tonight.' What was so wrong with me that I couldn't stand up to him and tell him what we needed, and repeat it until he understood?

"Why didn't I tell him how much I needed to be loved and how it hurt the kids to have such a remote, emotionless father? Why didn't I recognize how important he was to our future, before things went this wrong? Was my keeping the peace and keeping things smooth all the time worth this? By being quiet and doing nothing, haven't I put all of us at risk?"

Doris interrupted, and this time couldn't be put off. "Ed was not capable of being appealed to on those terms, Meg. You are assuming that if you had only asked him, he would have been capable of understanding what you and the kids needed. But he wasn't. Don't blame yourself for something outside his capacity to understand."

Meg gave her a grateful smile and spoke softly, "Thank you for that, Doris."

Doris said, sternly, "Then, *remember* it. It's not your fault. There's a lot of love spoken in your house; in fact, you really need a sign that says, 'Love Spoken Here,' just to remind you of what you and the kids do without even knowing you do it."

Meg nodded and said, "Well, what's done is done. And now I feel I've got a second chance to do something different. That place on the mountain is my new chance. But I want to assure you that the mountain house isn't built on any cliff. It sits on a huge mountainside overlooking this town and the valley. That Forest Service man told me that the property is almost pristine and surrounded by Forest Service land. As to living there, even though it's been years since I lived in the country, I'm sure that all those lessons Ma and Papa taught me about that kind of life are still inside me, and I've never really forgotten them.

"I think of what the kids could become—strong and independent, instead of sticking around here waiting for any little crumb of acceptance. No child of mine will be a victim! These are wonderful kids. And I want my own land. All these years I've lived on the edges of Ed's career and the scraps of his interests. It's my turn now.

"If this still sounds crazy, tell me; but if not, tell me it's okay to take a chance and try something different. I know people will talk and question my sanity. On the other hand, maybe this will finally confirm their feelings about me."

She sat back and waited, her face hopeful now. "But remember, I'm just *thinking* about all of this; I haven't made up my mind yet. I haven't the slightest idea how to go about all this; I've never bought property. I probably shouldn't have mentioned it to the kids yet, but I had to see how they really felt. And I did, didn't I?" She leaned forward expectantly. "Now, it's you I need to hear from."

Marc picked up the key ring from the table and spoke quietly and earnestly. "Forgive my initial response, Meg."

When she shook her head yes, he crossed the space between them and squatted down in front of her and took her hands in his. "My dear child. You are neither crazy nor will you or your children ever be victims of anything. I apologize for my teasing you. Doris should have kicked me senseless for getting so carried away. We've always said Meg Halverson had more guts in her little finger than most anyone we know, and that includes most of the men we know. We've seen what you've done with this house and your family, and we've known what you've had to put up with. Don't think we've missed a thing. Whatever you want to do, you just remember Doris and I are right behind you."

He placed the key ring in her hands, turning the bear face up, almost tenderly. Then he closed Meg's fingers over it with his own. Standing up and resuming his place beside Doris, he went on, "There's one thing more I'd like you to think over. Doris and I would feel privileged to be a part of this venture in any way you want us to be. Maybe we can go up and look around."

"Then come up tomorrow," Meg said. "They're putting in a new window in the afternoon, and I have to show them the way up. We'll take the kids. I'd love you both to see it, so you can give me your opinions."

Marc looked thoughtful, "Well, I don't want to press my advice on you, but we'd be honored if you would consider us a resource. In dealing with the real estate people, let me offer you my experience. And, supposing this all goes swimmingly, if, as Kurt mentioned, you need a new car, I'd be happy to advise you on those mysterious objects, too. It sounds like both you and Kurt need a few lessons on how to kick tires.

"Also, from the sound of this, it looks like your new venture would add a wonderful dimension to our lives. You know we're spending the summer in Seattle with the grandchildren, but we've got time before that, and all the time in the world after that." He gave his wife a squeeze and said, "Let's do it." He looked at Meg and asked, "Will you let us be a part of this?"

17

CROSSROAD

As Meg watched Tolly's bus pull out into the street and disappear, she was almost overcome by feelings of desolation, even abandonment—all of which she had never felt about her sister before. The bus was gone, and gone, too, was her chance to make amends and get Tolly's blessing. In all their years such a thing had never happened. They'd had disagreements, of course, but never this…this split, with Tolly condemning her for what she wanted to do. After all the years of doing Ed's bidding, she'd felt good about making her own decisions again, but now, standing at her crossroad, doubts dragged at her like a ten-ton weight.

She'd thought they'd talk at breakfast, and she'd gotten up early and made Tolly's favorite French toast. But it didn't take long for Meg to see that Tolly had erected a fence around herself that nothing could penetrate. Every one of Tolly's breakfast requests had been preceded with, "If you would be good enough to pass me the…" and ended with a dreadful, "You are so kind…" Meg wanted to shriek, "You're saying I'm so *kind* for passing you the—the *syrup*, for God's sake?" But she hadn't shrieked. Instead, she'd patiently gone along with it, thinking that Tolly would hear herself and stop all that baloney.

But Tolly didn't want to talk. In the car, on the way to the station, Meg had tried another tactic: commenting on Marc's toast to the love and support she and the family had been given, emphasizing the word support. Then she'd gone on and on thanking Tolly for her help. But Tolly, in a small, tight voice directed toward her window, had said, "It was no more than any other Christian would do."

To which Meg roared, "Toll-eee, what the hell is all this 'no more than any other Christian would do'? You were here during the worst crisis of my life. There are no words for all you did for us during this whole miserable mess." But Tolly had only shrugged, and the rest of the trip to the bus station was made in silence.

As Meg drove, she'd watched her sister out of the side of her eyes, observed her stiff, righteous posture on the far side of the seat, and the meticulous way she folded sheets of facial tissues into perfect little squares and put them in a special compartment of her purse.

When Tolly finished, Meg wanted to grab the purse, shake it out onto the floor of the car, mix it up with her shoe, squishing the tubes of lotions and defiling all those little lists of things. But she kept on driving—one part of her brain inflamed with total ground-zero madness, and the other part alert to the green lights, early pedestrians, and the easy progression of the traffic ahead of the car.

The bus had arrived on time, so getting the ticket was all a big commotion. Tolly, murmuring a barely audible, "Good bye," had climbed onto the bus all too quickly. And, once inside it, in the short time before the bus pulled out, no matter how Meg had tried to get her attention, Tolly was either fussing with her jacket, peering into her purse, or finding room for things. So there'd been no last minute reprieve, no endearing smile, no anything that acknowledged their bond or what had transpired these past terrible weeks. As the bus pulled away, Tolly didn't even wave. Nothing was mended.

As Meg backed out of the parking lot, she thought about the last time she and Tolly had been at this station. Everything that day had been so black or white, so right or wrong; she had cried for help, and Tolly, the bearer of the finest help any family could offer, had come to her rescue. Now it felt as though something even worse than Ed's death had happened.

In those days of Ed's disappearance, his death, and her breakdown, with all that was revealed and said, how could this have happened? And how could she erase what was said between them last night? After the frustration her spirit had endured as Ed's wife, she simply couldn't banish her thoughts about the mountain place or the sense of freedom she and the kids felt there. There was no way she could go back to Wyler and endure being integrated into her old life again. And she certainly couldn't fit into just being Tolly's little sister again. She thought about that. Was that the root of their problem? She recognized the tip of an old resentment she'd felt toward her small, but dominating sister. Though undefined and never dealt with, something tugged at her from their past.

On that note, she pulled out onto the main street and headed home. Clark Fork was just starting to stir. Stores were being opened and the sidewalks were already filling for the day's business. Even at this time of morning, people walked slowly, thinking of excuses to stand catlike, with their backs to the sun. On such a summer morning, it was easy to forgive Montana for its long, cold climate. In fact, a single chirp of a robin could instantly remove the most obstinate recollection of putting on tire chains or shoveling snow from the driveway.

At a stoplight, she was surprised to see Jill Handley and Nan Argonbright cross the street in front of her car, near enough to touch it. Both women had been at that miserable meeting Meg had abandoned, but neither had been to Ed's memorial service. Meg quickly rolled down her window, and called out, "Jill, Nan! Good morning! How are you?" For all of her trouble they gave her small, curt nods, as though to a stranger.

Meg thought bitterly, three out of three was a perfect score, and it wasn't yet eight-thirty in the morning. Perhaps they were like Tolly, doing their Christian duty in nodding at all. When the light turned green, in an effort to get away faster, Meg stalled the car and sat there swearing as she tried to restart it while impatient cars honked behind her. When the car finally lurched away under the sudden acceleration, she felt like the town idiot. Stung by her encounter, she drove only a little further before pulling up to a curb to get a grip on her emotions.

For a brief, bitter moment, she was tempted to pull up stakes and move up on the mountain just to give the wags something really concrete to talk about. In her present state of mind, it would be so lovely to see the town of Clark Fork at her feet, and show them—all bloody seventy thousand of them—how imperious Meg Halverson could really be. But that was silly and certainly not any reason to leave. If she stayed in town, given enough time, people would forget; and, given a little patience and endurance, she and the kids could get on with their lives here.

So, why did she even want the mountain property? Other than the big room they'd slept in, she hadn't even seen much of its interior; in fact, she'd only laid eyes on the place twice. It had been hard to admit that to Marc; no wonder he almost became hysterical. Could she do this just because she had fallen in love with a meadow and a log and the grove of trees that had rescued her? She didn't know. What if she didn't quite know the reason for wanting it and couldn't exactly define it? She shuddered at the risks.

Last night she'd told Marc and Doris about the town changing, but she had changed, too, and in ways that were harder to understand. As the mother of three growing children she had to be so sure that her actions were not impulsive or based on spite or some kind of idealistic drivel. Yet, as she sorted through her motivations, right now it all seemed to be just a whim. In light of what Tolly had said, she hardly trusted herself to make the decision. Tolly had said, "No!" and, for good measure, had thrown in the judgment of their long-dead parents. With no way to change Tolly's mind or get her support, who could help her make this decision? This afternoon, what if Marc and Doris should approve of the place? How would a man make this decision or, more importantly, how would another woman? She had railed against so many of Ed's decisions, but now, as the sole decision maker—and the one who would have to live with her decisions, along with her three children—she felt the full weight of possible outcomes. Dare she turn away from a conventional path and do this thing?

Meg felt pain in her hands and looked down to see the marks of her nails in her palms where she was tightly clenching them. She also felt a trickle of sweat run from her armpit down to the waistband of her jeans. She sat back against the car's headrest and took some long breaths as her scrambled brain searched through her experience for anything, anything, that might help her decide what to do.

As she wondered what her parents would think of her moving up to the mountain, her thoughts turned to the time when Ma and Papa had pried her out of Wyler and sent her to the university here. It was the very last decision that her parents had made for her.

. . .

Clark Fork was only three hundred miles from Wyler, but to her, having never been away from home before, it had seemed like the other side of the earth. With the amount of luggage she had to take, Papa and Ma had driven her in the pickup truck to catch the train. At the depot, when they were unloading her luggage, she, feeling a mixture of fear and homesickness, had decided she just couldn't go through with it. She had cried and begged to be allowed to stay home. She said she had a feeling that Tommy Southers was just about ready to make up his mind about marrying her.

But, even as she spoke those words, Papa kept on methodically transferring her luggage from their truck to the baggage cart provided by the railroad. When he was finished, he patted her shoulder, as though he hadn't even noticed her distress. Finally he said, "Hell, girl, you'll do just fine. In no time at all you'll have found your way around that school and know what you need to do to get yourself a brand new set of options. We have high hopes for you, Meggie, and you have our blessing."

For all her father's sureness, Meg had recognized the tiniest trace of concern in his eyes. But with the train warning its imminent departure, they embraced, and Ma had handed her a box of food for her trip.

Meg remembered how unstable her knees were as she mounted the steps into the train. She'd run up the aisle to stand by the window, waving and memorizing the picture of her two precious parents, standing tight together as always. As the train started to move, Papa had put his right arm up, just held it up in a jaunty, stiff "L" position, like the statue of liberty, without waggling his fingers. It was crazy how that picture of his right arm was always in her mind when she thought of him. It was his last gesture to her, and his eyes would never again see her face.

He had a stroke two months later, just before Christmas. Over the phone, Ma's heartbroken voice had told her that the massive stroke had affected his left side mainly, that Papa just lay there with his eyes closed. The doctor warned her it was the kind of stroke a person didn't recover from and it was only a matter of time. Meg caught a bus and rushed back to be with them all before Papa died.

Meg hadn't thought of that time in the hospital for a long while. But, now, as she sat in the car, the memory came sharply back. Her throat tightened as she remembered every detail of the hospital room: Papa's body inert on the bed; his labored breathing synchronizing the breathing of everyone in the room, as though she and Ma and Tolly could help Papa get air more easily if they all got into the rhythm of it. His lips were parted under the wild hairs of his moustache, and his hair, which had always been so neat, now flared out black upon a spotted pillow. A waxy look was already collecting under his deeply rutted skin…that skin that had stood against so many suns and winds, but would never be baked and parched by them again.

As one day blended into another, then another, he was never left alone. The three women worked out among themselves when they needed a nap, a break, or some food.

But there was that one strange day that would remain in her mind forever. On that day, Ma and Tolly had left her in charge so they could go down to the cafeteria together for lunch. She still remembered the pride she felt in having Papa all to herself.

As a child, she had rarely touched him, other than to give him a playful pat or a quick daughterly hug and kiss; but that day, she dug out a small jar of perfumed cream from her purse and rubbed it on his forehead as he lay there so unaware. In a little singsong way she crooned to him as she smoothed the fragrant lotion on his sun-scarred skin. It was a simple thing to do, a way to attend him in some way, possibly reach down into his unconscious brain to the Papa she had known. She also hoped the cream would dispel the hospital odors that so offended her.

Speaking mostly to herself, she'd said, "Hello, Papa. You're never alone. Right now it's only me here, Meggie. Tolly and Ma just went down to the cafeteria and will be back after they've had something to eat."

After saying that she just stood there, the millions of words she wanted to say to him just piling up inside her, along with her tears. Then a little song from her childhood, one she hadn't thought of for years, ran through her mind. She hummed it as she smoothed the cream softly onto his weathered skin, her fingers gentle, anointing, as she stroked it over his temples.

"This cream I'm rubbing on your forehead is my secret weapon, Papa. It's supposed to attract men. I don't know why I'm telling you this, but it works much too well." Then she said, "Oh, Papa, I've always loved you. I'm so sorry, so terribly sorry that when we said goodbye at the railroad station I didn't know it would be goodbye forever."

She was crying, and she bent and kissed his cheek. "Ever since the doctor told us you're going to...to go, I feel like I'm dying, too. I'll miss you; you have no idea how much. I miss you already. You always stood in front of my mind. And I've loved you the best." She thought a moment then went on. "A long time ago I promised you and Ma that I would always try to do my life right, but sometimes—especially lately—it doesn't seem like I'm doing it right—"

Papa seemed to stiffen at that, and Meg, wide-eyed and fearful, drew back and watched in amazement as he slowly and agonizingly raised his right hand—in that same stiff "L" gesture—and moved his hand slowly up to his lips and then to his ear and then to his lips and then to his ear, repeating the action again and again.

She still remembered how frightened she had been, how it felt like her heart had stopped, then thudded on, as though at the very last minute it remembered what its job was. She thought if Papa had raised his hand just once it could have been an accident. But where he had been absolutely motionless for three days, making those motions so deliberately, and for so many times, couldn't be an accident. She stood back from him, shocked, wondering what it meant and what to do. But finally, she reached out and touched his arm gently. As she did, she felt the muscles of his arm still wanting to make the motions; but she stroked it until he quieted.

She said, "Papa, I think you are telling me you can hear me. Are you telling me you can't talk yourself, but you can hear me? That's what you're saying, isn't it?"

She wasn't sure—she could never be sure—but she was convinced that that was what he was trying to tell her. So she began talking intently to him, desperately aware that this would be the only opportunity in the world to tell him what she had to say.

She thanked him for sending her to the university, for giving her some other options besides staying home and waiting for Tommy Southers. Laughing, she talked about her love for the mountains and land around Clark Fork and about her life at college and how much she liked school now. And she talked about her classes, the ones she loved and the ones she didn't. She told him she had changed her mind and didn't want to be an art teacher anymore. It was the music courses and creative writing she loved best. It was words she'd discovered, and her teachers were encouraging her.

All the while she talked, his hand lay quiet within her hand, and his breathing, that had been so tortured, had softened; she knew he was listening.

Then she told him about the boys she'd met, about one in particular who had already graduated from Yale and had come back to Clark Fork to be a professor. Her voice was troubled then. She told him that the man's name was Edward Halverson. She hesitated, wondering if she should tell her father more. Summoning her courage, she said, "He touched me, Papa. He is the first man I've ever let do that. He likes my long hair and…and I let him touch me, and…you know…we… But that's the trouble; I like how he makes me feel. Only, now it's so hard to decide if I like *him* or not. I'm so afraid of what I feel…and…I don't think you and Ma would like him, or Tolly either. But, I don't know. Oh, Papa, why do I have such a problem with my judgment since he made love to me? What should I do now?"

She had stood then, like she always had, waiting for his wise counsel. "Please, Papa, tell me what I should do about him. How do I leave him now? He's not like us. He comes from a rich family in Clark Fork and has always had money. He talks about different things than you and Ma do. He intrigues me, and I don't know what to do now. Please tell me what to do. Tell me how I can get away. And if I turn him away will there ever be someone else for me?"

While she was waiting for Papa to tell her, Ma and Tolly had returned from lunch. She had turned from him then and told them, with tears running down her face, what had happened and that Papa could hear.

She and Papa never got back to that conversation.

Two days later he died. But in those two days she and Tolly and Ma stayed by his bed, talking and singing the songs he had always loved. They sang until they were hoarse, and then they talked, about the past, the things that made them laugh, and the sad things that made them cry in just the telling. All he had to do was raise his hand an inch off the bed, and music and words poured out of the family in a torrent.

Then it was over. In his fifty-seventh year he was gone.

Meg often thought back to that day. Despite the doctor warning them that her father was going to die, she had expected a miracle. Why hadn't Papa opened his eyes and answered her questions? During her first year of marriage, especially, whenever she thought back on that strange day when she had told Papa all that was in her heart and asked him for advice, she felt a foolish childish anger at him. How dare he just lie there and not tell her to get as far away from Edward Halverson as she could? But he just lay there, taking it all in, then died before he gave her the answers. How dare he do that?

And why had Ma and Tolly come back to the room at just that moment? In all her life she had never had Papa all to herself. It was always Ma or Tolly or the wheat or the buildings or the horses or the farm machinery. It was always someone else or something else that had his attention, until that one last whisper of his life, and then he left too soon.

Even though she felt herself to be a reasonable adult, it went through her mind, unreasonably, like that. And, over the years, she thought about it, not once, but over and over again. Even today, the resentment toward Papa filled her—as absurd as it was to feel that way. That childish wish! How could she still hope that Papa could help solve her problems? As she started the car, she spoke aloud, "Dear Papa, I just couldn't believe that you could ever go away, that's all."

Once more headed for home, she thought again of the indictment Tolly had flung at her, that Ma and Papa would be shocked at what she wanted to do. Meg shook her head at that. Would they really now? Both Ma and Papa were as reasonable as most parents, but did a parent always have the perfect answer? And even if parents, in all their experience, *did* have the perfect answer, what should they do about it? Force it down their child's throat? Could Papa have said anything that could have stopped her from continuing on with Ed? No, she thought not. Once she and Ed had slept together, once she had felt the beckoning ecstasy of making love, her judgment was impaired.

Meg looked over at the empty seat beside her, at a little folded square of tissue that had somehow escaped Tolly's purse, and she stubbornly spoke the words she'd wanted to say to Tolly. "Maybe I am impulsive, but maybe that's all right. I might dream wrong dreams sometimes, but I carry things through and make things better. I can't wait for everyone's approval or permission. Even if I decide wrong, it's my choice."

She laughed a ragged laugh. The children were undoubtedly waiting for her to return home. At one o'clock, with the glass truck following, they were going to take Marc and Doris up that "new" road to see the mountain house. From there, things could move fast. But wasn't that what she wanted? Again, Meg spoke out loud, "Tolly, I love you so much and thank you so much. Sometime soon, please wish me luck."

And those words rattled around inside the car all the while she drove home.

18

THE VOTE

Meg felt like a coach as she paced up and down before her kids sitting on the edge of the sofa; she sounded like one, too. "Okay, you guys, Marc and Doris are going up to the mountain house with us in a little while. They've offered to check out the place. We need their opinion because it's a big decision, and they've had way more experience buying houses than I have. Marc is going to check out the heating system; check out the water and the plumbing; and check to see if the house is built okay. And I want Doris's opinion on just what our living there might be. I wish there was time to walk around the whole piece of land and get to know its borders, but we can do that later. We need to hear what they think because...maybe we can't see what's wrong with it. If Marc and Doris think it's not what we should buy, we need to hear that before we try to buy it. It will be hard but I want you to be quiet and let them advise us." Meg stopped talking when she saw that both Callie and Sara were close to tears.

Sara said, "But, Ma, they aren't little and don't play anymore. We gotta tell them why we gotta buy it."

Meg squatted down and caressed Sara's cheek. "Oh, honey, I know what you're saying. If Marc and Doris don't like it we'll all be sad, but it wouldn't be the end of the world. Maybe we could find some other place that's better. We have to let them see it without putting a lot of pressure on them about how we feel. That means I have to be quiet, too. I told Doris that they should see it for themselves, so I've decided to leave them alone and not say anything either. What I'm asking is I don't want you three guys to act like a bunch of super salesmen. That would only make it harder for them to feel out the place for themselves. Do you hear me?"

Callie, in the same desperate voice Sara had used, asked, "Can't we show them the fallen-down cabin and the springs?"

Meg smiled. "Of course you can. They'll want to walk around in the meadow, too. But if you start pulling them this way and that, and tell them how neat everything is, it won't help." She laughed good-naturedly. "I'm your mother, remember? I know how convincing you three gorillas can be."

She smiled ruefully. "Besides, it's a little late in the game, but the four of us need to actually see the place ourselves. I can't believe that we're even considering this place and we haven't seen what's behind all those doors or upstairs or downstairs, or seen what the kitchen looks like, or—" She stopped talking when she saw Kurt's face. "Or am I a little late? Kurt? You saw the house while Sara and I walked down the mountain, didn't you? Even though I told you not to, you opened those doors and looked around. Why, you rascal." She made a grab for him and laughed. "Come on, confess. I'll forgive you this one time, as long as you tell us what you found."

Kurt hesitated then said proudly, "Well, there are four bedrooms on the balcony level and that other door goes upstairs to some other rooms, and there's a bathroom up there. And I counted four bathrooms off the balcony bedrooms, and another one downstairs by the big workshop. Down there is a workbench and a neat space under the stairs that I'd like, and a room filled with all kinds of junk and lumber. There's room for three cars in the garage. And there are three other rooms down there, and one of them already has a bunch of wood for the fireplace."

Meg's head was in a spin at the thought of all that space, and she wondered how they would ever fill it up, let alone clean it. As the Forest Service man had said, Albert Turner must have liked to build things and didn't know when to stop. She just had to ask Kurt, "And the kitchen, what about the kitchen? You didn't say anything about it."

Kurt paused over that one, looking like he wished she hadn't asked. Finally he said, "Well, it's big and it's real blue."

"But I love blue, Kurt, and so do you. My bathroom's blue. I have blue towels."

"Yeah, I know, Ma, but it's a different blue. And the counters are awful skimpy." He looked at her, deeply worried. "Maybe you better not show them that room, Ma. At least not until we fix it up a little." He added, "If they get thirsty, can I take them to the spring, so they don't have to go into the kitchen right at first?"

Meg said, "Oh, dear, that bad, eh?"

"Yeah, it's real blue."

She couldn't imagine a shade of blue that would worry him like that, but she admired the workings of his mind in warning her of it. She took what he said to heart and decided she'd delay their going in there as long as she could. Then she was dismayed at herself: she was just as bad as the kids were about anything that might cause Marc and Doris to be negative.

Looking at each of her children, she said, "Think you could manage to kind of fade back a bit in the car going up? Maybe just sit there quietly and pretend you're going to the dentist or something? And when we get there, after we've looked around the house a bit, could you just go watch the men putting in the window until Marc and Doris have finished checking things out? Is that possible?"

She looked at them seriously, and they looked back at her seriously—for about three seconds, before all four of them broke out laughing.

. . .

With everyone taking the instructions to heart, it was a silent group that walked around the house, upstairs and downstairs, and around the outside. Neither Marc nor Doris spoke to each other as they trooped from room to room. Marc hummed a few bars of a tune Meg had never heard of as he made his various examinations. And Doris was stony-faced as she tagged after him. Meg noticed there was some reaction when Marc and Doris saw the rock fireplace wall, and she saw their hands caress the wood of the bookshelves and paneled walls a little longer than necessary. Generally everyone was keeping their opinions to themselves. Meg's stomach ached and she wondered how the kids were holding up—off somewhere and having fun, she hoped.

The kitchen was the last place they examined; and, as Kurt had indicated, it was truly dreadful. At first glance, Doris said, "Oh, my!" And Marc, with a disdainful quiver of his nostrils, didn't need to say anything. Coming into it after the magnificent woods and stone of the great room and balcony, the kitchen had an antiseptic look. It was covered with some kind of shiny wallboard of a malevolent purpley-blue color—good for morgues or submarines, Meg supposed. She mentally added the kitchen to the list of transgressions that had been perpetrated against Albert Turner. She could imagine his saying, generously, "Alice, you go ahead and decorate the kitchen, and I'll do the rest of the house."

Besides its color, the room looked downright sad. Obviously, it had never witnessed the clutter and mess of chocolate cakes and children licking the beaters, or of their helping assemble cinnamon rolls, with much of the cinnamon and sugar underfoot. No soup bones had been simmered in this place, nor had the spotless oven ever provided eager noses with the tangy, intoxicating smells of homemade bread or lasagna or pecan pie. But, given the chance, she and the kids would change that!

While Marc and Doris walked around, peering into the kitchen's four undersized cupboards—which couldn't hold a quarter of Meg's kitchen equipment—Meg went over to the kitchen's large north window to see the view it offered. One peek was all she needed to know that this window would be her favorite. From it she could see the gnarled apple tree and the old rock wall. If the children loved that place like she thought they would, she would be able to see them playing from here.

In the clearing a breeze was caressing the grass in the meadow and ruffling the branches of the trees around it. In the middle of the meadow a single tall tree stood alone. On a jutting branch near its top two large hawks were resting. Was one of them the soaring Red-tail she had proclaimed as the very symbol of this place on her first day here? It had to be! As she spoke, one them lifted off the branch and went skimming off down the slope. Meg watched it, thrilled to see its brown back and its reddish tail. Pressing her hands and cheek against the glass, as if to embrace this view of earth and sky, she thought, If only this place will be mine. If only Marc and Doris can see beyond the house's rough exterior, the miles between this place and town, its wildness, the improbability of a single woman with three small kids living up here, and this dreadful kitchen…if only.

She drew back when she realized that this had to be the very window where Alice had watched the solitary figure of Albert "walkin' around, walkin' around" below her. Alice would not have stood in full view, but peered from the side, pressing her bony body tight against the blue walls—no doubt finding comfort and safety in something she could scrub clean should she make an inadvertent human smudge on all that shiny blue. Meg chided herself for her scathing thoughts of that woman, even as she vowed that should she be so fortunate to call this kitchen her own, she would erase all traces of Alice Turner from it.

· · ·

After the Websters finished their rather depressing inspection of the kitchen, they accompanied Meg down the stone steps to the living room level, ran their hands over the beautiful stones of the fireplace, and looked out the windows again. Then they went outside to talk things over.

Kurt and Sara and Callie were already sitting on the stone step, quiet, with their eyes downcast. Doris said, "Is there room for three more bottoms on this step?" The children scooted over to accommodate the adults, but they moved like three mute automatons and resumed their positions on the rock without speaking. Doris shot a worried look to Marc and Meg.

Meg smiled faintly and cleared her throat.

Marc asked Kurt how the window repair had gone, and Kurt dug a bill out of his pocket and handed it to his mother. "The window's all fixed and the men left." Without another word, Kurt rested his arms on his knees and gazed off into the meadow. The two little girls looked over at him and rested their arms on their knees, too, and looked off into the same distance.

Marc studied the three of them and finally said, "Is it a fair supposition for me to make that some of the enthusiasm you three expressed yesterday has worn off?"The two girls shrugged and looked over at Kurt, who was kicking at a little clump of grass. Kurt shrugged, too, then shook his head and said, "No."

Marc raised his eyebrows and asked, "No? Are you saying, 'No, it isn't a fair assumption that the enthusiasm has worn off?'"

Kurt looked over at Marc and said, quietly, "I'm not sure what you mean." Giving his mother a pained look, he said, "We don't want to make you like it if you don't." He swallowed with effort. "The kitchen's pretty bad, isn't it?"

Marc looked at Meg and said, "Ahhhh! I see a mother's admonishment at work here. Yes, indeed." He rubbed his chin and was silent for a full minute. No one breathed, audibly at least. Finally he spoke. "For what it's worth, in my humble opinion the kitchen is the only bloody disaster in the whole place. But, given your good taste and fertile imaginations that can be remodeled. Usually, the one thing most kitchens lack is space for such changes. But that certainly isn't the case with that veritable auditorium in there." He went on, "Granted, the exterior of the house lacks certain esoteric refinements that we might require of a house in town. But, all in all it's a really sound house, made of good materials and constructed like a fort.

"Furthermore, it's my opinion that its furnace would serve a hotel; its water system would be the envy of any hospital; its insulation is sufficient for the next ice age; the windows are all double-paned; the workmanship is excellent; and there's enough room to house, toilet, and bathe an entire battalion. As to the land, by God, I wish I were fifteen years younger! What a beautiful piece of land. Of course, we've only seen a fraction of it, but what an incredible place to live. I now understand what you all were so excited about. Meg, you said the Forest Service chap told you that federal lands surround the place? That being true, my God, what luck! And then there's that cabin…

"Make no mistake, there would be problems living here. You all would need a lot of determination to put up with the inconvenience of that road—that you optimistically keep referring to as 'the good road.' I just hope I don't have to drive on 'the bad one.' You'd have to have a four-wheel-drive vehicle that you can depend on. You'd have to make every trip into town count—really change your buying habits, stock up and all of that. I'm sure there's a lot more to living successfully up here than meets the eye but, by God, it would be a temptation to try. Yes, indeed."

To Meg, his opinion was a vindication, and she felt giddy. With her eyes bright and suppressed excitement in her voice, she said, "Then you think we should do it, Marc?" When he shook his head, yes, she turned to Doris. "And you, Doris? Tell me what you really think."

Doris was stroking the back of Sara's head, and before she spoke, Sara, with a look of anxiety in her eyes, turned her face up to Doris and said very solemnly, "Ma told us kids that because you love us you'll tell us the truth. Would you like to see the fallen-down wall and the spring down there before you tell Ma? It's awful pretty."

Doris grinned down at her and gave her a squeeze. "I'll tell you even before we see it that I think this would be a wonderful place to live. It's your kind of place. I think it's been waiting for you. I really do." She looked at Meg and smiled, "Well, Meg?"

Meg took a long, shaky breath and looked around her—looking down into the meadow, out across the valley, and to the mountains just across from them. In doing that she allowed herself, for the first time, to think of the place as a solid home for her and her family.

Seeing them all waiting, she gave a small shake of her head and spoke, slowly and carefully to the three kids. "Like I said last night, this can't be just my decision. Because part of your Halverson inheritance will be going into this, I'll expect you to help make the decisions around the place. Think about it. There aren't any kids living across the street. You'll have to go to a different school. It's going to be a big change in how we live, and some of the changes will be hard to get used to. It could be a lot of fun living here, but it won't be easy. I vote yes, but it looks to me like you three kids are the ones who are really going to have to make this decision."

She was interrupted by, "Yes! Yes-yes-yes-yes-yes," and the kids whooped and ran around until everyone was laughing and pounding on everyone else.

Marc said, "I hate to break up this riot, but if you were to ask me, I'd suggest we make an appointment with the realtor today. Let's hear what they have to say and, if it's anything you can afford, make them an offer and give them a check. You don't want to lose this."

Meg fairly gleamed. "Yes, Marc. Yes! Let's go back to town right now and see if we can buy this place."

19

TWISTING PATHS

The real estate building had a large shocking-pink banner draped across its front bearing the message, "RAINBOW REALTY: Find Your Dreams at the End of the Rainbow," written in giant black letters. Marc read it aloud as Meg parked the car, adding a droll, "This era isn't without its subtleties."

Looking at Meg with concern, he said, "Now get that worry off your face, Meg, and look relaxed. Buying property is a bit of a game, you know. Just keep your cool, and remember that the realtor earns absolutely nothing if the client doesn't buy anything. You're the one in the driver's seat. I'm here to back you up if the need arises." He led the way to the door, holding it open with one hand and gallantly gesturing Meg and Kurt through it with the other.

Once inside, they stopped. Arching above them and dominating the whole room was a huge, brilliantly striped wooden rainbow—obviously homemade. It was anchored to the high ceiling by a chain. Attached to it, by various lengths of transparent line, hung a meteorological miracle of grey clouds and large drops of water, cut from paper-thin aluminum; and these tossed and spun at the least movement of air within the room. In fact, even though they had closed the door and were standing stock still, the contraption still rattled and whirred. It was hard not to laugh at it, but they managed to be respectfully quiet.

While they waited for someone to acknowledge their arrival, Marc whispered to Meg, with a sardonic laugh, "Just remember that this is going to be a snap. All you'll have to do is sign your name, pay the bill, and move in."

Meg laughed along with him then whispered, a little breathlessly. "It's just that there's so much riding on this, Marc. I don't want to disappoint the kids, and I don't even know what Mrs. Turner is asking for the place. I'll relax as soon as I see my name on that dotted line." At that, the three of them gravely studied the noisy object above them.

Just as the apparatus was settling down, a heavyset woman appeared from a side room. She was dressed in a bright red jacket and had a large pair of glasses balanced on top of her blond head. She introduced herself as Golda Dubois. After they had shaken hands all around, she gave the rainbow a wicked glance and led them as quietly as possible to a round table positioned directly under the largest end of the rainbow. Once they were seated, they had to wait for the rainbow to quiet down, but this time they laughed.

Golda said, "That wasn't my idea, by the way." With a self-deprecating gesture, she explained, "Other than it's distracting, I told the manager that a woman of my size with the name 'Golda' shouldn't be sitting under it. But Rainbow Realty must have its rainbow, you understand."

Disarmed by her candor, Meg felt herself relax, and she, along with Kurt and Marc, eased back comfortably into their chairs and awaited the next step.

Golda quickly and accurately assessed each one: the determined-looking Mrs. Halverson had to be Ed's widow. Marc Webster, who first appeared to be a lawyer, but now appeared to be a family friend, was here to lend her moral support. The boy, Kurt, with his amazing resemblance to Ed, was young, but obviously had an interest in what would transpire here. Both he and Mrs. Halverson looked hungry for something, with just the right amount of fear on their faces. That was always a good sign. At least she didn't have to guess why they were here: it was about the Turner property, of course.

Singling Meg out Golda said, "Whatever brought you folks here, you look like you mean business. What can I do for you, Mrs. Halverson? I'm assuming that's Mrs. Edward Halverson." As Meg nodded, Golda said, with great sincerity, "I so enjoyed working with your husband and Art Stroud. Ed was very bright and he knew a lot of people. His name was magic here in the business world. I'm sorry about his accident."

Meg dropped her eyes to her lap and uttered an uncomfortable and barely audible, "Thank you for saying that. We appreciate it." She then hurried on, looking first at Kurt and Marc for encouragement, "Mrs. Dubois, there's a piece of property we're interested in. It's on the side of a mountain just south of the canyon road. It's Alice Turner's place."

"Yes, of course, the Turner place." Golda chuckled, "You know, we're supposed to ask our clients just where they heard about a particular piece of property, but, in this case, it's quite beside the point, isn't it?"

Meg looked puzzled. "I'm not sure. I heard it was for sale from Mrs. Turner herself, if that's what you mean. I had to pick up a key from her and we got to talking and she told me her place was for sale. That was before we saw the For Sale sign at the bottom of the property, with Rainbow Realty's name on it. In fact, I still have Mrs. Turner's key. I'm afraid it's all very complicated."

All the while Meg was explaining this, Golda was nodding her head politely, anxious to break in. When Meg had finished, she said, "Yes, yes, of course. I'm sure it is. The important thing is, you've finally met Mrs. Turner and survived the experience. Now, there's a woman who likes to talk." She smiled impishly. "I'm sure she couldn't discourage *you* with all that talk, but for other clients, it's best she doesn't meet them."

Even more puzzled, Meg said, "Yes, I suppose if I had never seen the place before talking with her I wouldn't have gone up to see it. She wasn't very happy about living there, but I ended up feeling sorrier for her late husband."

"Sorry? Sorry for Albert Turner?" Golda looked doubtful. "Surely, Mrs. Halverson, you can't mean you're sorry for that man. He was so very, very obstructive to us. They were an unlikely couple, but now that he's no longer in the picture..." Laughing, she went on, "Now that the property is hers...well, with some of my clients I feel I provide only a little knowhow—as the keeper-of-the-keys and the writer-of-the-forms—but with others, I am reminded of the absolute necessity of having people such as myself doing their selling for them. Some people—and Mrs. Turner comes to mind—should never be allowed to open their mouths, if you will permit my saying that." She looked at Meg with mock apology.

Meg gave Marc a bewildered look, as Golda Dubois went on, speaking in a confiding voice, "When I listed the place, I told her I'd just as soon she left town while we're trying to sell it, in case someone called her for details about the place. No prospective client should hear her blow-by-blow pictures of the wind blowing over trees onto the power lines and cutting off the electricity for days at a time, or about the water system freezing up periodically or her horrid stories of being snowed-in and not finding anyone to plow them out, or of skidding sideways down those icy roads." Golda was laughing now. "And her description of all those mice coursing through the house—*unabated*, if you will excuse the pun—as well as all those other *interesting* animals walking by the outside of the house at all hours. Those kinds of facts wouldn't do much to help the sale…of…that…house…would…they?" Golda stopped speaking. She had missed something she shouldn't have missed. Meg Halverson's face was white, her lower lip was quivering, and she was looking at her son like she was going to cry.

Golda watched in horror as Meg pushed back her chair and spoke to her son, "We can't do it, Kurt. I really hadn't thought it out, about what winter would actually do to the roads. Getting you kids to the bottom of the canyon for school every morning, then picking you up. I just didn't think it out thoroughly. I thought we could, but we can't. Mrs. Turner told me a lot of things, but she never talked about those things in detail, or maybe I just didn't want to hear what she was saying. Your Aunt Tolly was right. There's no way we could live in that house."

Golda fairly screeched, "What do you mean 'live in that house'? Surely you aren't considering *living* up there!"

Angry and disappointed, Meg turned on her. "Of course, we were, at one time. What did you think? But trying to deal with those things—being snowbound with three kids to get to school—broken power lines—no water—I couldn't cope with those things by myself!" Meg picked up her purse and got up from her chair. "Come on, let's go."

"But you mustn't leave!" Golda slumped back dramatically in her chair with her hand on her heart.

Seeing her distress, but unmindful of it, Meg snapped, "I'm sorry to say this, Mrs. Dubois, but I don't understand in the least why you'd think we weren't going to *live* up there. What you told me hardly matters now; but if I might say, if you are all that interested in selling the place, I think *you* are the one who shouldn't be allowed to open your mouth." She softened her voice a bit. "I apologize for that. I guess I needed to know what living up there would really be like, so thank you for telling me, and thank you for your time."

Golda said, "But let me explain—"

Kurt, still sitting, begged softly, "Don't go yet, Ma. Please. Can't we find out more about it before we go? You know I can help you with things."

"Oh, Kurt, we can't. You couldn't miss school. And remember me, the person who knows nothing about a car? We can't live up there alone. We'll find some other place—one I can manage."

Marc soothed, "Now, Meg, don't panic. Remember what you told us? You don't have to know how to do every damned thing yourself. You can always hire someone to help you—a couple, a hired man. Hell, put 'em up in that cabin and—"

"But I was just dreaming, Marc! There are things a person *wants* to do and things a person *can* do. Living up there isn't one of—"

Golda interrupted, "Mr. Webster's right, you're being hasty, Mrs. Halverson. Please, just sit down. There's something you need to know."

Meg kept standing, hugging her purse to her body and waiting, while Golda, blinking rapidly and panting, regained at least a part of her composure, and in an earnest voice said, "I'm so terribly sorry I upset you, Mrs. Halverson. Believe me, I had no idea you'd want to live up there. Ed was only interested in the land, not the house. If you'll recall, he was going to tear down the house and put the sawmill where the house was. So I just naturally assumed that *you* were only interested in the land, too. Yet, now that I've had a chance to think of it, by relocating the sawmill somewhere else—perhaps in the clearing—and headquartering out of the house, you could certainly supervise the development of the property better."

Meg backed up and plopped down into the chair, dropping her purse as she did. Collecting herself, she said, "Supervise the development of the...?" She drew air into her lungs so fast she squeaked, then coughed, and, in the struggle to clear her throat, finally squeezed out, "Supervise the development, right." It was on her face to say more, but she clamped her lips shut and put a restraining hand on Kurt, who was groaning.

Golda looked apprehensive once again, but continued on cautiously, "I was going to say that it's interesting that the Turner property has suddenly gotten to be such a popular place. Someone else wants that property and last night Mrs. Turner was presented with his offer." She added, "Another agent wrote it up; it wasn't me. Mrs. Turner told me about it." Seeing the look on Meg's face, she said, "I thought you'd be interested. Now this offer—which Mrs. Turner hasn't accepted as yet—is *supposedly* conditional on him—that is, the *other party*—getting financing. But, his being the developer...I mean, it's absurd; his offer is too low. He knows its worth. It's pure speculation on his part." Golda stopped and waited.

Another groan came out of Kurt, and Meg just sat and blinked.

Marc spoke up, helpfully, "Well then, if you expect Mrs. Halverson to make an offer, we're going to need more facts. We don't even know what Mrs. Turner is asking for her place."

Golda licked her lower lip and, tipping back in her chair, she allowed her eyes to linger a moment on the rainbow above them. Then, directing her reply to Meg, she said, "Mrs. Turner is asking a million dollars for it." She saw Meg and her son react to her words, but went on briskly. "I know that's a hefty price for land in these parts, but, as you well know, it's a unique property. There are 1,028 acres in that parcel, and those are pristine acres with old-growth timber and a number of deep, reliable springs. The property is completely surrounded by federal lands. By that I mean protected from encroachment by anyone or anything else. The feds also provide undisputed access across their lands into the property. With what you'll be doing with it, you already know how valuable that is." Golda's eyes gleamed as she thought to add, "Then there's that house and the cabin on its upper side.

"But, let's first talk about the housing development and what Ed suggested Stroud do with it. Assuming you are here to carry out Ed's wishes, shall we say, *independent of the bank*, I need to know what you know about it. So, if you could tell me what Ed told you then I'll be able to fill in any blanks. We can save a lot of time that way."

Meg stammered, "I'm not sure I can say," and looked helplessly at Marc.

Marc cut in, "Well…hell, Mrs. Dubois. It's asking a lot for Meg to speak of this, with her husband's death and all. Would it be asking too much for *you* to review for us what Ed and Art were going to do? You understand."

Golda gave Meg a solicitous look. "Of course, of course, I wasn't thinking." She continued, "You are undoubtedly aware of the heavy expenses associated with the initial development of any property. But this property, as your husband and Art Stroud recognized, is unique because it has a natural flow of marketable resources to help offset these costs. The trees are the key to the whole thing, because selling off that amount of timber will bring in a big chunk of money right away. You have to get to the trees with the trucks and equipment before logging can begin. So, the first thing is beefing up the access roads.

"I can't remember exactly how many board feet Ed estimated would be pulled off that place, but it was plenty. I do remember he figured they'd put the temporary sawmill where the house now stands and stockpile the logs in that clearing below the house. But you seem to have other thoughts on that. As I recall, Art's Kladstone paper mill would contract to buy all the slash. I'm sure Ed left you all those figures.

"Anyway, once the trees are out of there and the majority of the land is cleared, the sawmill would be dismantled and it would just be a matter of dividing the land—with careful planning, of course—into two- to five-acre parcels, then building a few houses—large, showy ones, to set the trend—and marketing it as an upscale development for those who want to live out of town but not *that* far out of town."

Golda stopped and turned to Kurt and in a syrupy tone said, "I bet you and your little friends would want a pony, or maybe a big, big horse."

Kurt nodded politely while averting his eyes, and Golda went on, "A new school and a moderate-sized shopping center would be built somewhere on the lower part of the property—closer to the canyon road, no doubt, which could service it more easily. Of course, this will open up the canyon floor to development, too, making your property all that much more valuable. Does this sound like what Ed had in mind?"

Meg swallowed, then said, "Ed and Art thought of everything, didn't they?"

"Oh, yes, Mrs. Halverson, those two men were thorough, as any good businessmen should be; in fact, quite a team. Your husband's death has to be a real loss to Art Stroud, no doubt about it."

Meg thought for a moment. "You know, Mrs. Dubois, there's something I guess I never exactly got straight. I'm pretty busy with the kids, you know, and don't always pay attention. Why didn't Ed and Art Stroud do this earlier? Before Albert Turner died?"

"Why, because old man Turner wouldn't sell it to them. He was going to; he was thinking about it, but when he found out about their plan to develop the place he stopped the sale. But now with him gone... As they say, 'He who gets there first-est with the most-est gets a plum for the picking.'"

Meg asked, "Well, then, why isn't Mrs. Turner doing this developing—"

"By herself? I don't think her husband ever told her what went on in those talks last fall. But even if she knew, she just wants out. In fact, I've had a hard time getting her to think of it in any positive way at all. When I spoke to her about listing it, she was surprised it had any value. Mentioning the money helped—she and her friend Sadie have thoughts about moving to Las Vegas—but I can tell she really doesn't believe she'll ever get the money to go." She stopped and laughed. "If you want to know, I'm the culprit who keeps telling her to hold out for top price. But it's a fair price, considering the eventual return. Also, of course, it's my listing and I'd like to be the one who sells it."

Meg persisted, smiling now, "Well, why isn't Art Stroud interested then? Mightn't he still want it?"

"Art Stroud. Hmmm..." Golda tapped a scarlet-nailed fingertip on her lower lip and looked steadily at Meg as she spoke, "At the risk of repeating myself, Mrs. Halverson, I judge that *the man* making that low offer was thinking there was *no one left* who had the knowledge or the interest or the foresight to know that the Turner property has such a unique value. In my opinion, yesterday's offer doesn't in the least reflect the land's true worth. Forgive me for saying this, but for all its grand size and the view it has, the house doesn't add much to the land's value…or detract from it, I suppose. It's the value of the land itself: its timber, its water, its ready availability to the town of Clark Fork, where its value lies."

She stopped then, letting all her words soak in. Seeing that they had, she added, "I can't tell you what the other offer was—that question is on your face, Mrs. Halverson. But I must tell you that at my insistence Mrs. Turner assured me she would hold out for full price, at least, for a little longer. So, anyone making a better offer will get it. Let's hope she doesn't change her mind. Now, I really can't say any more, confidences being what they are in this business."

A smile flitted over Golda's face, and again she looked up at the rainbow. Then her eyes returned to Meg. "So, Mrs. Halverson, shall we write up the offer? I can deliver it to Mrs. Turner for her signature and be back here by, say, four o'clock? Then it will be all yours. Tell me, what is your pleasure?" She sat back and folded her hands on the tabletop and smiled sweetly. It was time to be quiet and wait.

Meg took a deep breath and held it, then let it seep out while she stared at her own hands on the table. She longed to scrape back her chair, make her excuses and leave. How could she decide what to do with the rest of her life in full view of Golda Dubois? The room was stifling and nothing stirred, not even the restless aluminum clouds and water drops above her. She longed for their jiggle and whirr now; it might signal a change in this air—which smelled of old ashtrays and carpet cleaner and, she supposed, the paint on that damned rainbow. She could feel a trickle of sweat slide down her neck and into the crease between her breasts.

Kurt fidgeted; she could feel his questions and knew what they were. She turned and cautioned him with her eyes to sit still. To Marc she gave a painted look and wondered where that simple task he'd mentioned was—sign your name, pay the bill, and move in. She met Golda's eyes for a microsecond then looked down at her hands again.

Of course, it was Art Stroud who had made the low offer on the mountain property. And if she didn't buy that beautiful place its very essence would be destroyed by every device known to a developer. That fact changed everything: canceling out her trivial concerns about icy roads and trees blowing down over power lines; and, as a matter of fact, even its one million dollar price tag.

What made her think she was the first to discover the Turner place? The name had sounded familiar when Ellis Brodie first mentioned it that day in the truck. But she would never have thought to connect the beautiful place she had inadvertently found and gotten such comfort from to the Turner place that she'd overheard Ed and Art discussing months ago. In recalling that, her old argument with Ed surfaced—the one she called "land ethics" and he called "progress." Except this time there was no flinging back the last word and stalking away—it was hers to solve, and the kids were looking to her to do it.

She cringed inwardly at the very thought of Art and Ed looking at that spot of pure loveliness with the same callous greed she'd seen in their eyes and heard in their voices over the years. Unfortunately, she *could* imagine them admiring the trees, not for their beauty, but for the number of board feet of lumber they would produce. She could imagine them looking at the house, not for its robust defense against the weather and the spectacular view it provided, but merely as an accessible location for a sawmill. And she could easily imagine them planning where to put the roads and how they could divide the cleared-off mountainside into subdivision parcels. It was nauseating. How could it be that when she first stumbled across that place—feeling so much, feeling so grateful for its solace—she had not felt the mark of destruction they had already placed on it? She had only felt peace and joy—her own and, later, that of her children. Why was it that some viewed the earth—lying so beautifully serene—with their inventive brains eagerly concocting methods of ravaging it and bending it to their will?

"Meg?" Marc tugged at her sleeve and said, "Mrs. Dubois, my friend needs a breath of air. We'll walk by the river. Give us an hour."

Golda's face changed from smiling confidence to something grudgingly bestowed upon strangers. She tapped her watch and muttered something about another appointment and reminded them that Mrs. Turner would wait only so long. But faced with Marc's determination and Meg's uncertainty, she allowed them an hour's reprieve and excused herself.

Marc led Meg and Kurt outside, guiding them to a small shady park alongside the river, where they found a bench in the late afternoon sun.

They sat idly listening to the water's low, contented chuckle, their eyes drawn to a fisherman below them, parting the river's dark green current with his knees, and pulling hypnotic loops of fishing line from the surface, again and again; the line flinging stray diamond-bright droplets into the water at every cast.

Marc spoke first. "I feel like I just climbed out of a washing machine. How about you two?"

Meg's words exploded out. "Talk about learning more than I ever in my life wanted to know!"

Marc patted her hand, "You're doing fine."

"But their plans for that place!"

"You're doing fine, my friend. Just a little switch in motivation, perhaps."

Kurt asked, "Do we have that much money?"

Meg said, "It's a lot of money, but with one thing and another we can do it."

Kurt smiled for a moment then spoke accusingly, "You never told me about Dad and Mr. Stroud wanting that place. Is that why you want it now, to build a bunch of houses? I don't want that. I want the place like it is now, and so do Sara and Cal."

"Don't worry, dear, I want to keep it just as it is, too." She reached over and unclenched his hand and started stroking it gently. Looking at him directly, she said, "I'm sorry we've been talking about things your father was connected with. His job was buying land then developing it, so Mr. Stroud's bank could make money. And he was very good at that. But I want you to understand that he and I felt very differently about those things. It might not have sounded like it, but what Mrs. Dubois said was news to me. I pretended like I knew it because I needed to know everything she knew about it. I was being kind of deceptive."

Kurt nodded with relief and they smiled at each other.

She continued, "Frankly, what I'm having a hard time with is trying to decide just how deep my convictions are about that place. Those weren't halfway things Mrs. Dubois was describing. While she was talking about it I could almost hear the whine of chain saws and the crash of trees falling to the ground. Those beautiful old trees would end their lives in a slash pile, or lie on the ground, cut into lengths, and hauled off to who knows where. I pictured road graders, with their relentless screech of metal against rocks, obliterating the springs, and pushing things into huge piles to be burned. Then the land would be naked. Someone would come along and mark the mountainside into squares and put down concrete and strips of asphalt, and all around would be cars and roofs and garbage cans. There'd be nothing to hold off the sun then. I saw the sun as unobstructed heat sending up shimmering mirages from the roads and sidewalks and—and, you know, Kurt, I felt like I was going to throw up."

She leaned back and went on, "I don't want that to happen to that mountainside. I want to get to know those trees personally. I think of that old silver log that's been lying on the ground for a hundred years, and that group of trees around it, living their quiet lives next to each other. I would like to give them continued life, because I think that's what we owe them. There's something about that mountainside that I can't put into words. It's almost like it's is trying to tell me something, or ask me something... Oh, I don't know. What I do know is I don't want us to get rich off it, even though Mrs. Dubois feels that any *really good businessperson* would use it for something. I don't even think in those terms where the mountain is concerned. I want us to get to know it, then live with it as it is. It would be our little piece of land to think about and care for."

Kurt looked at her and said, "Yeah," very quietly.

Marc said, "Meg, I'd say your convictions are quite deep enough. Shall we go buy that place now?"

. . .

Meg met Golda Dubois' eyes and said, "I shall pay Mrs. Turner full price, *in cash*. I can write out a check now for half the amount. After my lawyer checks everything out, I'll give her the rest." She took a deep breath and added a little foolishly, "You won't have to call the bank to verify this check right at this moment, will you?"

A shrill laugh escaped Golda. "*Ask Art Stroud*? Heavens no! There's no reason for that, Mrs. Halverson. Best we girls leave well enough alone. Like I said, 'He—or *she*—who gets there first-est with the most-est—'"

Meg finished it: "'gets a plum for the picking!' I promise, my check won't bounce." She threw back her head and laughed giddily.

Golda had long ago learned the art of breathing deeply without moving her chest in the least, and this was one of those times. No, she thought, pulling down her glasses and settling them firmly onto her nose, this time the sale was not going to go away. She dug a pen from her jacket pocket, pulled a long, familiar form from the depths of the briefcase beside her chair, and started asking questions and writing in answers quickly and accurately. The rick-et-y-pop, rick-et-y-pop of her heart had quieted down, and for that she was thankful. Selling big properties was a risk to her health: disappointment one day, selling it the next, and all the while the paths turned and twisted and one never knew what was around the next corner.

Art Stroud would be furious, she thought. But he deserved it, after making that ridiculously low offer. He deserved a little one-upmanship. Play games with Golda Dubois, will he? While she checked through the paperwork, one corner of her mind was already figuring out the commission she would get from this sale. It was going to be a great year.

Meg, looking first at Kurt then at Marc, silently mouthed, "We're buying it." Marc smiled and nodded his head slightly, inclining it to her purse and making a writing motion with his hand.

Seeing that, Kurt dived into her purse and got out her checkbook, then fumbled his way to the bottom again to come up with a pen. He watched his mother write out the check and counted all the zeros, just to make sure.

As Golda inspected the check, she asked as casually as she dared, "And your house, Mrs. Halverson? Now that you're buying the Turner place, are you selling your house here in town? Have you listed it with anyone yet?"

Meg realized she hadn't even thought of that, and answered impatiently, "I'll be more than happy to talk to you about that later, after Mrs. Turner's signature is on this document. Please, call her. We just have to know we're the ones who get the place. Please. Right now." She squeezed Kurt's knee under the table.

Golda said, "Yes, of course, but I want you to think about it. I might already have a buyer for it, a new dentist. But they need a house very soon. They've been living in a motel with their children. But, first things first: I'll call Mrs. Turner and tell her what I have in my hand."

20

BETWEEN ERAS

Meg reached out from beneath the covers and turned off the alarm, then settled back for another thirty minutes before she had to face the noise and excitement of moving day.

In these last private moments she looked around at the room where she and Ed had spent their nights for the past eight years—the dimensions and geography she had long since memorized. She wondered if her whispers still existed, like hopeful little jewels lying unnoticed among the ugly, unkind things that never made sense. All those she would happily leave behind with the new owners. Perhaps she should warn them.

Pulling the comforter around her ears, she congratulated herself for buying this new bed. The other big one (upon which so much marriage had been conducted), along with its huge bedding, she'd sold to a grateful young couple for practically nothing. Actually, she had felt embarrassed by the sale. What was more intimate than a bed? It seemed akin to selling one's underwear. Before they changed their minds, she offered to help them uproot it from its spot against the wall, then struggle it into their truck—and out of her life forever.

After just one night, her new queen-sized bed (virginal and without allusions), its lace-trimmed sheets, and the thickest goose-down comforter she could buy, already felt like hers. But the subject of the bed exposed something she had put off thinking about since Ed died: namely, her emotional life from this point forward. By moving to the isolation of the mountain, far from any social possibilities in Clark Fork, she was acknowledging that, from here on, her efforts would be for her family and her mountain property—and these she would be doing alone. Even so, her resolve triggered an older grief, and she stared at the future bleakly. As she lay there, aware of her breathing and the warmth and softness of her thirty-eight-year-old body, her need to express the very tenderness that Ed so wantonly thwarted came to mind. There had only been Ed, never another, and even though she had given birth to his three children, she had never been allowed to experience feelings of satisfaction with a man. Now she never would.

At the furniture store where she bought her new bed, the salesman spoke at great length about the construction of the mattress, ending with, "It's made for sound sleeping—" and adding, with a leer, "if that's what you're after?" That comment and the arch of his eyebrows had nearly scotched the sale, and he hurriedly resumed his discourse on mattress firmness being essential to a healthy back.

If she'd known for sure that she could have controlled her emotions, she would have told him that he couldn't know what his comment meant, that when a woman has been found to be neither attractive nor lovable, she wasn't going to risk further rejection. Of course, she'd told him no such thing.

Her thoughts turned to Golda Dubois. Once Alice Turner accepted her offer, things moved fast. The very next day, Golda listed and sold Meg's house to the new dentist, on the condition that they could occupy it in two weeks. Marc's lawyer had looked over both transactions, and the deal was done.

With the kids' educations very adequately provided for, Meg made a list and set money aside in anticipation of the things she wanted to do to the house: redo the kitchen; replace many of the fixed windows with ones that opened; bring electricity and running water to the cabin, put in a small bathroom and a stove, and install cupboards and finish it nicely inside. All that was in addition to a liberal fund for things she hadn't thought of yet. What money was left would supply a steady, adequate no-frills income. She would always have to watch her spending, but that she could manage.

She had gone to the bank to retrieve some papers from her safety deposit box and literally bumped into Art Stroud coming out of his office. The stack of papers in his hand had gone flying and she had dutifully helped him pick them up. After a stiff exchange—the first words since he and his wife had so unkindly and abruptly left Ed's memorial service—Meg put on her game face (good old H.U.) and, placing the papers in Art's hands, had told him brightly that she had just bought the most marvelous 1,028-acre mountain place above the canyon road, and she and the kids were so looking forward to moving into the house and settling into their new life in the wilds of Montana. She trilled, "From what I hear we saved that pristine mountainside from sure destruction." His only response was to remind her to have her new address printed on her checks, adding a sour, "If such a place even *has* an address." Before she could answer he ducked into his office and closed the door. For her it was a good moment.

Reluctantly throwing off the covers, she chuckled contentedly to herself. At this time tomorrow... *at this very time tomorrow*, she'd be cozy as could be in her mountain bedroom, and the kids in theirs. She imagined what the sunlight coming in that eastern bedroom window would look like, with its view of sky and giant trees. Oh, it was going to be so lovely! She and the kids would be living with cartons and boxes for a while, but what did that matter. She pictured herself going into that odd blue kitchen tomorrow morning and cooking their first breakfast, and imagined the kids happily clattering down the hall when she called them. All that mattered now was to get their possessions up to the mountain house and then relax. There was only peace and tranquility ahead.

· · ·

It was amazing to see the wiry little man heave a heavy container up onto his shoulder and march out the door to the truck, as though the load was his greatest joy and he would only lay it down with an argument. "Shorty" wasn't more than five feet tall or a pound over one-hundred-and-twenty. When she met him at the door and he had announced that he and his three partners (who weren't all that big either) were the movers, Meg stammered around, trying to make it clear that she had a house full of heavy furniture, and the mountain house had several levels and lots of stairs. The way she said it implied that perhaps someone at the moving company had made a mistake and sent kids to do a man's job. Shorty just looked up at her with a great kindness in his brown eyes, and muttered, "Beg pardon, Missus," and darted past her into the house.

Within minutes Meg was aware that she was in the presence of a master mover who knew more about it than she ever would. But still she gasped when she saw him hoist a heavy carton of her most precious dishes onto his shoulder. And she was again moved to explain just how rare and totally irreplaceable the contents were. During her explanation, Shorty lowered the carton to the floor and gave her that patient, kind look again, but didn't say anything. His gaze sent her scuttling away into a corner of the house where she wouldn't be tempted to express her anxiety, or be the recipient of one of his tolerant, wordless stares again.

In the next room she could hear him explaining to Kurt that lifting didn't require brute strength, that it was legwork and balance—just tip the box, get under the load, and rise up straight. Meg thought, oh, sure. But apparently Kurt took it all in, and he passed her in the hall carrying a box of books on his shoulder. She heard him bantering with Shorty and the other men in a way she hadn't heard him talk before, other than with Marc. It was a good time to back off as a mother. At age eleven, he could do an amazing amount of cooking, turn out salads and spaghetti sauces that had real pizzazz, keep an orderly room, wash windows, scrub toilets, and vacuum; but he had been slighted in the world of men.

. . .

There were three things Meg had decreed as absolutely essential to buy, even before they moved in: a Jeep, a whole carton of mousetraps, and a tin pail of peanut butter for bait. With a little speech, Meg made the anti-varmint project appear of greater magnificence than the actual doing it would be. Then she recruited the Littles. She showed them how to bait the traps and remove the mice, and bought a box of rubber gloves to use while doing it. The Littles, having had no choice in this job, presented her with a speech of their own: they would keep a tally of how many mice they caught, and their mother would pay them a nickel for each mouse. In view of just one 24-hour-catch, Meg named it "The College Fund."

After the family's experience with being marooned that night on the mountain, buying the Jeep was their highest priority. Because Kurt had a keen interest, it made sense to have him know as much as he could about it. Meg decided that she would be "just too busy," and enlisted Marc and Kurt to go to the dealer, decide on the best model, buy it, and learn all about its mechanics. Of course Marc was in on her plan and, once the Jeep arrived (painted a deep metallic blue, at Kurt's request), the two began their study of what made it work. Kurt carried the Jeep's manual around with him and even studied it in bed at night. During the day he and Marc spent every possible minute under its hood, or lying beneath it, identifying its parts, listening to its motor, tracing its wires, and working the gears and pedals.

So it was that Meg learned about their new vehicle from her eleven-year-old son. When Kurt finally brought his mother into the act, it was he, with very little prompting from Marc, who made sure she connected the sounds coming from it with what was actually happening under its hood. By this time, the manual had been relegated to the glove compartment because it had been memorized. Kurt now talked about four-wheel hubs and gear ratios in much the same way he once talked about the chain and pedals of his bicycle.

It was a big moment when the male contingent finally invited the female contingent to accompany them on a test drive, and Meg was to be allowed to drive it. Of course, the main selling point had been the Jeep's ability to crawl slowly uphill, using its powerful engine and gears, and all four wheels instead of two. Meg could hardly contain her joy as she drove the marvelous machine up the mountain road the very first time. The whole trip made them all feel confident that they could handle whatever road conditions were ahead of them, especially when winter came.

That night at dinner, Kurt said that Marc had offered to teach him how to drive the Jeep, once he and Doris came back from their trip to Seattle. Kurt explained carefully that he was already tall enough to reach the pedals and it would help if he could drive around the place, hauling wood or whatever. In his argument he added with great earnestness that other "ranch" boys drove at an early age. Meg, who had been shaking her head, yes, all the time he was making his case, said, "I agree. That's wonderful." For this she received a rare, unexpected hug and a kiss from her son.

Doris remarked to Meg that it had been years since they'd been so excited. While the Littles worked on the mice, Doris helped Meg clean the house, and Marc, always with Kurt's help, brought a man up from town to check the furnace and water system thoroughly, and figure out how to bring water to the cabin. Marc had gone over these issues with Kurt and Meg so they would know what to expect, and get acquainted with the idiosyncrasies of the house long before winter arrived—winter always seemed to be some kind of threshold in their minds, and would probably remain so until they experienced it firsthand.

. . .

Meg took a break from vacuuming behind the disappearing furniture to see Sara bustling to the front door with her arms loaded. The two girls were seldom apart and Meg wondered where Callie was, but didn't ask. Instead, she leaned against the wall, stretched and yawned at the thought of the work ahead of her up on the mountain—all without the help of Marc and Doris. How she would miss them! There was no doubt about it, they were family. They'd spoiled her so, helping with everything they could before leaving. Of the many bedrooms in the mountain house, Meg had given them the largest room on the third floor, and it would remain theirs. They had already brought up many items from their house in town. Everyone was delighted.

Yesterday, before they left for their annual visit in Seattle, Doris had located a high school girl named Marty to help Meg for the first few days. She would stay in the Webster's room and keep an eye on the kids and help in whatever capacity she could. Meg was looking forward to Marty's help, and would enjoy her company.

. . .

Looking tired and cranky, Callie walked in the door and came over and leaned against her mother. "I'm thirsty, Ma. Do we still have glasses?"

Callie felt a little warm, and her face showed just how disruptive the move was on everyone. Meals had been sketchy and out of whack and so had bedtimes. Meg said, "Yes, dear, I have some paper cups. Come on." They went to the kitchen and Meg filled a cup twice for her. Meg looked at her and asked, "Are you feeling okay?"

Callie answered, "I'm sleepy, and I—I just want to get there, Ma." She almost sobbed.

"I know, dear. It's taken so long, hasn't it? Most everything is out of here and in the van. All we have to do is go pick up Marty and we'll be on our way. Why don't we take your little blanket and spread it out on the back seat of the Jeep so you can take a nap."

Callie sounded quarrelsome, "My blanket and stuffed animals are already in there, Ma. I've been sleeping there already. I just came in for a drink." Meg gave her a distracted kiss and a pat on her bottom, and Callie headed outside to the Jeep again.

. . .

Meg finished the last-minute tasks and, after one more look around, closed the door. She was putting the key under the rock by the front step when she saw Marty coming up the walk. Meg said, "Why, hello, Marty. I was just coming to pick you up. We're all ready to go. I hope the kids left you enough room in the back seat."

Marty rolled her eyes and shook her head. "I'm sorry, Mrs. Halverson. I decided I just can't go. Not up there."

Meg said, "Oh, Marty, you can't mean that. I really need your help."

"I-I'd like to, but I have something else I have to do. And Mother wouldn't—you know—let me, and my boyfriend might come over and—"

Meg had gotten the message. She bit her lip and, over a constriction in her throat, said, "Of course, I understand. But would you by any chance know of someone else—anyone else—who might—?" But

Marty was shaking her head no and had that "not up there" look on her face again. Meg smiled and said, "Well, thank you for coming by."

Shorty was walking toward Meg and passed Marty in the breezeway. By the looks of him, he was impatient to get going. She told herself: We'll do just fine. Just fine.

When Meg crawled into the Jeep, barely finding room for her feet among houseplants and brooms and food from the refrigerator, Sara and Kurt both said, almost at the same time, "Callie's sick." Meg turned around to the back seat and one look was all she needed to know that, indeed, she was. Callie's cheeks were flaming and her eyes were red. But Callie raised her head and smiled and said in a shaky, fever-drifty voice that sounded like she had a mouthful of marbles, "I'll feel okay when we get there, Ma."

"Of course you will, dear." Meg reached back and stroked her little face, and thought of calling the doctor, then wondered grimly how she would do that with the phone inside *this* house disconnected. Thinking ahead to the mountain, she wondered how she was going to care for a sick child while moving and settling in. The beds and bedding were somewhere in the middle of the van, and who even knew where the damned thermometer was. Her mind suddenly veered to all the other things that could go wrong. If she took Callie to the doctor now and had to give Shorty directions, what if he took the wrong fork and tried to drive up that other terrible road? Where could he ever turn around? Meg's feeling of being stretched to her limits was now joined by a growing fear that her family would all too soon face big challenges of living up on that remote mountainside.

Looking behind her, she saw that Shorty had the van running and was drumming his fingers rapidly against its door. With no other choice, she started the Jeep and pulled away from everything they had known, to head into their unknown future.

Part Three

21

NO BEARS

When they finally turned onto the fork that led up the mountain, it was as if a rubber band connected the van and the shiny blue Jeep. When the heavy van slowed to negotiate a particularly sharp turn, the Jeep—wanting to race on up the road—stopped and waited impatiently. Then, when the van at last heaved itself up onto a less-steep part of the road and was in danger of catching up, the Jeep bolted ahead for a short distance before Meg again remembered she was showing the movers the way.

As they approached the gap where the Canada lynx had been, they saw a familiar green truck bearing the Forest Service emblem parked by the side of the road. The man was there too, bending to the little spring, scooping up water over his face. Sara announced, "He's the one who calls me Punkin!"

Meg slowed the Jeep to a crawl then stopped and everyone hung out of the windows with big smiles on their faces and said "Hello" to him—even Callie.

Ellis Brodie blotted his face with his sleeve and waved in recognition and walked over to the Jeep,. "Well, well, well, look who's here. Does this mean you're going to give this place another try?"

Everyone laughed, and Kurt said, "We've been here lots of times."

"I've never seen you, and I'm doing a timber survey right around here. Or maybe I just didn't recognize you in that new rig. That's quite a machine, but it means you won't need rescuing anymore."

Sara beamed. "Maybe we can rescue you the next time."

He gave Sara a wink then turned to Meg and chuckled. "Maybe I'll just have to let you do that."

Meg said proudly "We bought the Turner place." She gestured behind her. "And those grinding gears you hear back there are coming from the moving van with all our stuff. This is our moving day."

He looked incredulous. "Whoa there, you're going too fast. You say *you* bought that place? I heard the place sold, but I didn't know who bought it. That's really great. Congratulations." He stuck his big hand through the open window, grabbed Meg's hand and pumped it vigorously. He winked at her. "This means you won't have to break in now."

Meg finally extracted her hand and laughed with pleasure. "Your words of welcome are nice to hear, Mr. Brodie." Looking over her shoulder and seeing that the van was catching up again, she added, "I'm afraid we're going to have to leave now. My youngest daughter is running a fever and we need to get her settled. It was nice to see you, and thank you again for helping us that day." Smiling broadly, she ducked her head back inside the Jeep's window, and after a flustered grind of gears, she once more pulled on ahead. In the rearview mirror she saw him looking after the Jeep, a grin still on his face.

. . .

As they turned onto the final stretch of road, where the old wagon road left the clearing, Callie, sitting right behind Meg, called out. "Is that the Canada lynx?" She pointed over Meg's shoulder to the trees on their left.

Meg jammed on the brakes and stopped the Jeep just as Sara said, "No!"

Kurt said quietly, "That's not a lynx, Cal, that's a bear!"

Meg didn't see it until it moved its head to look at the van behind them. The dark brown bear, with a small patch of white on its chest, was there at the edge of the trees, no more than fifty feet from the car. In the shadows, and with the underbrush up around its legs, it was hard to judge its size, but there was no doubt about it being fully-grown. Shorty saw it too, and honked his horn. At that, the bear stood up on its hind legs and looked from one vehicle to the other. Then it dropped back down onto four feet, in a measured motion that sent a ripple through the muscles of its shoulders and along the fur on its back. The bear looked to its right and let out a short "woof" and two tiny cubs came tumbling toward it through the brush. By the time they reached their mother, she was already moving, and the three of them ran quickly up the road ahead of the Jeep, in the direction of the house. Turning a bend, they disappeared from view.

Within the car there had been a sharp intake of air, in unison, when the bear stood up, and a jumble of "Ohhhs" when they saw the cubs. But now there was a heavy silence, as everyone considered the possibilities of what they had just seen. Callie put her hand on Meg's neck. In a strained voice that sounded like she couldn't quite catch her breath, she said, "You said there weren't any bears up here."

Flinching at Callie's accusation—or what she interpreted as an accusation—and assuming that Callie had pretty much spoken for everyone in the car, Meg took a breath and answered, "I did say that, didn't I? When I told you that I didn't think bears would be this close to town. I'm afraid I spoke without knowing for sure. But I still think they are too smart to want to hang around people. You saw how smart that mother bear and her cubs were, running away from us."

Callie said, in a constricted voice, "But they're going to our house."

Trying to recover, Meg said, "I'm sure they will turn off into the trees before they get there. But now that we've actually seen one, we're going to have to be careful, like we always are."

As she started up the road again, she thought, what Callie didn't know—or anyone else, for that matter—was that no more than an hour after reassuring Callie, that night after the picnic, she had found out that there certainly were bears here—at least one. In fact, it was near this very spot, and, quite possibly, it was the same bear.

But what had she brought her children to? An occasional glimpse of a bear was one thing, but a mother bear and her cubs in the vicinity of the house put a whole different light on the children playing as they had that first day they saw the house. She wondered now what other dangers were awaiting her children? Here they were, not even in the house yet, and already the rules for living here had changed.

As she drove on, even though no one said anything, she could feel the children looking behind every tree and clump of bushes they passed—anticipating another glimpse of the bears. And she did, too, as though keeping the bears in view would keep them safe. When the road ran along the top of the clearing, Meg slowed down even more, and they strained their eyes to see if the bears could be there. As they approached the house she expected them to be there ahead of them, maybe even guarding its entrance. But the bears had disappeared without a trace. The vegetation, orderly and still, was keeping their secret.

When Meg stopped the Jeep to climb out to unlock the garage door, she tried her best to hide her nervousness. Kurt and Sara bounced out of the Jeep and disappeared into the garage. She heard them pound up the stairs into the safety of the house. Callie now lay on the back seat holding her blanket up to her closed eyes, sucking fingers that hadn't been in her mouth for years. Meg, now feeling almost sick herself, let her stay there while she unloaded the stuff in the Jeep, dumping it anywhere inside the garage. And, behind her, she watched the van begin to position itself across the road, like some giant's gate, to start the unloading process. She wondered if she dared leave the garage doors open through all of this. Would the bears just walk in? She finally decided, no, they wouldn't.

Once she finished unloading the Jeep, she scooped up Callie and her blanket and carried her through the garage and up the stairs. By the time she got to the top of the stairs in the dining room, she knew she was going to have to turn right around and go back to town: Callie was in trouble. She was limp in Meg's arms, having difficulty breathing, burning with fever, and her eyes, when she did open them, were no longer holding steady. Meg carried her into the kitchen and laid her carefully down on the kitchen counter. Callie just lay there, not moving, and Meg spread her little blanket over her, trying to think what to do first. Call the doctor. She advised the operator it was an emergency and asked to have the doctor call back immediately. Then she called loudly for Kurt and Sara to come quickly. They clattered downstairs, having heard the alarm in their mother's voice.

Meg said, "Kurt, go get Shorty. Tell him to come up right away. Callie's really sick and we've got to drive back down and get Callie to the doctor. Tell him to have one of the other men move the truck so it isn't blocking the road. Hurry."

Kurt ran down the stairs and out the front door.

To Sara, Meg said, "That stack of towels we brought here to clean, find some of the ones we didn't use and take them to my bathroom. Run about six inches of cool water into the tub. I've got to give Callie a cool bath to bring down her fever fast. I'll stay here with Callie because the doctor is going to call me back. Do it now, Sara."

In a few moments, Shorty and Kurt came into the kitchen. Just as she was about to explain, the phone rang and she gestured for them to listen to what she was going to tell the doctor.

After hearing Meg's description, the doctor told her to bring Callie to the hospital immediately. Meg told him she was forty minutes away from the hospital. He advised her that there was no time for a cold bath and suggested she wrap her in wet towels for the trip down.

After she hung up the phone, Meg stood there rocking Callie and looking indecisive. To Kurt and Sara and Shorty she said, "I have to take Callie to the hospital, which means we have a problem here. Shorty, you need to unload our furniture and I have to leave. What I'm trying to figure out is how to do all this."

Kurt said, "Ma, you and Sara take Cal in and I'll show Shorty where the furniture and stuff goes. Can't we read the labels on the boxes and figure things out?"

Meg said, "How can I leave you alone here to do that? I might be down there a long time."

Sara said, "Ma, let me stay here too. You take Cal. We'll be okay. I can help."

Meg looked imploringly at Shorty. And before she could say anything more. Shorty said, "I've had young-uns of my own, Missus. You trusted me with your dishes and I reckon you can trust me here with these young-uns of yours, too. Now you take that sick little-un of yours to the doc and leave the rest to me and the boy here. We'll keep good track of this little gal—maybe she can find us something to eat and dig up some coffee. I'll help her."

Meg had no reason not to trust this man, but to leave Kurt and Sara behind with him? She said, "But I don't know when I'll be back.

What if I don't get back until late?"

"Ma, don't worry about us," reassured Kurt. He looked around and smiled. "We're here, aren't we? This is the best place in the whole world."

"Sure, bears and all—"

"Gee, yes. Isn't that neat? Sara and I ran upstairs to see if we could see them from the windows upstairs. But we couldn't. Maybe tonight they'll come out again."

Meg blinked. When the two of them had torn off like that she had thought they were afraid. "Listen to me, those bears know we're here now. If we're careful and respectful of them, we'll all get along fine. But you stay away from the road until I get back. A mother animal is really aggressive and might assume you want to hurt her cubs. Promise me you won't be foolish. Until we decide how to live near them, you must be very careful."

She chewed on her lip as she studied the serious, upturned faces of her two oldest children, then studied Shorty's earnest face, too, before making her decision, "Yes, Sara, you can stay here with Kurt. I have no doubt it will be best. You keep an eye out for the boxes labeled "bedding" and put them by the beds. The food for the refrigerator is in those ice chests. While you put it away, find something to eat. Remember, that's a gas stove over there and you've never had a gas stove. Shorty, could you please show them how it works? You kids have good sense, so use it every minute. If you don't know about something, ask Shorty or each other first. I can leave you only if I think you'll be all right." She stopped talking and drew a big breath. "Kurt, if you build a fire make sure you open the draft first. Oh, you know that. You two kids are the greatest. I'll be back just as soon as I can."

She turned to Shorty. "For all I care you can drop all those cartons down both flights of stairs, but these two kids... Please keep an eye on these kids for me, will you?"

Shorty rubbed his hand over his chin and said, gravely, "I'll watch 'em, Missus. But I tell you, I gotta leave real soon after we unload. I'll stay as long as I can, but I got to get the truck to Kooskie, Ide-ho, by morning, to pick up another load, and it's a long haul gettin' there. We'll wait as long as we can—maybe wait here 'til 6:00. I don't hardly know how we could stay longer, and still get this rig to Ide-ho on time. Will these young-uns be all right if we leave at 6:00?"

Meg said, "Yes. If you could just stay until then I think Kurt and Sara will be fine. I'll appreciate anything you can do before you leave. But now, I have to take care of Callie."

. . .

Meg was almost down the mountain when she saw the man's Forest Service truck heading toward her. As it drew alongside she slowed and, leaning out the window, said, "I can't stop. I'm taking my daughter to the hospital." She accelerated and sped away.

Callie didn't even try to open her eyes now, but lay curled into the wad of wet towels on the seat, fighting for every breath. Meg looked at her when she could, without slowing down. "Callie baby, you hang on. Please, please, please, don't let anything happen to you. I couldn't stand it."

Never had any of her children been this sick before. She had thought it was the usual sore throat that heralded a cold, but this was something altogether different. Callie was fighting for her life, her little lungs struggling for air.

. . .

Once in Clark Fork, she slowed at every stop sign and light, but only long enough to be sure nothing was coming. It didn't take long to get to the hospital, and she stopped in front of the emergency entrance, gathered Callie up, and rushed inside. When the nurse saw Callie's labored breathing, she called for help. Meg placed Callie on a gurney as a doctor strode over, shouting orders.

After a hasty examination the doctor opened Callie's mouth and carefully looked inside. "Her tongue is red and her throat is almost swollen shut. There's a real war going on inside there. We can't wait for a culture, so I'll have to guess on this one. I say she has a strep infection, a particularly virulent one. As long as she's not allergic to anything, I'm going to start her on a broad-spectrum antibiotic." He gave Meg a direct look. "If we're lucky, this will get it; if we're not, well, we'll have to intubate her before her airway shuts. Don't worry. We'll watch her like a hawk. There'll be a nice comfortable rocking chair right by her bed for you, Mrs. Halverson. You can relax in it while you watch her."

But once they got Callie to her room and into her bed, Meg tucked the blanket around her and picked her up, being careful not to disrupt the IV in her small arm. By feeling Callie and hearing her, she would be the first to know of any changes that someone else might miss. And besides, having her child lying against her was something she understood, and Callie would understand it too. When the nurse saw the look on Meg's face she didn't argue.

As the two of them rocked back and forth in the chair, Meg looked at the translucence of her daughter's eyelids and thought of Papa. She couldn't help him, but Callie was different. She watched the drip-drip of the IV solution going steadily into Callie's arm and judged her every breath, envisioning molecules of O_2 and CO_2 moving through membranes, and listening for any strictures to the process. As she did this a little thread of a song struggled to form in her mind: George Gershwin's song, "Summertime." She knew the tune, but searching out the words was like restringing a necklace: the words lay like a scattering of beads and the melody was the string. Soon she had them all put together and it was a whole song, and she sang it—small and self-consciously at first, because people were coming in and out of the room. But when she had to repeat it, she sang it stronger and surer.

Back and forth she rocked, back and forth, singing her song-wish, making her promise for Callie's life with it. At some point, Meg asked the nurse in charge to call the house for her, but what time it was she couldn't say; her watch was still on the kitchen counter. She was relieved when the nurse reported that everything was fine there.

The light in the room altered, lights went on, and people peered down at Callie, listening and measuring. They could see her breathing easier, and when they touched her forehead they knew she was much cooler. Twice Callie's eyes fluttered open, and she smiled and reached up her hand to her mother's face; Meg bent down to kiss Callie's little palm. Meg shifted Callie's small body a bit now and then, easing a cramp, but still she sang or hummed or whispered all those words over and over again, *"—But 'til that morning, there's a-nothin' can harm you, so hush, little baby, don't you cry."*

Martha, the nurse, came in carrying a small can of juice, and, for what seemed like the hundredth time, listened to Callie's breathing and took her temperature. She showed Meg the thermometer reading, but Meg didn't have to see it to know that Callie was better. Martha said, "I think you can put her down now and get up for a stretch. She'll sleep fine now. She knows you're here. Go ahead. I can't sing to her, but I'll stay with her."

Meg finally agreed and got up with difficulty, relinquishing Callie to the bed and covering her with the cool, crisp sheet. Standing up felt so good. Working the kinks out of her arms, she creaked into the bathroom and back.

She told Martha that she needed to call her other children and asked where that phone was located. "And what time is it? I took off my watch when I was bathing Callie and never put it back on."

"It's night, Mrs. Halverson. It's almost 10:30."

She hadn't been aware of time. Sara and Kurt would be asleep by now and she wouldn't call and wake them up. All day her thoughts had hardly strayed from Callie, but now that she had laid her down, concerns for her other two flooded her mind and tore her in two again. Martha's report that the kids were fine had helped, but she still felt suspended between valley floor and mountain slope, hospital and home, Callie here and Kurt and Sara there, even though she could only do one thing at a time.

When she told the doctor that she had left her other two children alone on the mountain, his face hardly hid his harsh judgment of her. She told him, "I had to decide what to do. You don't know my kids." Even so, he had turned his face away.

She remembered how Ma and Papa had just plain trusted her. When their trust wavered, she wavered; but when their trust was strong, she never doubted she could do what was expected of her. Kurt and Sara and Callie were normal kids and could be scamps at times, but all three were obedient and trustworthy. Living up there on the mountain was going to be like this, hopefully not as bad as this, but *like* this.

Greatly reassured by the sight of Callie sleeping, Meg said to Martha, "I need to see my two other children at home. Would Callie have a setback if I left now? If I was needed, I could be back in two hours. The desk has my phone number."

Martha said, "By all means, go. We'll take care of her. But, first, wake her and tell her you're going."

Meg leaned over and called softly until Callie opened her eyes. She croaked out a "Hi, Ma." Swallowing with difficulty and talking in an uneven kind of verbal shorthand, Callie said, "You…sing…to…me." Her eyes looked around the room and she raised her eyebrows, rather than ask.

Meg said, "Yes, honey. We've been here for a long time. You are in a nice room here in the hospital, and this nurse's name is Martha, and she'll be right here. I want to ask you something, Callie. I need to go and see how Sara and Kurt are. Would you mind if I went back to the mountain tonight to see them?"

Some tears squeezed out of the corners of Callie's eyes and plunked into the pillow. "I…remember…I heard." She nodded her head and swallowed with difficulty, then looked intently at her mother and asked, "Back tomorrow?"

"Yes, I'll be back tomorrow, first thing."

"—Sing Summer again?"

Meg laughed down at her and said, "Sing *Summertime*, yes. I'll sing it until you're absolutely sick of it." Callie smiled at that. Meg added, "You keep getting well so we can get you back to summertime on the mountain."

Callie again spoke with difficulty, "Will…bears…come…again?"

"Yes, I'm quite sure we'll see them again." Meg asked her, seriously, "Is that scary?"

Callie croaked out, "No. Better than bears…in books." She smiled.

Meg laughed, "You're going to be okay, you little imp."

"Tell Sara and Kurt 'Hi.'" She gave Meg a long hug before settling back.

Meg whispered, "Good night, my little sweetie. I'll see you tomorrow. Sleep well. Get better. How will we ever get unpacked without you?" But her last comments had been wasted. Callie had closed her eyes and was making soft sound-asleep sounds.

22

THE NIGHT

With the last lighted window far behind her and no other reminder of the civilized world, the Jeep felt like a spaceship, bullet-shaped, its headlights hollowing a tunnel in the night. The eerie green of the dashboard dials and the low, incessant throb of the engine only intensified the feeling. Once Meg crossed the boundary that marked the beginning of her property and began the steep climb, the tunnel of light crumbled off into space on either side of her and she felt airborne.

The ping of a rock hitting the front fender, followed by the startling materialization of two mirror-eyed deer at the road's edge, warned her to slow down. She told herself one more time that the faith she had placed in Shorty was intuition-born, not casually given, and she would get to the house and find Sara and Kurt were all right and blissfully asleep. Even the nurse, Martha, had reassured her that this was so. So it was going to be all right, and she didn't have to hurry.

As she drove more slowly along the dark road, she had a quiet laugh on herself. This late June night was all that remained of a day she had imagined so differently. She had often pictured this first day of living on the mountain. In that picture, her children were always playing contentedly in the meadow, while she, arms outstretched, like some kind of dark-haired, blue jeans–attired Julie Andrews, was walking slowly through the grass toward them. With a song on her lips and the strains of a full orchestra accompanying her, she would possess this wilderness, her eyes looking around, owning every blade of grass and leaf and rock and tree. In that picture she had appeared huge and powerful on the mountainside, but tiny in the giant bowl of this part of Montana, and hardly visible in the greater scheme of things on earth.

Even so, she would announce, "Well, I'm here." Then she'd stand there, waiting for some kind of recognition for her accomplishment—but from whom this could come she didn't know.

She scoffed at her impudent imagination and, with an ironic chuckle, compared that fairy tale to the crashing realities of this moment. Here she was: weary beyond weary, clothes wrinkled, body sweaty, teeth scummy, famished and thirsty, deeply lonely, and hunkered over the steering wheel of a Jeep moving through a darkness that she was uncertain of. Add to that, somewhere on the other side of the Jeep's windows, roamed a bear that made her skin crawl.

The thought of its existence had been manageable until this morning when she actually saw it and its two cubs. Despite her attention to Callie's struggle to breath in the hospital, one corner of her brain kept replaying the image of that animal. Each time, the mother bear's eyes looked at her in recognition, and said, "Oh-ho, it's you. We've met before. Remember?" And Meg could only nod in confirmation.

She had guessed the animal was of medium size until it stood up and whirled around and came jolting down—all claws and power and that ominous rippling of the fur-covered muscle along its back. Once the bear and its cubs had disappeared down the road she was shocked to realize that what she had thought of as her children's fear was, more precisely, her own. The children—as Callie had reminded her a short time ago—were hardly beyond the bears-in-books stage, while she—one human mother and three children—was looking at the reality of sharing a mountainside with one bear mother and two cubs. Not a pretty thought.

She vividly remembered her fear the night of the picnic, when circumstances had forced her to leave the security of the group and, equipped only with that failing flashlight, push her way through that mess of underbrush to a road she hardly remembered. Her very worst fears had come true when she had become aware of the presence of the bear. Yet, the bear had turned away from her, even though it must have sensed her fear and knew it was bigger and more powerful than she was. It had chosen not to confront her—not out of any charity, but probably from some built-in instinct about not confronting humans if at all possible. Hopefully, in the future, she could depend on that.

Despite the property's proximity to town, it lay on the edge of a virtual wilderness of miles and miles of forestlands to the south and east of her property; and she knew of no other roads nearby, other than the two on her property. With all that, so far she had seen one bear and two cubs, a Canada lynx, many deer, several elk, and often heard coyotes. She knew there were mountain lions in the area because there had been newspaper reports of sightings and stories of their wandering into Clark Fork over the years. She thought back to that day of the picnic, of her feeling of being observed, even though they had seen nothing but birds. Considering how skillfully animals could avoid being seen, she estimated that the number of wild animals on her 1,028 acres was probably great; and, by now, those animals couldn't help but know she and her family were here. The word "co-existence" popped into her mind, and she stored it for future reference.

To a person as fearful of the dark as she was, that word was strangely comforting. She looked at the deep darkness outside the Jeep's windows. In town, she could imagine herself saying, "What a lovely night!" But up here, with night being so pitch-black and so frightening, would it ever appear to be lovely?

She had pushed the thought of the darkness away like an untidy detail she would solve in the future. But now she looked at it. Would nights up here mean she would always have one ear cocked for the slightest noise? Would night be a scuttling from one safety to another—the Jeep to the house and then fourteen miles of uncertainty between the house and town? Would night be a house full of lamps blasting their light? Would it feel safe only with a gun by the door? Would it be eight hours of huddling under the covers until dawn lit the rooms with safety? Could she live like that and risk passing on her fears to her children? She thought not; it would diminish all their lives. If there was even a remote possibility that nights here would be a time of terror, they would all be better off under the ever-present lights of the town—and they had chosen to leave the town.

Somewhere in her mind she realized she had already begun to come to grips with her fear of darkness, but she needed to challenge herself to be sure. She slowed the Jeep to a crawl and looked uncertainly outside its window. Even in town, night had seemed to reduce her to a possible victim, having removed her sense of sight and reminded her that her nose only supported breathing and spectacles, being quite unable to sniff danger.

About a quarter of a mile from the house, at the very place where they had spotted the mother bear and cubs, she stopped the Jeep and turned off the motor. Then she turned off the headlights. She rolled down the window, peering out from the safety of the Jeep, seeing the darkness as a curtain, but trying to think of it as three-dimensional and feel what it contained. As her eyes became accustomed to the dark she saw the great hulking shapes of trees on either side of the road. She opened the door and touched her feet to the ground tentatively, then willed herself to leave the car.

Shutting its door quietly, she stood beside it, still resting her hand on the door, like a wary umbilical cord. Finally, she let go and walked boldly five steps away and just stood there. She held her breath and listened for any sound that might indicate danger, trying to sense movement or the physical presence of danger as she had that night of the picnic.

Finally, she exhaled and laughed. In the soft, still, pine-fragrant night, her laugh was a small sound, but the biggest one around. She took another deep breath and held it, listening attentively. Off to her right the scrambling of a tiny creature, a falling leaf, a bird flutter, a distant "who-who-who," a string of tiny croaks, and more little rustlings. She laughed again and relaxed, thinking, if I can try not to breathe I can hear the night. At that, she strode further from the Jeep and felt her body relax..

Above her, the night sky, away from any competition from the lights of town, spread out blue-black and star-punched, with even the tiniest garlands of stars visible and brilliant next to the formidable giants known to her. From her viewpoint, the stars appeared to be eternally constant—visible at night, invisible during the day, seen or unseen, but always there. It was the earth that was ever-changing as it kept to its path through the sky—exploding, eroding, evolving, buried in ice, flooded, dinosaured, then mammaled, and now overburdened with too many people and facing a dubious future. Yet, whatever had gone on before this moment, she, as an earthling looking at the vastness above her, felt a connection with all those uncountable billions of earthlings who had gone before her; who had gazed upon these same stars and asked, "Who are we? What are you? Are we connected and, if so, by what?"

She said to the sky, "Well, here I am." Her words sounded like they might not quite reach the stars, but they sounded fine to her. So she said it again, a little louder, a little braver, "Well, here I am. I made it."

A shiver ran down her spine at her question. She wondered why she was standing on this mountain, and why she was alone. Was it only an accident that she found this particular mountainside that day and found such comfort here? It never seemed like an accident. Rather, it seemed that every step of her life had been moving toward being here, and that standing here in the middle of the dark talking to the sky was all a part of it, too.

Maybe it couldn't be explained. Maybe it didn't even need explaining, but it seemed to her that this particular mountain had pulled aside its curtain of green and beckoned her to come inside, as a mother would who recognizes her child's sounds and needs, saying, "This is my child." And Meg thought, "Oh, Mountain, comfort me, protect me, as I shall try to protect you. Restore me to fullness in this touching earth, touching sky place."

She stood a little longer in the lovely gift of night then returned to the car to drive home to her new beginning.

23

HOMECOMING

As Meg drove the final stretch of road, she could feel her excitement rising. She was finally going to her very first, very own home, and not even her present weariness could lessen her anticipation of the fun she and the kids would have arranging every last detail as they wanted—put this here and that there and no need to justify it to Ed or anyone else ever again. She could hardly put into words why making such decisions were so important, but they were. She couldn't wait to put her signature on everything.

At age 38, she felt it was about time she had her own place. She'd gone from living in Ma and Papa's home on the farm to the Halverson House, and to the house she'd left. And in none of those places was she free to make her own choices. All the decisions in the original Halverson House had been made long ago and change was not an option. In fact, Ed had advised her that should she wish to change a faucet or update the water closet (that's what they'd called it and that's what it was), she would have to apply to the local historic preservation committee. Although she was the one who had forced their move from that red brick monstrosity to the big, new house in the town behind her, Ed had seen to it that the final word on its decoration was all his. He'd hired decorators from Spokane to decide on colors and fabrics and furniture, and then used their suggestions for the placement of the furniture. In a silent battle, if she moved something she could count on it being returned to exactly where it had been. Such things were little defeats, but defeats nevertheless. But, now, this was all hers and she was overjoyed with the opportunity to make it all her own.

Turning the last corner of the road, she saw a tiny, welcoming spot of light coming from the window facing the road. It was obviously for her, and just the thought of Kurt and Sara placing it there before they went to bed lifted her as nothing else could. She guided the Jeep toward it, as though to a beacon.

Drawing closer, the Jeep's lights picked out a strange car parked in front of the garage. It was small and old, and it should not be there. A hundred concerns raced through her mind: Were the children all right? Had they not locked the door? Was something else wrong? There were no neighbors around. Had one of the movers come back? Her apprehension grew when she saw, beyond the lamp and deeper into the room, the form of a man illuminated in a flicker of light.

Despite the fears she had dealt with back on the road, a new concern flashed into her mind: the front door was undoubtedly barred on the inside, so she would have to enter the dark garage and make her way up the stairs to find out who he was. She felt unprepared to do that, but, of course, she would. She was fumbling for the key to the garage when she heard the sound of the front door opening and a man's voice called out, "Mrs. Halverson, it's me, Brodie. There's no need to go through the garage. Come in this way."

She answered, "Mr. Brodie? Then that's your car?" She walked uncertainly toward his voice. When she saw him framed in a jagged stab of light in the doorway, an odd, unwanted thought came into her mind: that the fears she had just taunted were not behind her on the dark road, but might be here. In an unsteady voice she asked, "Are my kids all right?"

"Sure, they're fine." He held out his hand and helped her up the stone step. "In fact, I just checked on them and they're so sound asleep a grizzly bear couldn't wake them. How's your little daughter?"

"Callie's much better, and she's asleep. That's why I could come home. But, Mr. Brodie, you really should have called and told me you were here." She knew she sounded irritated, and she was sorry about that, but she didn't want people she hardly knew to feel they could walk into her house unannounced and without permission—that was part of what Shorty had promised. Otherwise, how could she protect her kids? Still troubled and unwilling to let it go, she went on, "How long have you been here? When I asked Callie's nurse to call, she said that a little girl had answered the phone, but she didn't mention your being here."

As he closed the door behind her, he gave her an impatient smile that could only be interpreted as overly paternalistic. "If I've upset you, I'm sorry. Things were pretty hectic here, with the movers and all."

"I'm sure, but you know how mothers are. Or do you? I remember you telling us, that day on the road, that you didn't have any kids of your own, so you might not understand how I feel about this." She hated how overprotective she must appear, and, judging from the look on his face, he clearly thought she was. Other than the fact that he worked for the Forest Service, she knew nothing about him. Then again, she supposed she'd just have to go with her first impressions of him, which had been good. And he'd surely been helpful. She sighed and asked, in her calmest tone, "Have you been here long?"

"Most of the day, yes."

"But your job, your wife? Do you live close by?"

"I live in town and I'm not married. As for my job, I have a lot of comp time coming to me and I wanted to help. Moving the furniture and boxes gave me a great workout." He gestured proudly around him, as though showing her around his own house, and began an enthusiastic explanation of why he'd put the couch in front of the bookcase and had the movers switch the big sideboard to that particular wall of the dining area on the balcony, rather than where Kurt had wanted it. He was beginning to tell her where he'd put some of the lamps when he realized he wasn't getting any response. He looked closely at her and asked, "Are you all right?"

Still feeling fractious, she said, more to herself than to him, "Just give me a minute. I wasn't expecting—"

"You weren't expecting me to be on this side of the door, I'll bet."

She gave him an ironic nod. "You're right there. But forgive me. I'm tired and it's late and I've been in a state all day, what with Callie's emergency and my having to leave my kids up here alone with strangers. My motherhood has been greatly tested today." She added, almost wistfully, "And, to tell you the truth, I wanted to be here for the move...you know, just be here, to see my things transferred from there to here. I've waited a long time for this."

"I'm afraid I don't know the feeling, having never owned my own place. But I'm happy I could help, Mrs. Halverson."

Meg looked at the earnestness on his young face. "I'm sure you did. Thank you." Now that she knew for sure that Kurt and Sara were okay—that everything was okay—well, she'd have to give this young man credit. He really had helped. In thinking that, she felt herself relent a bit. After all, it wasn't his fault she was so protective of the kids and so possessive of the house; he didn't know her history.

With that, she turned to see what he had done to the room he was so proud of—this room she'd wrested from Mrs. Turner, and from Art Stroud, too, and that she held a paid-in-full receipt for. Even if she hadn't been the one to actually do the work of moving into it, this room, lit in pretty firelight and the glow of the far lamp, offered the very same promise of safety it had that first night they'd found it. And, despite the chaos of unpacked cartons stacked against the walls, and furniture grouped uncertainly about it, there was no doubt that her life and that of her children was now firmly ensconced in this odd but powerful house. After all, she and the kids could still make the real choices. She ran her hand over the fabric of a loveseat, her favorite, that was pulled invitingly near the fire. But she resisted the impulse to sit down, saying, "I really need to see my kids." She hurried up the stairs to the balcony and headed to their rooms.

First she went into Sara's room. Without turning on the light she laid her hand on her cheek, feeling it warm and soft as it moved with her breathing. Satisfied that she was safe, Meg kissed her. Then she went in to see Kurt. He was out of the covers and as she lifted the quilt over him he looked up sleepily. "Hi, Ma. Is Cal okay?"

As she assured him that Callie was, she knelt down and kissed him. He said happily, "We got moved in. Did you see?"

"Yes, dear, I saw. You did such a wonderful job. Thank you." At that Kurt turned over and was again asleep. Meg closed the door, relieved beyond words, and walked back down the stairs to Ellis and the fire. In words filled with gratitude, she said, "They *are* fine," and sat down on the edge of the loveseat. Seeing him still standing, looking shy and uncertain now, she said,"Forgive me. Please, sit down and tell me about all this."

He hesitated before answering,"Well, like you said, it's late and I better get going so you can get some sleep."Yet, in spite of his words, he began clearing off the seat of the big chair next to the loveseat, then pulled it closer to the fire and settled into it.

Meg said,"You obviously met Shorty. Did the move go well? Were the kids helpful?"

"Yes to all your questions. But, look, Meg... May I call you Meg? You call me Ellis. Before I get into that, I unearthed this fancy bottle of brandy when Punkin and I were looking for a frying pan. I helped myself to it after I got the kids to bed. Could I pour you some to make this welcome official?"

With only a nod Meg watched him splash her expensive and potent, special-occasion brandy into his cup, and then into another cup, which she could only surmise was there in anticipation of her return.Taking the cup politely, she couldn't help remarking, with more irony than she would otherwise use,"You move *my* furniture and greet me at *my* door, and now you offer me *my* best brandy. Are you always this generous?"

Unfazed,he raised his cup in salute and said,"Doorman,bartender, babysitter, furniture shuffler—and all along you probably thought I just drove around counting trees."

She answered, "We've had no opportunity to get acquainted, other than the obvious things. I have no idea what you do for the Forest Service." She took a big mouthful of the brandy and held it in her mouth for a moment, then swallowed it slowly, feeling its delicious heat all the way to her stomach. "This might hit me hard. Other than a can of juice at the hospital, I haven't eaten since this morning at the house in town—how can it be that long ago? I seem to have lost track of time."

She looked at her cup and took another swallow. "I'd forgotten how good this is, and so is this fire.This is more of a homecoming than I expected." She touched her head briefly to the back of the loveseat's cushion, then thought better of it and sat stiffly forward again. "I expected to check on the kids, plan out what to do about tomorrow, and go to bed." She tried to speak with the authority the situation seemed to require, but with weariness dragging at her every word, and now the brandy, she felt the last of her reserve slip away, and she relaxed back into the seductive softness of the cushion.

He said, "The kids filled me in about Callie and what the doctor said. When I saw you on the road—"

"It was scary getting her to the hospital. She was struggling to breathe. But I got her there in time, and they knew just what to do. She's going to be fine now." She gave him a smile. "I interrupted you. You were telling me about your being here."

"Yes, right after you sped past me I came up to see what the situation was. Shorty, the mover, was at my truck before I even turned off the ignition. The Forest Service emblem on the door helped a little, but there was no way I'd get past him into the house. When your kids came out and identified me, Shorty relaxed and allowed me a few words with them, but only as long as he was there, too. He wasn't about to trust anyone. What did you tell him?"

Meg smiled proudly, "I asked him—a perfect stranger—to watch over them. I'm pleased he did. But you stayed on?"

"Well, after talking to the kids and hearing Shorty say he would have to leave by 6:00, I thought my time could be better spent up here. So I went back to headquarters in town and checked out and came back."

Meg nodded and, sincerely thankful, said, "You've been a great help. In fact, it looks like you rescued us again."

He laughed, and after a moment said, "Those kids of yours were all business. Kurt checked off the furniture on the lists the movers had made and issued directions as to what went where. And Punkin, she made sandwiches and soup and something *resembling* coffee for us, even though she could hardly reach the counter. She kept pulling a chair around to stand on. Shorty and I had to laugh. With those two kids there was never any doubt as to who was in charge."

She smiled at him. "They're so great...I can hardly say how I feel about them." As she spoke she was embarrassed to feel a constriction in her throat, and tears that had been hovering dangerously in the background all day spilled from her eyes. Unable to stop them, she put her head in her hands and just let them come. In a moment, Ellis was crouching in front of her and she felt his hand on her arm. Just knowing he was there triggered another wave of tears.

At last she pulled herself together and spoke, interrupted by an occasional catch in her breathing, "Forgive me. It usually takes a lot for me to cry. It's partly from feeling sorry for myself. The hardest thing about today was that I had to make a choice. With Callie so sick and the movers here, I couldn't be both up here with Kurt and Sara and down in town with Callie. And now I'm home and *all* my kids are okay, and-and it's so nice to be here in front of this fire…and not be alone." She wished fervently she hadn't said that, so she laughed and said, "Good Lord, I *am* feeling sorry for myself."

Ellis, sitting uncomfortably on his heels in front of her, reached out his hand and gently pushed a wet strand of hair off her cheek, then dug out his handkerchief and applied it awkwardly to her wet chin, before handing it over for her to do. When he stood up he asked, "Feeling better?"

Wiping her face and dabbing at the front of her blouse, she nodded, "Yes, I'm fine. The brandy might have helped bring that on, but I guarantee it wasn't the cause."

"I better get going. I have a long drive ahead of me." He put out his hands and helped her up. Still holding hands, and looking at each other, he said, "You're beautiful, Meg," and he bent down and gave her a quick kiss.

She let go of his hands and backed away, even though she longed to be touched again—oh, yes, be touched again, his hand on her face again, and another kiss, but longer this time and holding her tightly against him. She said a little breathlessly, "I appreciate your coming back and helping, Ellis. I'm sure the kids appreciated it, too."

As he was going toward the door, he stopped and turned to her. "Look, you mentioned you hadn't eaten since breakfast. Your daughter and I positively identified a box of food and put it in the refrigerator.

You go wash your face while I round up something in the kitchen. Go ahead. Go on. Let me do this."

Still conflicted by the emotions his being here had created, but aching from hunger, too, she searched for the words to refuse his offer. Unable to summon up anything reasonable, she went up the stairs to the balcony and, turning to the last door there, went into her bedroom.

Once inside she stopped and looked around. Her new bed was set up just where she wanted it, next to the window looking over the back porch, the one she had thrown the rock through those many weeks ago. And it was all perfectly made up and ready. Sara's ancient pink rabbit with the one frayed ear had been tucked carefully into it, its head on the pillow and the sheet and comforter pulled up to where its nose used to be. Meg smiled at that, guessing that Sara had put it there to welcome her home. It was a generous gesture, considering the fact that Sara never went to bed without it. Meg also knew that someone had helped Sara make the bed, and that could only have been Ellis Brodie.

On her bathroom counter she found a clean hand towel and one of her new bars of soap, unwrapped. Beside them lay her hairbrush and cosmetics, all neatly unpacked and orderly—and she knew that neither Sara nor Kurt, as thoughtful as they were, had done something as precise and personal as that. She stood blinking at them, trying to sort out her feelings. Having someone else—and a man at that—even think of laying things out for her touched her in a curious way.

When had that ever happened? It certainly had never dawned on Ed to do that. But, aside from that, to her, Ellis Brodie had crossed some arbitrary line somehow, just as his being here and showing her around her own living room had. And then that damned kiss, and him using that "beautiful" word on her. And in that moment, she had longed for more, longed for his arms around her, longed to be touched by him, longed to be cradled and crooned to... That confident young man, tall, blond, good looking, and utterly incorrigible... How could all those traits come in one person?

Even so, everything he did seemed to upset her. New tears filled her eyes, and she quickly grabbed the towel and buried her face in it, scrubbing her skin hard to distract herself from crying. She couldn't remember when she'd been so bewildered: feeling angry and resentful one moment and, in the next, feeling giddy and nearly undone by that briefest of all kisses—even though he had no right, and she hadn't asked for him to do that.

In her current state, she had about as much resistance as an iron shaving confronting a magnet—and that was the trouble. How in heaven's name could being around a little testosterone throw her into such a state? Was this what the world of men and women would be like now? After being married and out of things for eighteen years she guessed she'd forgotten. In fact, she hadn't realized just how safe she had been as a married woman, who didn't need to wonder much about the underlying meaning of things. What she did know was where such things could lead—her marriage was testament enough to that. She shook her head and shivered. Ellis Brodie couldn't be thirty yet, while she was… She didn't finish the thought. Maybe she was right in feeling that stab of fear when she had recognized him in the doorway earlier and felt she might be safer outside in the dark.

Confounded, she seized her toothbrush and furiously brushed her teeth, then splashed cold water on her face until it started to go numb. While patting it dry, she examined her reflection for the tiredness that had dogged her all day. She was appalled to see what excitement had done, as though someone less than cautious had taken over her skin. She brushed her hair until her scalp tingled, then fastened it with her favorite silver clip. Before she left the room she tucked her blouse into her jeans, applied a trace of lipstick, smiled toothily into the mirror, and went back out quite refreshed.

Ellis—whose eyes said, well, look at you—was just emerging from the kitchen. On a cookie sheet he balanced two steaming mugs of soup, some toasted sandwiches, and an apple cut into chunks. Understanding just how ravenous she was, Meg ran down the steps ahead of him and pushed a sturdy carton in front of the loveseat for the cookie sheet, then moved the food around on it so they could sit side-by-side and eat it. Sitting in the short space of the loveseat and touching each other was awkward at first, but in the homey comfort of the moment it seemed the thing to do.

After one bite of the hot, crunchy sandwich, with its runny, melted cheese, she declared the food a feast and insisted he add "kitchen wizard" to his list of accomplishments. Without another word they ate until everything was gone.

This time it was she who took everything, save the brandy and cups, back up to the kitchen. And it was from that vantage point that she saw Ellis move the box away from in front of the loveseat, then bend to add another log to the fire. And rather than sit in the big chair, he resumed his seat in the loveseat and poured the last of the brandy into their cups. Seeing him do that, and anticipating what it might lead to, a feeling of reckless pleasure filled her, even though she mistrusted having something less than reason draw her toward the warmth and beauty of the scene he was creating.

But as she descended the steps, a feeling of caution made her choose to sit in the big chair instead of beside him in the loveseat.

Sipping their brandy slowly and studying the fire as though each of its pops and crackles was important, it was Meg who finally broke the silence. "I have the nicest memory of this room and fireplace, the night we broke in and slept here."

"You mean the night you vandalized this place."

"I never did! It was cold. I was thinking of my family."

His eyes glittered wickedly. "*Mrs. Halverson*, you're a vandal."

"Well, maybe so, but I confessed before you had to grill me," she chuckled. "That brandy, now the food. I'm sinking fast, Ellis. I have to get to bed. I have no idea what time it is. All I know is I've got just a couple hours before I get up again."

Ellis said, "About tomorrow, I mean today—whatever day it is—" he gestured at the boxes "you'll want to be with Callie, so you'll be faced with the same problem of the kids staying here alone. I'd like to help out here again."

"But you've already done too mush. I mean too much. Oh, dear, I can't say the words."

"Call my offer a housewarming gift."

"I guess I couldn't refuse one of those."

Ellis waited a moment then smiled."Thank you for not refusing it. And in view of the long trip down to town, I was wondering if I could stay here tonight?"

Meg inhaled sharply."Oh, I don't think that's the best thing. Really, I don't. You better go home now." Seeing the disappointment on his face, she reconsidered, telling him, "You're right, it's late, and... And with you here I could leave early and wouldn't have to wake the kids." She added quickly,"Somewhere in all this jumble there's Callie's room and bed, and I'm sure we can find you a sleeping bag or something."

He said,"If you mean that room next to yours, Punkin and I made up that bed, too."

A tingle of alarm ran through her, sobering her mind."Your list of talents goes on and on, doesn't it?" Her words ran together no matter how carefully she spoke."Now that that's settled I'm going to bed."

Yawning and stretching comfortably, he said,"Sounds good to me."

As she got up she tripped over the box they'd been using for a table. He reached out and steadied her and they eyed each other warily. He lifted his eyebrow and said,"That's a big dark bedroom up there. Would you like a little company tonight?"

Meg pulled away and gave him a hard look. "I can handle that big dark room all by myself, thank you." She turned away carefully and began turning off the lamps.

Ellis was using the poker to push the log more firmly behind the andirons when she came back; they stood there, together in the dark, watching the few coals. Finally, they left the fireplace and went up the stairs, Ellis first and Meg following, holding tightly to the railing and pulling herself up. After saying "Goodnight" they went into their rooms and closed the doors.

24

ELLIS BRODIE

In the early morning light, Meg longed to look around the house, go down the stairs and open the door to the outside, and fully experience this, her very first morning on the mountain. But here she was, headachy and standing before the door of the room next to hers, distrusting her motives for awakening the man inside it. But she had to leave for the hospital and see Callie, and she had to remind him to listen for the kids and fix their breakfast. And, after last night, she just needed to look him in the eye and explain things—if anything needed to be explained. As helpful as his offer was, to stay over and watch the kids, she had to admit she wasn't comfortable with the arrangement and now wondered if Kurt and Sara should come to the hospital with her. But, now that she'd agreed, how could she do that? If only she'd stuck to her guns and told him that his staying the night was a poor idea.

This whole damn move was so awkward now. If her stomach wasn't so queasy and she had the time, she'd be leaning against the kitchen counter putting food and coffee down her throat or, better yet, sitting outside on the stone doorstep with a plate of toast and eggs and having a whole pot of coffee herself. Maybe then she'd be able to make clear decisions again, like the ones she'd been making since she'd bought this place.

She couldn't remember being so confused—torn this way with Callie and that way with Kurt and Sara and now wondering if she needed to apologize to a stranger about her behavior. She stared at the mug of coffee in her hand, hoping that it and her instructions about the kids were good enough excuses to knock on his door.

After she'd knocked she heard nothing for a full minute. But after knocking quietly again, and whispering, "Mr. Brodie, it's me… uh…Meg?" She heard a large thump, an oath, and then his voice. "Meg Halverson. Yes. Of course." That was followed by a number of other thumps, and then the door suddenly opened. He stood with a sheet wrapped around his lower body and everything above his waist bare. Smiling broadly, he explained, "My clothes are in the bathroom. Sorry."

Meg blinked at him, her one hand still poised to knock again, and the oversized mug of coffee clutched in the other. Looking worriedly at the sheet, she whispered, "It's very early. I'm sorry to wake you, but I'm taking off now. The kids are still sleeping, but if you could listen for them? Tell them I called the hospital and Callie had a good night. I asked when I could bring her home, but the nurse didn't know. Tell them that for me. And feed them, please? Oatmeal and toast, maybe? I laid everything out. They'll eat anything. Tell them I couldn't wait for them to wake up. Now I've got to go." She looked down at the mug. "This is for you," and handed him the coffee.

Keeping his grip on the sheet, Ellis took the cup in a one-handed exchange, and whispered, "Listen, Meg, before the kids wake up could we talk?" At her hesitation, he gestured to a box just inside the door. "It's all right. Just come in and sit down on that for a minute."

She hesitated, cocking her head and listening for any sounds from the kids' rooms, then nodded uncertainly. "Just for a minute." She sat down on the box like someone whose body was present but whose mind was safely somewhere else. She tried not to watch as he gathered the sheet more securely around him before sitting back down on the bed. Peering around the obstruction of the door she laughed for a moment then cleared her throat and told him, "You really look darling in that."

"I'd hoped you'd noticed." At that he reached his bare foot over and pushed at the door to get it out of her way, and before he could stop it, it closed with a decisive click. He said, "Leave it!"

Meg sat back and looked at it, chewing at her lower lip. "I really need to get going."

"Don't worry. You can leave in a minute." Laughing coolly at her concern, he said, "What's that line? 'Here we are alone at last.'"

Without her answer, he took a quick swallow from the mug then handed it to her. She took a sip and passed the cup back and, without another word, they finished it. When Ellis sat the empty mug on the floor he looked genuinely sorry it was gone.

She said, "There's more of that in the kitchen."

"Thanks, I'll catch that later. How's your head?"

"Actually, pretty bad. How's yours?"

"Ugh. Any chance you could locate some aspirin before you leave? I don't remember unpacking any yesterday from your case."

She looked down at that, frowning, and mumbled, "It was in my purse. I'll leave you some on the kitchen counter when I go."

He looked at her quizzically, "You're not feeling good."

"I'll be fine. I was a little sick to my stomach last night, and I'm still a little queasy. When I found the brandy bottle I knew why. That's potent stuff and we seemed to have polished it off." She shook her head. "What I really need is some solid sleep. I'm sure you need that too."

He nodded. "I heard you get up in the night." With a chuckle, he added, "I went to sleep figuring that you were just a few feet and a closed door away—"

She listened to his words solemnly but didn't respond.

He added with a smile, "So near and yet so far. Someone said that, too."

"Yes, I know." She gave a nonchalant shrug but couldn't keep from smiling.

He said, "About last night—"

She interrupted, "Yes, about last night. There are things I don't do. Drinking too much is only *one* of them. Feeling sorry for myself, and asking for sympathy are two of the others. I want to apologize for—"

"Apologize? For what?" Ellis gave a short laugh then shrugged. "Come on, Meg, alcohol had nothing to do with you letting go, if that's what you mean. Maybe you just found a sympathetic ear for a change."

Meg shook her head. "Parts of last night are pretty hazy, and I'm not happy about that. In my book, levelheaded women don't get drunk with strangers. And they don't cry in front of them either."

"I don't understand the 'stranger' part of that."

She looked hard at him. "Call me old-fashioned, but you don't know anything about me and I don't know anything about you. Before last night I'd seen you three times on the road, including when you got my car going—which I appreciate—but I'd say we're strangers."

He said, "You might not know much about me, Meg, but I know a lot about you."

"No, that's not true. You know *something* about me, from the house here and the kids and my sister Tolly and from my last name being Halverson. But that's all you know. And, other than the fact that you work for the Forest Service in some capacity, I don't know any of the really important things about you." She laughed. "Other than you occasionally wear sheets." Turning serious, she said, "At the risk of sounding discourteous, what's your background? Where do you come from? You're in my house and you've been here with my kids, but I really don't know anything more."

At her words, Ellis studied her playfully, with narrowed eyes, then grinned widely and answered, "There's no one special in my life at the moment, if you don't count Punkin."

They both laughed quietly at that and he settled back against the headboard more comfortably. He said, "Okay. I'm twenty-nine years old. I weigh one ninety-five and I'm six feet two. What else? I'm a native-born Montanan. I'm probably more conservative than most. I'm the only kid in my family. I was raised in and around Glacier Park. My father—he's retired—was in the Forest Service, too. My mom—I call her Glacier Lady—is a retired schoolteacher. They presently live in a cabin on the edge of the Park, in Polebridge. My degree is in Forestry here at the university. Let's see, what else?" He gave her an apologetic smile. "Oh, yes, I truly hate parsnips in any form: fried, boiled, or over ice cream. And I prefer blonds, but they don't prefer me, so I usually get stuck with tall, grey-eyed, soft-haired brunettes like you. Am I inspiring your trust yet?"

All the time he talked, Meg's face was poised for and reacting to each word. She answered, "Me trust you? You've got to be kidding! Here you've skillfully cut the distance between us to three feet and a closed door, and you're wearing a sheet and God only knows what else." She looked down at her hands a moment then said, "Those are just your statistics, Ellis—and good ones, I'll admit. Seriously though, if we decide not to be *strangers*, there are a lot of other things we need to get straight."

She looked up at the ceiling then began counting on her fingers. "As for my statistics...well, we needn't mention my weight or height—neither of which I'm ashamed of. I'm a native Montanan, too, but I'm most definitely *not* one of the conservative ones. Unlike you, I come from the central part of the state where trees and water are at a premium. My Ma and Papa farmed wheat there, and my sister Tolly, whom you met, and her husband still do. Our parents died young, within a few weeks of each other. That was years ago, but, if you want, I could count up the exact number of years and months and hours they've been gone—I miss them that much. You're lucky you still have your dad and your...Glacier Lady."

Her words faltered, then she gave him a steady look and spoke quietly. "I'm thirty-eight, and I'm a long-time mother, a short-time widow, and I've been long-time unhappy in the wife department."

She paused there, unhappy that she had told him that, but surprised, too, that she'd summed up her situation so precisely. She went on, "Even though my marriage wasn't all that great, my husband's disappearance and death hurt me and my kids very much. Moving up here to this mountain...well, it's a clean slate of sorts, a chance to start over, and I take this starting over very seriously, just as I take raising my kids very seriously." Speaking that directly to him had embarrassed her, so she finished in a lighter tone. "Now you know how much of an old-timer I am."

"Some old-timer. What if I told you I had figured you to be about that age the first day we met on the road? And, right away, I knew you must be Edward Halverson's widow. I'd read about what happened. You made quite an impression on me, telling that story of breaking in here and spending the night in front of the fire with your kids and sister, then walking down for help. You never once complained about that." He added, with his voice mimicking a distressed female, "*Or just about fainted, or could have cried at the thought*. You didn't seem to think there was anything remarkable in how logically you did what you had to do.

"But about your living here, it's rare enough for a man to choose to live this isolated in the mountains, but a hell of a lot rarer for a woman to do that. When I was told it was you who bought this place, at first I was amazed, but then I figured that it all fits. This is one of the sweetest pieces of land I've ever seen, and on a north-facing slope. With better than a thousand acres of virgin timber around this big clearing and near a decent road, well, you've got a great place. This big house isn't overly pretty, but a person can forgive a lot if it's well built and keeps you out of the weather. Yes, I've thought a lot about you."

Meg's face had changed from a look of pride to one of bewilderment. She said, "Wait a minute. I don't understand. You just said, 'when I was told it was you who bought the place.' But, on the road, when I told you, you were really surprised. You even said you'd heard the place was sold but you didn't know who'd bought it."

He looked confused for a moment. "I said that?" then added, forcefully, "No, it was just yesterday that I knew. You're the one who told me—on the road, with the moving van coming up behind you."

Seeing that she still looked puzzled, he said, a little lamely, "Well, I might have heard it before then, but what does that matter? The important thing is you bought a good piece of property and I'm glad you're here. We'll be neighbors, with my Ponderosa seedling research being conducted around here. I'll drop in from time to time, just to check if you are doing okay. You and I will be friends." He stopped talking and winked at her. At that, Meg started to get up. He put out his hand, as if to delay her leaving, and said, "So, are you feeling better now, beautiful?"

In a dispirited tone she said, "Yes, yes, I'm fine, thank you. I'll be even better when I see Callie." She chewed on her lower lip a moment then said, "About what you just said, you called me beautiful. Beautiful is a big word to me, Ellis. I don't like flattery or those kinds of compliments that don't mean anything, and are said for reasons other than what's really true. I've spent too much of my life saying those things to people I *had* to say such things to. When those words are directed to me, well, I don't know what to do with them. So I'd rather you didn't call me that."

He said, "You don't know that you're beautiful and desirable? Surely your husband told you—"

"The word for me is capable, Ellis. *Capable*. I don't want to talk about this, but my husband was a busy man, and he had ways of letting the kids and me know that we were pretty extraneous. What he found in me was competence, to always be there, to handle all the little details that made his life go smoothly, to feed him and clean his house and iron his clothes and run his errands. And not dispute his authority, of course—no questions, no comments, no personal views. And, most certainly, I was not to have any expectation of getting any compliments or any of those little encouragements that make everyday life satisfying." Her last words were the bitterest she'd ever made against Ed, and they shook her. She stopped talking and turned her head away from him as she felt her tears threatening to come again. In an agonized voice she said, "See? I just did it again."

"You did what again?"

"All this damned self pity. My God!" She took a deep breath. "I apologize for that and for my being so...so out of control last night—which I have to assume I was."

His laugh was loud before he thought about the sleeping kids and toned it down. "What the hell are you talking about? We got a little drunk, but—"

"But I hate being hazy about last night. I remember crying, but I hate not knowing exactly what I said after that."

He tried to interrupt, but she went on, "The funny thing is that this talk of ours has been very instructive, at least to me. I seem to have a problem that I really wasn't aware of. Every time I open my mouth about my past a lot of ugliness comes out. I think it puts you in a difficult spot, making you feel you have to compliment me, and console me somehow. I'm truly sorry about that."

Ellis looked at her for a long moment before he spoke, "It's all right, Meg. Don't worry about it. Last night I understood that you were tired and lonely, so I knew it was up to me to do the thinking for both of us." Watching her closely, he added, "You're probably resisting the thought, but what went on last night had nothing to do with that brandy. And it doesn't matter how short a time we've known each other or about you being thirty-eight and me twenty-nine, or anything else. We'll be—"

"Stop! Don't finish that sentence!" She jumped up and shook her head. "Better yet, let me finish it. 'We'll be *friends*.' That's what you were going to say, wasn't it? We'll be friends. And we *will* be friends. There are so many things I want to know about this mountain. Maybe you can educate the kids and me. My dearest friends, the Websters, are going to be away the rest of the summer. Until they come back, it will be good to have a friend drop by now and then to see us. I'm sure the kids would be happy about that, too. I'm a pretty good cook. We'll trade a few dinners for some of your mountain know-how. How does that sound? Now I really have to drive to town and see my daughter. I just wanted you to be sure and listen for the kids."

She opened the door and, looking back, laughed at his struggle with the sheet as he tried to stand up. "No, please, just stay there. Get dressed. Listen for the kids, and tell them that I'll call them from the hospital, and that I'll be back a lot sooner than I was yesterday. I promise." She smiled, "And be sure and eat a good breakfast yourself. I'm going to need your muscles to move that big sideboard back where I wanted it."

25

A NEW DAY

He left his shoes and socks off for a reason: he could pad around a lot easier in his bare feet, stepping over and around the half-opened cartons that lay all around the ungainly kitchen. And, of course, he could be a lot quieter. He didn't know anything about little kids, and the longer he could put off dealing with them the better. What was he thinking, agreeing to take care of them today? Yesterday things had gone fine, like he'd told their mother. But yesterday was yesterday and today might be a lot different.

A lot of things didn't faze him in the least, but being alone with kids did. While he thought wildly about what a kid might like to do, he ran his hand across his forehead and stared at the moisture on it, as though seeing what fear looked like. He went over to the sink and splashed water over his face, blotting it with a paper towel, before returning to the stove to give the oatmeal a stir.

What did kids talk about? They weren't old enough to talk about things he was interested in. He'd think of something. If he had some food ready to throw into their mouths when they hit the kitchen, it might quiet them. Maybe he could con them into eating breakfast outside on the front doorstep. Hell, if that didn't work, and they were still unhappy, he might try taking them for a ride. At this time of morning there was a good chance they'd see some deer or elk. Then again, they'd probably seen enough of those things and would be bored silly. If they got really desperate he could always drive them down to the hospital to find their mother. Throwing in the sponge wouldn't gain him any points with her, but, hell, dealing with the ladies was a gamble any way you looked at it.

Listening at the kitchen doorway again, his ears strained for the sound of feet or the flush of a distant toilet. But there was nothing. His thoughts returned to the night before, about where things could have led with Meg, but didn't. When he'd heard her Jeep drive away earlier, fast and spitting gravel, he hoped she'd remember that a dirt road and switchbacks weren't made for speed. If she were as concerned about her kids as she said she was, she'd have to think of things like that now. Nine years older than him, or not, that was one hell of a woman. She had stirred him up the first time he'd met her and Punkin on the road; but last night and again this morning in the bedroom, with the door closed, well, she'd really gotten to him. Too bad she hadn't taken him up on his suggestion for a little company last night.

When she'd sped past him yesterday on her way to the hospital, he'd thought he might make a few points by giving her a hand with the move; and he wanted to satisfy his curiosity. He hadn't been inside this house for a year now. He was as curious as anyone to know why Halverson's widow and kids left town, and to find out what they were going to do with the Turner place. That's when the possibilities of her and this place became a lot clearer. That changed when she'd come home late last night, all annoyed that he was here, and questioning him in that superior lady way. Then she'd let down her guard and cried like anyone else after a tough day. As usual, he was getting ahead of himself, but who knew where it could wind up?

Actually, when he thought about it, yesterday with Kurt and Punkin hadn't been all that bad. Like he'd told their mother, when he saw them, especially Kurt, taking charge of things that he thought only an adult could do—talking to the movers and making decisions and always good natured—he was frankly impressed. And that little Punkin! Her peanut butter sandwiches were okay, but her cooking—she hadn't diluted the canned soup enough, then had only heated it to lukewarm. He'd never tasted bean with bacon and tomato soup mixed together. It sat in their cups like pink pudding until he and Shorty and his crew dipped their sandwiches in it until it was finally gone. And the coffee was so strong you could have served that up as pudding, too. But, with her eyes shining and proud, Punkin offered all of this to them as food, and they took it as that. Kurt was all right, too, for not getting on Sara's case about the soup. Judging from the way he'd examined it, the boy knew it was pretty awful, but he ate it like everyone else.

Best of all was when Punkin helped him make up the beds—her little hands smoothing and folding the sheets on Meg's bed, and her prim little voice saying, "See, ya gotta make hospital corners of the sheet like this, Ellis, so it won't pull out. And ya gotta tuck in the sides." He laughed when he thought about it.

Then she'd said, "My Ma doesn't wear jamas. She likes to sleep in her bare skin. Not like a bear that walks around, like the kind we saw by the road, but like the kind of bare that's naked. See it's a joke, Ellis. When you say 'I'm going to sleep in my little bare skin,' people laugh, you know. Ma sleeps in her little bare skin, but the rest of us don't cuz we get uncovered at night and need jamas."

It was a statement of deep logic, and while she talked she tucked a large, dirty, worn-out toy rabbit into her mother's bed in the same way he imagined a mother tucked her kid in. It was done as rationally as that, as though Meg needed it to be there, but with no explanation to him as to why. The once-pink rabbit had only one ear and no nose, and Punkin positioned it lovingly into that expensive cream-colored, lace-edged bedding as though she didn't notice that it looked like it had been used to mop a dirty floor recently. Hell, maybe it was Meg's rabbit from her childhood and she couldn't get to sleep without it. Big girls, and little ones, too, were puzzles he couldn't waste his time figuring out.

He'd have kids of his own by now if he'd succeeded in connecting up with a girl during his days at the university. But, for one reason or another, the two opportunities he'd had fell through: Bethany—his first real love—had accepted a job in Milwaukee. Hell, what would he do in Milwaukee? He still heard from her. She wasn't married yet, and nothing had changed in her job, other than it had gotten more important. Tears and games—.

And then there was Carol. In the ten months they'd lived together, she wanted more attention, more understanding, more touching, more loving, more goddamn everything than any one man could supply.

Tears and games there, too. When she went back home to Billings and married her old boyfriend he'd felt nothing but good riddance.

He always laid the blame for his continued bachelorhood on the fact that trees and plants were a hell of a lot easier to deal with than women, although the rewards were less.

But a rich older woman, with a valuable piece of land, a new Jeep, and a readymade family—that was something worth putting a little effort into. Maybe fate was saving him for this. He let his mind linger again on how nice those cool silky sheets must have felt on that hot lady's little bare skin last night and wondered just how soon he would feel them on his little bare skin, too. Getting into those sheets and showing her just how beautiful and desirable she was, was a prospect he would enjoy thinking about. Well, he was ready. Let the games begin!

He was already in a great position: she was grateful for his help with the move, and she had already promised some future dinners in trade for his knowledge about the area. If she needed them to "get better acquainted," he was up for that. And if it was more time she needed, he'd give her all that, too. But, if she thought she was going to call all the shots, well, for a sexy older lady she sure didn't know much about men.

He stretched his wrists way out and saw the blond hairs on his muscular arms pick up the light. Strong arms. Willing arms. He grinned. All this place needed was someone strong at its helm, someone like himself. He'd first thought that when he'd run into that realtor lady, that Golda Dubois, who was removing the For Sale sign off the tree in the canyon and told him who had bought this place. Yes, he could do them all a favor.

After listening for the kids again and eager to get the show on the road, he picked up the cookie sheet and clanged it loudly against the stove. While he waited for the noise to get a reaction, he went over to the east kitchen window to see if anything was moving outside, ducking his head around to get a clearer view. It was from there that you could get a look at the large game trail just inside the thick stand of trees that formed the eastern border of the property, some sixty feet from the house. It was in the morning that the two male bears made their trek back up the trail after their overnight orgy down in the canyon's campground garbage dump.

Last year, he and Al Turner were standing at this very window talking about that big game trail and the bears that used it, when Al jabbed him hard and said, "By God, would you look at that!" The two black bears were slowly coming into view, in that now-you-see-it-now-you-don't way of wild animals. When they were just opposite the window, they stopped, and, from the safety of the trees, they peered nearsightedly at the house, looking both curious and indecisive, as though they had some unfinished business there. When they'd finally shambled on up the trail, Al said he'd caught sight of them many times before, and figured they lived somewhere on the ridge behind the house. Because they were always together, they must be brothers. Al, having talked to the campground's keeper, found out that in the summer, around 11:00 at night, the bears showed up at the campground but were gone by morning. Al, clearly enjoying himself, surmised that they were peaceable enough, but a person wouldn't want to surprise them. "Considering how many bears there are here, this place should be called Bear Mountain."

Remembering that remark, Ellis made a mental note to tell Meg that they'd better get a dog to warn them when a bear was nearby.

With nothing moving on the trail, Ellis went to the kitchen's large north window and stood admiring the scene directly below him. It was by far the best window from which to view the clearing. He'd always envied the Turners this view, wondering how it was that Alice Turner never got hooked on watching the hawks and ground squirrels or the larger game animals that you could see from it. But then, Alice Turner was afraid of goddamn everything.

Nothing was stirring there either, although about half way down the clearing he could make out the pair of Red-tailed Hawks waiting on their dead branch of their favorite tree, a towering Western Larch standing alone in the meadow. From the way the hawks were hunkering down, he could tell they were anxious for the sun to heat things up in the meadow below them. Once the ground squirrels got warm and began to feed around their holes, the hawks could begin their hunt. Graceful birds. He never got tired of watching them. They and their youngsters made a good living off the clearing.

. . .

The oatmeal was cooking dangerously near the top of the frying pan by the time Kurt and Sara bounced into the kitchen. They stood quietly and solemnly beside the stove, watching the thick grey mass rise as a whole up the side of the pan, like some kind of woolly animal fighting for breath, then the clump exhaled and sank to the bottom, and the whole process started all over again. After being assured that Callie was doing fine and their mother was with her, finding Ellis cooking oatmeal in a frying pan seemed to amaze them more than his continued presence did. They seemed to accept his method of cooking the cereal as the way a man did it, as opposed to the method used by a mother.

Ellis was seriously buoyed by their interest and smiled hopefully. They were still night tousled, but fresh and bright, and damned fortunate to have had almost ten hours of sleep, compared to his two. All in all, they were pretty cool—no tears, no need to drive them to the hospital to see their mother, and this oatmeal watching continued to get their attention. Another day with them might go okay after all. Ellis realized he was just standing there waiting, and they were standing there, too, looking up at him in a friendly, but clearly puzzled way. What they were all waiting for he hadn't the foggiest idea, so he smiled, and they smiled, and then he said, "Well, let's get to eating," and turned off the stove.

Punkin immediately offered to set the table, but Ellis, hoping it wouldn't hurt her feelings, said he had other plans. He got her busy feeding bread into the toaster and buttering it, and adding to the already teetering stack he'd been working on.

In vain, Kurt scrounged through boxes for some glasses, then rinsed out three of yesterday's cups and poured in the orange juice. The three of them drank it standing by the kitchen window, using the wide sill as a mini table. Ellis noticed that even this intrigued them, prompting the two of them to exchange mysterious looks and smiles that gave him the uncomfortable feeling he had broken some family rule and might be held to account for it at some future time.

With a little help he filled three bowls with the hot cereal, then loaded them and the plate of toast onto the cookie sheet and maneuvered it and the two kids down the balcony steps and out the living room door for a first breakfast on the front doorstep. There were a few trips back for spoons and a knife, then coffee, then sugar, then jam, then mugs of milk, then some torn-off sheets of paper towel for napkins. The kids laughed at him when he couldn't think of anything more to go back into the house for.

The cold that the rock had stored from the previous night leached into their bottoms through the thin cloth of their pajamas, and both kids rocked back and forth to get warm. Punkin, just before they started eating, and after first looking at Kurt in that same secret way, asked Ellis, "Are you *sure* we don't have to get out of our jamas and into our clothes before we eat breakfast?"

Ellis said, "Naw. Your mother gave me strict orders about that. She told me, 'Now don't you dare let those kids get dressed before they eat. We'll have none of that up here. Even if they kick and scream, you march them outside and set 'em down in the sun and show them how they're expected to eat up here in the real world." Winking at Kurt, he lowered his voice and added sternly, "This winter, you'll find that eating outside is a little harder to do, but by then you'll be tougher and have grown fur."

Sara collapsed in a fit of giggles, while Kurt, obviously too old to laugh at such silliness, just looked pleased.

After that, everyone calmed down and began scooping the cereal out of their bowls with oversized spoons and crunching their way through the mountain of toast. As they ate, all three of them wiggled their bare toes into the few threads of grass on the otherwise bare earth at the base of the stone slab. Something about it triggered a memory of when Ellis was a little kid himself, with his dad. How could he have forgotten that feeling? And why had he been so worried about today with these kids? When he looked down at them, sitting beside him, all he could think to do was to laugh. They looked up surprised, thinking they had missed something, and laughed, too, before getting back to the business of eating.

While he ate, the word Meg used in describing Halverson's relationship to her and the kids came to his mind. Extraneous. He thought it meant being irrelevant, unneeded, unconnected; and that didn't apply to these kids. These kids wanted to be right here, sitting close beside him—touching him, in fact—despite all the room on each end of the stone step. And their closeness gave him a confidence he hadn't experienced before, and he certainly wasn't going to leave them anytime soon.

He looked over at Kurt, who was hunched over, balancing his bowl on his knees, his serious young face looking out over the scene before him. Conscious of Ellis's eyes on him, Kurt looked up and gave him a hesitant smile that blossomed into something bigger before he'd looked away.

And then there was Punkin, in her pink pajamas. At the moment she was sitting on her hands, rocking back and forth with her legs outstretched and her big toes overlapped. Her silky hair reminded him of Bethany's, the way it had somehow fallen neatly into place without being combed. Now it swung back and forth whenever she moved. He'd been deliberating if he should tell Punkin she had a smudge of jam on her cheek, but she looked so cute he decided not to. From time to time she looked up at him from the corner of her eyes, shy and friendly, then turned full toward him and gave him such an adoring smile his chest hurt—and had from the very first day on the road. He picked up her hand and put it between his own big hands, making a sandwich, then pretended to take a big bite out of it. When he let go she smiled up at him, then looked down at her knees. He'd have to admit these kids were okay. And, again, it occurred to him—but with something like an ache this time—that if things hadn't gotten all screwed up with Bethany, he would have his own kids by now. That fact now felt like a loss.

26

MEADOW LESSONS

They drew the meal out as long as they could, assiduously removing every crumb and sticky trace of it, then placed the empty dishes and utensils on the cookie sheet. Once the food was gone, both children looked up at him, awaiting his next move. Although they were silent, he could see their questions flit across their faces: Should they take the dishes inside? Should they get dressed now? Was he going to put them to work unpacking? Anything he wanted would be fine, just ask.

As Ellis delayed a little longer, the two kids sat back, too, clasping their knees and sighing contentedly. This reluctance to leave wasn't only because of the charm of being together, or even because they'd been given a reprieve from the world of work awaiting them inside the house. It was the morning unfolding itself in front of them that entranced them, and it was as compelling as the image on any giant movie screen.

To their east, the sunlight had been sifting through the trees, throwing a network of shadows over the meadow. In the bare spots of the mountain just across from them, it was fascinating to see the same thing happening; but seeing it from a distance, it was easier to understand. Ellis commented that this sharp-shadow, deep-color time of morning was always a favorite time. Pointing to the town far below them, he declared, "You now live on top of the world, and everyone down there lives in a hole. Up here the sun is yours first and the town's second."

The kids nodded at this idea, seeing that it was true. The town was deeply buried in blue shadow cast from the mountain on its eastern side. While around them the sunlight fell like strands of warm gold over their faces and arms and knees. The kids' faces registered both pride and satisfaction in this new order of things.

Caught up in his success, Ellis picked up a stick and drew some lines in the dirt in front of him, saying, "If the Indians and mountain men could make their maps like this, we can too." Kurt and Sara nodded expectantly. He said, "This is what we're looking at. This wiggly line here is this range of mountains we're in. And here we are, right here." On the first curving line he drew a little square for the house and put three dots in front of it to represent the three of them.

"Okay, now, this line running along here is the range of mountains that's shading Clark Fork right now. See, we're part of that range." They definitely saw that. Drawing furiously, he said, "And this great big area is the valley the town is in, right here. And here is the river that runs through it and eventually joins this other river that we can't see from here, but it runs on to the Pacific Ocean, right here."

Big ocean. Right. The kids nodded their heads eagerly.

Out of the blue, Ellis asked, "Have you ever been to Glacier Park?" By this time both Sara and Kurt's eyes were hypnotically glued to the point of the stick and, since it was still in the Pacific Ocean, they didn't raise their eyes, even though they both shook their heads no.

Ellis continued, "Well, I used to live next to Glacier Park, in Huckleberry Ranger Station. It's way off there to the north." He marked a small "N" on the ground, then busily drew in more lines for mountain ranges, and finally reached way over and drew a dashed line and informed them that it represented the border between Canada and the United States. He then drew a big square that represented the park and pointed to where he lived by it. Finished with drawing, he tossed aside the stick.

The children's toes were curled uncomfortably against the front of the stone step—so they wouldn't accidentally step on a mountain range or erase a river—and they blinked at the stick, lying some distance away, and looked at each other, then at him, completely dazed.

Ellis fairly shouted, "It's wild, wild, wild, and the most beautiful country I've ever seen. It's old, sacred Blackfoot Indian country. Glacier Park is called that because there are many, many glaciers in that area—

you know, snow and ice that never melts completely over the years. It was a great place to live. I went to a one-room schoolhouse, and my mom was my teacher. For a long while I thought everyone lived the way we did—you know, in a cabin in the mountains with all the animals nearby. Then, when I was about thirteen, I went with my mom to Minneapolis and saw my first city and realized that the way I lived in Montana was very different.

"I grew up knowing about bears—mostly grizzlies—and mountain sheep and goats, moose, elk, deer, coyotes, fishers, martens, mink, weasels, and all the rodents, like picas, marmots, ground squirrels, and chipmunks, and all the birds. My dad knew all about animals' behavior, what they were doing and thinking, and where an animal was in relation to its food supply at any given time of the year. I'm telling you this because I want you to know that you kids are the luckiest kids in the world to live here." He gestured widely around them, then laughed and shook his head in wonder at it all.

All the while Ellis talked, Kurt's eyes never left his face. And now Kurt said gravely, "We all wanted to live here and were afraid we couldn't. We almost didn't get this place because someone else wanted to buy it. But Ma and I bought it. She let me come to the real estate office to help her, because Sara and Callie and I own this place, too. And when we have to decide something about it, all four of us talk about it and decide."

He looked away, but continued quietly, "We've always lived in town. We used to have a neat place to play—you know, when we were little—but someone built a house on it." He turned and looked right at Ellis, and spoke earnestly, "Anyway, we didn't want to live there anymore. Our father left us, and when he died our mother got real sick and we thought she was going to die, too. We had to live at the Websters until she got better." After a moment he added, "Because of a lot of other things, we didn't want to live in town anymore."

Sara said, "Kurt means cuz the kids we used to like now *hate* our guts!"

Kurt said, "Don't use that word, Sara. Remember?" Turning to Ellis, he said, "Yeah, even Chip didn't like me."

As curious as Ellis had been about the Halversons, the kids' openness made him feel like an intruder and he wanted to turn off the conversation. The picture the family presented, of easy talk and teasing humor was a protective covering. Meg's words about the clean slate now seemed loaded with warnings not to mess with this family. His plans for a grand seduction shrank in view of the hurt dealt by Halverson's death.

Sitting back a little, he watched the two kids looking out at the land before them. They had a look of wonder and pride on their faces that he hadn't seen earlier. He saw this country almost every day as he worked around this area but, today, along with the kids, he saw it fresh and new. It was a new day for all of them.

The sun was rising higher now, the morning growing older. Even so, time felt as suspended as the two hawks wheeling high above. While they watched, Ellis identified the two-dimensional silhouettes as Red-tailed Hawks. When they plummeted down and skimmed over the meadow below them, the morning light polished their shoulders and illuminated their red tails before the birds shot up to lie on the air once more. As they watched the hawks hunting for their breakfast, Ellis remembered a game his father had invented for him when he was a little boy, about Punkin's age. The game was meant to introduce him to thinking about what was going on around him. To the kids he said, "Close your eyes and just listen for a while and tell me what you hear."

Sara was quick to close her eyes and put her head on her knees. Kurt hesitated, a little too sophisticated to hurry into anything, but he finally did. Neither one said anything for a minute then Kurt said, "I don't hear anything except Sara's stomach gurgling. She ate too much."

Sara's answer was muffled. "I did not, Kurt. You had two more pieces of toast than I did. You hogged it."

Ellis laughed as he reached out and put a hand on the back of each one of their necks and gave them a squeeze. "Okay, you two. Do as I say or else."

This time Kurt listened, then asked, "What's that weird sound?" He looked up into the sky. "What's that?"

Ellis said, "Those piercing sounds are the hawks calling back and forth to each other. Surely you've heard hawks before."

Kurt nodded his head, yes, but looked doubtful.

Sara said, "I heard some squeaks, too. Did I hear squeaking, Ellis?"

"You did. Now I want you both to watch the meadow and listen this time."

The hawks were high in the sky and everything was silent and still—a leisurely scene, pleasant to watch: the light-grey ground squirrels eating quietly in the grass or standing sentinel-straight in the early warmth beside the mounds of earth near their holes.

Ellis said, "Now watch and listen to what happens."

Both hawks dove down; and the moment they did, the meadow was filled with the sharp chipping squeaks of warning and an explosion of movement as the ground squirrels scrambled for safety and jumped into their holes. Luckless, the hawks again shot high into the sky and began soaring lazily once again.

The kids watched spellbound now, as one by one the ground squirrels started peeking out of their holes again and moving warily around, nibbling on this and that, while others resumed their sunbathing stance beside their holes.

Ellis said, "Don't think for one minute that the ground squirrels don't know exactly where those two hawks are. Okay, let's do it again. Close your eyes and tell me what's happening."

This time both children put their hands over their eyes and listened carefully. Long minutes went by, but they waited.

Then Kurt said, "The hawks are over the meadow right now."

And Sara said, "Yes, cuz everybody's squeaking."

Both children uncovered their eyes just as one of the big birds glanced off the ground and labored off with a wiggling ground squirrel dangling from its talons. Kurt gasped and Sara put her head behind Ellis's arm, horrified. Almost apologetically, he said, "Looks like we're not the only ones who are having breakfast this morning." He watched the children closely for their reaction.

Kurt swallowed and said, "Aw, we've seen that plenty of times."

Sara said sadly, "Yeah, but I don't like that bad hawk, killing our ground squirrels. Can't the hawks eat something else, Ellis?"

"Well, Punkin, how would you feel if the hawk had just caught a snake?"

"I'd like that because I don't like snakes. Yuck."

Ellis said, "Well, I'm not too fond of snakes either, although the ones up here are harmless. But every living thing has to eat. What I'm saying is, if it's a ground squirrel that gets caught we don't like it, but if it's a snake, it's different. I don't think it's ours to choose, Punkin. We can't say a hawk is bad because he is a hunter. And we can't say that the little ground squirrel that became the hawk's breakfast shouldn't have died. I want you to consider this: one of those hawks is a mother and the other is a father and they are raising a family of baby hawks in that big tree down there in the middle of the meadow there," pointing. "They have been hunting on this mountainside for years and years. Now that you're living up here you'll have to try to understand what you see in a little different way.

"Look at the beauty of that other hawk soaring up there—probably still hungry. When I see a big bird floating along like that, not flapping its wings, but turning and rising on the currents of air—and remember, that hawk is able to do that just by understanding those air currents and flexing the feathers on its wings and tail—I think I like watching a hawk even more than I like watching a ground squirrel. But that doesn't mean I'm going to gather up a pile of ground squirrels to feed the hawk just so it can keep on flying up there.

"To us, ground squirrels seem like cute little creatures who stand in the sun and make squeaking sounds. But I'm quite sure that hawks and bears and coyotes see them very differently. To them, ground squirrels must look like little tan grocery bags full of food. Unfortunately for the hawks, those little grocery bags are equipped with four feet that can run fast and sharp squeaks to warn the other grocery bags. Occasionally, the birds can outwit one of those grocery bags, but most often they can't. We have to understand that both the hawks and the ground squirrels live here together and have for hundreds of thousands of years: the squirrels eating the plants and roots from the meadow, and the hawks eating the ground squirrels.

"In spite of this, both the hawks and squirrels are still around—there's a balance between them. It's people who get all screwed up in their thinking, putting big labels on things—the 'Good Guys' and the 'Bad Guys'—and deciding to change that balance in favor of who they think the Good Guys are. They shoot the hawks and eagles and coyotes, then they wonder why the ground squirrels and other rodents are eating up their crops.

"We can watch them, Punkin, but let's try not to choose whose side we're going to be on. When we see something like we just did, let's think of it as something we were privileged to watch, and not as a tragedy. Does that make any sense?" He tweaked her nose.

Sara nodded and gave him a huge smile.

Kurt, who had quietly listened to Ellis, laughed and said, "When a bear carries you off, Sara, I'm going to tell him, 'What took you so long?' It'll be neat to watch you screaming and dripping blood all over."

Sara let out a howl and reached around Ellis's back and hit Kurt. "Kurrr-t, if you do, then I'll get a big hawk to carry you off. Cal and I'll cheer."

Ellis said, "Whoa, you two."

Sara, with a doubtful look on her face, pointed at the road where they had seen the bears. "Ellis, I don't want those bears to eat us. When you lived in Glacier Park, did your dad have a gun and shoot them so they wouldn't eat you?"

"No, Punkin, but we had to be careful, especially since most of the bears there were grizzlies. You see, Punkin, bears are very unpredictable. Like I told you yesterday, I've seen that particular mama bear of yours many times before and she never looked like she wanted to stay around long enough to hurt anyone. But, with her cubs now, she's going to be protective of them and a little more aggressive to anyone who surprises her. And that goes for the other bears that live here." He almost missed seeing the look that went between the two kids when he said that. He thought for a minute. "Your Mom needs to get a dog."

Kurt said, "She already said she wants one."

Sara interrupted, "Yeah, Ma always wanted one. Only our daddy didn't like dogs or kittens. He didn't like any pets, cuz he said they were dirty. So we never had anything. But now we can cuz he's gone."

Embarrassed again, Ellis put his finger over her lips and quickly said, "Well, I never had a dog either, because my mother said I couldn't, for the same reason your father said. I don't know much about dogs, but I don't think you'd want a little housedog, or one who would take off and run after a bear or chase the deer. What you need is a big dog with a big enough voice to get the bears' attention, a dog they wouldn't want to tangle with. And neither would the coyotes. Coyotes won't hurt *you*, but they've been known to kill a dog if they can lure it away and gang-up on it. You need the kind of dog who would be your friend and stay around you all the time, the kind who'd let you know if there was something like a bear around."

Kurt's face had taken on a look of dreaminess. "Gee, I've always wanted one of those big, wavy-haired, grey and white sheep dogs, with its eyes looking out from under its hair."

Ellis looked doubtful. "Well, I don't know. With all this brush up here, you might want to think about something you wouldn't have to be brushing the tangles out of all the time. You might want to consider a dog with a shorter, sleeker coat, a dog that's known for its good hearing and good nose—and can *see*! What about a German shepherd? That breed might be just the kind to have in a situation like this, especially a female who would stay at home. German shepherds are people dogs, as well as watch dogs. Tell you what, when your mom comes home we'll ask her together. Wouldn't this be a great place for a dog to live, too? It wouldn't have to be tied up all the time. If she says it's okay, maybe I can help you find one. Until then," he stood up and stretched, "you know what we gotta do, don't you?"

The two children groaned in unison and Ellis laughed. "Yeah, I thought you'd know. Come on, troops, let's get to it." He picked up the loaded cookie sheet and headed into the house, where Kurt and Sara heard him say, "For heaven's sake, if I've told you once, I've told you a million times, you kids can't eat breakfast in your 'jamas. Didn't your mother ever tell you that it's not only impolite, it's agin' the law?" If there were more words, they were lost; he was already in the kitchen.

Kurt looked at Sara and they shrugged their shoulders, then laughed and ran in after him.

27

PROSPECT

Meg surveyed the living room from the loveseat and sighed contentedly. This elegant room! In the weeks they'd been here they could have made more progress settling the rest of the house, but at least this room was finished. Outside, the evening was stealing what was left of the sunset, and the thin light coming from the windows gave a general impression of the pictures and books and furniture; but it was the firelight that defined their edges and bestowed the glow of life onto the leathers and brass and the waxed wood beneath the intricate patterns of the oriental rugs.

On the low table beside her a vase full of mountain flowers drooped toward its reflection in the glass tabletop, the bouquet little changed from the clutching of Callie's small fist. Meg smiled at it: a valued gift picked during the family's evening walk to the cabin and to the remnants of the long-ago woman's camp near the apple tree. That place of antiquity drew them—not so much as something they owned, but as something precious deserving their care.

She loved this time of evening. Relaxing against the loveseat's back, she felt encircled in comfort and peace. This place satisfied her, as she knew it would. The children were happy, relaxed, alert, and curious, and they rarely quarreled. They had not only adjusted to the differences in living here but were fully invested in the adventure. Arriving home from town, they spilled from the Jeep, carrying the packages and books into the house, and helped put things away with few complaints. From there, they hurried outside or to their various haunts: Kurt to the shop in the basement and his special room under the stairs, and the Littles to the big upstairs room at the top of the house. Around the house they were helping her more with household chores and the cooking. Kurt, having relinquished his salad making to Sara, was showing more interest in how foods went together—breads and stew and sauces—and Meg couldn't be happier with his help.

They'd started walking together in the evenings and had invariably discovered something new. Yesterday it was a young buck deer browsing at the edge of the meadow. He was aware of their presence, raising his head and eyeing them from time to time, but he still kept on daintily nibbling at the low bushes. When he left they went to the spot, curious about his choice of food and wanting to discover why he chose this plant to eat so intently, but not another. Then, this evening, they had watched with awe a group of ravens freefalling and tumbling in the air currents above the ridge. It was evident that the birds were playing some sort of game because they did it over and over for no apparent reason. With envious eyes they had watched the birds' joy.

Still caught up in her own joy of the experiences they were having, Meg looked down at the sleeping child nestled against her and felt the tiniest twinge of guilt. Callie was fully recovered, but she had started coming back downstairs after Sara and Kurt were asleep, and now it was an evening ritual. Meg remembered her own craving for the undivided attention of Ma and of Papa, so she understood Callie's need.

Meg shifted her leg and said softly, "Hey, sleepy head, you can't stay here all night. It's time to wake up and go back to your bed."

Callie's eyes popped open and she smiled up at her mother. "You thought I was sleeping, but I was listening. Did you know the fire hums songs when it's little like this? And sometimes your stomach squeaks when you breathe. Maybe something needs oiling in there, or maybe you've got mice, too." She made a tiny squeaking sound.

Meg said, "You don't suppose I accidentally swallowed one?"

"Oh, yuckky!" Callie made a face and reached up and took a strand of her mother's hair and tickled Meg's nose with it until she shivered and pushed her hand away. Playing an old game, they squeezed their eyes into little slits and looked at each other fiercely, then ended up laughing.

Callie scooted away from Meg and lay back into the opposite corner of the small couch with her arms behind her head and one leg crossed languidly over her knee. Watching the fire she said, "Do you remember when we slept on the floor here a long time ago, Aunt Tolly and us? That's Sara's and my mostest, favoritest night."

Meg laughed at her words and nodded. "Goodness, yes, a bunch of puppies. But it wasn't that long ago."

"It *has* to be long ago, Ma. I don't even think of living in our other house anymore. Sara and I pretend we've always lived here. We like how we can just walk out the door to do things. Guess what my favoritest other thing is."

"The spring?"

"You're supposed to guess, not know. How did you know?"

"Because it's one of my *favoritest* places, too. When I see you heading up the hill I know just where you're going. Next time, come get me. We'll go together."

"Okay. We'll lie under the bushes and look at the sky and think about things. That's what I do. The wet rocks are so pretty and the water tastes so good. I like it cuz Kurt hung a cup on a bush so we can take drinks."

"He makes a lot of things handy, doesn't he? He likes making things in his shop."

"Uh-huh."

They were quiet then, just looking at the fire, until Callie sighed loudly. "Is anyone *ever* going to visit us, except Ellis? When are Marc and Doris going to be done visiting their kids?"

"After school starts, maybe in time for my birthday."

Callie frowned. "I wish it was sooner. They don't know where we put our furniture and stuff, or about all the mice we've caught, or where the Indian Paint Brush flowers are growing in the meadow. Aunt Tolly hasn't seen how I fixed up my room. She doesn't even know that Sara and I don't sleep in the same room anymore. And I want to show her the little schoolhouse in the canyon that we're going to go to. Will Aunt Tolly and Uncle Charlie ever come here to see us? Or is she going to be mad at us all our lives? We're not mad at her, are we?"

Meg said a hasty, "No, not at all! I miss her and love her just like I always have. I bet she feels the same way. We just had a misunderstanding, that's all. Your aunt and I get a little stubborn at times. But you're right, I better write her to say how much we want her to be happy with us. After their wheat is cut, maybe she and Uncle Charlie will visit us, now that Old Flint is with them. I'll write her that you wondered if we were still mad at each other. Okay?"

Callie nodded happily and looked thoughtfully at the fire, chewing on her lower lip. She finally said, "Ellis looks at you funny. Sara says that's because he's going to be our daddy. Is he?"

Meg rarely blushed, but she felt her face get hot and hoped Callie would think the red was from the fire. Instead of answering, she reached over and walked her fingers up all the buttons on the front of Callie's pajamas, while Callie tried to fend them off in her extra-ticklish spots.

Callie was still giggling when she asked, "Well, is he? Sara saw him kiss you by his car the other night. Sara says that proves it."

"Proves it? Proves what?" Meg looked uneasily at Callie, then thought to say, "Marc and your Uncle Charlie kiss me when they leave, but that doesn't mean they're going to be your daddies."

"But they're different from Ellis. They're old and they're already daddies. Sara and I want Ellis to be our daddy."

Meg rolled her eyes. "Callie, Ellis is just our friend. And he kissed me because he was leaving for home, that's all." She took a deep breath and changed the subject, "Just think of all the things he's taught us up here."

Callie nodded and smiled. "Sara and I watched the hawks hunting the little grocery bags again today. We listened to their squeaking first."

Meg chuckled, "The *grocery bags*... Ellis told me about that. He knows a lot of interesting things about animals, doesn't he?"

"He knows ev-ery-thing about here. Daddy didn't know fun things like that, and he didn't laugh all the time like Ellis."

"Your father knew about a lot of other things, Callie. But we're not going to talk about that. I think it's time for someone I know to go to bed."

"But I want to talk about Ellis. Why does he always have to go home? Couldn't he stay over so he could be here all day? Sara thinks he'd stay over if we asked him, or you could."

Meg burst out laughing and reached over and tousled Callie's hair until she could get herself under control.

Callie looked at her, puzzled and hurt. "But I mean it, Ma. Couldn't you ask him to stay over? Sara and I know you like him cuz you fix him good dinners. He's so neat. Couldn't you tell him we want him to be our daddy?"

Meg looked deeply into Callie's eyes. "I know your kids would like a father around, and it would be great for me to have a little help with you guys, but..." She didn't finish the sentence, but Callie's smile told her that she didn't need to. Meg continued, "But, asking Ellis to stay over isn't the way it works, and I don't want you two to ask him either—not a word! You girls have to understand that as much as you'd like him to be your daddy, *becoming* a daddy is more than giving a woman a kiss goodnight and staying over."

Callie's heartfelt questions had made Meg sad, and she reached over and caressed Callie's cheek with the back of her fingers. Speaking almost to herself, she added, "I honestly don't know how to get you a daddy, Callie. When you and Sara get to be big women you'll learn that there are many things you can't figure out ahead of time...that you have to kind of *live* them to find out." She stood and pulled Callie to her feet. "But we're not going to talk about anything more tonight, young lady. It's up-the-stairs time." She herded Callie up the balcony stairs. At the top, she put her arms around her and said, "Callie dear, you know I love our evenings together by the fire, but you're not sick anymore and you need to get to sleep when Sara and Kurt do. No more excuses. What do you think?"

Her question sounded a little sad and it was matched by the look on Callie's face. The phone ringing below them stopped their conversation. With an impish smile, Callie offered to go back down and answer it. Meg gave her a quick kiss and a little swat on her bottom and told her to get right to bed. She'd tuck her in later. When Callie's door closed, Meg went down the stairs, and resumed her seat in front of the fire before answering it. It was Ellis.

"Kids asleep?"

"Pretty close to it. I just got Callie to bed. She's gotten a little spoiled and needs some special attention before she can get to sleep."

"She's not the only one. I hope you gave her a kiss, too."

"Umm hum."

"But not like the one you gave me, I bet. That kind keeps you awake."

"I don't think I *gave* you a kiss as much as you *took* it."

"Gave it, took it, who cares? It was sweet. I can still taste it."

Meg sighed audibly. "Could we not talk about this on the phone? Was there something else?"

"It's been a couple days since we've talked. Everything going okay?"

"Yes...yes, mostly. It's so lovely up here. Something new always pops up. Today we watched some ravens playing, and that led us to wonder about the air currents, both up in the sky and down here. When we take our walks, in some places the air always feels cool, and then, right next to it, it feels warm. We wondered why is all. Sara is convinced that you can explain it."

"You could coax it out of me with another dinner."

"I don't recall that you take much coaxing. Tell you what, we'll start writing down our questions and present them to you all at once. A big list should be worth both pot roast and an apple pie."

"I'd prefer one question at a time and macaroni and cheese, followed by another kiss."

"You're terrible!" She couldn't help laughing. "You better be good or you'll have to settle for creamed parsnips on crackers."

"If it comes with a kiss."

Meg smiled to herself while she searched for a change of subject. "Speaking of ravens and air currents, this place has really fired our imaginations. In fact, when we go into town to pick up supplies, the Jeep just naturally heads to the library on its own. It's amazing the books we've found there. This place is turning us all into reading fanatics."

Ellis said, "Facts and numbers are what I live on. You can't miss as long as you have the facts and numbers."

Hurrying on, Meg said, "Well, anyway, yesterday we hiked up behind the spring to check out a patch of huckleberries that Kurt had found. It's so pretty up there. We hoped mama bear and her cubs wouldn't decide to do the same thing. They didn't, probably because the berries aren't even close to being ripe."

"By late August they will be. But, Meg, don't bother with those small patches. I'll show you where the really big patches of berries are, higher up on your property."

Feeling a little stir of exasperation, she joked, "Since Kurt found the spot, well, sometimes it's more fun to discover these things ourselves. They are more *ours* when we do."

"I'm just trying to save you time. Huckleberries are a pain to pick, but if you really want them, you'll thank me for steering you to the best spots." Then he added, "You haven't told me the not-good part of your day yet."

She hesitated a moment, then said, "I don't recall mentioning something not being good."

"You implied it."

After another long hesitation, she said, "Well, I've had problems with the workmen doing the cabin's remodeling."

"I assumed that everything was going great with it, now that you're in charge"

"Let's just say that I'm learning."

"Learning what?"

Picking her words carefully, she said, "I'm a little frustrated in trying to make the cabin into a habitable place. The men I hired seem incapable of thinking of the cabin in anything but its most utilitarian sense—a place to retreat to or hunt out of—while I want their work to match the craftsmanship Al Turner put into it. Their work is shoddy. I told the foreman my Papa's old saying, 'If you don't have time to do a job right, how are you going to find time to do it again?' Yesterday, when the foreman kept on giving me excuses, I paid them all off and told them not to come back. I hated to see them go, but at least they'd finished the hard work, getting electricity and water to the place and plumbing its little bathroom. But their carpenter work will have to be redone. Unfortunately, my plans for getting a couple to live up here and help us will have to wait a while longer." Her voice trailed off.

"That sounds more like a big problem than a little one. My offer to take that job on still stands, Meg. I know I could find the right men to do the work."

Dispirited, Meg said, "I know, and I thank you, but I still see it as something I want to do."

"Time's flying, Meg. The first snow arrives in October, maybe even September."

"I'm aware of that, Ellis." When she thought of the snow, she felt an odd lift to her mood. "I can hardly wait to see snow up here. I haven't picked out a stove for the cabin yet, but I keep thinking how beautiful it will be in winter: smoke curling out of its chimney, light shining from its windows, the trees all snowy and looking like a Christmas card. I keep a sleeping bag down there and I've taken a couple naps on that old iron bed under the window. Just before I drift off—"

"You hear the breeze whispering through the trees—you've already told me that, and you still sound like an advertisement. But it's those trees that are causing the problems. They need to be removed. Forcing the men to work around them made their jobs that much harder. No wonder you're having trouble."

Meg hummed ominously. "This isn't a good topic for us, Ellis. Those trees aren't coming down."

"Damn it, Meg. You're stubbornness has hurt more than the work there; it's hurt us."

The word "us" rattled around in her head, avoiding her heart altogether. She spoke cautiously. "You accuse *me* of sounding like an advertisement, but when you talk about trees *you* sound like a textbook! You talk so brilliantly, so eloquently, about hawks and ground squirrels and deer and elk, but the trees you speak of seem to only have a commercial side. To quote you, 'Those Douglas Firs and Ponderosa Pines make fine lumber, and those Western Larches are good for veneer and posts.' I seem to have forgotten which trees make the best turpentine. I wish you were as interested in the beauty of a *tree* as you are an animal."

"I like a tree just as much as you, but I can look at it objectively, see the end of its usefulness—"

"That *end* you speak of, who, exactly, decides when a tree is at its end?"

"The person who owns it, as a matter of fact! I just don't get it. You own that place, so you better start thinking about those things, Meg. Those trees by the cabin aren't your only trees at the end of their usefulness. This sentimental streak of yours really surprises me. You're so practical otherwise. If you can't make those kinds of decisions yourself, you better find someone who can."

The fight had almost gone out of Meg's voice, and she spoke softly, "Talk like this just kills me, Ellis. I don't want to fight."

"I don't want to fight either, but you keep forgetting that land management is what I do. Think about it, Meg."

"Okay, okay, I will. Are we done talking now?"

Ellis softened his voice. "I know you're mad at me, but wait a minute. The reason I called is that a lot has been happening that you need to know about. I even have a surprise for you. But first, we still want a dog, don't we?"

Meg heaved a sigh before answering. "Yes, *we* still do. When we were looking for huckleberries, I kept thinking that if we had a dog with us I'd feel a lot easier. It's not that we're afraid, but I'm always wondering what we should know about ahead of time. I've been calling kennels, with no luck, but tomorrow I'm going to call Spokane—"

Ellis interrupted, "But I found a dog today, at the Humane Society. A big German shepherd, female, mature, all black—someone found her and a cat together, both half-starved, and brought them to the shelter. A couple days ago I'd called and told the man in charge what we were looking for, and this afternoon he called me back and told me about her. I just got back from seeing her. She's just what we want, so I asked them to hold her for you and the kids to see. She's too thin and needs rest and lots of food at the moment, but I know you'll like her. Why don't you all plan on driving down and meeting me there on Sunday and we'll look at her together?"

This was good news, but Meg had to work hard to sound as eager as he was. "It's nice you found her, Ellis." To her ears her words sounded wooden. "Sunday's fine. The kids will be thrilled. They're so impatient for a pet. Whatever dog we get better not be afraid of being over-loved."

"Good. Now, there're two more things. You heard about the big fire near Glacier Park. The district here is sending me to help out up there. I leave on Monday. I have no idea when I'll get back."

"I heard about it on the radio. That fire sounds dangerous."

"It is, but I won't be on the fire line, just on the control desk. I've done it before. I'll enjoy it, actually. But I wanted you to know. As for the surprise, tomorrow being Saturday, you and I can finally go on that hike we've talked about. I'm especially anxious to show you around the eastern side of your place, then the high country. We'll take my forest service map and see if we can locate the corners of your property. You'll love it.

"Now, I can hear what you're thinking, Meg. You're thinking it's impossible because the kids can't be left alone. But I took care of that. There's a couple I know who'll stay with them. Jeannie Young is a secretary in my office and her husband Paul is with the Post Office. They'd like to see the place. I'll drive them up first thing tomorrow morning."

His voice changed, becoming low and intimate. "A hike will give us a chance to see the parts of your land that you never see from the road, Meg. And we need to get away…and be alone for once. You know, get to know your place a little better, just the two of us… before I go. I'd like that and I bet you'd like that, too. It'll be a chance to get better acquainted."

When Meg heard that, something like panic replaced the tension their tree conversation had rekindled. The panic had nothing to do with his leaving for the Park fire; it was spending a whole day alone with him that she feared; that and maybe being pushed into something hasty. Yet, how strange that was, for not a day had gone by that she hadn't longed for the opportunity to be alone with this young, sensual, maddening man. Now, just thinking about it—and especially since he'd kissed her again two nights ago—her mind and body were adrift in a sea of delicious imaginings. For the second time she felt her cheeks flare from the direction her thoughts had taken. Before, there'd been no opportunity to be alone with him; but now, he'd made that opportunity, and the temptation to explore their attraction would finally be there.

His voice pried her from those thoughts,"Meg? I'm waiting.You're not going to turn me down, are you?"

"I don't know." Still casting around wildly for her answer, she said, "No, I'm just thinking. I'm sorry you have to go to the Park fire, and the kids will be sorry, too. I hope you'll stay safe.About the couple—the Youngs—I'm sure they're fine, if you say they are, and the kids would like showing them around.About the dog..." Unable to resist the feeling of annoyance that had overtaken her, she said, "It's crazy, Ellis, but you always knowing how to do things and being the one who introduces me to things..."

She took a deep breath."First you showed me that my car wasn't dead.Then you showed me the right road to this place.And you were even in this house ahead of me and served me my brandy and my food that first night.You even showed me the elk and deer at the salt lick above my house. And next month it'll be all those gigantic patches of huckleberries. Now, tomorrow, you want to show me around my land and point out where my property lines are.And, as if that weren't enough, now you've found the perfect damn dog. Have you left anything for me to discover? I feel like a guest here!"

She could feel her anger all over her body, but, hearing her last accusation, an overwhelming feeling of shame came over her.After a moment of silence she gave a short laugh to try to make her words into a joke.

He joined in after a few moments.Then there was only embarrassed silence, with each one aware of the other's thoughts, despite the miles between them.

She shook her head, exasperated at herself."Oh, Ellis, I'm sorry. Forgive me.That came out too strong. I'll admit I'm a bit envious over what you know about this place, but—"

"It sounded like you meant it. You forget I'm only trying to be helpful."

"And you have been.You are. I don't know why I said that. Please, forgive me."

"It sounds like I should be the one who apologizes.You've had a bad day, Meg. You're forgiven, if I am. Let's leave it there, okay? But you haven't answered about the hike. I've been looking forward to a day alone with you, and I hoped you—"

"I want to go. I want to see my land."

"Then agree and we'll make a day of it."

She looked at the phone cord she had just twisted into a hopeless tangle and took a deep breath. It was a hike to see her land, and that was all it would be. Wouldn't it? She finally answered, "Okay, tomorrow then. You're right, I've been hoping for a day like that, too." They finished by planning the food and the time they'd start in the morning.

28

AFTERTHOUGHTS

After Ellis hung up, Meg held the phone against her throat a few moments before removing its cord, shaking out its tangles, and plugging it in again. She had to admit that before the phone call, in spite of her pleasure at how well everything was going up here, she had felt a shade isolated and a bit lonely, even though the loneliness wasn't anything new, having scarcely changed from when Ed was alive. But, now, a feeling of dissatisfaction was threatening the peace she had felt earlier. She wondered why this happened so consistently with Ellis?

The room was dark now and she left the loveseat and went over to the window, switching on a table lamp on the way. Its soft intimate light restored a focus to the room without obliterating the last view of the world outside the window. There was little more than a faint afterglow on the western horizon, and the lights of the town below her were fully on. Funny to see them down there like that: lighted streets she used to drive about on at night, to the grocery store for milk or ice cream, or the quick emergency runs to the drugstore when the kids were sick—more cough syrup, a prescription, a rub. And, of course, somewhere in those strings of lights were the streets that Ed had driven back and forth on each day and each night—to the bank, to home, to the bank again, or, quite possibly, to some other street to see a woman with long hair: a woman who was still unidentified. Meg didn't think of that very much anymore—whatever her life had been down there, she no longer felt connected to it. Now there was Ellis.

She remembered thinking that in moving to the isolation of the mountain all her hopes for love were gone. But on the very night she'd concluded that, Ellis came into her life and, in a single touch of his lips, had awakened her. Also, in spite of her need to protect herself that morning in the guestroom, she had revealed to him her deepest vulnerability, sketching her shattered life as though drawing a picture and placing it in his hands—feeling it was safe with him. The source of her present anguish was not knowing what he was doing with that information.

She closed her eyes and leaned her cheek against the window frame and thought of Ellis's energy, enthusiasm, and knowledge—and her powerful attraction to him…that lovely, nine-years-younger golden man. Where that attraction would end up she hadn't a clue. Her words to Callie, about having to live things you couldn't figure out ahead of time, now seemed remarkably wise. But it was far easier to say than to do. The question wasn't where Ellis fit into the kids' lives, but where he fit into *hers*. That's what she wasn't clear about. She knew that the children were crazy about him, and she was beginning to understand how entwined Ellis was with them. "Ask Ellis!" had become their byword, because he was there to answer. He had become a fixture around the place the moment he'd helped them move in. After that was his stopping by at dinnertime, giving her little choice but to ask him to stay. Now it was impossible to see the house and the land without somehow connecting it to him. When his work took him to another area, he'd call her—just like he had tonight—to say where he was going and when he'd be back, just to be sure she'd put that fact into her schedule.

How petty she'd sounded tonight! How could she fault him for his knowledge, with all she had to learn up here? And, now, he had even found a dog, a perfect dog. While she'd been calling kennels as far away as Idaho that had new puppies and half-grown dogs, but no mature watchdogs for sale, Ellis had been logical and successful right here in Clark Fork. And the dog would be perfect—things were always perfect when they came from Ellis; all three kids would attest to that. Even so, it had irritated her that he'd referred to it as "our" dog. Where had that come from? Didn't there have to be both the man and the woman agreeing to that word? Had the kids, in their great romance with him, granted him the right to be part owner of these things? If so, she'd better check to see if she still owned the damned house!

She shook her head and allowed herself to feel relieved that he was going away to Glacier Park for a while. The word "relieved" teetered dangerously in her thoughts. Relieved about what? Their skirmishes over her cabin? Their fights over her trees? What strange things to fight over when her body, in its most perverse way, was in this acquiescent state.

Defensively, she turned her mind to the problems they'd had over remodeling the cabin. It had started when he'd said, "You're too busy settling the house to handle that. Why not let me help there?" He'd been so helpful with other things and, once she told him what she wanted, he took over the project. But far from lessening her workload, his involvement had complicated it.

Those trees! Ellis had a way of thinking of a tree as nothing more than a tube of bark holding its valuable splinters together. Despite his deep knowledge of wildlife, he often talked of game animals (the ones he could hunt) like that, too: bones and fur, nutritional requirements and behavior patterns, each animal's ecological niche, and whether they were useful or not useful. After hearing the kids rave about all he had taught them, his seeming double standard surprised her.

She remembered how appalled she had been when, once the plans for the cabin had been decided, he had brought his chainsaw to take down the six trees closest to the cabin. When she objected, he gave her every practical argument why they had to be removed: they were overgrown and messy, they showered the building with needles and twigs, the branches were a hazard in a big wind, they were a fire hazard, they blocked the light, and they would complicate things when the workmen were trying to dig the trenches for the water lines, as well as interfere with the electrical line.

Not wanting to have to remind him that she owned the place, Meg tactfully argued that, besides being home to a large number of birds and squirrels, the trees added charm and character to the cabin. She suggested that, if they were a fire hazard, the branches nearest to the chimney could be selectively trimmed back and a spark retarder installed on the chimney's opening. When he still insisted that they be taken down, she defended the shade they provided and their lovely piney smells, then spoke at length about the wind making soft whispery sounds when it blew through them. She'd said, "It's enough that the big house has no trees near it, nor any windows that open to the air and sounds and smells of the trees. At least not yet, that is."

Still he argued, saying that there was no middle ground regarding them and accusing her of acting like some kind of modern day Pocahontas, willing to throw her body over old trees to save them instead of admitting their hazard. That comparison finally did it and she was ready to bow to his authority; but, that night, she was jarred awake by a dream in which Ed and Art Stroud, sitting under a huge rainbow, were discussing ways to take the land away from her. The next morning she told Ellis she wouldn't permit the trees' destruction and the work would just have to take place around them. And that was that. Ellis, not willing to compromise, had backed out, and much to her relief the cabin project became all hers again. If that episode had left her discomfited, Ellis was hardly fazed—his jolly, helpful self and his access to her property remained intact.

Meg's thoughts jumped to tomorrow's hike and how such an outing had come about. During a dinner conversation a week or so after they'd moved in, Ellis had spoken about a small herd of elk that lived in the upper reaches of the property. He said that they usually gathered at a natural saltlick in the evening. (A natural saltlick? That was news to Meg). Meg decided the outing would do them all good, including Callie. When the question came up as to whose car to take, Ellis suggested the Jeep, and, without a word to her, climbed into the driver's seat. Meg sat beside him, with the three kids in back, hanging over his shoulder.

The saltlick, high on a steep hillside southwest of the house, could be viewed by driving up an obscure trail off their main road. (Meg hadn't known about that trail either). The trail climbed up through the trees and brush onto a bench of land, ending just below an opening on the slope. As he drove, Ellis explained that the trail was used by hunters in the fall, and, in fact, he had shot a yearling bull elk from this very spot the previous year, and intended hunting from it again this coming fall—which had been news to Meg.

No animals were visible at first. While they waited inside the Jeep, Ellis explained that during the warmer months the elk hung out here in this high country because it was cooler. The onset of snow would force them to move to a lower slope, where the wind blew the snow from the bushes and shrubs and grasses that comprised their diet. As he talked knowledgeably of these things, the children looked at him in awe, taking in every word. He knew so much about the animals and the land they lived on.

It was then that Ellis unfolded the U. S. Forest Service map he carried in his pack, along with his binoculars. It was the first map they'd seen of their place and it helped them understand how large an area their 1,038 acres covered. Besides all the familiar landmarks—the road, the springs, the bench of land containing the house, and the line of trees just outside their back porch—the map showed the saltlick and rock formations and other different things that Meg was eager to see first hand. As for her property, it looked even more important when represented so officially on a green government map. Callie said their clearing looked like a funny shaped cookie cutter had taken a piece out of the green dough of forest surrounding it. Everyone agreed that she was right.

With a proprietary finger, Meg traced the straight lines and sharp corners of her place—all tucked neatly inside the federal lands—then laid her hand over it protectively, as though she could feel the trees and rocks and folds of earth through the paper.

Ellis watched her do it and, shaking his head in disbelief, he scoffed, "You haven't seen it on a map before this? Surely you didn't buy it before seeing a map of it?"

His question made her feel that she'd been reckless or worse, and all the doubts she'd had about buying the place rushed at her, even though she felt he didn't have the right to question her like that, in front of the children or alone. Still, in a confusion of defensive words, she said, "No, I mean, yes, I—I don't know. If there was a map to this place, I never saw it. We just wanted to live here."

On cue, the children chimed in with their reassurances, and Ellis returned to his jovial, bantering self. That was when he'd made his offer to take her on a hike. Pointing at the map, he devised the route that would give her a feeling for her land and the federal lands surrounding it. He'd bring the map along and identify some of the landmarks of the area, and see if they could find a corner or two of her property. She'd nodded soberly and, smiling tentatively, agreed to go on the hike sometime—sometime meaning when the house was settled, when Callie was all better, and when she could get away.

Kurt was the one who spotted the string of elk filing to the salt lick, looking like slow moving ghosts. There were thirteen cow elk and calves, and four deer. The animals seemed mesmerized with the salt, patiently and methodically licking at the ground and a few tree stumps sticking up from it. Ellis explained that the wood had taken up some of the salt and minerals from the ground over the years. He'd passed his binoculars around so they could take turns watching.

It was during that evening, with her family in the car, that everything seemed possible to Meg. In the low, bantering talk between Ellis and the children, she could hear their relief at having so neatly made their escape from the unanswered questions in town. Outside the Jeep, their new environment was hugging around them, making them feel invisible, even conspiratorial, as they watched animals unaware of being watched. While they were there, the dew fell in a delicate spattering of fine droplets on the windshield, its fresh, woodsy fragrance mixing with the rare, musky smell of Ellis.

With the kids so engrossed with his binoculars and the animals, Ellis had looked over at her and his eyes had wandered around her hair and neck, as if she wasn't there, before he'd smiled. It was enough to allow Meg to linger on the prospect of having a man in her life again, and all that that implied—love and companionship for herself, a father for her children, and a helpmate for this wonderful piece of land. With it came the realization that the companionship Ma and Papa had were what she'd always felt deprived of, married to Ed.

Ellis's knee was inches from hers, and his hand—she could have reached out and caressed his hand. In fact, she had tried dodging her head around Callie so she could catch his eye. But by then his eyes were again on the elk or joined to his binoculars, and his hand was gripping the Jeep's steering wheel or adjusting its mirrors to suit him. With the children so in love with him—and she beginning to feel the same—why couldn't he have turned to her at that moment and, with that roguish wink of his, told her, in some subtle way, how special this moment with her was? But, trying to understand Ellis was like falling farther into a tunnel.

Two nights ago he had kissed her again, but fiercely this time, before driving off to town. As his car's taillights disappeared, she'd stood there stunned, rubbing her wounded lips and wondering what had just happened. There had been no preamble to this kiss—no soft declaration, no caress—but just a grab and kiss, and he was gone. Her first inclination was to be amused at his lack of finesse, to want to offer suggestions—or lessons—on what kissing was all about (as though she knew anything about that). But the ache of her arousal had stopped that kind of thinking.

Since that first kiss the night of her homecoming and his suggestion that he accompany her to bed, he hadn't once touched her or let her touch him. Using some strange rules known only to him, in all the times they had been together—with or without the children, in the kitchen or in the casual moments they were next to each other—Ellis had never so much as laid a finger on her. In fact, he had consciously avoided her hands, twisting out of the way twice, so that she had stopped trying to signal him in that way. She wondered if, in the time she was married to Ed, people had decided they shouldn't touch each other anymore—no small caresses, no fingers lightly touching a face, no hand resting on a shoulder or an arm like she touched the children, in those wonderful, quick, reassuring caresses that said so much of care and interest, encouragement and love. To her, not touching the people in your circle didn't make sense. And, between a man and a woman who were attracted to each other, didn't touching help drain off energy, like a lightning rod does in an electrical storm? She tried to imagine Ellis's viewpoint, but couldn't. Not touching her was a game, perhaps, something useful.

It was his eyes that he ran over her, invading her, as though they were hands. And she, as much an observer as a participant, allowed him to do it, feeling her body respond. When he was around she was in a watchful mode, restless, easily startled—and waiting for him. Pent-up air exploded from her lungs. Was he waiting for her to do the same thing—look hungrily at him, want him with her eyes? That must have been what prompted Callie's comment: "Ellis looks at you funny." If it was those looks her two little girls had intercepted, she must make him stop, for it was a perverse way to express emotion.

The kids were so wrapped up in him. In the many offbeat ways kids said it, all three had expressed their yearning for a father—having never really known one, with Ed's penchant for absence and neglect. They seemed so in love with Ellis; and why wouldn't they be? Not only did he woo them with his stories and his good-humored laughter, he wooed them with his very availability.

The picture of the Littles plotting to have him "stay over" made Meg laugh again at the absurd innocence of such an invitation. But it demonstrated what she was up against, too. Getting the girls a daddy sounded like something they expected her to do—like getting them an ice cream cone, only faster, please. As for Kurt, well, she wasn't as sure about his wishes on that, with his quiet reserve and his many interesting projects in the basement, which he didn't mention to Ellis. The thing that stood out in her mind was Kurt's resentment when Ellis drove the Jeep. Where Marc had generously involved Kurt in its workings, Ellis enjoyed it for its power and for what that power conveyed; and none of those things had anything to do with Kurt.

Before Ellis, she had relied on herself; and now, she felt betrayed by her body and confused by her thoughts. If only Doris or Tolly were here—Doris, with her even-headed, earthy objectivity, and Tolly with her homey assurances that promised order and respectability. If they were here, they'd laugh with her about it and put it all in its proper place, and put Ellis there, too. But those two women weren't here and she had to work through this tangle by herself.

One way to do that was to call off the hike; she simply wasn't up to it. She'd call Ellis now, using the excuse of too little time to prepare for it. Kurt had always shown an interest in the hike, so they'd wait until Ellis came back from the Park and bring Kurt along.

Calmer now, she dialed the phone. But his line was always busy and she finally gave up. She thought, "This is absurd. Ellis and I are reasonable people, so, of course I'll go. I'll have a lovely day with an incredibly interesting man who knows the area so well. I will enjoy every minute of the hike."

She tidied up the room, turned off the lamp, checked the children, and went to her bedroom, determined to get a good sleep, even though it was earlier than her usual bedtime. The sheets felt delicious on her bare skin. She moved her toes into the corners, seeking pockets of coolness, and all the while trying to free her mind for sleep. But she was not in the least tired. It was her nightly routine to go out and sit on the rock doorstep and listen to the mountain's evening sounds—sleepy birds calling back and forth, the nightly howling of the coyotes, two owls whose conversation she'd begun to recognize. Her mind yearned for that distraction, but she turned over and tried to sleep.

Resting there, she imagined the feeling of fresh air sliding through an open window, but then her brain began a tally of the windows she had to replace with the kind that opened. After that, it leaped to the impossible kitchen—what to keep and what to remove and how many new cupboards and what kind of countertops. Oh, to make this house as wonderful as she knew it could be! It was going to take time and a great deal of money, and judging from the cabin, she'd made a poor start. Where would she find the highly skilled workers she needed? Confronting these tasks was overwhelming. Maybe Ellis would know. Oh, Ellis, where do you fit in all of this?

After an hour of this, she threw off the quilt and stood staring out the glass that sealed her from the mountain she loved. As she watched, the stars appeared soundlessly as they had the night of her homecoming. Why had she been so afraid of the man she saw inside her house that night, even when he assured her who he was? Was it a premonition? Was it possible that that lovely, virile man was playing some kind of game with her and the kids?

It came to her that she couldn't stand another night of this kind of questioning. She must use tomorrow to seek out the answers to the riddle of Ellis. She prayed that her loneliness hadn't altered her judgment, that she hadn't been so hurt by Ed that she couldn't see things clearly anymore. Aware of being chilled, she returned to bed and once again snuggled under the down comforter. Perhaps now she would be able to sleep. And she did, but it was an uneasy sleep wracked by dreams.

She woke up tired and drawn. After starting coffee, she went outside and searched the perfect blue sky for any hint of bad weather. But there was nothing as wonderful as a black cloud to interfere with the hike. When the children joined her, she explained where she and Ellis were going and informed them that his friends would be here in her place.

They were not overjoyed at the prospect. "It isn't fair," they chanted. "You and Ellis going on this hike without us." Their protest encouraged her to ask herself why she was leaving them alone with total strangers, and she told them she wouldn't go then. But Kurt—that noblest of sons, as fair and straight as a parson—spoke up in her defense, reminding the Littles that she had been working pretty hard and it was about time she went somewhere herself. He added, "And once Ma knows the way we can all go on a hike, too."

Meg nodded and headed for the bedroom. There she dressed in her oldest jeans—the pair with the frayed knees and the pink enamel splatters—then dug out the shabby shirt with its high-buttoned neck. She caught up her hair tightly into two little pigtails, ending with mismatched barrettes on their ends. She slathered sunscreen on her face and lips, and removed her earrings. When she was done, she studied the apparition in the bathroom mirror and declared, "This isn't Halloween!" and took off the old clothes and dressed instead in a better pair of jeans and an old but reasonably respectable shirt. She combed her hair in her usual style and added some makeup—but not much.

Back in the kitchen, she remembered to tell the children about the dog Ellis had found, and that sealed it. The kids started to plan where a dog would sleep and what it would eat. They finished breakfast in a hurry and took off downstairs to see if there was anything for a dog in the "Treasure Room"—the room stacked high with old junk and the unbelievably wonderful odds and ends collected by Al Turner.

Jeannie and Paul Young were like their name and full of enthusiasm. As they were being escorted around the house and outside and being impressed by the lurid details of the mother bear and her cubs and the Canada lynx and the ravens and the Red-tailed Hawks and ground squirrels, Meg put together a lunch. Ellis packed it and a small coffeepot and two cups and other odds and ends into the small pack he would carry. And while he talked more about the fire in the Park and the possible dog, Meg looked at him secretly—this golden man in a fresh blue shirt, looking well rested and full of teasing words and laughter—this man who occupied her wakeful evenings, then her dreams—this man whose eyes had already moved over her body without touching her, and to whom her body had responded—this man who had smiled to himself while he calmly cleaned up the mess and broken pieces of the coffee cup she had held out to him with her hand trembling—this man with whom she would spend the day—alone—no children.

29

THE HIKE

Meg assumed that the hike would start somewhere lower on the mountain, where her property started, and in a place that could only be reached by car. She imagined that they would get out of the car, pull on their daypacks, decide who would carry the lunch, make sure they had the map, and lock things up. From the car they would walk some distance into the forest, commenting on the beauty around them, the little glimpses of perfect sky, and their good fortune with the weather, all the while avoiding looking at each other and bound together by anticipation. When they'd hiked a mile or so, Ellis would say, "Let's stop here, Meg." And she, having already built a picture of "here" in her mind, and knowing exactly what "here" meant, would stop.

But that wasn't the way it went.

The hike began with Ellis saying, "Let's go!" And with a tight, inscrutable look on his face, he walked out the kitchen door, down the back porch steps, and across the sixty feet of open ground separating the house from the wall of trees. There, well inside the trees, he turned right onto a wide, well-worn game trail that Meg hadn't known existed.

Meg was scrambling after him, still trying to get her right arm through the strap of her pack, when she remembered that her sunglasses were still on the porch step. She yelled, "Wait up, I forgot my glasses!" He was moving fast and she didn't hear his answer, but she ran back and retrieved them, kissing the kids goodbye for the second time. Before reentering the forest, she turned and waved again to the forlorn figure of Sara leaning back against the screen door. Then the path turned, and the thicket of plants and trees, like a giant chlorophyll curtain, closed off the sight of all that was familiar and dear to her; and changing her mind—for whatever reason—was no longer an option.

Somewhere far ahead of her she heard Ellis calling, "Meg, come on!" And with the same impatience she shrilled back, "I'm coming, I'm coming. Wait up!"

Seeing the large game trail that close to the house really gave her pause, but no more than the intimidating stands of trees on either side of it did. Even though she and the children had explored much of the property close to the house, no one had yet ventured inside this eastern segment of the forest. On the other side of the house, the western side, the forest flowed gracefully down from the ridge top to the clearing and there encircled it, tenderly, trimming its edges with low, colorful shrubs and saplings before resuming its downward journey to the canyon floor.

But here on the eastern side of the property, the forest rose up in an unyielding line, with no soft blurring of plants around its feet, its giant trees pressed elbow-to-elbow and toe-to-toe, as if guarding the entrance to this side of the mountain. Here the trees were so numerous that when one of them died, it spent its decaying years propped upright against another until it collapsed in a shower of powder and chunks, to lie in a heap in the small plot allowed it.

With Ellis somewhere far in front of her, Meg entered this place alone, walking into it like a person entering a darkened room—feet thrust out, feeling for obstacles—until her eyes got used to the change in illumination. Once inside, she looked around, surprised. As inhospitable as the forest had appeared from the outside, here it was like entering a cathedral, with a muting of both light and sound. It affected Meg deeply, for with everything else in her world in motion, these silent trees and the tranquil earth beneath them were as far from chaos as anything could be. She smiled at them in recognition—these old trees—she was among friends again.

If Ellis were here she'd tell him, "This is what I mean. Listen, their silence is telling us something." But he was already far ahead, calling out an impatient, "Meg! If you don't hurry we're not going to get anywhere!" She moved on, hurrying toward the sound. They could talk of this later, maybe when they took a break, or over lunch.

From their starting point, the game trail went gently uphill; but very quickly it began to climb, with only a few interspersed flat areas. These she welcomed, for it took a while for her to catch her breath. Judging from Ellis's voice—always ahead of her and commanding her to hurry—she wondered if she could keep up with him if he was going to walk that fast. She'd have to ask him to slow down. Yet, from the glimpses of him, he was looking neither left, nor right, nor back for her. She guessed she would have to adapt to the speed he'd set. This was going to be a day of hurry, with no "listening to what a tree was saying."

Ellis was examining the trunk of a large tree beside the trail when she finally caught up to him. He surprised and delighted her by reaching out and pulling her against him, to see what he was looking at. Three long gouges had been scratched into the bark and, from them, a rumpled flow of yellow sap, like melted wax down a burnt candle, oozed to the ground.

"A big bear made these," he announced, "and judging by the depth of the slashes, you can imagine what he's capable of."

Not knowing what would happen next she only nodded and tried to concentrate on the tree. Being next to him like this and being held so close was just as she'd imagined it would be. She was about to ask him how he knew a bear made them when he pulled her even closer against him and kissed her forehead, declaring, "Umm, you taste salty." Leaning down and tipping her face up with his free hand, he asked solicitously, "You doing okay? Can you handle walking this fast?"

Laughing up at him and feeling bolder, Meg said, "It's fast, but I'm doing great. Now that I've gotten my second wind, I'll be fine."

At that, he put both arms around her and, pressing himself tightly against her, said, "Oh, woman, you feel so good against me." He leaned back a little and spoke urgently. "We're going to have to do something about this, aren't we?"

Unable to speak, Meg closed her eyes, waiting for his kiss. As she moved her arms around him, he pushed her away. Grinning wickedly he said, "There'll be time enough for that later. We have a lot of ground to cover if we want to get to the top of the mountain by noon." With that, he gave her an encouraging pat and started up the trail again, just as rapidly as before.

The timeout had given her a chance to catch her breath—at least from running up the trail. But her breathing from the excitement over what had just happened was another matter. The way his body felt against hers lingered in her mind. To have touched him at all was a dream come true. How long had it been since she'd felt this way: eager and alive and filled with a longing that started low and traveled all the way up to her ears. And his delicious implication that somewhere further up on the mountain they "would do something about this." It was finally out in the open; he wanted her just as much as she wanted him. She sighed, thinking about the pleasure they would give each other. There was no question in her mind as to how she was going to handle it.

As she tried to keep her mind on her feet and not fall over anything on the trail, she watched him, ahead of her, with longing and envy. He glided over the trail like a single graceful machine—bending smoothly to avoid the branches, stepping effortlessly over fallen logs, and fairly hopping over the rocks and roots littering their path—while she felt like a bag full of odd parts. Nothing had prepared her for this kind of brisk hike. But then, Ellis did this every day, while she did little else but push furniture around, unpack endless boxes, cook and clean, and drive up and down the mountain road—and, regrettably, in that last activity, only the Jeep got any exercise.

Why she'd just assured him that she was able to handle this pace was a puzzle. It seemed a triviality, but if she were another woman—the helpless kind, the kind she wasn't nor ever could be—she would have said, "Surely you don't expect me to hike up this trail this fast." And that woman would be treated gently and, perhaps, be considered more desirable for having asked him that. So, why couldn't she ask him, or any man, to make an accommodation for her? She guessed she just needed to prove to Ellis that a thirty-eight-year-old woman could keep up with a twenty-nine-year-old man. So she wasn't going to beg him to slow down; she was just going to keep up with him. Besides, it would get them to "there" faster.

Now that they were moving along together, Ellis started to talk. "You've never mentioned seeing the two male bears that use this trail to get around. It's my guess that one of them marked that tree back there."

"Two *different* bears…?" Meg's voice broke up in her rapid breathing.

"Yeah. I was just wondering if you've ever seen them from the kitchen window? They're easy to spot. In summer they use this trail every night to get to the garbage in the campgrounds, then come back up each morning. Since this trail swings close to the house, you—"

Meg interrupted, "If you're talking about *different bears* from the sow and cubs we've seen on the west road, no, I can't say I've seen the two you're talking about." She stopped talking and tried to take in this new information—two other bears passing close to the house, regularly.

What else but big animals could have worn this trail so deeply into the ground? She had long accepted the thought of bears living here, too, but she'd rather hoped they'd taken up their lives *away* from the house now that the Halverson family had announced its presence.

He continued, "Well, you might be on the lookout for them and keep the kids away from here until we get our dog. Two old male bears can be a little tricky. The Turners often saw them. Alice was scared to death of them even though Al kept telling her that the bears' biggest concern was too much mustard on the hotdogs they scrounged up or rancid peanut butter." He laughed. "Al said that he could almost set his clock by them each morning they returned up the trail—at around this time, as a matter of fact."

"Great!" was all the reply that Meg could manage as her mind locked on the words *around this time!* The need to move quickly away was like a hand pushing at the small of her back, and she seemed to have run out of saliva. She wondered what a bear coming up from behind would sound like. Or maybe it didn't make any sound until it was too late. She took a quick look over her shoulder, even though she truly didn't want to see anything.

Ellis continued, "You're sure to recognize them. They're both brown, but one's got a ruffle of blondish fur around his front feet.

They've lived on this side of the property for a long time. Al figured that they sleep up around here during the day, but he never found exactly where."

She made her voice calm. "I'm glad to know about them. Thanks for telling me." The whole conversation was hard to believe—Ellis chatting about two large bears the same way another person discussed two eccentric but generally lovable relatives.

As she craned her neck to see around the trees they were passing, she noticed that the trail itself was nearly obscured by the low-growing plants along its sides, and the forest seemed full of watching things. She considered asking Ellis if she might walk in front of him for a while; but she finally decided she'd just stay close behind. When her foot caught on his heel and nearly tripped him, she backed off, but just enough to feel safe.

Ellis was saying, "—so you're smart keeping your garbage cans locked in the garage and away from those two old garbage hounds."

The word "hounds" softened the teeth-bared, claws-out image she'd just conjured up and she managed to pant out, "Guess we've been lucky."

His answer was lost when he ducked under a tree leaning over the trail. As she fought her way through its branches, she considered plotting the bears on a map, as to which ones went with which side of the property. She should be grateful that her little strip in the middle was uncontested, at least so far. That dog Ellis had located better show up! Without that prospect, with the kids running all over the place, she wouldn't have a tranquil moment.

As disconcerted as she was by what he'd just told her about the bears, she truly enjoyed hearing his stories about these mountains. He was a fount of strange facts and valuable information, and she, along with the kids, hung on his every word about these things. Every time he came to dinner he had a story and, if it was true, it offered its own set of instructions. Yet, from the casual way he talked, either he was trying to impress her and the kids, or he really had no idea just how little they knew about things up here.

It was the beauty of the terrain they were hiking through that finally quieted her worries about encountering a bear. Here, the only sounds came from the pound of their feet on the trail and the brush grabbing at their clothing. Everything she saw delighted her, and the trail itself was intriguing.

Her first impression was that the well-worn game trail meandered willy-nilly through the trees, but there was nothing haphazard about it. From the many smaller trails joining or exiting it, indeed, this trail was the best way to travel here—a kind of throughway, when an animal was pushed by season, storm, or the need to escape, or in need of water and food, or to reach the protection of a favored resting area. Seeing that, she could understand that an animal's predicament was the same as a person's. All manner of beings used these trails; perhaps the long-ago woman had walked on this very trail. It was nice to think about as they hiked in silence.

With her interest caught, she studied the trail itself. In its dampness between Ellis's boot prints she could see a scuffling of animal tracks—hoof prints and coyote tracks as well as those made by animals she couldn't or really didn't want to identify. Even so, she was fascinated, just as she and Sara had been that day they saw the lynx.

The trail went up and then down, up and down, up and down. When they were climbing, the mere task of lifting her feet and placing them accurately on the uneven ground was difficult enough, but it was worse when the trail headed downhill. At first she welcomed the change, until she found that gravity threw her forward and it was up to her tired knees to keep her from careening headfirst.

Most often, the trail went through cool, darkened stands of timber. Wherever the sunlight broke through the tightly locked branches above her head, its angled shafts of light chose to illuminate single plants—as if the sun were picking favorites and bestowing prizes. When the trees pulled back to reveal an open meadow, the trail looked newly hewn from the brilliant, summer-lit grasses and bushes of snowberry and huckleberry that bordered it. Then the trail reentered the darkened forest, with its fluttering light again erasing its edges. The forest air flowed cool and moist into her nostrils and smelled like a blend of growing plants and decaying wood, of mushrooms and damp earth, of balsam suffused with a sharp animal musk. In the trail's deepest, most undisturbed recesses, the air, as though trapped in a bottle, still held the thought of last winter's snows.

Within the first hour they passed a good-sized spring close to the trail. They hadn't packed water, so when she saw it she expected Ellis to stop. But he bypassed it without even asking her if she was thirsty. Obviously, he was thinking about another spring somewhere up ahead. With a wistful look back at it, she added "stopping for water" to the list of things she wasn't about to ask him to do, and she stayed right on his heels.

What puzzled her was his passing up interesting land formations, without so much as a word or a gesture. If he could speak at length about bears and garbage, surely these landmarks were worthy of a few words, as well as identification. So far, there'd been no mention of looking for the corners of her property, as he had talked about doing, and she wondered what he was waiting for to bring out his map. Between gasps for air she managed to call out to him, "Can you show me where we are on your map?"

Without breaking step, he looked back and said, "I didn't bring it—just another thing to carry."

"A *folded* map? I'd have carried it! There are so few things in my pack." When he didn't answer, she reached out and grabbed his sleeve and stopped him. Looking at him and panting furiously, she managed to say, "You should have told me, Ellis. Remember how interested the kids and I were when you first showed us the map? And when you talked about our going on this hike you said you'd show me my property lines and find its corners. Surely, you'd need a map if you'd really intended to do that."

"I guess I should have brought it. Sorry." He started to walk away, but she grabbed at his sleeve again.

She demanded, "At least tell me where we are. Is what I'm standing on now *my* land? I want to know where I am and what's mine."

He gestured vaguely. "Well, we've crossed back and forth between your land and the Forest Service land. It's hard to say right here who owns what, but the place we're going to is located on your property."

That hardly appeased her, and she wished she'd spoken up sooner—not that it would have changed anything, she supposed. She gave him a shove to go on; and for the next half hour she chewed on her disappointment. At least she didn't have to wonder what coming on this hike was all about: a grand seduction and not much more. Seeing his actions back on the trail in that light, he now seemed—not exactly callous, but certainly manipulative, holding her tight to him that way and arousing her, then pushing her crudely away and putting everything on hold. She heaved a sigh at the conflict of her thoughts. What was she supposed to do, stand there like a stick and not respond? He had to know just how vulnerable she was. As for him—always keeping himself out of reach, playing on her weaknesses—it had a familiar feel to it.

But if he was a master of teasing, she was a master of exaggerated hope. Her angst of last night was such a stupid waste of time. At least she was learning something about him today. Now that her emotions had cooled down, she just felt foolish, galloping dutifully behind him as if toward some kind of reward.

Disheartened now, she slowed and had fallen farther and farther behind. It was no use pretending that she could keep up. With that thought, she stopped and looked hopelessly at Ellis, a couple hundred yards ahead of her. She called out to him, but her voice came out dry and hoarse. Why couldn't he just turn around and notice that she'd stopped? All morning, except for an occasional backward glance, he appeared to give no thought to her well being, never breaking the pace he'd set. She called out again, "Ellis! Stop!" And this time her voice carried and he turned and waved at her. Then, after making a few hand gestures that she hadn't the least idea how to interpret, he ducked into the underbrush alongside the trail. By the time she'd blinked some stinging sweat out of her eye, he had disappeared. Undoubtedly, he needed a toilet break. Well, so did she. She left the trail and took care of herself, all the while keeping in mind the place where he'd vanished. When enough time had elapsed for him to have decently finished, she walked up to the spot, calling out to let him know where she was.

Waiting, she gratefully sank down on a fallen tree. With her feet sore and the muscles in her legs and knees in a rage, and being hot and thirsty besides, she unbuttoned a couple buttons of her blouse and pulled the cloth away from her damp skin to let the air work its magic.

When ten minutes changed to fifteen, and she'd still heard nothing, she got up and yelled at the top of her voice, "Damn it, Ellis, where the heck are you?" After listening hard, she again yelled, "Are you playing some kind of joke, leaving me..." to which she added, quietly, to herself "to cope all by myself, for god's sake? Too bad I'm not being attacked by one of those bears you love to frighten me about. Or is it *you* they're lunching on?" With a rueful laugh, she checked over her shoulder, wondering if she might be in any kind of danger, then shook her head in disgust that she'd even done that.

But where Ellis was and what she was supposed to make of it made her furious. Insufferable man! Was she supposed to just wait here until he came back from god knows where? Was that what all those hand signals were about? Couldn't he use his voice, for god's sake, and have a little consideration? Or had something really happened to him? She thought not, and wondered if this was some kind of setup: his hoping that she'd beg for his protection, along with food and water? Perhaps he was close by this very minute, hoping to see her worry and squirm. If that were the case then he would be very disappointed; as long as she could move she'd go calmly on, but this time at her own pace.

The problem now was should she turn back? She was hungry and very thirsty, and it was his pack that held the food. She had to find water soon, but just stopping had helped clear her mind. As for her thirst, she remembered reading somewhere that putting a small stone in your mouth could ease thirst, if only to distract one from thinking about it. She picked up a small flat, nickel-sized stone, wiped it off on her jeans and popped it into her mouth. It tasted just like she imagined a rock would and laughing at herself distracted her from her mounting worry.

Finding water was her most pressing concern. She could turn back and, keeping to the trail, find that spring they'd bypassed earlier. But, in reality, her best chance for water lay ahead—that was what Ellis was aiming for. Besides, she thought she could smell water up ahead, so she'd just follow her nose.

By her watch, they'd been walking for over two hours, and they had seemed to travel in a giant loop. But where she was now, other than very near the top of some mountain, she had no idea. Once on top, if she could see the valley, she'd hopefully know where she was in relation to the house. Glancing over her shoulder, through a break in the trees she caught sight of the very mountain she saw across from the house every day. She knew where she was! If she had to turn back, by using these bearings she could find the house. This discovery restored her confidence.

With a laugh, her concerns over the day fell away. She'd ruined last night with her worries, but she wasn't going to ruin this day, too. Actually, she was having a wonderful time. Last year at this time, as Mrs. Edward Halverson, she'd been locked into a world where her weightiest concerns were whether her dress would match her shoes, or who might be insulted by having to sit next to Mrs. So-and-So at an upcoming party. But today—today she'd not only learned something about her physical endurance, but by walking on the very skin and bones of the mountain, she thought she'd heard the voice of the mountain itself, saying, "Look at me, listen to me, smell me, examine my heart; this is what I am."

Remembering the shafts of sunlight falling around her in the darkest part of the forest only confirmed the impression that she'd been given a guided tour. Ellis had led her there, but he was no part of it. Now, his having left for points unknown didn't matter in the least. What mattered was that the hike had peeled away some of her old scars, leaving her feeling strong, and restoring her faith in herself, and she had even been stirred by emotions she hadn't felt for years. She couldn't say what was ahead of her today, as far as Ellis and she were concerned—she'd deal with that later. But today, now, she was having an adventure, and reveling in it!

Rested, but pushed to find water, she started walking up the trail again. She chuckled in satisfaction that she wasn't looking back over her shoulder any longer. There were animals around—it was more than a hunch; she could feel them through the small traces of their musk in the air and even sense the air still bumping against itself from their passage. When the trail took a sudden jog, and a few uneasy hairs stirred on the back of her neck, she dubbed it coexistence—a word that she had certainly considered many times since moving here.

She put out her hands and touched the tree trunks and bushes she was passing. Their rough textures and leaves tickled her palms and finger tips, but not as foreign objects. These were something familiar. "My land! My land!" She said it over and over, even though she knew it was hers only in the sense of holding title to it and of making future decisions concerning it, at least for the while.

Pausing, and looking around her, she knew that owning land was a weightier thing than owning a house. A house could be built, lived in, and torn down if need be, but a great chunk of land like this was different. It could be said that she owned it, but, in reflecting back on her parents and their farm, in reality it was the land that owned her.

A memory of her parents came to her mind—of Papa and Ma and her on an evening walk. Her parents, looking the very picture of steadfast stewards of their land, were standing on the highest little hill overlooking their wheat fields, and Papa was pointing out something to Ma. On his face was a look of absolute love for the land before him, his precious land. He understood everything about it—where the water collected and the snow drifted, where the soil was the deepest and the thinnest, what to plow and what to leave undisturbed. He saw the land as pieces and parts of the whole, and saw himself as the one who coaxed it to flourish. If he ever cursed it—as a caretaker curses the certainty of his task, or for having to trade his youth and energies for what little he was able to wrest from it—she never knew.

But there was more in that particular picture of her parents that called for Meg's attention. It had been just the three of them moving up the hill. The hill wasn't steep, but it was a good climb. Occasionally her parents stopped and turned around, patiently, to see if she was coming. (She was always looking for arrowheads in the plowed fields, having found three of them before.) Papa and Ma were still young at that time. Even so, she recalled how slowly the two of them had walked: moving together, in step, right feet, left feet, talking together, their laughter low and intimate, Papa's hand around Ma's waist, or on

Ma's arm, or offering her his outstretched hand to steady her over the little breaks in the field.

What Meg took from that soft and lovely picture was that there was never a separation between them; they always seemed in step. It wasn't just Papa, or just Ma, but was Papa and Ma together. Each had his or her individual tasks around the farm or their small community, but they were always a unit. There was never a contest between the two of them. There was no Papa setting a pace and Ma panting to keep up. Between the two of them there was kindness and love and nothing to prove.

Just recalling that almost brought her to tears, and she tucked the memory back into that safe recess of her mind again—to remember it, to use it, and to have it always.

30

CAMPFIRE

As Meg made her way wearily up the trail—still following the scent of water—she wondered if Ellis might be waiting for her at the spring, wherever that was. She couldn't imagine he would have just left her to find her way home by herself, if for no other reason than the difficulty of explaining it to the kids. She laughed at that, letting her imagination run rampant over possible scenarios. He could tell them, "A bear ate her! So sorry! But we have to consider the poor bear, that had apparently run out of ground squirrels." She was laughing aloud at her thoughts when she almost walked into Ellis, standing just off the trail, half-hidden behind a tree. She jumped when she saw him.

He looked at her quizzically and said, "Well, well, well, so you're still with me. I've been wondering if maybe you decided to go back home."

"Well, well, well, yourself." She looked at him coolly.

Reaching out, he wiped his fingers across her damp forehead and held them out for her to see. "I don't know why you're sweating, walking so slowly. I've been watching you."

"Now there's a nice thought!" She shook her head in disbelief. "After you took off I decided I'd take my time and enjoy the view. Where did you go?"

"There's an elk meadow near here, and I thought I'd take a side trip to check it out. There're lots of tracks but no elk."

"You went to see some elk? Was that what all your hand signals were about? Couldn't you have told me where you were going? Did it even dawn on you that I might have liked knowing where you were going?"

"Poor Meg! Were you afraid I'd get lost?"

An unreasoning anger welled up in her. "I'd rather hoped your concern might be for me. Last night on the phone you were all excited about this hike giving us a chance to be alone. Remember? Well, we've been alone all right. You've been alone, and I've been alone, but until this minute we haven't been alone together!"

He laughed at that and put his hand under her chin and looked into her eyes, as contrite as ever. "I'm sorry. Are you going to forgive me?"

She brushed aside his hand. "You say 'I'm sorry' too easily for me to believe you mean it." Clearly disgusted, she said, "I'm thirsty, Ellis, *very* thirsty. How much farther to a spring?"

He said, "When we passed that spring earlier, I half expected you to ask to stop."

"Then I must have disappointed you." Her head had begun to ache and her legs had turned to rubber. Speaking as matter-of-factly as she could, she said, "Are we going to stand here and play games? I'm thirsty and hungry and tired. You have the food in your pack and you know where the damn spring is, so it looks like you hold all the cards. If you've been waiting for me to say that, well, there it is."

Looking genuinely at a loss, he said, "Just up ahead there's water, along with a pretty spectacular view of the whole valley and the mountains to the north. And there's a flat area beside the spring to build a fire. I was thinking we'd brew our coffee there and eat lunch. The water there is unbelievably cold." He had turned to walk on, but hesitated and said, "You'll be happy to know the spring's on your property."

She acknowledged that with an impatient nod, but having no choice but trudge behind him for an unknown distance was irritating. However, the prospect of getting to water was reason enough to do it.

She felt the spring's moisture on her face and then heard it, before catching sight of its silvery water falling prettily and musically down a miniature stair step of moss-covered rocks. The water emerged from a ferny crevice in the wall of rock and, after descending, it gathered into a little pool. From there it wandered its way through a tumble of rocks for a few feet before vanishing, as though its wet skeins were needed elsewhere.

For a long moment she stood silently, watching the water and listening to its diminutive sounds. Slowly she began to comprehend what Ellis had said, that this place was on her property. She thought, I'll paint a picture of this magical place, my land's first portrait. When I bring the kids up here to see it, I'll bring my paint box. Oh, they'll love it, too.

It was only then that she could lie down flat beside it and begin to drink, where the water splayed over a flat rock. As she drew in the water her tongue and lips explored the rough moss covering the rock's surface. It took a long time to drink enough and, when she was through, she laid one cheek, then the other, on the rock, letting the tiny current dam up against her temples, then each closed eye. After that she drank again. Cooled at last and dripping, she pulled herself up, aware that her anger had disappeared with her thirst. Seeing that Ellis was watching her—in fact, was smiling broadly at her—she said, "I might have left you some."

"It's me who left you some. I had my turn a while back."

"It's perfect here, and you're right about the spectacular view." Looking beyond the trees to the valley and the several layers of mountain ranges that this high view afforded her, Meg confirmed what she had intuited earlier—where exactly she was. But the spring puzzled her. As she headed tiredly to a tree in the flat area and sat down against it, she said, "You're the encyclopedia, so tell me about this spring and those near my house. The snow has long since melted, so how can such icy water be flowing this high on the mountain? And then it just disappears. Where does it go?"

He said, "The very fact that it's just as cold in winter as it is today is a clue. There's running water deep inside this mountain. It works its way between seams and layers of rock, then surfaces here and there before heading back down and moving on. As to where it comes from, I doubt that anyone but a hydrologist could tell you that. Most likely all these springs come from a single source, but I don't know. It's fascinating to think about, isn't it?"

Meg nodded in wonder. "It's a gift from this mountain. It's offering us refreshments just when we need them most. But it's not just for us—there's a beautiful set of fresh elk tracks right where I was drinking."

"I saw that. Elk and deer hang out here, no doubt about it. And why wouldn't they, with a stopping place like this? Look, Meg, you relax while I get a fire going for the coffee. But, before you get too comfortable, maybe you could catch some of that water in the coffeepot while I'm rounding up some wood."

While he went about his task, she opened his pack and took out the coffeepot and began filling it slowly and patiently at the spring. As she did, she marveled at the dainty waterfall and the beauty of this cool little glen nestled so unexpectedly into the mountain's face. Remembering the day she'd walked home from that last committee meeting—the day Ed had died—she'd pictured herself up on a mountaintop such as this, but not even *her* imagination could have thought up anything this beautiful.

Once the pot was full, she regained her seat against the tree and loosened the laces on her boots and removed them, along with her socks. Instantly feeling better, she massaged her feet while she watched Ellis's preparations for the fire.

From the assorted rocks alongside the spring he brought three large flat ones to the open space near Meg. From this site he first cleaned off the accumulation of pine needles and the scattering of brush and grass, setting aside the driest of these for fuel for his fire. With a small flat rock he took his time scraping out a narrow but deep depression in the ground, and then meticulously settled the three rocks into a triangle, overhanging it. Into the very bottom of the hole, he tucked twists of dry grass, dried moss, and leaves, and a layer of tiny twigs. Next, he searched through the pile of wood for the smallest, driest sticks, snapping them into small sections, and placing them on top of the dry tinder. To these he added slightly bigger sticks, stacking them layer-by-layer, as if building a log cabin, until he had made a perfect little house of wood. When it was all in place, he lit it with a single match stuck carefully into the dried stuff at its base.

Feeling her approval, he grinned as he tucked the box of matches back into his shirt pocket and patted it.

Meg smiled over to him and said, "Gosh, after all that, I was expecting you to use a flint and steel to light it."

They both watched a thin trickle of white smoke work its way up through the pile, then saw a tiny flame appear, as though deep inside a lantern. It wandered shyly up through all the kindling, then suddenly made a lunge at the bigger fuel and settled into its task. Ellis continued to add bigger and bigger pieces of wood, and when he had a solid base of burning wood he balanced the coffeepot on the three overhanging stones.

He sat down across from her, close to his supply of wood, saying, "Now, as your local Forest Service representative, I'll see if I can boil our coffee water without burning down anything important. I wouldn't want this to compete with the drama going on in Glacier Park."

Meg laughed comfortably. "As the land owner, I'll certainly go along with that." After a moment she said, "It's a treat watching you do all the work; building a fire is usually my job. The way you fixed the rocks to hold the coffeepot is something I'll remember. I could tell you've done this before. Doesn't the very thought of coffee make you want to add that packet of coffee to the water right now?"

"Something like that."

"Well, can't you hurry it up?"

He laughed along with her. "You need to be patient like me. The water was cold and this fire's not that big."

While she waited she began to yawn and, unable to resist the fire, she stretched out on the ground, propping up her head on her hand. It was pleasant watching Ellis—his tanned, muscular arms with his blue shirtsleeves rolled way up, and his face, so intent on the fire and so satisfied with it. As she watched him she became absorbed with his hands pushing a stick slowly into the fire, then seeing the fire's leisurely response. She had never realized just how sensual the act of fire building was, and she felt her face blushing at the direction her thoughts had taken.

With the fire going well, Ellis stretched out across from her. And for a time, without speaking, the two of them—with their eyes like those of sleepy dogs—lay captive beside it, their faces reflecting the sounds and smells accompanying the fire, as well as lulled by memories of other camps and other campfires.

Meg broke the silence. "Having a dad who was a Forest Service ranger must have been a great influence. He must have been the one who taught you how to make a campfire."

Ellis nodded. "Yes. He's always been a great one for campfires, having spent his life in the woods. He's one of those old school rangers—somewhere between a naturalist and a 'board-footer.' My job is a far cry from the work Dad did in those backwoods field stations, with his mule strings and trail crews. With all your talk about old trees, you two would get along famously. I keep telling him that his *naturalist* type of forestry has been replaced by high-tech science. He and I can talk about the old days but we can't talk about the specifics of the kind of forestry I do."

His words brought back hers and Ed's old argument and she fairly itched to follow that statement up with a question or two. But wary of starting an argument, she settled for, "Following your father into Forestry must give your parents a lot of satisfaction."

"Yes, Dad's pleased, but Mother still resents it. She had plans for me in Minneapolis, I guess. Her family manufactures hardware. I didn't want to disappoint her, but there was no chance I'd ever go there and do that." Happy to change the subject, he asked, "What about you? Have you done much camping?"

Meg nodded happily. "Yes, as a girl, for two weeks at a time. Camping was one of the high points of my life. Two weeks was never long enough, but with hiring someone to come in and feed our animals and do the milking, it was as long as Papa could get away. We always put in our camps in the Little Belt Mountains where we'd never see another human being. And we always camped beside a little creek."

Ellis nodded for her to go on.

"We had a big wall tent—the kind with the ridge pole and all those crossed braces. It made for a strong tent that we could live in for a long time, even during storms. We didn't have cots, so we slept on the ground, inside the tent. Papa fashioned a king-sized frame out of four logs and we filled it with grass and moss and all the soft ends of boughs from the trees he'd cut for the tent poles. We didn't have sleeping bags, so we piled all our blankets and comforters into it. It was a little lumpy and hurt our backs in spots, but my sister and I didn't care. We all slept together, with Tolly and me in the middle and Ma and Papa on the sides.

"One of my best memories is our singing in bed in the dark—the four of us trying to harmonize those old songs we loved so much. Can you imagine an animal passing our camp at night and hearing the sounds coming from the tent? It might have scared some animals, but I'm sure the coyotes understood." She laughed at that.

"Anyway, I remember feeling all snug and safe lying there at night, and looking out at the fire—Papa tied the tent flaps open so we could see it. But even with the fire, I remember worrying that something could creep up and get Ma and Papa, because they were lying right up against the tent's cloth walls. That's the thing about camping, that mixture of being scared and thrilled at the same time—like you might be tested in some terrifying way—but if you came through it okay you'd be a better person."

She looked at him for understanding and they laughed together. "Papa and Ma always got up ahead of us. When Tolly and I woke up, the first thing we'd hear was the creek, and the first thing we'd smell was coffee and the fire—like now, only better."

While she was talking, the water had come to a rolling boil. Unhurried, Ellis pulled out some of the wood to quiet it then leisurely added the coffee grounds without it boiling over. Almost immediately, its delicious smell drifted around in the space between them. He pushed it to the back of a rock for the grounds to settle. He removed their lunches from his pack then poured the steaming brew into their cups, using an old hot pad Meg had thrown into the pack at the last moment. Ellis sat down beside her and they began to eat.

Still wanting to talk about camping, Meg spoke between bites. "Papa was the one who taught us so many things about the mountains. He taught Tolly and me how to fish. And Ma showed us how to cook over a campfire using her old cast-iron Dutch oven; I mean, cook *real* food, like corn bread and brownies, beef stew and biscuits, and chicken and dumplings. That Dutch oven is mine now; I chose it from among the things left behind when they died.

"Anyway, that's where I learned to love a campfire so much. My husband didn't like things like that, but I've taken the kids camping when I could. They're regular little troopers. In fact, since we moved here, they call their play down in the meadow 'camping.' I have to admit that sometimes when I go down there with them I feel like I'm a kid playing again. Living where you did, your mom must have enjoyed that kind of thing."

"Glacier Lady, with Dad and me?" Ellis uttered a derisive laugh. "No way. My parents are two extremes. Dad's like an old flannel shirt and Mom's like cold satin." Looking embarrassed, he stared vacantly into the fire, then went on, "To me, Dad has always seemed to be in the right place at the right time, while Mom...well, when she met up with Dad, I think she was in the wrong place at the wrong time. I've felt sorry about that, and a little guilty. If it hadn't been for me she would have gone back to Minnesota, and Dad would have found someone a little more suitable for his lifestyle."

At a questioning sound from Meg, he continued, "Mom's family's well-off. The summer she graduated from college, she came out to Montana to work in the dining room of one of the big hotels in Glacier Park. For rich girls like her it was the thing to do, for a little change of scene, I guess. Anyway, Dad had also just graduated—from the School of Forestry in Clark Fork, of course—and he was on his first assignment in the Forest Service, in the district adjacent to East Glacier. It all must have looked pretty idyllic to Mom. To make a long story short, they got married that first September and I was born seven months later. Yes, I'm one of *those*."

Meg said, "You're not the first *early* baby, Ellis. These days there's no stigma in that. Your folks came from different backgrounds, but it sounds like they made a good life out of it. And with her background in industry and his in Forestry, it seems like you've had the best of both worlds. Coming from a farm, I might understand a lot about growing wheat, but I know nothing about manufacturing."

He nodded somewhat reluctantly. "You're right, but there was a lot of negative stuff: her family never once visited us, so it was Mom who made the yearly trek back home to Minneapolis—it always had a real pull on her. I went with her when I was little, but, once I was in high school, I stayed home with Dad.

"I grew up feeling that no one was happy—she loved the city, Dad loved the ranger stations, and I was in the middle, being pulled first this way and then the other. She never complained, mind you, she just put up with those little ranger stations in those backwoods places my dad always put in for."

Ellis looked like he didn't have anything more to say, and just fed more wood into the fire; but then he said, "Did I mention that she was my teacher until I went to high school? It was a mighty small school. Being a farm girl, you must have gone to a little school, too."

Meg answered enthusiastically, "Yes, in Wyler. The town's very small, with only thirty-five families in it. There were three grades to a room, and I never had more than two other kids in any of my classes. My fifth grade teacher was a man and he liked volleyball and woodworking a lot better than teaching grammar. It was my mother and sister who taught me about verbs and nouns and prepositional phrases. What was it like being taught by your mother?"

He got up and moved some dry wood closer, then sat down across from her before he began speaking. "As a teacher, my God, she taught with a vengeance! She was always bringing her background into those little hick schools—as though she was the kids' only hope—and mine, too, of course. She was one determined teacher!" He laughed, then looked serious. "You and I know how great it is for kids to grow up in a little community, with all that freedom to learn things on your own. But Mom was pretty contemptuous of that; she never saw the adventure in it and never joined in on anything there—unless she thought she had a chance of *changing* something. You might say I got a unique education."

He laughed again. "When we lived at Huckleberry Ranger Station, I remember one day, my six classmates and I were sitting outside on the step of the little rundown cabin we called our schoolhouse..." He stopped talking for a moment. "I'm not sure where I was going with that... Oh, yes, about our school. None of our parents wanted us to be bussed to the grade school in Columbia Falls—about thirty miles away—so they decided they'd make a school for us right there—on the only flat place in those parts, between the river and the road—and Mom would be the teacher.

"The cabin that became our school had once been a line shack on a nearby cattle ranch. The only reason the rancher got so generous was because that old broken down building had serious condition issues. After locating it, they just hoisted it onto a flat bed truck, hauled it to the riverbank, and dropped it on a platform of logs they'd laid there for that purpose. That old school was heated by a cook stove and it had one window, but, by God, it had a city girl for a teacher!

"Keep in mind, that school was smack-dab in the middle of a big willow bottom, and that willow bottom was home to about six moose during most of the fall and winter and part of the spring—which was pretty close to being the whole school session. When we went outside for recess, we had to keep pretty good track of where those moose were—doing a regular head count, so we'd know where they were in relation to us.

"You never want to tangle with a moose—they're big, but more than that, they're unpredictable. With their long legs they can cover a lot of ground fast, and, for no reason that's apparent, they'll chase a person. And they can growl—no kidding! People think moose use their antlers as weapons, but they don't. Their weapons are their front legs and hooves. They'll rear up on their hind legs and come crashing down on anything they've decided doesn't need to live anymore!

"Anyway, there were two things those moose knew. First, they knew damned well that that willow bottom was theirs a long time before the school came along. And second, they knew that, with the kids and all, the willows around our schoolhouse would turn out to be the most entertaining place to eat, especially if they also needed to take a nap. I'll tell you, recess was broken off short more than once when a moose decided to trim up our shrubbery. But by that time we'd learned just how much time it took to hightail it back inside the school. At times, we cut it pretty close.

"You spoke about learning grammar. One particular day a moose was browsing outside the schoolhouse, eating this and that, chewing on the tips of the willows under our one window, and occasionally bumping the walls and brushing against it—actually moving the building a little. That day while all of this was going on, Mom, very typically, started telling us about the industries associated with the Great Lakes barge system, as though Lake Superior was just fifty feet away, instead of our river and that critter. She had that knack of counteracting whatever was going on around us, rather than tying her teaching to it.

"When a column of mountain sheep clattered by on the hill just south of the school, you could almost count on Mom deciding that it was time to learn how to diagram a sentence. You'd be amazed what my brain connects with prepositional phrases! And if we were studying geography—well, the most obvious thing would have been to simply go outside and make your point there because, out there, the whole lesson book was in front of our eyes—that great range of mountains towering above us with its glaciers still sculpting and carving away the valleys outside our school. The hillside itself was glacial till, grinding against an incredible jut of striated sedimentary rock. If a person knew what he was looking at, he could probably read the whole history of life on earth from that piece of rock.

"With all due respect to Mom, if it didn't come out of a book, if it couldn't be tied to some kind of culture or business or planned industrial growth, well, it just didn't count. That's probably the biggest thing I hold against her. That, and the way she made us feel guilty for letting our eyes wander from the lessons—as though what was outside didn't count for anything." He leaned over and picked out a couple sticks of the remaining wood and threw them into the fire, as though they were exclamation points.

Wondering how he resolved it, Meg asked, "But what about your Dad in all of this?"

"Oh, he knew—I moaned about it often enough. But his way of dealing with my *teacher* was to get on his horse and go off and work on some backwoods trail for a few days." His face brightened. "Overall I'd say I benefited. Mom warned me that those hicks I called friends were ignorant and wouldn't amount to anything, because they wouldn't make the effort to better themselves. Most of them are still there, hicks and drunks and bums."

Meg was aghast at his reasoning, and said, "That's a pretty harsh judgment, Ellis. Do you know that for a fact? Is that what you think? Or is it your mom's assessment? Surely you could be more charitable."

Ellis shrugged but said nothing.

She was silent while she watched him add more wood to the fire. His conclusion was so disappointing…and troubling. His upbringing—however different the setting—sounded too much like the pushing and pulling of her and Ed that her children had experienced. And Ellis's comments about the backwoods school worried her about what might be in store for *her* kids, now that they'd been going to a more rural school in the canyon.

Despite this, she could only say, "Be sure and tell the kids about those moose around your schoolhouse. They'll love it. Knowing them, they'll be disappointed if they don't have moose around their schoolhouse in the canyon. We all like your stories, Ellis."

Now that the food was gone, Meg yawned inelegantly and again stretched out by the fire. In the far distance she could hear the sound of a small airplane, a sound that always made her feel genuinely content, although she never could decide why. She was about to comment on it when Ellis reached over and picked up her foot. Taking his time, he examined it closely, peering intently at a small blister then stroking each toenail thoughtfully before declaring, "That polish is called 'Pink Pearl.'"

He had her full attention now and she laughed in surprise. "You know your nail polish."

He acknowledged her words with a slight shrug and moved his fingers slowly to her heel, then under the cloth of her jeans to her calf, kneading the muscles lightly, knowing just where they were the tightest. In a quiet voice he said, "I bet that feels good."

Meg closed her eyes and nodded from the pleasure of his fingers on her skin and from how it was awakening her whole body. As his hand moved higher, she laid back and relaxed, giving in to the sensation and aching for more.

Then, with a start, she opened her eyes and pushed his hand away, and regained her seat against the tree. When she felt calm enough to speak, she asked, "So where does a big outdoorsman like you learn about nail polish?"

His face had reddened and, in a controlled voice, he asked, "Why did you pull away from me? I know you want that, Meg. I could feel you quiver."

"I'm not prepared to go there, Ellis, that's why."

Very deliberately Ellis moved away and sat down across from her before asking, "And when will Mighty Meg be prepared for *that*?"

She echoed the words, "Mighty Meg?" and wondered if that was the phrase he whispered to himself at night, Mighty Meg, with her land and…what else?

He hadn't answered and they sat silently, staring into the fire again, each with his own thoughts. Meg's eyes traveled in a covert line between the fire and the man. For all his potent force, it was a boy's face she saw—the petulance around his mouth, the teasing eyes downcast, and looking every bit ten years younger than her thirty-eight. What did he know of pain or loss or sick children or responsibility, beyond that of caring for himself?

A lock of his hair had fallen forward—a usual state—and she suppressed the impulse to reach over and push it back into place, as though it were her right. How easy and dangerous it would be to give in to his lovemaking. All she'd need do to start that happening was to lie back and give him a signal that she was ready—maybe unfasten a single button of her blouse, or run the tip of her tongue across her lower lip. Then all that she had been yearning for would be hers—his male hands gripping her body to his, and the hollowness in her mind and belly filled by a live man instead of a distant memory… And this time he wouldn't twist away, of that she was certain.

But she wouldn't do that. She shook her head to push that fantasy away, and held her hands to the fire, despite the warm day. As she did, Ellis looked up and said, "So, what do you think?"

Meg's thoughts raced wildly around, finally she said, "Trust me, Ellis, you don't want to know!" Then, more collected, "You never answered about where you learned about Pink Pearl polish."

"You can't expect a man to reveal his sources about things like that."

"Well then, let's talk about why you *really* wanted me to come on this hike? You got me up here on the pretext that you were going to show me my property lines. But when you didn't bring the map—"

"That damned map! If you're going to hound me about it—"

"Well, forget the map then, and tell me what you want, Ellis. You want something, but in all the weeks we've known each other I don't know what it is."

"I want the same thing you want, Meg. I want more of what we were just starting to do a minute ago. If you want me to be more specific, I'll show you." With a half smile he made a move as though to grab her foot again.

She made a great show of folding both legs under her, Indian style, then looked at him seriously. "Maybe I do want the same thing as you. But diving into that kind of relationship without any idea of where we might end up..."

He held up his hands as if they could stop her, and scoffed, "Okay, okay, now come the conditions."

"*Conditions?*" Meg sighed audibly. "My god!" She looked at him, and in a sad voice, said, "I don't like your 'conditions' word, Ellis, if I understand what you mean by it. Surely there's nothing between us that could be *traded*. I want a thousand things from...from a lover, but I can't imagine putting any conditions on him. What I'm saying is that things between us aren't at that point. We haven't known each other that long, and...I don't get the feeling that you care how I feel. You don't look me in the eye. Was the point of this hike for me to watch you run up a game trail, disappearing then reappearing at will, until we got here? And now that we're here, we can—can get down to it—make love up here by this spring? There's got to be more than—than just sex. A woman needs...I need..." She looked directly at him, determined to wait out his reply, no matter how long it might take.

He said, "Okay, 'conditions' was the wrong term. What do you need to convince you that it's okay to make love here? We couldn't have a prettier place, and we both want it."

Seeing his hands gripping each other tightly, Meg was quiet a moment. Then she said, "I'd like to talk about campfires."

"Campfires? We've already talked about campfires."

She went on quickly, "It was beautiful watching you make this campfire. I could tell you've had a lot of experience with them; you know what they need. You chose a certain spot and dug the fire pit and selected and placed the dry smaller stuff so artfully then the bigger sticks. Then you lit it. At first all we saw was that little trace of smoke. It took a while before we could see the flames leap into sight and start looking like a fire should. Then it got hot."

She looked over at him questioningly, wondering if he would somehow catch her metaphor. Again speaking slowly, she went on. "A *campfire* takes so many things to be a success. It's only a chemical equation: Dry Fuel + Oxygen = Kindling Point + Match = Fire. We both know all the steps—not that we necessarily put a name to them each time we...uh...we build a fire. We just know what a good fire needs. Don't we?" Again she waited, but without his answer she went on, instructively. "To have a successful fire, every part of the chemical equation has to be just about right, so that the kindling point is reached... so it can become a successful campfire. So I was just wondering—"

"Wondering what? What are you talking about? What's your point?" He sounded quarrelsome.

Meg looked off to the mountains in the distance and wished that little airplane sound hadn't gone away. "Oh, I don't know, Ellis. Whatever it was, it doesn't matter." Hearing that dangerous catch in her voice, she stopped talking and wondered why dreams die so hard sometimes. They'd first died with Ed, and now with Ellis. It must be her fault, not knowing what to say to get the things she wanted. She shouldn't have stopped him a while ago. What was wrong with her? If only he could think of looking at her and holding her like he did that first night. Maybe he needed her tears to think of doing that. Of course, she wouldn't stoop to that kind of ploy. Anyway, it was all so awful now. Her body felt cast in ice.

She finally said, "Sometimes I think that it's not me you want, but something else. And I have no reason to believe anything different. All those looks you give my *body*, while you avoid my eyes… Why don't you look into my eyes, Ellis? And…and you haven't touched me since that first evening at the house."

"I wouldn't say that. I kissed you goodnight a couple days ago."

"That was taking not touching!"

"Maybe I don't trust myself around you, Meg."

"Really, now! I don't believe that. In all this big, dry, overhanging forest, you built this perfect little fire so carefully, coaxing it, caressing it, knowing just what to do. Then, with just one match, you lit it. I felt a little jealous as I watched you. So, I don't believe what you just said, that you don't trust yourself. I suspect you know exactly what you're doing every minute; it's just that the feeling isn't there. If only you'd reached out and touched me a few times and let me know what you were thinking." She paused for a moment, than added, "I need a lot of words, Ellis, and a lot of touching."

"Touching!" He pounced on that. "I've wondered about that. I've watched you with your kids. You don't realize how much you're always draped over one of them. You're touching their hair or you're patting their shoulders or their arms. Don't you know that all that touching weakens a person? Think about it: someday those kids will have to stand all by themselves. It was all right when they were babies, but they aren't babies anymore. What happens when the person doing all that petting is gone? My mother didn't do that, not if she could help it." He gave a short derisive laugh. "My dad taught me a lot of great things, but it was Mom who taught me about the real world."

Meg sat forward, blinking and seriously affronted at his questioning her motherhood. And she wondered how in heck the conversation had just jumped from her instructions about…making love…to the *real world*, as defined by his mother? Then again, maybe it was something she needed to think about. She eased back against the tree and was about to speak when Ellis blurted out, "Are you going to give marriage another try?"

Meg nearly jumped at his question. As much as she wanted to tell him, "no," she said, "I guess I've thought of it. Someday I suppose I will, but—"

Ellis interrupted,"Until recently, I never thought I would. What do you think about marriage?"

Meg swallowed, wondered wildly if he was proposing. "Gosh, I–I don't know. I probably have a pretty idealistic view of it. My parents' relationship looked pretty ideal because it worked with them. In Ed's and my case...well, the whole world was allowed in on that." In a hesitant voice, she asked, "And you? What do you think of marriage and families? Why haven't you married?"

He answered, almost to himself, "My job has kept me pretty well tied up. There was a girl in college, Bethany, and another one, Carol. Carol's married now, but Bethany...we still write occasionally. She's in Milwaukee, working. By now, she's like my mom was, a regular city girl. Anyhow, I'd have kids of my own now if things had worked out with her."

Meg was surprised at his candor, going over his words thoughtfully in an effort to understand. She said, "Yes, you would by now. I'm sorry you don't have your own family. My kids really like you, Ellis. But you don't need me to tell you that."

"Yeah, they're great." He laughed. "That little blondie Punkin... and Callie, with her dark curls. They don't look anything alike, but, my god, those two can think up more things to get my attention. I've never been around kids, so I didn't know they were like that. Bethany's a blondie, too..." He stopped talking, but his face carried on his thoughts.

Meg looked at him kindly, "It sounds like Bethany was pretty special, and she still might be."

"Yeah, she was. But it didn't work out and she moved away. I guess I never met the right woman...before you, that is." Speaking roughly, with his eyes looking at the fire, he said, "I was thinking that you and I should think about getting married some day."

His words stunned her. In spite of her wildest fantasies about him, in truth, she had never imagined those words coming out of his mouth, and she wanted him to stop talking. But she sat there, unmoving, waiting to hear him out, and waiting for his declaration of love.

A minute went by with no other words, and she finally understood that there wouldn't be anything further. She said,"I'm surprised, Ellis, because there haven't been any…any indications that you were thinking along that line. I'm really surprised. Thank you for asking me, but I have to say,'no.' I really don't think we've connected since that first night."

"But you can't be *surprised*, Meg. I helped you get settled. You've had me to dinner often enough. We've done a lot of things with the kids. I've called you. We were going great on the cabin until you got on your high horse about those trees. Now we're getting a dog."

"There's a big difference in our ages, Ellis." Looking for any recognition of this on his face, and wanting to talk about it, she finally sighed deeply and, keeping her voice soft, said,"Anyway, what about love? You haven't mentioned love." Without his saying anything, she went on,"I don't think you even like me, Ellis." Her voice began to rise and she spoke accusingly."There *could* have been love, if you'd let me know in some way. Did you expect me to read your mind? You can't have thought I was ready for this. A woman is like this campfire, you know, she has to be brought to the kindling point—in her mind, first, and then her body. That's what I was trying to tell you, Ellis."

"Why are you yelling at me? Stop yelling at me!"

Meg's response caught in her throat, so she softened her voice. "Am I doing that? I don't mean to." As untimely as ever, she felt tears in her eyes. When she got her voice under control, she stood up and stretched. Walking behind him she touched her fingers briefly to his shoulder, asking softly,"Shall we finish off the coffee?" Without meeting her eyes, he nodded and handed her their cups. She walked over to the spring and rinsed them out, then came back to the fire and picked up the coffeepot that was pushed to the side of one of the stones. While she poured in the coffee and handed it back, she looked down at him—that lock of hair hanging down again, making her fingers ache to push it back.

In that moment, she thought about tenderness, feeling the size and extent of the tenderness inside her—untapped, never tapped by anyone but the children. Why didn't a man know about all the tenderness waiting for him—tenderness that he could swim in if he chose? All he had to do was reach out and touch her gently and look deeply into her eyes and smile and say the tiniest of words. If a man ever did that she felt she'd burst into bloom—maybe release a perfume—and any little thing he wanted he could have. She felt like she was standing on her toes, poised for some eternal moment, as though the entire direction of her life and the children's lives and the land's life would change, if only a man did that.

If she were granted just one wish, she would wish that this beautiful young man could be everything she had wanted him to be. But he wasn't. After making love what would she and Ellis have? As she watched him sitting there, the phrase "careful with fires but careless with women" came into her mind. Wasn't that what her memory of Ma and Papa had warned her of earlier? Making love was no casual thing, at least to her. Making love had a way of holding her in thrall, of making her a captive to it. And making love to the wrong person could change her resolve, might even render her helpless, like what had happened after Ed first made love to her.

In her eighteen years with Ed she'd had enough cavalier treatment to last her a lifetime. Even after he'd had satisfying sex (at least to him), he'd turned away. Even in his death in that Idaho river, he'd turned away. What gave her any hope that she could trust love, should she ever be given that choice with another man?

As for Ellis, he didn't want the same things as she did—hadn't he proved that over and over? She saw clearly that the anger she so often felt around him came from her hunch that there was little else between them but the hope for sexual gratification. Given enough time he might become the attentive lover and partner, who saw the land as she did and would help her raise her children. But having sex would be pushing the clock. Anyway, he'd given her no indication that he could evolve into that role, with his clumsy kisses and hurtful games. His enjoyment of the kids was real, and theirs of him, but that wasn't assurance enough. She had no more idea what tugged at his innards than she had ever had. This intriguing man of her homecoming was just as attractive and just as obscure as ever, an enigma.

Seeing his shoulders hunched up and his body all sharp points and angles, Meg sat down across from him and breathed a tired sigh. As they watched, the fire sank back into the coals, the last few wisps of smoke hovering for a moment before going to nothing—like a sob—leaving the coals grey and cold against the earth.

Meg looked at her watch. "Let's clean up here and head back. I'm concerned about leaving the kids any longer. Let's go back the very shortest way, rather than the way we came. Without a map—well, I just want to get home." She threw the dregs from her cup into the coals, where it sizzled briefly. When she stood up, the stiffness in her knees warned her of the downhill hike ahead of her.

Ellis got up too, and after stretching, came up to her and put his hands on her shoulders. Looking down at her, he said, "So you need more touching, eh?" He ran his hands hard down her arms and down her waist and down her buttocks and pulled her roughly to his body, and bent and kissed her, hard, on the mouth.

When she got a chance to catch her breath she pushed him back. "No, not that, Ellis."

"Damn it, Meg, you wanted to be touched!"

"The touching I need is a lot different than—than that," and she felt alarm at the huskiness in his voice and the urgency in his hands.

"What the hell do you mean by that? We've waited long enough, haven't we? Isn't this what you want? It's what I want." He jerked her blouse out of the way and slipped his hand into the front of her jeans.

Meg could feel his fingers move beneath the silk of her panties and slide into her wetness, beckoning her to open up to him. For a moment she yielded, feeling the eagerness of his body's want of her, and of her own.

But she couldn't do it. She said, "No, Ellis! I can't!" and twisted out of his grasp. Calming her voice, she said, "I really can't, Ellis. And if that doesn't mean anything to you, it should."

He backed away angrily and looked at her, clenching his fists and working the muscles in his jaw.

She stood looking at him for a long moment, before bending down and picking up the coffeepot and throwing the grounds onto the coals. She filled the pot with water, as patiently as before, to drown the coals. Wordlessly, Ellis jammed everything from their lunch into his pack then watched Meg stir the sodden coals. When everything was dead out and the rocks kicked back into the water, they shouldered their packs. And without a backward glance they left.

PART FOUR

31

LETTERS

Wyler, Montana

Dear Meggie,

I cannot tell you how much it meant to get your letter and hear all your news. I was thinking you wouldn't want to talk to me again after I left you at the bus station that way. When Charlie brought your letter into the kitchen I had just started to knead my bread dough, but I tore open the envelope anyway and stood there reading it. Well, you know how it is when you're kneading bread: you can't put the dough aside for a minute. But I couldn't put off my blubbering either, so the dough had to take all my tears—splash, splash, splash.

At supper, when I was slicing the loaf, I told Old Flint that if the bread tasted extra salty it was Charlie's fault for bringing me your letter right when I was kneading it. Of course Charlie had to say that after all these years my bread finally had enough salt in it to suit him, and he was officially volunteering to make me cry any time—you know Charlie!

When we stopped laughing, Old Flint looked at his bread with the oddest look on his face, as if he saw my tears in it and was relieved along with me. He knows how upset I have been over our tiff when I left that day. Charlie knows about my regrets, too, but Old Flint always sees things a little differently. It was a wonder he did not jump up from the table and go get his camera and take a picture of that slice of bread. When he gets that look on his face it is usually time for his camera and, before you know it, there is a "click" and whatever it is will be there forever, leastwise on paper.

His pictures are not like anything I ever take. He never wants people to dress up in their Sunday best and stand in a line and smile, like I do. He uses that old-fashioned black and white film, but his pictures turn out awfully good anyway.

He took one of me a couple weeks back. I'm in the kitchen—kneading bread, of course! I'm wearing Ma's old bib-top apron with the green trim, even though it is awfully raggedy. When I realized that Old Flint was bent on taking my picture, I told him I needed to tidy up for it first. But he said, "Now, Tolly, you know I don't want tidy, I want real, and the light coming from the sink window is right and is just catching your hair, and the dough is so pretty. You just keep on kneading that dough." Old Flint says things like that. It's almost enough to turn my head!

As it ended up, I also had some flour on my nose, but it is a real nice picture that you've got to see. That big lump of dough I'm working on puts me in mind of when I used to take care of baby Johnny. I could almost cry that that time of caring for a fat little feller like him is gone from my life. Maybe that is why I like making bread. The dough is so alive and new, and when it is all kneaded right, it always feels like a baby's soft round bottom to me.

Before I get off the subject of Old Flint's pictures, the other evening Charlie and I walked him out to the little family cemetery in the middle of our wheat field. We wanted him to see where Ma and Papa and baby Norma are. Charlie wanted to check its fence, and we needed to pull weeds and just neaten up the place a bit. Of course, Old Flint took his camera.

My, that's a pretty place. Makes a person hope that those dear people, who were such an important part of our lives, know how good we are taking care of where we laid them. It makes me happy that there are still places like that, where we can take care of our own, instead of laying them in a place they never walked on. I was telling Old Flint that I wonder how many times Papa steered his plow and his combine around that little plot, being careful not to hit one of its fence posts. I can't help but wonder what Papa's thoughts were as he did that. Did he wonder when he would end up there? Did he even wonder who would get there first, him or Ma? It would have shocked him, being taken so young, and then Ma joining him so soon after.

Anyway, when we got there the sun was just resting on the whiskers of the wheat. From there our house always looks half buried in grain, and the Little Belt Mountains are just tiny blue humps off to themselves. I love to see the wheat fields at this time of year. In that whisper of breeze, those uncut stretches of wheat move together like a big friendly animal breathing, its coat yellow as butter and smooth as velvet. I half expect those fields to purr.

Just like I knew he would, Old Flint set up his camera and began fiddling with this and that and deciding on the light and such for the longest time. Then he took just the one picture, figuring he'd got just what he came for. Oh, Meggie, the picture he took will just break your heart when you see it. I was telling Charlie that Old Flint's pictures always make me see what I feel instead of just what I see.

My heart has been so heavy since I left you at the bus station. There you are living up there on the mountain and sounding so happy, while I am nothing but a foolish, stubborn woman! Things just went to hell in a hand basket between us when you decided you wanted to move to the mountain instead of coming home to the farm with me. Even now, no matter how hard I think about it, I cannot discover why the thought of you going up to that mountain upset me so much. Bad times between us sicken me in the worst way, and this time it was me who did it. I can't ever tell Charlie exactly about my feelings. But Old Flint, he understands. I guess I told him all there was to tell about you the day he took that picture of me. Probably more than I should have.

The men are coming in for lunch. There's so much more I've got to write you about. I hope I have enough stationery.

I'm back. I am mighty thankful you had that Jeep when Callie was so sick. It puts me in mind of how little ones can get sick so fast. You just know they're going to die, but just as quick they get well. Of course, we are lucky to live in a time when there are antibiotics and Jeeps.

That little grave on the other side of Ma—I don't know what our sister Norma died of. Ma never could talk about it. But it could be Norma was taken because there weren't any shots for things then and because we lived so far from a doctor. All I recall now is that it was winter when she was taken. I'm sorry you never knew Norma. If you had been there, maybe between the two of us we could remember what she looked like. Now, all I remember is her hands. She got very sick one day, and was gone so fast the next day. One day I had a sister and the next day I had nothing but the memory of her little hands in mine as we danced around the kitchen. Maybe that is why I loved you so much when you finally came along three years later. I was so afraid you would be taken like Norma and by something I could not do anything about. Maybe that is why I would not let you out of my sight.

You mentioned that young Ellis Brodie was away fighting that big Park fire. I most certainly remember that he and his truck rescued us so kindly that day. When he comes back you tell him hello from me. Write me a long, long letter next time, Meggie, so we can catch up.

Now, I have got some good news and some bad news. Our Johnny quit college and has got himself married. He and Trish Stellerman eloped. They will be back in about two weeks. They want to come in with us here on the farm. I do not know if you ever met any of the Stellermans, located three farms to the north of us. They are a nice family and we like Trish, although she is barely seventeen. I should be happy, but I wanted Johnny to finish college and maybe decide on something else to do. Farming is a hard life, with more bad years than good. With all this, well, I'm worn out arguing about this (to myself). I'd like to tell them they are too young, but Charlie and I did the same thing, only I was even younger. As much as Charlie tries to respect my feelings, I can tell it is just a dream come true for him. Johnny and Trish are going to live in that little old house in Wyler that Charlie and I lived in years ago. It's all but falling down, but Johnny and Trish are young and in love, and they won't even notice.

For the bad news, everything is going to work out fine except for Old Flint. I can hardly bring myself to write it. We've got to let him go now because this farm cannot support more than two families. Meggie, I got something to propose, so read on.

When I visited you right after Ed disappeared, we were so busy with one thing or another, and we never had a chance to talk about Old Flint. He arrived in Wyler with only one bag and a box. Where exactly he comes from we don't know. And he got a real discouraged look on his face when we asked. He's from a city in the east is all he ever said.

As to why he ended up in Wyler, well, it seems like he just wanted to come west. When he first told Charlie that, Charlie told him right off that if he wanted to go west he best stay right here in the middle of Montana, because the actual West that he was thinking about, pretty much peters out at Montana's western border. After Montana and the littlest strip of Idaho, the West turns into cities real quick, first Spokane, then Seattle. Afterwards, whenever Old Flint talks about this, he says that it was that information and my cinnamon rolls that kept him from going further.

We put Old Flint up in the bunkhouse and, the first night he was here, Charlie admitted to me that he couldn't help but hire him. Seems the two of them got talking in the Wyler café, and even though Charlie mistrusted the newness of this fellow's hands, he liked him. In just the way Charlie said it, I could tell right off that Charlie would forgive Old Flint for the newness of his hands. He was right and, after these six months, his hands look a little more used. They're nice hands. I especially like it when he pulls that camera strap over his head and settles the camera in front of him. His hands hold that camera of his so gentle and loose, kind of like the way one holds the reigns of a favorite pony—soft, like they don't have to do a lot of explaining.

Now, just the thought of him having to leave is a sorry one for Charlie and me, a real sorry one. We have not yet told him, but I think he knows something is up. He might have overheard us talking and put two and two together. He walks around real quiet like he is saying good-bye to things but doesn't want to say it out loud just yet.

All this talk about Old Flint is for a reason, Meggie. What I am getting at is if you could hire him, then we wouldn't have to exactly say good-bye to him. It would be more like we were *relocating* him inside the family. You mentioned in your letter that the work on that little cabin hasn't turned out too well, and that you want to do some remodeling in the kitchen. Old Flint would be real good at things like that. Like I say, he is real good with his hands and with his head, too. He has been such a help to us. It seemed to have surprised him just as much as it did Charlie that he could do such things as he does around the place. But once he knows how something works or is used for, he gets the hang of it. We've never had someone work for us that we've enjoyed so much. He might not like to talk about his past, but I think he misses being part of a family. We gave him his board and room and paid him for all that he did. But, except for all the photography things from Great Falls, he did not spend anything that we ever saw. He does not ask for a whole lot of money, but he is worth a whole lot more than we ever paid him. It's real hard thinking about him having to leave. Let me know as soon as possible if Old Flint could come to work for you. I would like to tell him he has a new job. As an extra incentive, I'll tell him that your place is still in the good part of the west, and that you make cinnamon rolls as good as mine.

I hate to mention this, but did they ever find out who that woman in Ed's car is? And have you seen any wild animals yet? Hello from Charlie.

Love from your sister,
Tolly

· · ·

Rt. #1, Canyon Rd.
Clark Fork, MT
August 4th

Dear Tolly,

It was so wonderful to get your long letter today. The kids were thrilled with theirs and are hard at work on their answers, so be prepared.

Johnny married? How wonderful! Before you know it, you'll have some grandbabies of your own around the place. That's just what you need. I'll drop Johnny and Trish a note and a check, so they can pick out just what they want for their house.

Of course I forgive you—but what's there to forgive? I love you, Tolly. You are the nicest sister in the entire world. The things you said in your letter touched me deeply. It told me exactly why you were so scared for us living up here. You always took such good care of me and tried to protect me. Our only problem is we never learned how to really talk something out. Growing up in a happy family has its problems. Whenever we disagreed we didn't want to disturb all that tranquility by expressing it. So you and I have never come to grips with our differences. The important thing is we love each other and always have.

About your plan for keeping your Old Flint in the family, it's a wonderful idea! By all means tell him we can use him up here. Please have him call me collect. Tell him I'll pay him well. He can stay in that darling cabin, even though it isn't finished. But it's winter proof and has electricity and a toilet and shower. I've even ordered a cute Vermont woodstove for it. Tell him we would expect him to take his meals with us, just as he does with you. I could really use his help, especially with school starting soon and the kids having to be transported back and forth.

Oh, I've missed you so much. I have so much to tell you. The kids will write you about our new pets, but I'll give you my version of them, too. When the Humane Society rescued them they were half-starved. The farmwoman who owned them had died. Before we even saw them, we were told that we had to adopt both of the pets or neither of them, as they could not be separated. When we saw them, the black, giant-sized German shepherd and the yellow tomcat were sitting together way back in the corner of the wire dog kennel, looking as forlorn as anything could be—like it was the two of them against the whole world. My knees went weak, probably because they had the same refugee status as the four of us Halversons did.

The kids and I had no experience judging if they would be good pets, but Ellis looked them over and thought they would be okay. The only cats I remember were the feral ones at the farm, and they kept to themselves. After just one look at this cat's orange eyes, I was tempted to say, "Forget it!" But of course there was the dog.

At first glance, the dog seemed big enough for the watchdog we wanted. But then her gorgeous brown eyes fastened on me, and she asked, just as plainly as if she could speak the actual words, "Please remove us from this cage immediately! Take us away from here!"

By this time, the girls had been thinking up names for the cat (Muggins won out over Spot), so I found myself pledging to the keeper that we would love, honor, and obey both animals until the end of time.

Kurt and I named the dog Erda while we were in the store getting huge sacks of pet food, cat litter, some catnip toys, and rawhide bones.

The Jeep ride home was not without incident, and then there were the pets' baths. While everyone recovered from that, the two squeaky-clean animals inspected the place. We finally found them outside, sitting happily together on that lovely stone doostep. Now their only problem is enduring all the fussing and petting and unusual treats from my pet-starved kids and me.

Very quickly Muggins went from being an outside cat to a dedicated housecat after a close call with one of our red-tailed hawks. Although Sara explained that it was perfectly normal for the hawks to behave this way, she is the first one to reprimand anyone for leaving the door open, should Muggins dare go outside and try to walk in the meadow again.

Both pets are a lot of company for us. In fact, the Littles, especially, keep reminding me that their entire lives started the moment Muggins arrived. Even I, the non-cat lover, have to admit that he is kind of intriguing. Now, if he starts catching mice I'll bow down and worship him, as we are a bit overpopulated. As to our lovely Erda, she seems more like a person than a dog. Her German name means "Mother Earth" and comes from a theme in one of Wagner's operas.

In answer to your questions—yes, we've seen wildlife around here, and, yes, we're careful. Erda seemed to know what her job was on the first day. She goes with the kids whenever they go outside and is easy to spot in the meadow. If she isn't playing with the kids she's off to the side watching them attentively. When she senses some critter is around that she doesn't like, she barks furiously and simply rounds up the kids, nudges them into a bunch, and puts herself between them and whatever it is she's unhappy with. I'll never know where she learned this technique, but however she came by it, it's thrilling to watch.

At first, the kids thought she was just playing a game with them, barking. Then, understanding she was serious and something they didn't know about was near by, they got a little scared. But it didn't take long for them to revel in the fact that they have a loyal personal angel, with big ears, a great nose, a huge voice, and a glittering set of teeth. She's impressive. I certainly wouldn't want to cross the line she keeps drawing around her three precious child-pups.

I would trust that dog with my life any day. She has an uncanny awareness. Although she doesn't say a word, she seems to perfectly understand my concerns for the kids' safety. Our partnership is palpable. Since she arrived I've relaxed, and this she senses. But then, we talk to one another. Just recently I bought a big iron triangle, like the one on the farm, and hung it by the back door to call everyone in. When my gang comes in, Erda, after a day of guard duty, gives me a quick look that seems to say, "Thanks for ringing that thing. I needed a time out." Once inside, she seeks out a quiet corner in the kitchen and is asleep in a second.

I love the graceful way she lowers her body down without a sound—there's no sudden bag of bones flop and sprawl. When the kids are playing inside, she assigns herself to me, padding around softly with little clicks of her nails on the wood floors, and occasionally making a point of touching my leg with her nose. Twice she has very gently taken my hand in her front teeth for just a moment, in what I have interpreted as a lovely gesture of possession. Both times touched me so deeply that my eyes filled with tears. As I did, she looked up with that fleeting glance of hers, as if to reassure me of her good intentions. This is a big dog, Tolly, and she is very fierce when she needs to be. I tell you this to help you understand her gentle heart.

In the evenings, when I settle down in front of the fireplace in my favorite loveseat, she lies down, locating herself at the perfect distance for my hand to stroke her. At night she sleeps on a rug by the side of my bed. Oh, my elegant companion. I think she must read my mind.

Okay, Tolly Jefferson, you asked about Ellis Brodie. I've wondered what to write about him. He has been here many times for dinner. The kids are crazy about him, and he enjoys them—quite a change from Ed, eh? He knows all kinds of facts about these mountains and tells some interesting stories.

My thoughts about him are murky, to say the least. His appearance was so sudden and unexpected. I hadn't even gotten into the house yet and there he was. For a while, before going on a hike with him, I felt pretty much like the kids did—thoroughly smitten. But the hike gave me a clearer view of him, especially when he suggested that we get married—and that proposal came without any declaration of love. Frankly, when he's around it's difficult to separate my need for a friend from my need for someone in my bed. (And no, we didn't, we haven't, and we won't!)

The kids make my relationship with him so complicated. Sara and Callie told me that they expect me to provide them with a father and implied that it better be Ellis! I'm relieved he's gone for a while, as I need the peace of this place without him defining it in his terms. While he's on the fire in Glacier Park he said he would keep in touch, and he has, with written notes and a couple phone calls. I can't understand why he does this. I turned down his pitiful proposal of marriage, and only a fool would interpret my, "NO!" as meaning "Maybe." Problem is, he reminded me that I want male companionship. But at my age and living up here—it's just confusing. After all those miserable years with Ed—well, you know.

Do you realize that I'll be thirty-nine in a few weeks? Of course you do. And school will start before we know it. The kids are getting excited to go to their little school in the canyon.

I have no idea what to expect with the change of seasons. Will fall come earlier than it did down in town? And what kind of winter should we prepare for up here? And what about the roads? The summer is just speeding by, and time with these kids is so precious. We plan something special every day, so I'm learning to put off the nonessentials until they get in school.

I did find a workman to install a new window in my bathroom—so far, the only window in the house to be fixed like that. He had to actually make a bigger opening in the wall for it—not a small job! It opens up to the fresh air and the mountain smells and sounds. It's heaven. The other windows will just have to wait until spring, I guess. I have too many projects started at the moment.

Western Montana is having a bad forest fire season. Rain is on everyone's wish list. The sunsets are red due to the smoke particles in the air from the forest fires burning north of here. We wonder what poor mountain is burning up. With our house located in a clearing, we could save it at least. We're very cautious, but refuse to be afraid.

I often think about the woman who lived in the meadow a long time ago, with her pretty white and blue dishes. Whoever she was, I feel a spiritual connection with her. I can't imagine that she lived up here all by herself. It's a mystery. I wouldn't mention it to the kids, but on a little rise, near where she lived, I found a tiny mound with ten rocks placed on top of it. Even though the grass is tight around it, I swear I can see that the rocks form a perfect cross. I wouldn't think of disturbing it, of course, but when you wrote of tending our family plot in the wheat field, I wondered if we might not have one right here.

That leads me to think that, really, we're all the same, living our lives—lives that in the grand scheme of things no one would know about, or even care about. Then we disappear into the folds of time, leaving behind our little chips of dishes and our apple trees. Our graves end up as the only records of our being here. We think we're so important while we're alive—but only to those who knew us.

With all this talk, I want you to know that I'm wonderfully happy up here, even though I feel lonely at times. I miss you and I miss Doris and Marc. Doris called last night. She sounded exhausted. We talked for over an hour, because neither of us wanted to hang up and we kept thinking of things to say. They hope to come home around my birthday. You and Doris have made me realize that I need some serious girl talk. I'm getting to feel that the only things worth talking about are elk and deer and trees and carpentry and windows.

You asked about the woman in Ed's car. No, she is still unidentified. I've called the sheriff three or four times, and he's said that the divers have never found her purse or anything more. I've come to believe that we'll never know her name or what her connection to Ed was. Time and this gorgeous mountain (and that serene old log I showed you) are helping me put the past behind me. I am feeling whole again. Have Old Flint call me!

Love to you both, but especially to you, sis,

Meg

. . .

Wyler, Montana
August 7th
Meggie Halverson!

Forest fires and all the kids' letters talked about bears and other wild animals!! That is just what I meant. Are you all right? Can't you ask Ellis Brodie to come back right now? He will protect you, Meggie. Do you have a gun? You be very, very careful. Now don't get mad at me for saying that.

Oh, I'm so upset. Things have changed here. I am sorry to tell you that Old Flint left us yesterday. In the morning, after the mail and your letter arrived, we told him we could not keep him on and mentioned your job offer, and said for him to call you collect. He nodded then he went outside and never came in for dinner. When Charlie went out to find him he was gone. And so were the few things he had brought with him. We did not see him go. Oh, Meggie, I would have run after him if I had seen him take his bag and box down the road. Without saying goodbye! I am just beside myself.

He left a note, saying he did not need the money, and the note was on top of most of the money we had already paid him these last six months. He had hardly spent any of it. He wrote that we were not to worry. He said, "Thank you for all your kindness and help." He said, "I learned so much."

He left us a large picture that we had never seen before, of that gate on the long road that looks like it runs plum into the Little Belt Mountains. A large, flat package from the photo store in Great Falls came in the mail the day before he left. It must have been the gate picture. It has a fine walnut frame and is beautiful. I will always treasure it more than anything I will ever have in the house. The picture feels like he is telling us something, but what it is escapes me. The gate is open. I figure that if the gate were closed I could not have stood it.

So Old Flint is gone. I wanted him to go to your place and help out. I'm sorry to have built up your hopes. Charlie told me to tell you that you better get hold of that foreman and those carpenters before they completely disappear, regardless of their work. You will want to get that cabin finished before winter sets in.

Old Flint, I will miss him. Charlie and I both will.

Love from your sister,

Tolly

32

A SINGULAR DAY

One summer morning, years ago, as Meg and Tolly lay side by side surveying their world from the roof of Papa's garage, Meg observed that most days were not new at all, but merely reused. After all, like their mother said often enough, anything that had once worked right could be dusted off, given a new name, and be used over again.

At the time of that declaration, the assorted settings for their play, besides their garage-roof sentry post, were the wheat fields, the chicken-coop-turned-playhouse, the snow forts they and Papa carved from the big snow bank that formed each winter between the house and the garage, and the coulee. The untrammeled coulee, with its seasonal sprinkle of crocuses, shooting stars, and yellow bells was part of the small wedge of pristine prairie that Papa and his plow had spared from his wheat growing, mainly for his daughters' sake. Yet even with these exciting venues, Meg felt the days lacked distinction. She didn't mean the days were boring, but they were *all the same*.

Once she'd moved past those childhood days—of sleep, eat, play, sleep—and entered into days committed to work, she changed her mind entirely. She found that, for no discernable reason, there were days that stood above all the rest: days that from the first shout of dawn to the night's last sleepy blink, fairly tingled with portent. Today gave every indication that it was going to be one of those singular days. But then, yesterday had been singular, too.

. . .

Day after August day, mornings had been born hot and dangerous. With the sun twice its normal size in the smoky haze and blasting every timid cloud from its intent, the parched grasses and leafy plants hung head down in weak-want, in hope that something would take pity and squeeze some juice into their roots. When the huge grinning sun had at last melted off the edge of the day and slid behind a Montana that was burning in tiny imitation of it, night came on with the smell of smoke mixed with resolute dew, and fitfulness hung over everything.

The people on the mountain also suffered. During the day they ate little, quarreled often, and walked stiff legged around each other. Before bedtime, in consideration of the drought, they took hasty showers, all the while feeling vaguely guilty over the never-ending flow of water from their faucets, and fearful, too, lest its source turn capricious and leave them.

Meg, after an uneasy evening of being too apprehensive to build the nightly fire, and too squirrelly to read the usual story to her progeny, finally exerted her maternal prerogative and relegated the cranky children to their sweaty sheets. But she allowed their bedroom doors to remain open to the outpourings of the living room stereo. But even the cool fingers of Sibelius violins seemed cloying.

With Callie crying because Muggins was occupied somewhere in the basement, and Sara whining that Kurt was purposely kicking their adjoining wall, Meg, with a rare headache, slammed down her book and replaced Sibelius with an environmental disk entitled *Northern Minnesota Lake Sounds*. Before climbing into bed herself, she turned up the volume and listened—as rapt as the kids—to the slow swishing paddling of a canoe in a lake they could only imagine, to the lap of water and the occasional hollow clunk of an oar bumping against the canoe, and to the crazy liquid giggle of a loon that they could only compare to the cries of a coyote. Somehow, those sounds assured them that cool, wet, green things still existed, and they were asleep before the disk ended and the stereo clicked off.

· · ·

The storm hit at midnight. With a shriek of delight, the wind hit its fists on the east side of the house, shoving it west a fraction of an inch with a creaking of its nails and boards. The gale's great booming voice was followed by lightning and immediate thunder. In the din, all three children streaked down the hall yelping and hid under the quilt alongside their mother, who was clutching at her own pillow. Erda, too, leaped onto the bed and lay quivering among the other bodies. Meg half expected the cat to join them and, when he didn't, it crossed her mind that Muggins, with his orange-marble eyes reflecting the lightning, might be cheering on the storm demons from the living room windowsill.

As the hair on all their necks spun around, the children counted from the last strike with Meg—"one-thousand-one, one-thousand-two"—to sense the storm's movement. They counted through gritted teeth and with the light from the last strike imprinted on their brains. In real fear as the thunder sent shudders down through the earth, Meg laid her hands on the bodies around her, imploring the powers to spare them and Erda, their house and their land, and asking that rain be part of all this nonsense, surrounded as they were by tinder-dry grass and oily trees. As the giant fire maker repeatedly passed his flint over his steel, and the people awaited its jagged sparks, it became apparent that the high rocky ridge above them was taking all the strikes, leaving their fortress unscathed.

Mercifully, the noise moved on and the rain came. It began with a sudden gush of water, and turned into a long and steady pounding on the walls and roof. When the smell of its moist, reassuring offering drifted in through the parched pores of the house, the people and dog sighed. They were relaxing into sleep when Meg roused them and, with Erda's supervision, led the group away and tucked each into his or her bed in the wonderful coolness.

. . .

It was the creak of the big front door opening that awoke Meg. She burst from her bedroom, clutching her old blue robe to her nakedness. She found the kids and the dog framed in the doorway and looking outside. Beyond them lay a turgid landscape with a rare fog cuddling the meadow. The children grinned up at her as Sara announced, "Look, Ma, now we can build a fire in our camp and cook dinner there."

At breakfast on the step, even the animals got caught up in the good spirits. Muggins—who spent most of his time looking skyward (hawk-ward) whenever he was dragged outside—put the intricacies of his stomach on hold and allowed himself to be passed back and forth, secure in the thought that all these hands would soon get bored and allow his escape.

When Erda's exuberant tail sent Kurt's glass of juice flying off the stone step, where it smashed, she first looked at the pile of glass and then at the family, to determine if her tail had gotten her into trouble again. When she found that it hadn't, she was so grateful that she forgot the rules and slurped up the yolk from the fried egg Callie had carefully eaten all the white from, so she could lift it whole into her mouth for one final squish. When *even then* no one yelled, but laughed instead, Erda placed her nose rather imperiously on her paw and closed her eyes. She'd heard the word "camp" mentioned and needed to get her rest while she could.

· · ·

The morning sun had coaxed Meg into having her third cup of coffee on the doorstep. As she idly inspected the well-watered scene in front of her, she stroked the big dog lying at her side, pushing her fingers deep into the black ruff of the dog's neck, past the glistening guard hairs, and into the springy wool underneath. Ostensibly, the two of them were basking in the sun, but, from the movement of Erda's ears, Meg knew she wasn't the only one listening to the kids scrambling around inside the house: up the stairs, down the stairs, down the hall, doors slamming, then opening. And, all the time, their voices sounded like someone was playing games with the radio dial. Whenever any footsteps sounded nearby, Meg could feel Erda's body tense up, ready to lift her body up in that effortless, liquid motion of hers and become a part of whatever it was the children wanted. As the footsteps retreated, the dog allowed herself to relax into her dog-in-waiting mode and settled her nose onto her paw.

Meg gave her a sympathetic chuckle as she watched the dog's expression soften into sleep. Her canine life was a busy one. Just a few moments ago the dog had picked up the scent of an intruder in the trees near the back porch—Meg guessed it was probably the brother bears, it being nearly ten o'clock.Their interruption changed Erda into her *potentially* fierce guard-on-duty mode and, after raising her head and looking in that direction, she'd rumbled a warning, then a short warning bark, and listened intently. With her warning received, she had again rested her nose on her paw, mumbling little comments to herself as she closed her eyes.

Meg had seen the dog in her fully engaged combatant mode only once. And that once was enough to understand its potential—just like running a finger across a newly honed blade is enough. It had happened very soon after Erda arrived on the mountain. Whatever it was had not heeded Erda's preliminary growl and warning bark, so the dog had to confront it. Erda leaped to her feet and advanced slowly and stiff legged toward the animal in the trees. As she moved, the one-note rumble in her throat increased in volume and took on all the invitation of an opened steel gate, as her quivering lip, which just barely advertised her row of white weapons, drew farther back from her teeth. The now-roaring dog, in a posture of pure menace, moved rapidly toward the trees that obscured—what? She stopped when whatever it was changed its mind and left. Mission accomplished, Erda returned to her soft, friendly, sleepy self.

Meg tried hard to feel comforted by the dog's display; but she was disquieted by it, wondering what kind of animals, passing that close to the house, required all that fury. For the next few days Erda was pressed into establishing her territory—and her reputation—with her wild neighbors. It made for a noisy time. Erda's voice, echoing from the ridge above the house, sounded more like "Back, back!" instead of "Bark, bark!" Meg could almost hear the bears grumbling to themselves, "All right, all right, for god's sake! We won't walk *there* anymore, but may we please walk *here*?"

Meg's satisfaction at being close to this wondrous dog, of loving her and being loved back, filled her with sudden emotion, and she encircled the dog's neck in her arms and laid her cheek on Erda's head. The dog rumbled acknowledgment of the gesture and, as Meg moved her face away, the dog touched Meg's eyebrow with her wet tongue.

Theoretically, it was Meg who had rescued the dog from the cage at the shelter, but Meg, being so starved for love and in need of being touched and touching another responsive body, felt just as rescued. There was nothing Meg could think of as momentous as Erda coming into her life. The moment she had seen the dog in the cage, she knew she was witnessing an animal suffering. She had no way of knowing if this dog had ever experienced imprisonment before, but the way the dog's golden-brown eyes had held steadily onto hers spoke to her of the dog's grief and desperation.

The strange thing was that since that day the dog had never again held directly onto Meg's or the children's eyes. As Meg had gotten to know her, she understood that, to Erda, direct eye contact was either threatening, impolite, or to be used only in an emergency—as in needing to escape the cage. To all her humans, Erda practiced the quick look technique. It said lightly, "Okay. You are here and I am here and it's great. Whatever you want to do is fine with me. But remember, if I say something is around, you've got to trust me to take care of it. Remember, I've got a few talents that you don't have, and it's a jungle out there."

From where she and the dog were sitting on the doorstep, she could just see the top of the old fireplace down in the meadow and most of the apple tree where their camp was—their domain—and any minute now the kids would start their preparations for the upcoming meal. Once a day had been officially designated as a "Dinner-Cooked-in-Camp Day," it was all she could do to keep them from running down there right after breakfast to build their fire and start cooking the evening meal. It was that enthusiasm that forced her to ask some important questions of them: whether the upcoming meal was humanly possible to create and, in the end, digestible. Once that formality was taken care of, Meg was relegated to the sidelines, to eventually become their guest. Later, not wanting to miss a minute of it, she would stroll down leisurely and set up a lawn chair a short distance away from their camp, but within ear shot, and try to read a book—which entailed remembering to turn a page every so often.

The camp had not happened easily or without a lot of soul searching on Meg's part. Even before she found what she suspected was a child's grave there, she hesitated. What prompted it was her reverence for the unknown history of the long-ago woman and the possibility of losing the mortal scraps of one who might not otherwise be remembered.

Even before their actual move to the mountain, the kids were after Meg to let them make a permanent camp down there, so they could build fires and cook in the remains of the old fireplace. But when Meg looked at how the camp was losing its recognizable shape, without anyone knowing anything about the early inhabitants of this place, she was filled with an unbearable sense of loss. She saw the fireplace stones, the logs, and the rusting iron not as refuse of a wrecked early 1900s habitation, but as relics from a life that must be recognized.

Meg stalled their playing there until she could decide what to do. Finally, she explained that, with loving care and plenty of photographs before anything was touched, they could try to restore the fireplace's chimney on the one standing wall of the cabin by using the materials scattered around the camp. In doing that, Meg could see the possibilities of the camp, and she got as caught up in the project as anyone.

The hearth had held up, even though its chimney had collapsed. Most of its stones lay scattered, and Meg and the kids stacked and fitted them together with the same concentration and satisfaction as they put into a jigsaw puzzle. Then they wedged their own large iron grate into the hearth for a solid cooking platform. It worked perfectly and, as long as the fires were always kept well under control and supervised, it was a safe place to do outside cooking. Ellis had inspected it and insisted on four other precautions: no fires during dry or windy conditions, a fire screen must be placed over the smoke hole, a pail of water had to be at the ready whenever they built a fire, and someone must always be there with it. Fire safety up on the mountain was an absolute, not a vague suggestion.

When the camp was officially declared as finished, they held a special ceremony, placing the two pieces of white porcelain into a very special niche between two flat rocks protruding from the side of the refurbished chimney.They drank sparkling cider from Meg's crystal goblets then walked around inspecting the camp. Meg's conscience was salved.

When actually cooking a meal there, to save all the trips back and forth to the house, Kurt dug a deep hole near the old wall and half buried a large metal container he had scrounged from the downstairs Treasure Room. He explained that, with its tight lid, they could now store the camp dishes and utensils, salt and pepper, soap and towels, cooking pans, and a jar of matches right there in camp. His idea was that all they would have to do was bring the *ingredients* down from the house and get on with the cooking. It worked well just as long as they didn't count the dozens of trips back and forth. Callie, being the youngest, could usually be conned into being the local slave. Meg had to chuckle seeing her pounding back and forth on the trail between the camp and the house, arms full and face eager.

The one major stipulation Meg made was that food in any form must never be left in camp after a cookout.The resident bears needed no more ideas than they already had when it came to garbage. The Littles had found bear tracks in the dust around the camp the morning after their first meal there, but only that once. Either the bears assessed how slim the pickings would be or Erda had communicated a message of her own.

What the camp needed next was furniture. To this end, Kurt located a book at the library on ways to use rope to lash small logs and sticks together. His primary goal was to build a table near the hearth to serve as a food preparation surface—a kitchen table of sorts. For building material, he hacked down a small tree. Using a handsaw that he had also discovered in the Treasure Room, he neatly trimmed it and cut the wood into the lengths the pamphlet suggested. For the table legs he sharpened the four heaviest pieces into points and pounded them into the ground.To those he lashed other lengths near the top to serve as supports. On these, he laid a solid layer of thin branches for the surface of the table, lashing everything together with rope. It took a lot of rope and, since Kurt didn't know what the term "purist" meant, he used a lot of nails, too, contrary to the booklet's rules. When the table was finished, they all stood back in awe admiring his handiwork.

They all knew there were better tabletops to be had—an old card table, boards laid over boxes, that sort of thing, but that wasn't the point. Kurt had made this table from scratch. In fact, they forgave the table's saggy, bumpy faults (especially when they were cooking), for it was big enough and was where it should be and was just the right height. And it fit right in with the fireplace and the old tree nearby, both of which were full of aged lumps, and the tree had a couple "hands" on the ground with which to steady itself. Kurt considered taking his handsaw and trimming all the table edges even, but Sara and Callie sold him on the fact that they needed those irregular points to hang things on: hot pads and towels, cooking forks and spoons, sweaters, their cups, and a hundred other things that kept falling into the dust.

When they cooperatively rigged a rather intricate two-shelf cupboard, using the same lashing technique, and placed it up against the remains of the one low wall, the camp assumed an aura of permanence. Now they could turn out some really heavy-duty meals. To relieve the congestion of the table's points, Kurt screwed hooks into the cupboard's sides for cups and cooking utensils, making it even more perfect.

With such successes behind him, Kurt made a little washstand, with a short piece of log for a pedestal, to hold an old enamel basin. A sardine can, to hold a bar of soap, was nailed to the side of the washstand. On a small nearby tree, he lashed a chunk of old mirror, then strung a rope clothesline for the towels. Before each meal they made a great ceremony of washing up there. They stood in line (Meg, too) while waiting for their turns, making conversation about important things (a topic was chosen). When it was their turn, each ladled fresh water into the battered washbasin from an even more ancient bucket that they had filled from the lower spring.

The camp had many rules, but the most stringent ones were for the washstand. Towels must never be lopped over the line, but must be hung with clothespins at their corners to dry. The bar of soap must be set catty-corner on the edges of the sardine can so it "wouldn't fall inside it and get icky." And it was decided that there was "Good Water" and "Bad Water." Bad Water had soap and dirt in it and must be dumped away from the apple tree to keep that yucky stuff away from the tree's roots. Good Water did not have soap or salt in it and could be thrown around anywhere.

Kool-aid, coffee without cream, and the juice from any canned vegetable were all considered to be "Good Water." However, some of those drew flies, so part of the Good Water joined the Bad Water away from the camp; but not all of it. Any water that was hot was to be considered Bad Water—unless you cooled it and could remember right off what it contained. When Meg thought to ask what all the containers of water were sitting around for, the complicated answers led her to suggest that all "used water" be classified as Bad Water and dumped out over the hill. That one suggestion helped the Rules Committee considerably.

Watching the three youngsters scurrying happily around, Meg wished fixing up her blue kitchen in the house could be as easily done—and as much fun to use. Perhaps she should ask Kurt to "lash up" a few cupboards and counters for her, too. When Kurt had the axe in his hand, he got a powerful look on his face that suggested that all the women in the camp had to do was ask and he could chop down and lash anything together—perhaps a sofa or a coffee table—anything was possible.

When Sara and Callie were at the store in town assembling possible ingredients for their camp cooking, Meg noticed they were thinking in terms of ten- and twenty-pound units of such things as sugar and flour. On one trip to Safeway, she saw them thoughtfully fingering a whole slab of bacon. In fact, whenever a meal was being planned for the camp, something like an electric quiver ran through the kids. They made lists and stood a long time before the opened cupboard doors in the kitchen examining things they had never before paid any attention to—things like tapioca and corn syrup and bay leaves.

This activity reminded Meg of the feelings she'd had when she was a little girl, in the playhouse Papa had built for her out of the old chicken coop. There, Meg had only cooked mud-and-grass pretend foods on a pretend stove, and she canned weeds. She had spent untold hours sifting the tiny rocks and scraps of grass from the garden dirt with that old strainer of Ma's, then decorated the cakes with the purple flowers of tumbleweeds. But up here on the mountain it was the real stuff.

Today, it was Sara and Callie who were in charge of the meal, and they decided to make their favorite baked bean dish. Callie made her mother understand that if she were to bring a pan of cornbread with her, to go with the beans, they'd make coffee for her. Looking thoughtful, Callie had said, "Let's see, and perhaps you could bring a bowl of fresh peaches for dessert. Do you have any whipped cream?"

Meg thought, "Those little scamps, understanding bargaining at this age!" But an hour before their *very* early dinner, Meg fooled them and brought down the eggs and butter and fresh buttermilk and the rest of the mixings, and taught them how to make the cornbread themselves. They stirred up the batter, poured it into the Dutch oven, covered it, laid hot coals into its recessed lid, then laid it into the coals under the grate. It tasted wonderful with the beans. Erda liked honey and butter on it. Muggins ate a mouse instead, with predictable results.

33

TOUCHING EARTH, TOUCHING SKY

After all the food was eaten, the camp put in order, and the dishes cleaned up at the house, the four of them sauntered back down to the camp, in step and holding hands. It was that time of day when the sun hadn't even thought of evening, the time when the only thing to do was lie in the shady grass under the apple tree and digest their meal. As they lay there, the talk was about whatever came into their minds.

The conversation started with the lightning storm, about the ridge taking the lightning and sparing the house, and about their fear of the noise. Meg was asked to tell them again about the lightning balls that traveled along the fences at the farm. That led to stories of hail stones the size of walnuts and of her parents scooping them up and using them to freeze ice cream. Then the conversation turned to the spider hanging above their heads, rebuilding his web. Kurt commented—rather learnedly, Meg thought—that although all spiders were arachnids, some spiders looked like spiders, but others definitely looked like arachnids; the difference being that arachnids were sharp-cornered and spotted and acted dangerous, while spiders just looked busy. Meg was still thinking about that when Callie squirmed and asked Meg, from behind her fingers, if they ever drop—"You know, Ma, just let go and drop?" Meg told Callie she thought this one knew what he was doing and to think of other things if she didn't want to move out from under it. Sara named the spider "Charlotte" in hopes it was friendlier than it looked.

Callie pointed enthusiastically to the large group of puffy sheep-shaped clouds over the ridge then changed the subject to birds—especially the one that sang near the upper spring. Meg said it was a wood thrush. Sara said she called it "The Elusive Paradise Wonder," because of its voice. Meg thought, "Elusive? Elusive? That was a pretty big word for Sara to use. Hadn't Ellis used that word one night at dinner?"

Kurt wanted to know why baked beans made a person's guts grumble, and that led him into a rather explicit tale from last year's classroom, which Meg thought best discussed another time. There was a long discussion on where the spring's water came from. Kurt wondered why it was always cold, no matter how hot the day was, and why it never stopped running, not even before the rain when everything else was drying up. His observations fascinated Meg for being so like hers the day of the hike, but she wasn't about to bring Ellis's name or explanations into the conversation, for fear of any more "Daddy" talk. When it was her turn to speak, she mused eloquently about cool caverns full of dark water running under the earth and rising to the surface magically here and there. Callie said she hoped the caverns didn't have any toads in them because she just knew toads peed in water. Kurt and Sara groaned in unison.

Lulled by the day and the magic of the ground they were lying on, Meg had only a fraction of her mind on the conversation. Somehow, all three of the kids' heads were using her stomach as a pillow; and the heaviest head—Kurt's—was resting on her bladder. Even so, she resisted even taking a deep breath for fear of ending the moment. Yet with the kids making the conversation last longer and being slightly absurd, she knew that they, too, were aware of the singularity of this moment.

With only the smallest motion of her hand she could feel all three heads at once—an occurrence worth acknowledging. Yet, even in her contentment, her thoughts jumped to the future. A voice filled with motherly dread warned her that it was just a matter of time until one, then another, then the last of these heads would choose not to be under her stroking hands; would resist her twisting the threads of their hair together; would think it childish, her skipping her fingers down their noses; and would undoubtedly shun touching her or each other in this deeply familiar way again. When that time came, they would wrench away from this family clump—and from her. Then, necessarily separate, they would proceed on to their individual ways, to their other destinies, and she would be left on her own.

Well, she thought, perhaps this three-head moment was more a mother's moment after all, the culmination of her own destiny. Laying her hands reverently on the group of heads and pressing them lightly against her body, she wondered silently, "Will you remember this moment? Do you love it, too? Maybe you do, maybe you do. Only, don't leave yet. Not yet. I'm not ready for that."

It was then that Meg thought about this day being so singularly special—its clarity caught in some curious ray of light that caused her to feel a sense of excitement. She wondered, was this moment the reason for it? Or was this just a preamble to something greater? She didn't know, nor could she imagine what it was. When she had heard the thump of the front door opening this morning and had run to it, she had felt a keen disappointment when it was only the kids on the doorstep. But what had she been expecting?

She took a long, long breath, filling her lungs, exhaled, and then took another. In doing that she realized that her momentary reverie hadn't hurt the conversation. She found herself still "um-humming" here and there, with an occasional noncommittal, "You really think that?" thrown in. But she was pretty unnecessary to the present topic, the possibility of buying an elephant, and, before that, humans eating grass.

Why is it, she wondered, that in order to see the real stuff of the family, they had to be on some sort of neutral ground, away from all their little territories? It wasn't just being away from the house; this whole place gave her that insight. She stroked the heads and thought how wonderfully removed they *all* were up here. She had failed to get that across to Tolly, judging from her short letter today, instructing her to get Ellis back to protect them. Meg laughed ironically and thought, Oh, sure. If it were up to Tolly they would all be as dust-free as precious figurines inside a glass dome. Where was the fun in that?

To her mind, the only real difference between her sister and herself seemed to be that of outlook. Tolly tended the fences; Meg opened the gates. Tolly thought "Bears!" without realizing that free-roaming wild animals gave this piece of land a rare purity. Being surrounded by unknowns and wilderness made the kids cautious but not afraid.

By experiencing things personally they were more curious than they had ever been. Now they had a chance to hear their own voices, to observe, to question, to mull then draw their own conclusions. Perhaps they might even start to imagine what their eventual destinies might be. The kids might not think in those terms yet, but she did.

At this moment, they lay watching their familiar group of ravens taking turns tumbling down the drafts of air sliding from the ridge. Two days ago she had seen all three children lying on their stomachs for hours, studying ants moving in and out of their nest. She had watched them laughing as they tried to catch the main shaft of water in the upper spring with their hands. A few days ago, Callie and Sara had led Kurt and her into the forest to show them the tiny hoof prints of a fawn, using words that depicted the most precious find on earth. While they were looking at it, the Littles had drawn them to notice the sweetness of the air beneath the trees—"Just smell it here, just ssmmeeell it."

Oh, yes, she had observed these children touching the earth and touching the sky. Because of living here, would they be better prepared to deal with the world's problems later on? There had to be a connection between *knowing* the land, and making future decisions to protect it. How passionately would a person fight to save old-growth forests and pristine lands, watersheds and creeks, rivers and salmon runs, if that person had never personally experienced those things?

At that moment Erda stood up and raised her head, sniffing the air in the direction of the woods above them and giving a tentative growl. It seemed important enough for the dog to give her people a quick look—the one that said, "Stay!" Her low rumble kept them on alert until whatever it was had passed—probably a bear, as Erda only *watched* deer and elk.

When the dog again lay down, Kurt gently gathered one of her ears in his hand and brushed its black tip against his mouth, commenting that she was the only radar screen fueled by dog biscuits and cornbread. Erda leaned back against him and licked his face with her long pink ribbon and applauded his observation by pounding her tail on the ground. Callie sneezed.

34

TO KNOW ONES SELF

Meg lay back into the perfumed bubbles of her bathtub, as delighted in feeling luxuriously female as she had felt attentively motherly earlier, lying in the grass with her children. The water in the tub was deep and hot; she could just hear the cool jazz coming from her bedroom radio; and she knew, as she always knew, when lying in a tub, that warm water was the ultimate clothing for skin.

Regardless of what she bathed in—the round tin tub of her childhood or the various porcelain tubs of her later life—it was in a bathtub that she was forced to reflect on her whole self. Clothes had a way of isolating one's head and face from the rest of a body; while being naked in a tub, with nothing to hide behind, one was obligated to contemplate and appreciate the intricacies of the whole machine. She became aware of that fact at the moment she stripped off the last of her clothes and, caught awkwardly between fashion and hygiene, saw her whole self in the mirror—it was still a nice sight: she was still "in the pink" and, she had to admit, still a bit sexy.

Her bathroom, which had once resembled something straight out of a bus depot, was now a pretty and welcoming place; and it had taken little more than a new window to change it. Of course, it had also taken paint and new light fixtures and replacing the big, square sheet of mirror with a smaller oval one in a delicate gold frame. But the most important addition was the sturdy new window, which started near the floor and ended near the ceiling, and had two screened sections on its sides that could be opened to the outside with their little cranks. The way it had utterly transformed the room gave Meg hope as to what new windows could do to the other rooms of this chunky brown fortress.

· · ·

Given the room's southern exposure, the window provided a grand view of the bench of land behind the house and the ridge looming above it. And, just as she had wanted, it brought in the sounds and smells of the mountain. Listening, she could hear a raven's odd groak-groaking, along with the voices of smaller forest birds, which were just now beginning their melancholy end-of-the-day mantras.

When a slight breeze began nudging the towels beside the tub, she sank lower into the bubbles to escape its coolness, sighing contentedly. Here she was having a hot bath halfway up on a mountain, where she was a thousand times more likely to be observed by a bear or an elk than a person from her bathroom window. It was beyond luxury, and her gratitude was for Al Turner's wizardry in having brought the spring's pure water through that welter of pipes and tanks and heaters into this tub.

She lazily scooped the bubbles up over her breasts again and again, watching the bubbles slide down and spread out over the surface of the water. Peering over the edge of the tub at the dog lying half-asleep on the white rug, she lifted up a handful of bubbles and let them slide off her fingers and plop lightly down onto Erda's nose. The dog's nearest silver eyebrow lifted, revealing a fraction of an inch of glittery brown, and the tiniest tip of her pink tongue gave a bubble a taste then rejected it. Sighing loudly, the dog watched the bubbles turn to water and descend into the nap of the rug. She huffed and became absorbed in sleep once again.

Meg said, "Forgive me," and laughed apologetically. This marshmallow of a dog! To all the critters that stalked, climbed, hovered, howled and prowled on this mountainside, Meg vowed to keep the dog's secret. Inside this menacing black watchdog resided a gentle soul, more content to decorate a white rug than tear apart an adversary: a true sheep in wolf's clothing. Once the dog's human charges were safely deposited into their snug little cubicles, she became a cheery cherub, ready to trundle off to bed herself.

As Meg lay back into the bubbles, she studied the geography of her body: its half-sunk continents rising from the bubbly sea and mist; its group of recognizable islands; her twin volcanic breasts; the rounded hill of belly, with its small sunken lake at its center; and the long slope to the furry lowlands and steamy jungles. Beyond that were the peninsular thighs, two kneecap islands, and, cut off from the mainland, the two sentinels of her big toes—pink-pearl flagged and waggling. Her continent lay quiet until its need for the distant bar of soap caused a cataclysmic eruption, only to be calmed and soothed in heat and fragrance once again.

She touched her finger to a volcano's nipple and watched it change from its indistinct roundness to stand erect. Her mind wandered back in time to touching Ma's breasts in the bath. Meg must have been near Callie's age when she asked about them, as one comments on familiar artifacts—once known intimately, but now only vaguely remembered. Her little girl gesture toward her mother's breasts seemed more to be a question, "Will I have them, too?" In answer, Ma had pointed to Meg's own tiny nipples—two mole-like dots on her little chest—and reassured her that some day they would grow and Meg would be able to feed her own baby from them, just as she had fed Meg. The look on Ma's face had indicated that that was very nice to be able to do. At that early time, there had been no need for Ma to have finished the story; that breasts would advertise Meg's charms, reflect her thoughts, react to her passion, and, in effect, have a life of their own.

As Ma had prophesied, Meg's nipples first started to bulge and grow into tingling mountains—and this reassured Meg. But later, around the time the blood had so unpredictably and so ineptly arrived, she became a helpless bystander to her body's changes. Having grown from midget to giant, with a never-ending cycle of zits and hairy armpits (that extruded a telltale stain at first hint of self-consciousness), she secretly doubted that grace and beauty would ever be part of her body's transformation.

But, somehow, the ungainly growth slowed down and the tubbiness smoothed into surprising curves. Meg smiled in secret knowledge of the beauty she still possessed: full breasts, narrow waist, long legs, her body firm and strong, her skin juicy and springy to the touch. She pinched her thigh, and then let her hands flow sensuously over and around her breasts and belly. She remembered feeling like a huge pod as she was stretched to bursting with pregnancy...all four times (occasionally, she counted the other boy). Now that belly was gratefully at rest; its duty to posterity presumably finished.

But all the feelings that led to those babies were still there, and still raging. When would those desires—that hovered in her mind, but centered within that triangle of hair—ever be satisfied? Why didn't those wants end when her "duty to perpetuating the race" was finished? The sexual pleading within her seemed always like a conversation left off in midair, and she was drawn to think of words that would somehow keep that conversation going. That potent conversation, which had left off long before Ed died, had flooded back when Ellis had leaned over that first time and kissed her. It was as though her lips held an "on" button to the mysterious fountains within her.

Ellis. Just because she was lonely... How many times did she have to remind herself that there was no possibility of any future relationship with him? Although his being away relieved her, his letters (unanswered) and phone calls (received indifferently) kept the possibility of a relationship ever alive in the minds of the Littles, if not Kurt. Happily, they were occupied with their pets and they teased her less about providing them with a daddy. It was crucial that she keep him away. She determined, for the umpteenth time, that she would not invite him (or let him invite himself) to dinner as had happened all summer. And if he didn't take that as a hint...well, she'd just have to tell him again, "No, No, No!"

Her last view of him had been, frankly, embarrassing. The day after the hike they'd met in town, as planned, to see the dog. After helping bring the newly acquired pets to the house, and helping to bathe them, nothing would do but to invite him to stay for a cold supper, after which she'd walked him out to his car. There, he had almost begged for her, with his hands and words wanting her—not at some future time, but that night. He'd said, "Later, when the kids are asleep, I'll come back. We'll go for a drive. Anything. Bring a blanket, or we'll use the back seat. Stop holding me off!"

Hearing his words, she was both appalled at his desperation and exhilarated by that flush of raw desire they created in her. If only… if only there was something called "just a little bit of sex"… Like a furiously boiling teakettle, screaming steam and scalding droplets from its spout, wasn't there a way one could pour out a little, and afterwards, lean back and rest in the cooler, more contented part of the stove…just a little, only a little? In spite of the "Yes!" in her thoughts, she'd managed to tell him, "It's late and I'm tired, Ellis. You have to leave tomorrow."

He had said, "If not now, then you arrange it when I get back. I want to be in—"

She had interrupted, "—Yes, Ellis, I know just *where*."

She sighed a ragged sigh in remembering that, and moved her hand through the water to block that contested entrance of hers. As she did, an old memory came, unbidden, into her mind…a memory of ten thousand nights ago…

· · ·

…It was the spot near her face that so repulsed her. The anonymous spot had sunk into the worn fibers of that anonymous orange bedspread. The air in the room had smelled like an ashtray; and the motel sign, even with the blatant light coming from the bedside lamp, blinked hypnotically against the blind. Above her, on the ceiling, was another stain, ringed in brown with green crusts of paint hanging from it. Ed was above her, too, still wearing his silk shirt and tie and socks, while she was trying to pull the orange bedspread up around her nakedness.

Oddly removed from what was happening, she had fixed her eyes on the ceiling spot and wondered if other girl-children had been opened here. When she complained that it hurt, she was told it wasn't pain, but that a woman needed to *feel* a man. She tried to turn on her side. She begged, "Not again, Ed. And don't hold me so tight. I can't breathe." Yet, even as she said it she knew that it was too late.

Staring at the ceiling, she knew exactly why she was lying next to that orange stain. She had walked into the room, as willing as a schoolgirl walks into a classroom, ready for the new lesson. In his car she had succumbed to Ed's pleading and, after he lost interest in her long hair, she had let his fingers explore her. She was learning, too. His fingers had surprised her, bringing her to a panting state of madness. In her excitement, she had willingly walked through the door and lay upon the bedspread for the rest of the lesson, for the part that hurt. She had consented, and then it was too late.

She got pregnant between those two stains, and there was no one to ask for advice. Even as Papa lay in the hospital bed, not answering her, it was too late. Then he died, and Ma, alone in her rocking chair, grieved herself to death. Tolly was settling into the family farm and had her family to care for. There was no one at school she could ask, because she was too ashamed. Whose fault was it for letting a man she didn't like do that? It was hers. She could have told him "No!"

A tiny, half-formed boy, covered in blood, was the result. Living only a moment, he was a bathroom secret, never named and never counted by anyone but her. That tiny secret alive-for-only-a-moment speck of boy brought no grief, but only a puzzling relief, to his Halverson father. The Halverson ghosts would not look kindly on a "love child."

On her first wedding anniversary she burned her wedding gown. Just scooped it up and, in view of all the Halverson ghosts, stuffed it into the burn-barrel behind the red brick monstrosity of a house, lit it with a match, and stood there watching its agonized end; the veil still reaching out, gripping at the air, not wanting to go like that. She pushed it into the flames with a stick and told it, "You get in there!" She heard it scream as the flames devoured it; its seed pearls pinging against the sides of the barrel; the lace and satin ribbons sagging, grotesque, before turning into ashes. The whole mess sifting down into the old tin cans and broken bottles in the burn barrel. No feeling...feeling nothing, nothing...not even relief. The garbage men hauled the ashes away the next day, pouring all that remained of wedded bliss into the greasy mouth of their truck. From the kitchen window she watched it close its mouth, chew awhile, then swallow and drive away...

. . .

Erda heard Meg's sob and stood up, alert, and looked at her. Meg reached over and stroked her muzzle, saying, "It's all right, all right.

Just some ugly pieces of my past, pretty dog." It helped to turn her thoughts to her black, furred friend. But even as she stroked her, she wondered where in hell those *banished thoughts* had come from? Shaking her head furiously, she picked up the washcloth and soap and worked at the real job of being in this tub—scrubbing her knees and elbows until they hurt.

She stopped scrubbing and listened, gripped by that same strange feeling of excitement she had felt all day; and now a prickling down her spine. *Feet were walking. Feet were walking up a road.* What was it? Erda listened, too.

Hearing nothing from her early-to-bed children, she shook off the thoughts and slid back into the water, idly rejecting that this anticipation could possibly be caused from Ellis coming back. Or was it because of this wonderful break in the weather? The radio had reported that many of the fires were out. The sky looked clean of smoke again, so perhaps it would be just an ordinary sunset tonight. She thought, "Ordinary? Nothing is ever ordinary up here." She must hurry or she would miss it. She would quickly wash her hair and dry it on the front step. While she worked in the shampoo she began to think of the letter she must write Tolly tonight, about that old hired man. Tolly's comments revealed an interest in him—perhaps an itch in her own life. It was just as well he left the farm, poor man.

With her head in the water, she missed seeing Erda raise her head and listen, then glide silently out of the room.

Meg rinsed her hair and left the tub, towel drying her hair. She pulled on the old blue robe, and left the bathroom. Looking around for the dog, she called softly, "Where are you, Erda?"

The dog was already at the door, alert but not barking, staring at the door. She looked up at Meg questioningly.

Meg stopped and watched her people-dog. "It's a person out there, that's what you're telling me, Erda." She hesitated while she decided what to do then opened the heavy door carefully, letting the dog out ahead of her. Once she slipped outside herself, she stood close to the door, feeling its solidness at her back and the reassurance of the slab of stone under her bare feet. The two of them waited, the woman and the dog both searching the road.

The man walking up the road was caught in the giant sweep of colors from the sunset. In fact, he looked like he had walked straight out of it: walking, stopping, turning around and looking back at the sky, then turning and walking a little nearer, then turning around again and standing looking back at the sky. As the man made his way toward her, Meg watched him quietly, with her hand on the dog's neck, and her whole body again gripped in that prophetic anticipation. When she saw his face, she knew.

She said, "How did you find me?"

35

OLD FLINT

Meg, in her blue robe and her hair in damp curls, stepped toward him. He walked nearer and stood looking at her—far, far into her eyes. He didn't say it—no one said it—but she thought she heard the word "yes" when she looked at that face, that gentle, smiling face that calmed her so. When she heard the "yes" her shoulders sagged and the fingers of her one hand wandered around in the fur on Erda's neck, while the other one fingered a tissue in her pocket. Then she'd asked him that absurd question: not, "Who are you?" or "What are you doing here?" but "How did you find me?"

. . .

When Meg got back to him, after pulling on her jeans and a decent shirt and preparing a plate of sandwiches and a pot of Earl Grey tea, he was pretty much where she had left him, sitting on the front step, looking at the sunset. Meg felt embarrassed coming out the door at that moment, with the mindless clink of mugs against the teapot and a waft of garlic and horseradish from the roast beef sandwiches. But he seemed more than happy for the interruption. Standing up and smiling, he took the tray carefully from her and set it down on the ground at his feet before sitting down again. She sat down beside him and they were quiet again.

The sun had slipped behind the far rim of mountains, but with the sky's particular type of clouds, the sunset refused to quiet down. The color dimmed in stages, then a stray piece of light—thinking it could reverse the evening's process—would escape from below the horizon and turn the sky vivid all over again.

It was easy for Meg to guess the sense of awe going through this man's head as he sat there watching; she'd often felt it, too. Up here on the mountain, a person was in a position to comprehend the rhythm of earth's time-of-light and time-of-darkness. Seeing a whole day from up here was spectacular enough, but seeing an evening's quiet closing of a day shook one's soul.

It started with the light's gradual erasure of the color, then the fading details of the meadow and the valley. Then, just as it turned to darkness, there was that final spinning-off note. Adding to that the dimensions of the sunset they had just witnessed, a person was not only filled with humility about the real beauty of the earth, but had reason to believe it was being performed only for the person sitting on the stone step.

Through all this Flint sat quietly, his arms resting loosely on his knees and his hands slightly arched. Seeing him like that, Meg couldn't help thinking that if it were Ellis sitting there, he would have already jumped up, his wild gestures making the air around him dangerous, and said, "Look there at that blue cloud! Isn't that great?" Then he'd have gone on and on in a voice loaded with superlatives. And the quiet, contemplative moment Meg was having would have dwindled into something she couldn't even see through, much less feel.

But this man Flint was quiet. He took in the beauty before him with the reflection of it on his face, there not being any words for it. When something happened in the sky—like a cloud turning from rose to that deep gorgeous blue—a little tremor passed through him and he hesitated with his cup. Perhaps his heart paused too.

She felt his eyes open wider as the light faded and the town's lights below them started coming on, creating strings of white jewels, with occasional rubies and an emerald or two. The jewels ended abruptly at the town's far edge, as though someone had cut them off with scissors and dragged the leftovers to that little settlement west of Clark Fork. When Flint saw that, he exhaled slowly, as though leaning toward the best part of a movie and hoping no one in the theater would cough lest he miss something.

As the evening smells of pine and earth and cool, cool air crept in, Meg saw Flint's nostrils flare and he half-turned toward her to share his recognition of it, without the need to define it. She nodded and again thought of Ellis. He would have used that as an excuse to jab at her, to rattle her body, as if her sense of smell wasn't paying attention and needed a prod from him to get back into service. Then he might talk about the chemical formula that made pine trees smell like that and launch into a long dissertation on the explosive nature of those aromatic oils in a forest fire, or start to explain the turpentine industry. That was Ellis, all right. But this man Flint was quiet.

Meg had felt a little fearful at Flint coming up the road like he had, for she had no way of knowing then who he was. After he first introduced himself, she asked, incredulously, "You mean Flint from Tolly's and Charlie's farm?" She stopped there, not wanting to ask him why Tolly always referred to him as "Old Flint." Once her eyes had taken him in, it was clear that this man was in his middle forties.

He was taller than she, but not by much. His worn tan pants and nondescript shirt showed a thin, angular body with long bones. He had a high forehead and his ears were positioned close to a well-shaped head. His dark hair had a lot of gray in it and, although some of it was tucked behind his ears, the rest just brushed his shoulders. The skin on his face was fine-textured and deeply tanned. His expression was calm. He looked altogether ordinary except for his eyes. She thought his eyes were dark, maybe hazel, but she wasn't sure, for there was too little light to see. His eyes went with his hands, somehow, but she didn't know why.

From the very first, there hadn't been a lot of words from him. He was Flint and two days ago he had hitched a ride to Clark Fork. It was this afternoon when he began walking up the mountain. Yes, he could have looked up her phone number and called her, but he really wanted to walk and get the feel of the country gradually. The day was beautifully cool and there had been water in unexpected places: once in the canyon, and then, halfway up the mountain, at a spring by the road. As for food, in town, at the same store where he'd inquired as to where the canyon road might be, he'd picked up some nuts and a big bunch of green grapes, a slab of cheese and some muffins.

As to the walk, Tolly had pretty well described it to him back there in Wyler—well, it didn't seem quite as *dangerous* as she'd said, you know. He laughed fondly every time he mentioned Tolly and Charlie. He'd taken it easy all the way, being interested in the trees and plants that were new to him, as well as the animals that had left traces of their passing in the mud from the big storm.

Yes, he had to admit that the muscles in his legs were tired, that the flat country of the farm didn't prepare a person for mountain climbing, but the view he got of the mountains as he climbed was worth it. Perhaps tomorrow his legs might tell a different story. And, oh yes, before he came up to the house, he had dropped off his suitcase and a small box of his stuff in the cabin. They had been a pain to carry. About halfway up the mountain, he had thought hard about tucking his suitcase into a jumble of logs and rocks by the side of the road, to pick up later, but he'd thought of the bears Tolly had mentioned and, with his cameras and all, well he'd decided against it.

He hoped she didn't mind that he'd taken the liberty of washing up at the cabin. When Meg commented on the poor workmanship of the remodeling there, he laughed, just a soft laugh (soft like his voice), and told her it wouldn't be hard to make things right in there. He would enjoy doing it, as he enjoyed working with wood. Just with those few words he had removed the pain from that problem-laden project.

The closeness of the air around them pushed his smell into her nose. As she became aware of it, she thought that, from his long walk and being outside in the air and sun, he and his clothes smelled like a sheet that had been outside on a clothesline all day. Even so, there was a faint smell of sweat about him, too. Taking a last swallow of tea and setting her cup down on the tray she wondered why men smell different than women. Sweat was sweat, but on a man it came out open and frank, while on a woman it smelled a little guilty.

She felt an unreasoning desire to lean over and push aside his collar and touch her tongue to his neck to know what he tasted like, then to taste her own skin. She had to hold back from reaching out and running her fingertips over his face and nose and eyelids, like she touched her children. And this compelling need to touch him made her shy.

With the sky's light now gone, he whispered, "Night," and it was, and the wildness and solitude that the darkness provided were like opening up a new and different chapter. Now the town and its reckless electricity was an unwelcome oddity that their eyes could not help but fasten on. If it were possible, Meg would have reached up and pulled down a shade to obliterate it, to keep the mood. But a cloud drifted by instead—a rain cloud, judging from the few drops that fell on them—and it shut off the town's lights. They sat unmoving in the lukewarm night, smelling the delicious sweetness the rain had sprinkled over them.

In the continuing silence Meg wondered if she should jump up and suggest they go inside, build a fire, turn on a lamp. Instead, she said, "In the letter I got from Tolly just today, she said you'd left the farm. I didn't think you'd be coming here."

He only said, "Yes." So Meg added, "Tolly and Charlie love that picture of the opened gate you left them, and the others you shot. Tolly told me about them." She waited for his response then asked cautiously, "Are you a photographer?"

"Among other things," he said. "Charlie was working on some of the blank spots in my career." Meg could tell he was smiling. He continued, "Nice folks, Tolly and Charlie. Kind people. I wanted to tell them. With their son coming back... Well, it was hard to leave like that, without a goodbye; but easier, too. Good to leave before their kind invitation got used up."

Meg said, "From what Tolly and Charlie said about how much help you've given them and how much they enjoyed you, it didn't sound like that invitation was even close to being used up, Flint."

He didn't say anything to that.

She ventured, "Something in the way you speak sounds like you aren't from this part of the country. Is it the Midwest, or maybe East?"

He said abruptly, "Maybe East. A city. What's past is past." Laughing then, he said, less seriously, "Charlie was working on my words, too, but I failed at dropping my 'g's.'"

Meg laughed, "I call that 'sugar-talkin'. Charlie can really charm me when he gets going."

Flint laughed softly, too.

In the long silence that followed, Meg recognized that just that little peek into him made questions stack up alarmingly inside her, like she might drown in wanting to know. Remembering that Tolly had warned her about inquiring too closely about things like that, she guessed she'd have to wait for him to offer more information himself. Aware of his working over his words, she kept sitting there. But she soon got discouraged, and was about to end the evening by picking up the tray, when he said,"You've never lived in a city, Meg." It wasn't a question.

"No. No. I've visited them of course. But I wouldn't choose it. I had enough trouble living the last eighteen years among those lights down there. I seem to need great stretches of empty land, where I don't have to try to pretend what it once was, but instead, see what *it still is*. I'm a *land* person, a *mountain* person. Dents put in the land by careless men hurt me.This is what I need."As she spoke she noticed that their words, coming out of the dark now, with nothing of the speaker visible, seemed like words out of a dream, like they originated from a deep place and stood out honest and clear in the night.

After a long wait she heard Flint take a deep breath, and then his words began, like a thread being spun out of a wad and jumble of something that wasn't good to remember;that maybe hurt to remember. Starting slow, then gaining momentum, he said,"I walked up your road today and thought about the city I left. I lived in the northern part of the city and had to grab a commuter bus to get to work. I had to walk up the hill several blocks to my building, and part of that way, I had to walk under an overpass.Above me were eight lanes of traffic.The traffic made an unrelenting whine, shaking the concrete and steel that held it up, even shaking the sidewalk. It was dirty under there. Rain never reached under there, so nothing ever washed away the mess that accumulated—oil and the stuff that grinds off tires over the years; bits of glass and metal; wrappers and cigarette butts; and things that once had meaning, but have been cast away and mean nothing now. That stuff just piles up behind us. I hated walking through that trash; then again I was glad it didn't wash down into the water—the light stuff floating and the heavy stuff sinking deeper down and staying there—better it stays under that overpass than in the water.

"Today, walking up here, I thought about that. I patted my pockets to make sure that the food wrappers were still inside them. When I turned around and looked behind me, I saw only my footprints on your road, nothing more. And in a day or so even those will be gone." Turning to her he said, in a tight voice, "I don't know why it's important to me that you understand these things, but just now it is. You need to know, you and your sister and Charlie."

While Meg tried to grasp what he was telling her, he continued. "Under that overpass there were people living in the cracks. Not actual cracks, but in the spaces formed by the huge sloping concrete supports running diagonally to the columns supporting the roadbed. Into these shelters, the people had pulled their cardboard and rags and slept with their faces just inches away from the underside of the roadbed, feeling the rumble and vibration, hearing the same screech and whine that deafened me; only for them, it was closer and all night. I could never imagine how they lived there.

"As I passed by, they looked down at me, like rats peering out of their holes, sizing me up, and maybe looking for an opportunity... for, well, I don't know. Then I'd think they're people like me, who are only watching, much as I watch a bird, interested in its movement. But when a police car would drive by, they would fade back into their holes, and I was glad it was daylight.

"There was an old woman who slept in a dumpster near the sidewalk. She was on my same time schedule, like she had an alarm clock down inside there. In the mornings, as I passed, she often raised the metal lid and said, 'Hello,' very courteously. She crawled out of the dumpster like another person lifts off the blankets and crawls out of bed. But her being there worried me. I would think of her down inside that dumpster and, if I didn't see her, I would hope it didn't mean there were new garbage men on the route, who had picked up her bedroom ahead of schedule and dumped her into their truck while she was still asleep. I had this picture in my mind of her struggling to get out, screaming, 'I'm still inside!' And I used to wonder where her bathroom was, and where she ever washed her hands, and about the others living in those cracks above her dumpster."

Meg sat very quiet now, waiting, the pictures created by his words, clear and stark in the night.

He continued."The noise in a city takes its toll after a while. I knew silence as a kid, a long time ago, but in a city there are layers of noise you can't get away from. I can't understand the booming blast of car speakers, with the people inside the car risking their hearing and sanity; or the boom-box people, carrying their noise around with them—like hermit crabs carry their borrowed shells—and using that noise like it was their identity, letting it say,'This is me, and, if you don't like my music, you don't like me.'You'd think they'd seek silence instead.

"While I walked up your mountain I could hear my footsteps. It made me wonder if a person who hasn't known silence could know what's happening when all the noise gets worse. On Charlie's farm there is necessary noise, with his tractor and plow and combine reacting to the seasons: to plow, to plant, to harvest. In between those times, the land is so quiet—even the wind seems right—and the same is true up on this mountain.

"Today, at a spring, about halfway up here, I stopped and spread out my little picnic. I laid the grapes and cheese on a rock that had never seen soap or hot water, but was clean! After I cut the cheese I wiped my knife on a leaf; but then I wiped off the leaf. I spent some time there listening and studying the light and shadows on my pants and arms. I realized I'd never heard that particular stillness before. After I ate I lay down by the spring, on my stomach like a kid, and I watched small pieces of things get carried around in that clear water, as though a mighty force was moving them."

There was a long silence after that. Meg heard a jerking in his breathing and felt his hand move up to his face. Understanding that there was something hurting him, she cried quietly, too, remembering the day she, like someone drowning, had searched for solace here and had found it. Someday she'd show him the old silver log in the grove of trees. That would help him.

With an embarrassed laugh, Flint touched her arm lightly and said, "I've said too much. I'm beat. I better get some sleep. Do you have a flashlight I can borrow to find my way back to the cabin? Looks like I'll need to find some bedding, too. I saw the cot there."

The change in words took a moment to filter in and she said, "Oh, yes, yes. I'll walk you down, Flint. There's already a sleeping bag and pillow and an extra blanket there. I've napped there often lately. It's really nice to hear the trees there. I have a flashlight just inside the door here, and I'll get sweaters. Could you use one, even though it's mine? I have a big green one, a failed knitting project actually. It's huge!"

"Yes, please, if you don't mind. It's cooler than I thought."

They walked along the road, held together by the beam of light. Erda, padding sleepily beside them, bumped Meg's leg with her nose from time to time, to let her know she was there. Catching the light, the cabin door appeared suddenly ahead of them. Meg went in first, turning on the light, and leading Flint into the roughed-in bedroom. She pulled the bedding from an old chest and they unrolled it onto the cot together, plumping the one pillow and comfortably patting everything into place between them. That done, they smiled a little shyly at each other. Meg finally said, "There's hot water and soap and towels. But then you already know that."

"Yes. Thank you, Meg." His face looked haggard and he yawned. Bending to rub Erda's ears, he said, "You're quite a pet, aren't you? Thanks for not tearing me to pieces. If I'd known about you I wouldn't have walked up the road quite so casually. But you didn't even growl at me." He smiled at Meg. "I don't know the customs here. Now should I walk you back to your house?"

She touched his arm lightly and laughed softly, "Oh, sure! We can go back and forth like this for hours. No, no; I have this *ferocious* dog. We'll be fine. Please sleep in as late as you can tomorrow. You'll take your meals with us, of course. The kids and I will make breakfast whenever you come in. The front door will be open. Now that the end of summer is in sight and school will be starting in a couple weeks, the kids are really enjoying their loose schedules, which will be regimented soon enough. The kids will be surprised and pleased that you're here, Flint." The word "Flint" still felt a bit experimental on her tongue.

While she opened the window he looked around. "This is a nice place. I've been sleeping in Charlie's bunkhouse, so sleeping in a cabin under these big trees will be a new experience. Thank you. It's been some time since I laid my body out flat. Good night, Meg...Erda...and thank you."

. . .

For a long time Meg lay on her bed looking up at the dark ceiling, just like she had after Ed died, when she was so uncertain of the future. She thought of the great distance she had come since then, and tears of gratitude for making it this far slipped from her eyes and ran into her ears. She didn't cry much anymore. Maybe she should. It was hard to explain, but during her evening with Flint it had come to her, hard and plain, that she had never loved her husband. Even in the very beginning of their courtship, when she said to him and to herself, "Ah, yes, this is love," there had never been a real, breathing love between them. And in the years that followed, with her, it had been only a "staying with it" in the hope that they'd get through it somehow, that the big hopeless disappointing thing would somehow get better with age.

Talking aloud to the darkness above her, she said, "Ed, did we marry because we had no one else to marry, or was it because we were so hot? After the heat was less, you were always going away from me—happy to leave and using any excuse at all. Finally, I was glad you left. Even in the end, I was happy that you weren't coming back. For that, Ed, forgive me. I should have left you long ago, except you would have fought me for our children—not *for* the children, but to thwart me. They have always been mine, but you would have fought me for them, because you never could stand to lose anything, especially, lose anything to me. If only we could have quit our marriage, maybe we both could have found that one person to love."

She waited for relief from the pain of her thoughts, but the silence of the room only continued. Nothing seemed to produce any answers. The further she got into her life, the less she knew. The more she learned, the more questions she asked. She told the dark window above her bed, "I want to be the heroine of my life, but I don't know how to be. I've made such poor choices. Soon I'll be thirty-nine years old, but still I know nothing. I have never loved anyone but my parents, my sister, my children, and myself. When will I love a man? When will there be a man just for me?"

She wrapped her arms around her pillow and held it fiercely against her body and began to cry again. But this time she cried for her continuing loneliness; for wanting a man's eyes to look deeply into hers, for wanting his hands on her, for wanting to feel his need of her, for wanting him to take her somewhere—anywhere—and put his hands inside her clothes and run his hands into her juices—to want her like that. When she was ready, she would lie there and watch while he opened his clothes and took out that lovely man-thing and put it deep within her, holding her tight against him, and letting it hurt and plunge while she moaned for release. At that, the very power of her thoughts burst inside her, and she lay panting and throbbing—but still alone—and still in terrible need of closeness with another loving human being.

Calmer now, she spoke aloud, "Edward Halverson and Ellis Brodie, you lovely-bodied men with your heavy breathing, I want you to leave my mind. I want something that neither one of you could give me. If such a man exists, I want...I want...oh, I don't know what I want. But you two go away and let me wipe my slate clean of both of you, and start over."

She sat up and pushed the pillow back against the bed frame soberly, then pulled up the tangled sheet and straightened it out, folding its soft lacy edge carefully over the top of the comforter. When she slid back down, and pulled it all up around her bare skin, she caught a whiff of lavender and of her wild self. Then she turned over onto her stomach—like a kid in a book—and thought of the two and a half hours she had spent with a man who wept into pebbles. Old Flint.

36

SOMEONE NEW

With her coffee cup in hand and her mind filled with curiosity, Meg sat down to wait on the top step of the balcony stairs. Through the big west window she had a clear view of the road that went past the cabin. As she waited for a first glimpse of Flint, she was as excited as she'd been all day yesterday—and yesterday, she hadn't even known he was coming or, for that matter, anything about this man; this "old" Flint. And what was this feeling of anticipation all about? Perhaps last night had only been a dream.

Even with Tolly's virtual endorsement of him, Flint was the kind of man she wouldn't ordinarily notice. She tried to remember what he looked like—not too tall, lean, wiry, dark hair to his shoulders and showing lots of gray, long fingers and expressive hands—but his features? She closed her eyes and tried to put together his face, but it was the whole remarkable evening that came back to her: how she felt with him sitting close beside her, and how his words, about things she could hardly imagine, sounded in the darkness around them. In fact, his face was all mixed up in her impressions of him, his quietness and his curious restraint. When she'd helped him make up his bed, then left him in the cabin, she'd wanted to go back, maybe just to watch him sleep, hear him breathe, see the way his eyes looked shut.

Her value system had become so impaired in the years living with Ed. Despite her being reared on a farm where dress was casual and thrifty and style nonexistent, in Clark Fork the status of the men she knew was gauged by what clothes they wore: if they looked successful they were thought successful, and they were admired by men and women alike. Much to her discredit she, too, had judged their character by what they wore. Ed had been one of those, decked out in his fine French-cuffed shirts, silk ties, and dark three-piece suits, all of which fairly shouted his social standing and importance. That look of his—which she'd had a hand in creating—had given her pleasure, albeit a guilty pleasure, for having to acknowledge that the simple values she'd been raised by could be swayed by false gods after all.

Then, by assigning Ellis—with his youth and dazzling, sun-struck smile—all kinds of positive attributes just because of his external attractiveness, she understood that she had learned little from Ed's example. That first day on the road below the house, Ellis, leaning out the truck's window, had looked every bit a part of the wondrous forest around him. She and Sara had still been under the spell of the Canada lynx, so when Ellis gazed down at them, so magnificently blonde, it felt as though he could give them back the elusive animal that had just whispered by them.

With Ellis's beauty so apparent, how could she notice that his perfect mouth obscured an intractable single mindedness? And even when she found that they were at odds about almost everything concerning the cabin and the trees, something in her said, "Oh, no, he couldn't possibly be thinking those things, because he's so beautiful!" It was as though a feast for the eyes had removed her judgment!

Now, fearing her judgment, Meg steeled herself against disappointment as she waited for Flint to appear.

Of the many impressions she'd had, it was his crying and her own response to do the same that puzzled her. What had moved him to tears? And what of a man crying anyway? She remembered seeing Papa cry only twice. The first time had been the morning he'd found Jake, his favorite and last workhorse, dead in the barn. The other time was right after an August hailstorm had destroyed the wheat he had just begun to harvest. Ma had cried then, too.

Was it Flint's experiences in the city that affected him, or was it the silence he had found by the roadside spring where he had eaten? Perhaps it was that he needed that silence in some way? There seemed to be a kind of sadness in him; she'd concluded that last night.

. . .

When Flint finally appeared from the trees, she studied him intently: his clothes and shoes, the way he held his head and body as he walked, his very manner. He was wearing the same clothes he'd worn last night, clothes straight off Tolly's clothesline—nondescript, comfortable, and worn—but they looked right on him. He had tied his hair back with some kind of cord and, in the sunlight, his gray hairs looked like polished silver. As he walked toward the house, just as he'd done last evening, he stopped and looked around him, as interested in the effect of the morning sun on what was ahead of him as he had been last evening with the sunset behind him. Meg liked that, for she did that, too. But why this unremarkable man walking toward her so piqued her interest was a mystery.

Calming her excitement, she got up and walked down the steps to let him in. After greeting him warmly she said, "I'm glad you slept in a bit after your long day yesterday. Were you comfortable there?"

"Perfectly. I slept well, very well. I awoke to the different sounds of the birds, and to the kids' voices. I liked hearing them talking to each other and their laughter. Nothing like that around Tolly's and Charlie's place."

She nodded. "Those three rascals were under strict instructions to be quiet. Sounds carry well here; this place is a regular amphitheater. The kids' camp is down there in the meadow, just below your cabin. I predict that they'll find some excuse to come to the house now. One of them has to have been posted as lookout. I'll give them five minutes to appear. In the meantime, I made waffles for the kids and there's plenty of batter waiting for you, and sausage patties. I bet you're starved."

He smiled and nodded, "Very hungry," and followed her up the balcony's steps, all the while looking around him. Stopping in the kitchen doorway, he said, "This is an amazing house. It's exterior didn't quite prepare me for what's inside. Did Tolly ever see its interior?"

Meg shook her head sadly. "Not really, in the way you mean. She had a terrible introduction to this place—having helped me break into the house then being forced to sleep on the cold floor by the fireplace all night. I'm sure you've heard the story. From her latest letter, she doesn't sound as upset as she was. After all that happened to us in town, she was so set on us coming back to the farm to live. Of course, that wasn't possible. Someday, if I can get her up here again, maybe she'll understand how perfect this place is for us."

He nodded thoughtfully. "In every word she spoke about you, I could tell she's very protective of you. And then that farm, she's as rooted to that land as anyone could ever be."

Meg laughed, "When we were kids we had a game we called Touching Earth, Touching Sky. Tolly, being the oldest, always got to be the sky toucher, while I, having been assigned the role of earth toucher, ended up with my nose pushed down in the dirt watching her dance around. Who could have thought that she really didn't like high places like this, while I…well it's funny how things work out."

She poured coffee into two cups and offered one to him, gesturing to the sugar bowl and cream pitcher on the counter. Then, listening, she only had time to say, "Like I said, 'five minutes,'" as the kids and Erda came noisily through the big door below them and up the stairs to the kitchen.

As a group, they stopped and stood looking at him, smiling a bit shyly, but interested, too. Looking at them, Meg wondered when they'd ever stood in a line like that. And, after all her thoughts on assessing character by a person's appearance, she wondered just how a stranger would assess them, seeing as how "ragtag" would be a charitable description for their various getups.

They all wore jeans that had been clean two hours ago. Kurt's feet were happily encased in his brand new logger boots, and he was wearing his favorite grey hooded sweatshirt, from which his wrists stuck out of the badly fraying cuffs, and the elbows bagged like collapsing balloons. Sara was dressed in her cowboy boots and a blue-and-red plaid western shirt—her "Porcupine Shirt" (Meg didn't know why she called it that). Callie's small toe was visible through a hole in her right red canvas shoe, and she had on a disgustingly dirty green shirt of Kurt's, with the sleeves rolled to her elbows, both of which (the shirt and the elbows) had also been perfectly clean earlier.

Looking at their earnest expressions, Meg tried not to smile as she introduced her children to Flint, for she could so clearly read their minds. Other than Ellis, the workmen, and the young couple who'd taken care of them the day of the hike, the kids had not met one other person up here. Perhaps it was what she'd told them earlier, about Flint arriving last evening when they were asleep, or the look on her own face now, but they all knew there was something special (and a bit disconcerting) about his being here.

Flint took his time shaking each child's hand, speaking their names, and making a quiet, good-natured comment to each one. When the introductions were over, he said, "I know your Aunt Tolly and Uncle Charlie. I've been helping them out for a few months. I thought that maybe I could help your mother with her remodeling project for a while. You have a fine place. It must be interesting living here."

Callie was the first to speak. "Yah, there's everything here, our camp and the deer and the spring. Sometimes we're Indians. Ma helped us make a teepee, and one day she fixed cocoa and came inside and helped us drink it. We have a neat cat named Muggins. He's a boy. Do you want to see him? He upchucks a lot, so you shouldn't squeeze him very hard. I'll show you how to pick him up." She stopped talking and looked up at him. "Mr. Flint, did you really walk all the way here from town, like Ma said? I don't think anyone has ever, ever done that before."

Before Flint replied, Sara turned to her and said, "Ellis has done it lots of times!"

Callie said, "He never does that! He drives his car or his big green Forest truck."

Sara said, "Well, he could do it if he wanted to!"

Nodding toward his sisters, Kurt interjected, a little derisively, "We call them the Littles and they argue a lot." He reached over and stroked the dog's neck. "This is Erda. She looks mean, but she isn't. We adopted her."

Flint held out his fingers for the dog to sniff then caressed her muzzle briefly with the back of his hand. "I met her last night, and you're right; both her size and her gentleness surprised me. Up here, I'd say you'd want her to look mean, but she has a good heart. She's lucky to be with the right family."

Meg had plugged in the waffle iron and was now spooning batter into it. She said, "Kurt, why don't you pour us all some orange juice and we'll take Flint out to our doorstep to eat his breakfast. And don't think these waffles and sausage are for any of you guys. You've had plenty. I'm going to feed Flint just enough so he'll be ready for lunch in a couple hours, along with you."

. . .

After Flint had eaten and the dishes were returned to the kitchen, Meg turned to Sara. "I think it would be nice if you three cooked our dinner down in your camp this evening. I bet Flint hasn't had anything like that before. What do you think?"

Sara's face fairly lit up, "Can we make stew, Ma? And can we make cornbread again, like we did yesterday?"

Meg said, "Sounds good to me. But maybe you better ask Flint if he's available to come to dinner. Maybe he's planning to walk down the mountain and go to a movie or go dancing or something. And maybe he doesn't like stew."

Taking his cue, Flint waited, looking down at Sara expectantly.

Sara reached out and touched his sleeve. "Would you like to come to dinner at our camp and eat stew?"

Flint screwed up his face and thought a moment, "As long as there's cornbread I would. What time is dinner?"

Callie piped up, "We can do it now if you want."

Both girls leaned forward, waiting for his answer.

Flint pursed his lips, "Well, I don't know if I could do it right now, after eating those waffles— "

Sara said, "Maybe later?"

Flint smiled. "I'll look forward to it. Maybe your mom will tell me when."

. . .

After the girls and the dog had left to prepare the camp, and Meg had put out the stew meat to defrost, she and Kurt began to tell Flint all the things they wanted. After the cabin was all finished, they wanted to get rid of the kitchen's blue wallboard and to replace the windows with ones that would open. They wanted new cupboards and counters, sinks and stove. They wanted the kitchen to be friendlier. They'd need a new floor, too. And, if that weren't enough, Kurt told him that they wanted a woodstove installed in the corner of the kitchen, along with a table where they could eat breakfast, play games, and do their homework.

Meg heard the anxiety in her voice as she apologized for how complicated it would be. After the discouraging experience she'd had with Ellis and the carpenters, she could hardly face an even bigger project.

Flint took it all in without looking overwhelmed. He suggested that they first sit down and make a plan. While they were finishing the cabin, they could do the kitchen windows before it got too cold, and maybe take out the wallboard, so that they could take their time with the other kitchen things this winter. He said that it would save time and effort to order ready-made cupboards and storage units to fit their plan, rather than building them from scratch on site. "You've given me some ideas," he said. "Perhaps tomorrow we can begin to list these things, so we can begin searching for vendors and materials, and figure out a timetable. We'll need to locate some carpenters." He spoke apologetically. "My skills are not necessarily carpenter skills, but, after I know what you want, I can help supervise the men, check the quality of their work, and keep things moving along. Perhaps we can contact those same workmen again and get them up here to help us." With that suggestion, Meg felt herself relax and she and Kurt smiled at each other.

She and Kurt gave Flint a tour of the complete house—downstairs and up, which included the third story that contained the Webster's room and a big room holding a couple trunks and a lot of boxes that the girls had pushed around for a playhouse. Downstairs, they showed Flint the amazing furnace, cistern, water system, Treasure Room, main workroom, Kurt's workshop under the stairs, a bathroom, wood storage room, two small rooms that held nothing, and the huge three-car garage. The immensity of the place was almost embarrassing, reminding Meg of how small an area her family actually occupied. All that space was rather an oddity; there was no chance of turning it into anything manageable. Shrugging hopelessly, Meg said, "All I've done down here is attempt to clean it."

Flint gave her a wry smile and added, "At least it's good to have the space; that's usually the limiting factor."

When the three of them went up to the spring, Flint fell silent. With an uncomprehending look he stared at the upwelling water. He held up his hand to stop all conversation and listened to the bubbles breaking over the water's surface. Kurt, watching him, smiled proudly. Flicking a quick look at his mother, he asked Flint if he was thirsty. Before Flint could answer, Kurt took the drinking cup off the little wire hook he'd fashioned on a branch and, plunging it into the spring, held his dripping offering respectfully out to the older man.

It was her son who Meg watched as Flint drank: watched his lips and throat making sympathetic swallowing motions, and watched his eyes respond to Flint's pleasure. Meg wanted to reach out and hug the boy. It was a small thing he'd done, but, knowing Kurt, she knew it was a sincere gesture and might even be a signal of his approval of this unusual man. But there was something else that heartened her: Kurt's father would have never thought to do it. This offer of water came purely from Kurt's heart.

On the way into the house Kurt offered to show Flint the Jeep, or, more specifically, its motor. With the two of them peering under its hood, and Kurt doing most of the talking, Meg left them to see how things were going down in the camp. On her way she tried to think if Kurt had ever suggested showing the Jeep to Ellis and decided he hadn't.

With the feel of fall in the air and school starting in a matter of days, she thought that tomorrow might be a good time to take everyone down to the school in the canyon and acquaint them with the building and, hopefully, the schedules for the kids' classes. And that trip would include Flint, who she hoped might do some of the driving once school got underway. His unexpected arrival made everything seem better and possible. She couldn't believe it.

The kids were getting so excited for school to start—though they seemed a bit shy, too. But wasn't that the way it always was at the start of school, with everyone anticipating new classes, new books, new teachers, and all the new faces?

For reasons she couldn't explain, she felt the kids were going to do fine in their new school. A couple weeks back she'd met with the principal to be sure that everything was set for the kids impending enrollment (she'd written the school district earlier). She wanted to see the school building herself, as well as check to see that the principal had obtained their records from their former school in town. She'd had a good impression of the school and the principal. Even if he had recognized her name it hadn't mattered. The small, rural community in the bottom of the canyon had its own life, and she was looking forward to getting involved with it. How good it would be to be just one small part of a community again.

After talking to the principal about her kids, she spoke of the possible difficulties of getting them back and forth on the steep road during the winter. He had taken her comments about the road with a certain interest and promised to contact the County to ask them how much of the road they would snowplow. He said that the 4-wheel-drive vehicle she'd arrived in looked able to surmount most problems that they would encounter on their road. The whole conversation had given her a good feeling.

Her confidence in the kids doing well in the upcoming school year was built on more than that one meeting. The kids were different now and were no longer feeling like victims. All their experiences on the mountain had made them strong: their camp, their cooking and helping around the house, their interest in the animals and birds they saw, their dependence on themselves and each other for entertainment, their endless reading and game playing, their responsibility toward their pets, and their loving this piece of land as she did.

Their new confidence couldn't be broken by anyone's cruel or careless words. They were going to be fine. She smiled to herself. She might be wrong about this, but she was willing to bet she wasn't.

37

A PLACE TO HEAL

Meg put down the pick and dusted off her jeans-clad bottom when she and the dog caught the sound of the Jeep. Judging from the drone of its motor she could almost picture what part of the road it was climbing and how long it would take Flint to get there. If he hadn't eaten lunch in town, he'd most likely want it now, and so would she.

Before going inside, she looked around critically. It was slow going, but getting back into gardening again felt wonderful; that is, if one could put the name "gardening" to demolishing and rearranging the ancient piles of dirt and debris around the house's footings. Whatever its name, it was a task she'd ignored all summer. She wanted only wild plants up here—no green lawn or town flowers or anything that might interfere with the view—and she had the whole winter to plan how to do it. With that thought she removed her work boots and socks and went inside.

Meg smiled at the sound of Erda's nails clicking dutifully behind her, first up the balcony stairs and then into her bedroom. Once the dog determined that it was just a wash up and clothes-changing routine, she sank elegantly onto her rug, settled her nose on a paw, and closed her eyes. As Meg got out of her work clothes and laid out clean cords and an extra-heavy wool sweater, she eyed her companion affectionately. The dog was hardly asleep, and would rise up and be beside her the moment she was finished. It was a wordless conversation they had, and Meg relished every moment of it. With the kids in school all day, Erda had switched her attendance to Meg full time. Meg had almost dreaded school starting and the kids being gone, but, with the presence of Flint and the dog, the transition had been smooth and she'd never felt alone. On her way into the bathroom, she stepped carefully around the dog, trailing her fingers through her black ruff to let her know that she needn't move.

After washing her face and arms and combing her hair, she stood back and studied herself in the mirror. She liked her hair, shoulder length and curling on its own. She remembered the night she'd cut her hair and flung it into the bathroom wastebasket in town, thinking, "At last I'm rid of it!" and Tolly trimming it up afterwards. How far she had come from that awful night.

As she rubbed moisture cream vigorously on her face, she decided to try a little of the new blue-grey eye shadow on her upper lids, and maybe a skiff of the new rose lipstick. She'd had no intention of buying them but, once in the store to pick up a new bra, she'd wandered over to the cosmetic counter and spent a ridiculous amount for them, as well as the super-large jar of moisture cream and a flowery cologne. She had yet to summon the nerve to put on the perfume, but had added a drop or two on her pillowcases and the top sheet, and it really smelled nice.

She put her face close to the mirror to apply the eye shadow then abruptly drew back. Good lord! That telltale glimmer of hope in her eyes. If it were that obvious to her, it would be obvious to him and anyone else. She left the mirror and quickly changed into her clean clothes.

Erda had heard the Jeep's arrival and was already awaiting Flint at the door. On Meg's way to the kitchen, she leaned over the balcony's railing and called out, "Good girl!" Hearing the envy in her own voice, she reflected that a dog, in its straightforward way, had it so easy. When it loved someone it only had to wait by the door, then lick their face or hand and wag its whole body to broadcast its feelings. While a woman, with all the restrictions entailed in such things, had to carry on as though nothing extraordinary was going on inside her.

As she made fresh coffee and searched the refrigerator for leftovers, her mind stayed on Flint and on what Tolly had mentioned about his quietness. Today he'd been fine, but yesterday, when he'd come in for breakfast, he was in one of his quiet moods. He had hurried through his meal and left. By now she knew that that quiet preceded something resembling a kind of melancholy. It didn't last, so the word "depression" was too strong a word, and "melancholy" was no better, but, for certain, a look of pain moved over his face and he almost looked ill. Following that, he would make an excuse to leave—to work or be by himself, she wasn't sure which.

What was causing these mood shifts she had no clue. He appeared healthy and had a good appetite and the work was going well. He laughed and seemed to enjoy the kids' antics and engaged them all with his conversation and quiet bantering humor. But seeing him withdrawn like that, after her experience with Ed, concerned her, even though there was nothing else similar in Flint's character. With his reticence to speak of anything personal, getting to the bottom of these spells seemed impossible. She guessed she'd just wait and hope that it was nothing serious.

She had become so attached to their coffee rituals and meals together, and she felt he had, too. And those times they worked together on something... Last week they had installed the new Vermont woodstove in the cabin. It was fun doing it and the project had gone together easily. While he built a fire in it to see if the drafts drew properly and the chimney had no leaks, she went up to the house and brought back cups and the makings for cocoa.

What had begun as a test-run of the stove had turned into an all-afternoon talk-a-thon: first about stoves, then old movies, favorite authors and composers, and then his long, fascinating story about the building of the Brooklyn Bridge. That afternoon he'd spoken more words than he'd said the whole time he'd been here, at least by her estimation, and she'd teased him about it.

How one conversation could cover such diverse topics she didn't know, but time spent like that was what she'd missed for so long, in fact, for her whole marriage—the bantering, the interruptions, the can't-talk-fast-enough, the laughter, and the sense of understanding and agreement. To her mind, a person could get through the big stuff of life, but it was the absence of those little things that twisted one's heart.

When she'd left the cabin to drive down for the kids, Flint had accompanied her to the Jeep, had opened the door for her, and for a moment they had just stood looking at each other and laughing. As she'd driven down the road, she realized that his life had empty spots, too.

The next day when he was in town picking up a long list of building materials, he'd apparently stopped in at the music store and picked up a disk for her stereo. She found it among the receipts he'd handed her. A terse note taped to it read, "Listen!" It was choral music by Arvo Pärt, something she'd never heard before, and had drawn her tears. The choir and instrumental music was beautiful, but as haunting and sad as anything she'd heard. It was no casual gift. She had thanked him the next day; but her words were hardly adequate, especially after concluding that the music was telling her something about him—either by choice or by accident.

. . .

It was a genuinely gorgeous day, one that only a mountain autumn could create, with its jumble of golds and brilliant reds arrayed against its dark green backdrop. All traces of summer were gone now. Every morning there was frost on the ground, and during the shortened days the frost hardly had a chance to melt. Despite the chill, Meg suggested they eat their leftovers outside on the doorstep. Now it was just cold stone and, with the sun barely clearing the ridge above the house, it wouldn't be warm until spring. Still, it was the nicest place to be. Before bringing down the tray of food, Flint placed an old rug on the step for them to sit on, and Meg wrapped the coffeepot in a towel. Sitting close together and hugging their cups to their chests, they laughed at how clever they were.

Although they were sitting in shadow, before them the sun threw its net of hazy autumn softness over everything, changing the meadow's tan grasses to gold with ultramarine shadows, and tipping every bush and shrub in bright colors. Meg was pointing out the various trees and identifying them when she became aware that Flint was watching her. She turned to him and asked, "What?"

Searching for words, he reached over and began tracing his finger along the ridges of the corduroy on her knee. He finally said, "Both you and Tolly speak so passionately about the things you love—

she about wheat fields and windmills, and you about your meadows and mountains. You speak like poets, yet neither of you knows that. I come from a blasé place where it isn't cool for people to talk with that much emotion. I like it that you care deeply about the things you tell me about. You don't know how rare it is."

It was the first time he had said anything that personal, or had intentionally touched her. She couldn't trust her voice—the tears were already gathering—so, instead, she touched her finger to his, tracing his nail, then stroking his knuckle. He turned his hand and simply rested it on hers, his look inscrutable. She cleared her throat and finally squeezed out, "Poets, eh? Could you find a disk of music for my mountains and meadows, too?"

"Oh, I can think of a dozen composers that have already written music for you, Meg." Smiling warmly at her, he lifted his hand gently away and said, "You liked the choral disk? You thanked me, but that's all you've said about it."

She looked steadily at him. "I'm deeply moved by that music; the voices seem to be searching for something, reaching out for hope, maybe. Yet there's despair in the music, too. Is it a window into your soul, Flint? Is that *you* hoping and despairing? You seem to get very sad sometimes, like yesterday morning. Is something wrong?"

He studied the mountains across from them before answering. "I suppose I get a bit introspective at times, but nothing's wrong. That's an interesting question you asked—a window into my soul. I'll have to think about that."

"It's not just yesterday you've seemed sad; it's happened several times. You place your hand on your chest and get the saddest look on your face, and then you find some excuse to leave. When I see your face like that I can't help being concerned."

Flint made fun of her words, "Are you disparaging my face?"

Meg teased, "Well, allowing for *that*..." She became serious. "I know what melancholy looks like, and that's what I see in you at times. You have every right to say it's none of my business, but it is my business if I've been asking too much of you. A lot is resting on your shoulders, with the remodeling work, and now you're helping transport the kids to school every day or so. You volunteered to do it, but I wonder if you would tell me if it's all too much?"

"It's not too much, Meg. Being busy and involved keeps my mind occupied and me healthy. And I mean it when I say that driving the kids and hearing them talk on the way has become a high point of my day. I want them to be safe, and combining trips to school with buying supplies and getting groceries and the mail in town helps everyone." He patted her arm. "Which reminds me, I have the Jeep to unload." Finishing off his coffee, he smiled and thanked her for lunch and got up from the step. "Want me to take these dishes up to the kitchen?"

"Mr. Helpful. No, I'll get them. Thank you." Still not satisfied with their talk, Meg stood up too, and said, "Look, it's such a pretty day. There's something I want you to see. Take an hour or so and come for a walk with me. It'll be strenuous, but it's not far from here."

When he reminded her that there wouldn't be room for the kids if the Jeep weren't unloaded, she said, "I promise I'll help you do that afterwards. But now, come on." Seeing him still resisting, she put her hands on her hips and teased, "It's your job to humor me. Say, 'Yes, Meg, I want to go for a walk.'"

"My job, eh." He laughed then spoke seriously, "I'll hold you to your offer of help, and if this walk of yours passes anywhere close to the cabin, I need to stop and get my down vest."

"Then let's go." She hurriedly set the tray of dishes just inside the door and closed it. Then, with Erda at her heels, she pointed Flint toward the road.

. . .

Once they'd left the cabin, Meg began identifying the different plants for him. The leaves of the low huckleberry and Oregon grape had changed, and Meg told him, "Look, the road is rimmed in their crimson leaves. Isn't it beautiful?" Then pointing to the thick brush and downed trees on their left, she said, "Here's where we start." They left the road and began working their way through it.

Panting from the exertion, Meg said, "I don't want to brag, but the night we broke into the house I made it through here in the dark with only a crummy flashlight. Right about here is where I'm pretty sure I passed a bear. I heard it leave, but it really scared me. A lot of things scared me before we moved here, the dark night being one, and bears seemed part of that."

He grinned at her. "I'll remember that when I walk back to the cabin tonight. Even with my new flashlight I get a bit rattled ever so often." He leaned down and patted Erda. "I think I need another one of these." The dog licked his hand.

They walked in silence then, except for Meg's words of thanks whenever Flint offered his hand to help her over a log or held back a branch that would have hit her as she passed. Finally Meg stopped and leaned against a tree to catch her breath. Flint stopped too. She looked at him and said, "You know, for a city guy you're doing okay. You've been here for less than a month and you already look like a native."

He pulled at his hair and laughed. "First it was my face, now you're disparaging my hair!"

She looked serious. "It's nice. You aren't planning to cut it, are you?" Then, laughing, she said, "In about two years you can braid it, but it will take longer than that for you to *speak* like a native."

"You forget, young lady, I came here directly from a farm, where Charlie pretty much worked all the city out of me. But you're right about my speech. This morning Callie wanted to know if there was something wrong with my mouth. She's trying to get me to say 'ah' correctly. She said, 'it's not I-*dear*, it's I-de-*yah*'. First it was Charlie, and now it's your kids."

She laughed, "Surely you don't expect them to let you get away with anything?"

"You've produced three real charmers! On the way back from school I get to play teacher and make them tell me what they've learned. It's a lot of fun and I can tell they prepare for it. It's been a long time since I've been around kids."

"Then you have children?"

"No, I've missed out on that. I was speaking of the old days when I was in school."

She hesitated then asked, as lightly as she could, "Are you married?"

"I was married for ten years. She's back in New York. Her name is Annie. I wanted kids. She didn't. But there were other things. We were divorced just before I came west." He gave her a solemn look and added, "No second thoughts, no loose threads."

Meg took a deep breath. "It's too bad how things end sometimes." It had taken her a few moments to realize that he was talking about his personal life. Wanting more, she said, "Tolly wrote me about your coming west, but I've never heard how you got here."

"Ah, yes, my trip to Montana." Flint smiled at his thoughts. "Being raised in a city I was hardly prepared for Big Sky Montana. It wasn't that I'd never been west; I'd been to Seattle and San Francisco, but I'd only flown. For this trip west I was traveling by bus. My intention was just getting away, but the farther I got from the city, I realized I was shopping for a new place to live.

"I watched the country change from big cities to small towns to farms, then to farms getting farther and farther apart. I was heading for the *thought* of the west—whatever that was—and when I saw all that flat, empty land of Central Montana, stretching horizon to horizon and without so much as a speck of anything, I decided I was getting close and I got off the bus. I went in to that little combination gas station/café in Wyler—you know the one. Tolly said you worked there one summer. That's where I met Charlie. He was sitting next to me at the counter and we got talking. It came out that he needed help on the farm, and I applied for the job right there over coffee. He told me that my hands didn't speak well for what I'd be doing, but he thought he'd enjoy the training process."

Flint smiled then almost laughed in remembering. "He drove me out to the farm in that big truck of his, with all the rattles. I met Tolly, and the two of them took me out to the bunkhouse—apologizing all the way for it, of course. Before I knew it, I was unpacked, washed up, and sitting at their kitchen table. I remember my first meal there: fried chicken and mashed potatoes with cream gravy, green beans from their freezer, home-canned pears, and molasses cookies. After three days of eating the food you get at bus depots, it was phenomenal, to say the least. But, their kindness and trust is what I remember best.

That never changed. When I heard that their son and his bride were moving back to join in the farming operation, I knew it was over. It was hard to leave."

Meg said, "They took your leaving hard."

"Yes, well... With those cinnamon rolls of Tolly's I could have stayed there forever." They both laughed at that. As they resumed walking, he said, "Those two folks really got to me, especially their acceptance of the inconvenience of their life. Remember, I was seeing it from my New York City perspective, where you can get anything at any time. I concluded that people have to be born on a farm to put up with all the hassle. That one little store in Wyler offers basic things, but to buy most everything else, including hardware, lumber, medicine, clothing, movies, and all the rest, they had to drive to Lewistown, some thirty-nine miles away; and, for big items, to Great Falls, a hundred miles away. And those aren't easy miles; there's always the weather. In time, I came to accept this and to enjoy it really. Time is different in the country; it doesn't get eaten up by other things, but has a value in itself. Even so, it takes hardy people to accept an isolated life. I put you and the kids in that hardy group by the way."

Meg said, "After hearing you talk that first night you were here, it's the city people I'd classify as hardy, putting up with the noise and dirt and living close to so many people."

He shook his head. "There are many, many positives I could have talked about. But the contrast between un-peopled pristine land and the problems of too many people living in one spot hit me very hard that day. I felt moved to tell you, maybe to *warn* you."

He stopped walking and said, "I'm curious why a widow would choose to raise her children here? I worry a lot that you think you're living inside some kind of magic circle, and that you place too much trust in this dog here and pay too little attention to what could be dangerous. You have to keep those kids safe, Meg." His voice almost choked with his last words.

Meg was unprepared for the intensity of his words, and she replied defensively. "Their safety is uppermost in my mind, Flint. Don't ever doubt that. I agonized over the thought of pulling up our roots in town and moving here. It was a difficult decision. But we fell in love with this place and decided our lives would be better here. While I was worrying over whether or not to buy it, I found out that a developer had this place in his sights and had made a low offer on the land, to turn it into God knows what and ruin it. I simply couldn't let him destroy this place. By buying it, I actually saved it from destruction." She smiled. "I owe this mountainside a lot; it saved me, so I saved it. I think there's something magical about that, don't you?"

He nodded. "I'd never heard that story. I like it." He hesitated a moment. "But about the kids, I worry too much. It's a problem I have, I guess. I saw too much of the down side in my work." As he spoke he reached out and ran his fingers down her cheek, unaware that he was doing it. "I don't want them to change. They're different, but I can see you in each one of them."

She beamed. "They're easy to like." Deliberately changing the subject, she said, "What you talked about that first night really got to me. Is that the down side you mean?"

"It's hard to talk about." For a moment he looked on the verge of saying more, but he remained silent.

Seeing the log just ahead of them, Meg said, "This place is what I wanted to show you, especially this gigantic log resting here. I found this place on one of the darkest days of my life, and it gave me something positive to focus on while I struggled to recover from my husband's death."

"You weren't happy with him."

"No, we never should have married. We didn't see things the same way. I raised the kids alone because he was always gone, or busy, or some damn thing. There's nothing remotely similar between my life here and the one I lived with my husband in town."

"I can't picture you in any life but here."

"Me either." She raised her head proudly, "My heart is here, Flint." She sat down on the log and Flint sat near her. The dog lay down at their feet. She gestured around her. "I found this little glen quite by accident. Maybe any place would have helped me that day, but here I found what I needed to get my life back on track. I don't know how long this old tree has been lying here. It wasn't cut down, so it's lived its whole life right here and died of old, old age. Think of the storms it's survived—the violent winds and rain and hail and sleet and ice and snow. In the end it gave into the elements, I suppose, but it probably took a century or more to finally keel over. What it signifies, I couldn't tell you, but I find something elemental here, something natural and restful. Is it just me, or can you feel it, too?"

Flint said, "I feel something different here, too, but whether it's from your words or just this place, I couldn't say."

She looked over at him and spoke earnestly, "You probably guessed I brought you here for a reason. I think you're wrestling with something sad. If you can't tell anyone what's behind those spells of yours, at least you have this place if you need it."

He smiled kindly at her. "I suspected you had a reason."

"You're very good at keeping things all to yourself. You don't like to talk about yourself much. I assume you have a full name, but I've never heard it."

"My name is James Trevor Flint. I've been called Flint for so long, I now call myself that."

Running his names through her mind, she said, "James was my father's name. It's a nice name, but Flint fits you. I'm Margaret Lila, but I only answer to Meg." She looked at him and asked, "Is it a secret or something *why* you left New York?"

"Not a secret in that sense. I needed to get away from my job. My job was related to a city's problems, to it having too many people, that sort of thing. By coming west and starting over, I got away from those problems."

"You were a photographer there?"

"I took pictures there, but only as a hobby. It's something I've always liked, catching people as they truly are or at least how they appear to me, with none of those *posed* shots."

"Tolly spoke of that. I'd love to see some of your pictures sometime."

"First chance I get I'll show them to you. I've already taken some pictures here, some of the town's crusty old characters and some of the spectacular views up here. When I develop them I'd like your opinion. I suspect there's a market for such pictures. The other day I was eying one of those empty downstairs rooms of yours, in hopes of turning it into a darkroom."

"Yes! Consider it's yours."

With nothing else from him, she finally asked, "Where did you work in the city?"

"At a hospital."

After waiting for the details, Meg finally had to ask, "Why do you hesitate, Flint? If it's not a secret why can't you just tell me? I want to know more about you, but you only give me crumbs. Believe me, I know about wrestling with things. I also know the relief that comes from letting them go. My marriage ended in the worst way. There were a lot of questions about my husband's disappearance and death. He left us without saying goodbye, and a young woman drowned with him in the car. She's never been identified or her presence in his car explained. You can imagine how difficult that's been, especially since there was no note or any tangible reason for it. I was hurt in other ways, too. Having questions rattling around in one's head—well, I needed some place to let it go, and I found this place. I've moved ahead with my life." She looked deeply into his eyes. "If you could bring yourself to tell me what's going on with you, I'd welcome it."

He nodded. "You're right, Meg. I admit I get depressed over things, but it doesn't last."

Meg softened her voice and said, "What made you cry that night you were first here? You were telling me about the people that concerned you in the city, then about your lunch by that spring on your way up here. I couldn't figure out which of those triggered your emotions. I've thought a lot about that, wondering if I'd said something wrong or appeared to be prying...and here I'm doing it again."

Flint laid his hand on her arm and spoke in a tired voice. "You didn't do anything wrong, Meg, nothing like that. I was just so relieved to get here. Since I came west I have experienced more patience and kindness than I knew existed: there was Tolly and Charlie and you. There was the pleasant couple that gave me a ride all the way from

Wyler to Clark Fork. Then a friendly man who drew me a map so I could find the canyon road. And the woman who brought me a tall glass of ice water when I told her I was thirsty and asked to drink out of her garden hose. As I walked up the road that day, I was filled with gratitude. A lot of things happened all at once to me in the city. From the start, coming here has helped me."

"What things happened?"

He sighed deeply and leaned down and ran his hand over the dog's neck again and again. "I don't like to speak of them out loud."

"But, Flint, isn't that what you need to do? Just get it out?"

"I don't think an outsider like you should hear these things."

"Try me."

Seeing her hopeful and waiting expression, he gave her an almost imperceptible nod and continued, "A while back you identified some plants for me—the huckleberry and Oregon grape—which are turning red. When you saw them colored red like that, you said they were pretty because it was fall. When I saw them, in this strange shifting light, they looked like spattered blood."

"Blood? Whose blood?"

"No one I knew. Just some firemen who were doing their job, and some kids."

Meg waited.

As though she wasn't there, he said, "I wonder how long it takes to recover? I test myself with a question, 'Am I recovering?' To which I answer, 'Yes.' 'But am I recovered?' I have to answer truthfully, 'Well, I'm better.' But just thinking that those leaves looked like drops of blood made me doubt if I really am."

He went on. "It was a year ago now…yes, that long. It happened first thing in the morning, before we'd even made coffee. We were half asleep by then, lounging around after a fairly quiet night—a couple of cardiacs, some shootings, a scalded baby, a knifing, a hit and run, two overdosed kids. The report came over the intercom; a big warehouse was on fire and a large portion of its roof had fallen in. Many firemen had been on top of it. The ambulances were on the way. These are bad scenes that no one can really prepare for, Meg.

"Five firemen had died on the spot—as if anyone who's burned ever dies on the spot! Another eighteen were brought in as they were found, one or two at a time. Anyone seeing them knew that the five that were already dead were the lucky ones. Sirens screamed along with the firemen, and both Ruby and Sal were crying because they couldn't find any place to put their needles in. And I thought those two tough women had dealt with everything.

"Flesh gets charred but the heart beats on—as if it hadn't heard the news. Why, in light of all that destruction does a heart take so long to admit defeat? The unburned eyes that looked out of the blackened, oozing, bloody faces, asked me, asked anyone, 'How will this end for me? Please do something! This isn't a good way to go!' I was the one who was required to smile and say, 'Hold on, hold on. You're doing fine, son, you're doing fine. Hold on.' But, inside, I felt myself saying, 'Please die faster.'"

Flint placed his hand on his chest and said, "A doc friend of mine told me that I suffer from panic attacks. My heart starts to flutter and I get short of breath when I remember those questions in their eyes. But it wasn't just those firemen; it was all those others asking me what wasn't possible for anyone to answer or to change."

He closed his eyes for a moment. "That same morning, at the very height of that mess, another call came in. On the street corner of a nearby neighborhood, a drugged-out woman in a Cadillac deliberately drove up on the sidewalk and, at high speed, hit a bunch of kids waiting for their school bus. Unimaginably, she then shifted into reverse and backed up. But, even then she hadn't quite finished the job.

"It's this I see in my mind. Over and over I reconstruct it: school books and pencils scattering, children's bodies lifting into the air—their newly kissed faces, their hair still wet from a comb—falling, falling into odd positions, falling like bloody, broken rag dolls into odd positions—those sweet new faces, so recently and trustingly kissed.

"When the twelve surviving kids were brought in, there was no place to put them. All the gurneys held someone and were lined all along the hall. But we found room. Hell, we always found room. It didn't matter how few beds there were or how full the ERs and ORs and ICUs and CCUs were, we always found room. A trauma hospital tends a city's battlefield, so the hurt and the dying don't care exactly where we perform our miracles."

He looked over at Meg. "You've heard of the word 'triage.' A trauma hospital, like mine, has extensive services to offer. And in big emergencies and disasters, when an overwhelming number of really badly hurt people come in, someone has to assess the extent of injuries and gauge who will most likely die and who will live. On the surface, that sounds like a reasonable thing to do, and it is. There's a limit to what can be done and someone has to direct medical services to the patients most likely to respond to them. But to the person whose job it is to do that, it's more like being appointed God. I was that person, and that meant I had to remove help from those destined *not* to survive. I had to turn away and let them go, Meg, even though I'd promised them we were trying to help them."

"Oh, Flint. Oh, I'm so sorry. That's a terrible weight to carry."

He held out his hands in front of him and looked at her. "At the risk of sounding overly dramatic, these two hands could locate a fading pulse or reach into an open chest and bring life back to a patient. But no more." He sighed audibly. "After thirteen years of doing it, it got to me. One day I was doing fine, and then that one last day made me realize that I couldn't do it anymore. I hated leaving the team, but I'd had enough. It's called 'burn out'—a kind of battle fatigue, I suppose. I had to find a place where no one would ask me to make those kinds of decisions any longer. That's why I left the hospital and the city. Unfortunately, the pictures in my head came West, too. Some days they rush in at me. It helps to be involved with different things. Now I try to build things that I know will last."

Meg was shaken by what he'd told her, but when she tried to speak, he put out his hand, interrupting her. He said, "That's not quite all. When I finally got home that day, twenty-two hours later, I found something out about Annie, quite by accident.

"Annie was that one small island of sanity I centered on. I thought I'd told her that often enough, but apparently I was wrong. I wouldn't have known about it. I wasn't prying. I was just going over the statement from the bank, and felt I had a right to ask what she'd spent $1,500 on.

"We'd spoken of raising a family, at least I had, so she knew that I wanted kids. I don't know what you believe, Meg, whether you're pro-life or pro-choice. I happen to think that the courts have no business making those decisions for women, one way or the other. However, when you're married and your wife finds herself pregnant, I feel that the decision of having that baby or not having it is not something that only the woman gets to decide.

"That evening Annie admitted she had aborted our baby without my even knowing she was pregnant or asking me what I thought. She was good enough to tell me it was her fault that she had forgotten to take her pills the week we spent in the Bahamas. Sadly enough, it came out that it was her *second* abortion. We had a fight and there wasn't anything to stay together for after that."

He looked up at Meg with tears in his eyes. "That day was a bad day for losing people. That day I lost all of them!"

The whole conversation had sapped him and he slumped down and stared at his hands. Seeing him that way, and with her mind reeling, Meg got up and took his hands in hers. She said, "Thank you for telling me. Now I know why you feel all that pain. That music disk you gave me, with those plaintive voices, it *is* a window into your soul, Flint. And, whether you were aware of it at the time, I truly believe you wanted me to know that."

Looking into his eyes, she said, "I can't imagine what it took for you to do that job. But I believe that you can heal from those things—maybe by substituting other, better pictures for the painful ones. But, Flint, when those pictures come into your mind, don't walk away and suffer them all by yourself. Tell me, and we'll talk or listen to music—*hopeful* music. Or read me a story, or I'll read you one, and the kids, too. They love being read to. Don't walk away. Come and be with us. We're great company and, if nothing else, we'll make you laugh. Stay longer after dinner; offer to help the kids with their homework; ask them to show you how to play some of their games. Maybe you're a little shy about doing that, but I'll love having you around more.

"Don't feel guilty for leaving the hospital. After putting in all that time there, surely you earned the right to get away from it. You're human and you have limits. You gave your patients every bit of your compassion and skill. Even in the short time I've known you, I know you gave them that, because that's what you give us every day."

She closed her eyes in an effort to find the right words. "I'm not exactly sure what being in this place by this old log means, Flint, but I swear there's something we can learn from it. Maybe it's because this tree did all its surviving here and so can we. It's so beautifully quiet here. And it smells fresh and balsamy and clean. A place like this gives a person's heart and mind a chance to rearrange its molecules. In this kind of quiet, maybe you'll be able to hear something other than the pain and heartbreak you witnessed. Perhaps those hurt men and kids want to thank you for caring, thank you for all you tried to do to help. If you listen really hard you might hear them say, 'Your kind face was the last face I saw and, from it and the touch of your hands, I knew you wanted to help me.'"

Her words had affected them both, bringing them to tears. He stood up and opened his arms to her and held her against him, even as his tears shook him. He finally laid his chin against her hair and spoke, his voice still choked, "I like that, Meg. I like that." After a time he loosened his arms and just smiled at her.

Once she could control her voice she said, "Then we agree; I'll lend you this place, Flint." She flung her arms up in a huge gesture, scooped the air with her hands, and presented it to him. "Here it is. It's yours for as long as you need it."

Looking at him a little shyly then, she said, "So, what was all that talk about holding me to my promise to help you unload the Jeep? In about an hour *one* of us has to drive down and pick up those three rascals. So who will the driver be this time? Will *I* do it and we eat a supper of creamed cabbage on toast and canned fruit? Or will *you* go and I stay home and make Swiss steak, mashed potatoes and gravy, a lovely tossed salad, and an apple crisp with vanilla ice cream?"

He threw back his head and laughed, then said, "Why doesn't that sound like a choice?"

38

BIRTHDAY

Meg could say the word "birthday" without any trouble, but today she was having a hard time saying "*thirty-nine*," as though it wasn't yet in her vocabulary. The nearer she got to forty, the more she wanted to celebrate her birthday without anyone noticing it, either as a date on a calendar or in happening to recognize that the process called "The Effect Of Time" (regarding her skin and hair, and maybe her waist and hips, too) was unlikely to reverse itself.

The grey hairs sprouting from the brown were getting impossible to hide, especially since each was filled with a neon light that kept flashing the words "older-older-older!" And to those lines around her eyes and mouth—that she hoped were caused from smiling widely—she'd started applying copious amounts of moisture cream with the intensity she ordinarily used in scrubbing the bottom of a shower stall. As to her waist and hips, she had solved that by buying smaller mirrors that somehow missed those areas entirely. In consideration of all these, on this particular birthday, except for emergencies, like shaping her brows and applying lipstick, she was giving up mirrors all together.

. . .

It was Meg's intention—more a fervent hope—to celebrate her birthday just the way she wanted: more like a vacation. That meant doing minimum cooking and being allowed to settle into the loveseat and read the novel she had just started. As for food, she was thinking chips and dip and a salad. But one look at the wall of kids in front of her, all shaking their heads, no, was all it took to change that. She must have the kind of celebration they thought befitted her birthday—and that meant she was in for a day of heavy cooking. As to what the food would be, well, the Littles suggested those things she usually cooked for their birthdays, like leg of lamb or rump roast. Kurt—even though his eyes were alight with thoughts of stuffed pork chops and white cake with pineapple filling and fluffy white frosting—told his sisters, "Come on, you two, those are *your* choices, not Ma's." Then he asked, "Really and truly, Ma, what's your favorite? I don't think you've ever said, or were we just too little to ask?"

Meg looked at him with surprise, happy that someone in the family had finally recognized that. Nevertheless, she folded her arms stubbornly and said, "Come on, you guys, birthdays are for kids. You can help me whip up some kind of simple supper—waffles and bacon maybe, and afterward we'll take some popcorn to Flint at the cabin, maybe pop it there." But that didn't make it through the determined wall of kids, either.

Meg shrugged. "So I have to celebrate this thing, eh?"

They nodded. "And you gotta wear a dress."

"Okay, okay, but if I have to wear a dress, you guys have to dress up, too." Seeing them shake their heads in the affirmative, she said, "Now that that's decided, what I'd like to eat is...Cornish meat pasties... spinach salad...and, instead of a birthday cake, which I have to admit I'm not all that fond of, I want cream puffs filled with whipped cream and drizzled with homemade fudge sauce. My mother always fixed those for me on my birthday."

"Cream puffs for a birthday?" This was a side of her they had never seen before.

She wailed, "Well, you asked me!"

Kurt said, "But we don't know how to make those things."

"Oh, honey!" Meg gave him a hug. "Don't worry, I'll help. For the pasties, you can be in charge of cutting the steak up in little cubes, and you girls can help dice the potatoes and chop the onions. We'll all roll out the piecrust and make them. As for the cream puffs—"

Sara interrupted, "Can we make the cream puffs down in our camp?"

"Thanks, sweetie, but I'm afraid cream puffs are kitchen-oven things. But they're easy and I don't mind making them. You guys can stir the fudge sauce and fill them with whipped cream at the last moment. Is that all right?" She stopped talking. "Come to think of it, I don't have enough steak or eggs or whipping cream or spinach. Forget what I said I wanted. I do have stew meat in the freezer. You can make me a big pot of stew down there in camp—I love your beef stew."

Sara gave a martyred sigh, "If you really want that other stuff, you can drive us to town. But you'll have to wait in the Jeep while we go in and buy it." She added, "But we can't go down for a while, cuz we still gotta do a lot of stuff for your birthday. Just call us when you want to go. Okay?"

At that point everyone disappeared, leaving Meg mumbling rude words to herself over the trip to town and the work in making Cornish pasties. But when she thought of biting into a cream puff it made her salivary glands kick in and she guessed it would be worth it.

Cornish pasties were one of those non-recipe endeavors, needing "enough" steak, potatoes, onions, and "enough" piecrust. Her mother's roots were in the mining town of Butte. As she made them she liked to tell Meg and Tolly how the miners' wives would wrap up a big hot pasty in heavy paper and tuck it into the front of their husbands' shirts before they took off for the mine in the morning: The pasty kept the man warm on his way to the mine, and his body's heat kept the pasty warm enough for his mid-day meal down in the mine.

Cooking, at least to Meg, was a form of giving love. Gathering everybody around the table was absolutely one of the most pleasant parts of their lives. One of her wishes was that the kids would look back on the meals she cooked with the same feelings she had for the food her mother made. To promote this, Meg made a point of saying a long drawn out, "Ahhhh," whenever she took something wonderful out of the oven, hoping that her children would also want to say, "Ahhhh," when they took things, like homemade breads and rolls—and cream puffs—from the ovens of their futures.

She was still thinking all these noble thoughts when the day changed. Doris called, announcing that they had arrived home from Seattle late last night, "So we wouldn't miss your birthday, dear. And it was past time to come back. As much as we love our kids and grandkids, they have their lives, and we have ours. Marc is opening every window and door to let in this wonderful Montana air. Can you hear him singing? After we unpack and bathe we're coming up there to see you. Is our room still waiting for us upstairs? Can we stay the night?"

Meg chuckled in delight during Doris's one-sided discourse, mainly because she couldn't get a word in edgewise. Doris continued, "Don't you dare tell me you have other plans. You're going to have a birthday party. Just wait until you see what Marc and I got you in Seattle."

Talk of gifts made Meg uneasy and embarrassed, leaving her wondering how to respond to them, and the aptness of her response. She happily changed the subject to the menu, and told Doris she was just on her way to town to pick up the ingredients.

Doris said, "Instead of you making the extra trip, phone your order in to the store and we'll pick it up on our way there." And so it was all decided.

. . .

Meg was vacuuming the furniture when Ellis called.

"Guess what, pretty lady, I caught a ride back last night so I could help you celebrate your birthday."

Meg said, "Gosh—"

"Yes. I thought I'd line up the Youngs again so just the two of us can get away for a little celebration dinner." He laughed suggestively.

"I'm sorry, Ellis, but the kids and I have already planned a dinner. Marc and Doris—you remember my mentioning my friends—well, they just got back in town and are staying for the night."

He made a little disappointed sound then said, "But that's great. They can sit with the kids while we go out later. Just tell me what time dinner is and I'll be there. I'll bring something, maybe wine or flowers for the table? I already have something special for the sexiest girl in the world."

Meg felt perspiration on her neck. "Oh, Ellis, I don't know. With my friends here—"

"Come on, Meg. It will be perfect. Now, what'll it be, wine or flowers? Or shall I bring both? Yes, I'll bring both. How many bottles will that be, and what kind? Let's see, that's four adults, so we'll need two bottles. Right? And I'll bring something special for the kids to drink."

Meg said, "There's someone else here, a man named Flint. He's helping with the remodeling. So there'll be five adults, but two bottles of red will be fine."

"A carpenter? But he won't be staying for your dinner party. Won't he be going home?"

"Actually, no. Flint has been helping Tolly and her husband on their farm for the past few months, but now he's helping me. He came here the day after our big storm, just walked up from town, all the way up the mountain. Did you know we had a big storm?"

"Of course I heard about the storm. But, this Flint, this hired hand...surely, he won't be eating at the table and drinking the wine along with everyone else."

"Yes, Ellis, he will. He's not a 'hired-hand' in that sense. He's a friend."

"So you've known him before?"

"I've known *of* him. We met when he got here. He's not *exactly* a stranger."

"Sounds like you haven't *exactly* decided what he is. Is he just visiting like a relative or will he be there for the duration of the remodeling? Is he staying there in your *guestroom*?"

"He's settled into the cabin. He takes his meals here with us. But he helps me in the kitchen, too, because he likes to cook. He makes great salads. The kids like him. He's quiet and fun and has the nicest sense of humor."

There was a long silence on the phone. "It sounds like this hired hand of yours has really settled in—"

"Don't call him that, Ellis. He's not a servant. He's a delightful forty-five-year-old man." She laughed because she couldn't help herself. "He's seven years *older* than I am...well, six as of today. I think that's kind of funny with your being nine years *younger*...well, ten as of today—"

"So you discuss these things—who's younger, who's older, and by how much? I remember a conversation like that, Meg. Is this what the two of you talk about while you make your little salads and eat your little meals together? While you pour over your little plans for the cabin?"

"Surely you don't expect me to dignify that with an answer, Ellis!"

"What time is dinner, Meg? You haven't said. I'll be there. I've wanted to meet your friends and, of course, see the kids. How are they, by the way?"

"Why, they're wonderful—healthy, happy, silly, impossible, totally absurd, weird—you know how they can be. They love their new school."

At the end of a long silence, Ellis said, "Meg, I dare you to ask about me, to ask how things went for me, how the fires in the Park are, what the rains coming meant— "

"Oh, Ellis, of course I want to know that. There hasn't been time to ask. Think back and ask yourself when there was time for me to ask. Anyway, you wrote about that in your letters."

"My letters. Then you got them? I wasn't sure." His voice changed. "What time is dinner, Meg? Or am I supposed to be there? Would I be interrupting anything? Did you even invite me? I can't remember." Before Meg had a chance to answer, he said, "I'll bring three bottles of red wine. That will be enough for *everyone.* And I'll try to get those white chrysanthemums you mentioned you liked. Is that okay? Is my coming up at 6:00 okay?"

Meg assured him that 6:00 was fine, and the wine and flowers would be nice, and she was glad he got back safely and was relieved that the fires were now under control. She added, enthusiastically, "Don't you just love fall, with the leaves changing color?" She added, "That big storm changed everything, didn't it?"

Ellis let out a long pent-up breath and said, "I hope not," and hung up.

The click of the phone sounded hurt and angry and reminded her of that little pucker between his eyes and that petulant look—all of which she really didn't want to feel responsible for, especially on her birthday. This damned birthday! There would be eight people now; it was totally out of control and the house was a mess.

With the pressure mounting, she phoned in her grocery order, grabbed the vacuum cleaner again and called out to the kids to ask who would clean out the fireplace and who would help her straighten up the house. But anything resembling help was gone by then—as though erased off the face of the earth—with the sounds of Kurt's sawing downstairs, and the hushed girl-type whispers and scurrying between bedrooms, punctuated by the abrupt departure of Callie and Erda out the front door, along with a "Don't look!" flung over her shoulder. This could only mean that birthday surprises were well under way, and housework was not to interrupt them.

While Meg changed the bag in the vacuum cleaner, she thought wistfully about her earlier chips-and-dip-and-good-book idea then turned her mind to the cooking schedule for the complicated dinner. She was about to start the vacuum when the downstairs door opened and Kurt yelled that she wasn't to even *think* of coming downstairs. However, if she absolutely had to, she was to knock on the door five times before opening it. He went on to say that even when he opened the door she was not to look. "And, Ma, if the Littles want to come downstairs, tell them that all they have to do is knock on the door two longs and a short and come in." The door then slammed.

Meg leaned against the doorjamb and giggled. Then, just for the record, she found a pencil and wrote down: "Five for me, and still no, but two longs and a short for S & C," and tried to think what two long knocks would sound like.

Before she started to clean out the fireplace she stood on the balcony stairs—it seemed a neutral spot—and yelled at the top of her voice, "Marc and Doris and Ellis are back and will be joining us for dinner!" Kurt opened the downstairs door and Sara popped her head out of her room and they cheered, then the doors closed again and everyone got back to work.

. . .

The arrival of Marc and Doris turned everyone into a big clump of people holding onto each other, with little kids' heads sticking out everywhere, hands pounding away, and the air full of words about "how wonderful you look" and "we've missed you" and "so looked forward to—" It was a long time before everyone let go.

Even though Meg tried not to notice, both Doris and Marc looked older and a little bent around the shoulders. Their faces and eyes had a weariness that hadn't been there before. At the same time, Marc and Doris, remembering how strained and uncertain the family had looked when they had last seen them, smiled at *their* radiance and good health and happiness.

They looked approvingly at the house, allowing themselves to be led this way and that by the kids. They toured their rooms and closets, cooed over the tomcat asleep on Callie's bed, and were warned about his propensity to vomit. They were formally introduced to Erda. She was given the "big fierce dog" build up, with Sara pulling back the dog's lip to show off her teeth, then pushing up the fur on the dog's neck to show how she looked when something dangerous was around. Erda, after that demonstration, retreated to a distant corner in the living room and looked left out. Kurt went over and whispered something into her ear, and the dog licked his face and thumped her tail on the floor in thanks and looked happier.

While Marc and Doris were being pulled outside, to be shown the camp, Doris looked back at Meg. "I intend helping you with the cooking." Meg laughed and told her not to worry, she'd unpack the groceries and get started on the cream puffs. She added, "There's still plenty to do."

. . .

While Meg was beating the last egg into the cream puff dough, Flint knocked on the backdoor. He'd been out of sight most of the morning, busy on something of his own. He said, "I met your friends on the road just now, getting the grand tour. Tolly mentioned them so I knew who they were."

Meg laughed. "The kids have been looking forward to showing off the place. Marc and Doris will be staying the night." She gestured toward the coffeepot. "I was beginning to wonder if all this activity had scared you away from our usual coffee break. That's not a fresh pot, but there's enough for the two of us."

It pleased her that he now filled two cups, pouring just the right amount of cream into hers and stirring it before setting it down for her. Then he'd leaned comfortably back against the counter, arms crossed, his cup in one hand and the fingers of his other hand tucked under his elbow. She could easily imagine him looking at a patient this way, professional, inquiring, kind.

He said, "Looks like we both got letters from the farm yesterday. Of course yours was attached to a box, while mine was a short note from Charlie, telling me the price they got for their wheat and about the new kind of tractor he and Johnny are thinking of buying." He laughed and took a sip of his coffee. "A couple years ago, in my wildest dreams, I would never have thought that I would be interested in such things. But I was glad to hear it and flattered that Charlie remembered that that crop was partly my work." His eyes twinkled when he added, "Charlie keeps marveling about my finding my way up here, and his letter ended with the instruction that I give you a..." He stopped and smiled down at his cup.

Meg's face had reddened, and she looked at him shyly, then teased, "Give me what? A birthday hug? A birthday kiss? Sounds okay to me." She chewed on her lip as she waited for his answer, finally saying, "Tolly tells me that, too. I'm just happy she's speaking to me again. In fact, I think she regards me as a fully responsible adult now."

They both laughed.

After that they talked quietly about using real butter and vanilla in foods, and the benefits of rubber spatulas in cooking. He watched her work, interested, but without feeling he had to make a comment. His was a quiet she didn't worry about. Once she put the cream puffs in the oven she relaxed opposite him and finished her coffee. She told him, "I'm afraid we're heading for a real party tonight. I was trying to keep my birthday from being too much—from being anything, really—but things are really rolling now."

Nodding, he spoke quietly, "It's a lot of work for you, but it's important. Kurt and I talked about it. The kids can neither provide a party for you themselves, nor understand about the work, but they still want it to happen. You're giving them what they need." He smiled at her. "That boy of yours is good company. He's very bright, you know, and he has good hands. He's been helping me with something you might be able to use."

Meg laughed with the unexpected pleasure she felt. "Gosh, something for me, the newly thirty-nine-year-old?"

"A mere baby." He smiled and gave her a significant look. He spoke softly, "I've visited your granddaddy log a couple times lately. It hasn't moved an inch and it is still rearranging molecules."

Meg could hardly contain herself hearing that. A feeling of pure joy rose up inside her, and she beaming brightly at him. "I've noticed that there has been a lift in spirits of late."

He nodded. "The spirits are good." Without a break in his tone, he said, "I cut some wood and stacked it just outside the front door. Let me clean out the fireplace. After that there must be something else you need done. Otherwise, I'll go back to the cabin and start figuring out how I'll start doing what we discussed yesterday."

Meg said, "Thank you for your offer, Flint, but the fireplace was first on my list this morning. Go ahead and lay a fire, if you have time. Any chance you could make your spinach salad for tonight, with that wonderful bacony dressing? Dinner is at 6:00, so I hope you can come early."

"I'm not going to interfere with your party, Meg."

"I don't even know what that word means coming from you. You're part of whatever goes on here, Flint." Grinning broadly at him, she brushed a strand of her hair back from her eyes.

He smiled and nodded, "You reminded me of your sister just then, doing that with your hair. I'll be more than happy to make that salad, and that includes washing all that spinach there. I can do it right now if you think there's room enough for both of us there. After that, would you tell me where you hide the ironing board? My one set of party clothes has spent the last few months in a box and needs a touch-up."

At her look, he said, "Don't offer to iron them for me. When Tolly was helping you out, I inherited the ironing and cooking chores from Charlie—partly because I like to do those things and partly because I'm pretty good at them. If any of the kids' clothes need pressing, just put them by the ironing board. And tell the kids. It'll do them good to watch me. I'll give them pointers."

Setting out the spinach, Meg shook her head in wonder as she watched him scrubbing his hands and arms thoroughly with a brush. Grinning, she said, "I'd say you learned a few things at that hospital of yours. Could you please give the kids some pointers on hand scrubbing, too?"

When Flint left and she'd gotten back to work, Meg said to nobody in particular, "Oh, goody; he said 'party clothes.' It's going to be a wonderful party after all. I doubt if this house has ever seen one."

39

A LITTLE CLARITY, PERHAPS

To announce to everyone that the party had officially started, Meg put a disk of Schubert waltzes on the stereo and turned up the volume. It wasn't that she particularly liked his waltzes, but the music sounded like a party, and it seemed to orchestrate the clothes she had chosen: a knee-length dress of bright blue silk, with shoes that matched exactly.

The dress was not new. Ed had declared it his very favorite one day when she'd asked his help in choosing. When she was going through all the pain of sorting and packing up before leaving town, she'd actually put it into the Goodwill box. Then, just because Ed had liked it—a thought that amazed her—she'd snatched it up and stuffed it into the box marked "Save." Remembering that, she felt that stubborn resistant part of herself yielding—a sign of her healing.

The dress—what there was of it—draped deliciously and seemed to flow and linger at the same time. She kept walking around just to feel the silky material around her knees. It also showed an extraordinary amount of skin in front. After all this time of wearing blue jeans and cotton shirts, it was nice to know how beautiful, stylish clothes could make her feel sexy. Catching her reflection in the mirror, she admired the way her hair formed soft curls around her face and the back of her neck. Even though it was short, she'd pulled it back with the help of her mother's old-fashioned combs. Callie had put in the combs, and Sara had put in her pearl earrings, stabbing the posts through the tiny holes, and saying, "Yuk!" in a wistful, admiring way when she skillfully pushed each of the backs into place. Kurt was then called in and Meg was made to stand like a wooden soldier while all three children walked around and inspected her; after all their work on this party they didn't want any slipups.

Of course they were beautiful, too. Kurt was in slacks and shirt, and the Littles in dresses. Sara's had fit perfectly at the close of school, but now looked more like a tutu. While the only dress Callie could fit into was one of Sara's, and it was nearly below her knees. Despite this, their faces carried that "we're all dressed up" look that girls wear so easily and boys seldom do. Marc had used some of Doris' hairspray to slick back Kurt's errant locks; but it would take more than that to make the boy look ready for a party. His body was already rejecting his clothes and looking for the chance to let out a yell and disappear into the trees outside. In spite of this, Meg said they looked beautiful and they believed her.

. . .

Doris had just settled herself beside Marc by the fireplace when Ellis Brodie drove up (a half hour early); and what happened in the next ten minutes reminded her of a low budget movie.The Littles tore outside to greet him before he'd opened the car door. She noted that Meg also witnessed their greeting of him; but once it became obvious that the girls were trading birthday secrets with him, Meg quickly ran up the stairs and disappeared into the kitchen. Doris concluded that whatever it was that Ellis took from his pocket was the cause of the girls' jumping around happily. After he'd returned it to his pocket the three of them trooped into the house—the girls with the bottles of wine and pop, and Ellis carrying an extravagant and perfectly beautiful arrangement of white mums and pink roses.

Meg had reappeared and now stood leaning against the kitchen doorway with an expression that Doris could only describe as worried nonchalance.The girls trailed Ellis up the steps, still shooting questions at him and awaiting instructions as to where to put the wine. Once on the balcony, Ellis gave Meg and her dress a long, appreciative look, set down the flowers on the sideboard, grabbed her, and gave her as long a kiss as she would permit, which wasn't that long. Doris could feel everyone's reaction to it: a telltale gap in Marc's conversation with Kurt, and respectful, eye-blinking awe from the Littles.

Marc arose from his chair, anxious to understand what all the commotion was about, and Meg introduced Ellis to him and Doris. With that taken care of, Meg—like a puff of blue smoke—again disappeared into the kitchen.As much as Ellis tried to engage in polite conversation with Marc, it was apparent he wanted to be with Meg. After suggesting that the Littles go down by the fire, he picked up the flowers and disappeared into the kitchen. This only catapulted Meg out of the kitchen, followed by Ellis and his flowers.

Doris was completely mesmerized now, watching Meg and Ellis trying to decide the exact spot for the flowers on the table—with Meg always keeping the table between them. Once that was decided, Ellis lured Meg back into the kitchen, using the excuse of wanting to see what was on the menu. Doris heard Meg talking rapidly and convincingly about the cut glass dish she was going to serve the beet pickles in. With that kind of talk, Ellis guessed he'd go downstairs and have that cocktail Marc had spoken of. As he walked downstairs, Doris caught a glimpse of Meg in the kitchen doorway, scowling, and erasing what must have been another of Ellis's kisses.

As soon as Marc and Ellis were talking comfortably in front of the fire, cocktails in hand, and the kids were in the corner playing cards, Doris excused herself. With Meg hiding in the kitchen, it was obvious that she was needed up there.

Meg greeted Doris's offer of help with exaggerated gratitude, but, once she filled the sink with soapy water and the women started working, she retreated into silence and began chewing on her lip.

In a low voice, Doris finally asked, "Is there something I should know about that young man? When he came in…my goodness! I can certainly see what you meant about his being attractive. I'd say that man wants you, Meg. The way he looks at you, and that kiss—I could feel its heat all the way to where we were sitting. But as for you, I'm not quite getting a picture of idyllic joy. Has something changed since your last letter?"

Meg rolled her eyes. "I guess!"

"What happened?"

"What happened is we went on a hike in the mountains above the house, where I got a clear picture of him and changed my mind.

Amazingly, he actually proposed to me up there."

"My goodness, that was fast. And you answered?"

"I told him, no. It's been a relief with him gone fighting the Park fire." Seeing Doris' expression, she said, "It's not easy having a sexy, persistent man around. It just about drove me crazy. He kissed me the very first night I was here in this house, and that practically undid me. After that he started playing games with me, not touching me even though his eyes were undressing me—it's embarrassing to admit that. You have no idea how often I've thought of dragging him into my bedroom and getting it over with." She gave a wry laugh. "The hike turned into a bit of a test of willpower, but I managed to keep saying, 'No, Ellis! No, Ellis! No! No! No!'"

"You might have told him that, but from that kiss I don't think he believes it."

"That's the problem. He never takes no for an answer. That's what really bugs me. All month he's been writing us letters—the kind with long ropes that are meant to keep all of us tied to him—or maybe to keep him tied to us. Like tonight, he was the one who invited himself to this party, not me. I'd kind of hoped he'd disappeared altogether."

Seeing the question on Doris's face, she grimaced. "Oh, he's decent enough, but there's something I can't figure out about him. Even though he says he wants to marry me, I don't think he even likes me. And—and we never advanced in getting to know each other. It's hard to explain." She gave Doris a troubled look. "After Ed, maybe I can't judge these things anymore. I want...I want... Oh, who knows what I want?"

Doris stood back and looked at her. "Meg dear, Marc and I don't want you to end up alone here. You have so much to give a man. Marc says you don't know how attractive you are, and I agree. You're so pretty. I like your hair. You look younger. And that dress; blue is your color. And aren't you wearing a new perfume?" She paused then spoke thoughtfully. "But, dear, if you're sincere about not wanting to encourage Ellis, that dress says something else."

Even though Meg laughed, she covered her neckline with her hands, then tossed her head and teased, "But maybe I'm not wearing it for *Ellis*."

Doris looked relieved. "Well, for Marc then, and I'm sure he's already appreciating it. But let's not leave what we are talking about. You have to make the most of your opportunities. I know Ellis is several years younger than you, but May-December marriages can work. He seems like a nice young man and there appears to be a lot of good feelings between him and the kids. That's something they never had with their father. As for the rest of him, he speaks well, has a good job, dresses nicely, and has a lovely body with those tidy buttocks—my scoundrel, Marc, would use a different term. Now that I've met him and seen how much he wants you, I don't see how you can resist him."

Meg gave a shrug. "This whole thing is really confusing. A lot of years—a lot of *birthdays*—have passed since I was seriously courted. Even when I was young I never played the kind of games the other girls played with men. And now, I don't know the first thing to do."

Doris put down the pan she was drying and, searching for the right words, said, "There's no formula for men and women getting together. Maybe you're afraid of letting yourself go. Have you ever thought of not resisting him? You know, have a fling, get physically involved? With those barriers down you might reconsider his offer."

Meg giggled. "Good lord, so you want me to start wearing a big red 'A', do you? And to suggest that at your age!"

Doris's face reddened then she started to laugh, too. "I do not! On the other hand, Meg Halverson has been leading a very chaste life these many months. Maybe a little romp with Ellis is what that lady needs."

"I'm sure Ellis would go along with that." Meg stopped laughing and shook her head. "That wouldn't work, Doris. That's how I did it with Ed. Even though I had serious doubts about him, once I got sexually involved it was too late to get out. But all this is beside the point. After that hike, I never wanted to see Ellis again. Even before that I was on my guard around him. The more I knew him, the more I felt I should run *away* from him, as fast as I could go. You might not believe this, but I truly didn't give him encouragement. Even so, he was always thinking up ways to *help me out*. Frankly, I disliked most of his ideas and found him pushy. I told him what I thought, and each time he would capitulate and let things smooth over, until the next time I raised an objection. I've asked myself, why is he being so damned amenable?"

Doris ventured, "Doesn't that prove that he's trying to change for you?"

"Sounds good, but I felt that he'd zeroed in on me. One day I saw a coyote hunting a rabbit in our meadow. It was as though a string connected the coyote and the rabbit. No matter how fast the rabbit ran and darted this way and that, the coyote was right there, always making the right moves. In the end, there was no more rabbit.

"With Ellis, I've felt like I couldn't get away, like he's removed my defenses by always being so helpful, always being there, and always having the right answer. And I suspect that he's not above using his relationship with my kids to bolster his case with me! Add to that my feeling that he really doesn't even like me." She stopped and gave Doris a serious look. "Sorry about all my paranoia, but I do have a question and I want your opinion. If a man came along that I *could* love, would I recognize him?"

"You'll know, dear."

"But what if he's hesitant or has had a bad experience with a woman in his past? Would it be me who says something first, or would I have to wait until he does?"

There was something in Meg's face that made Doris pause before she answered. "If it's mutual, you'll both just flow into it; it's nothing you can stop. And you'll both know exactly what is right to do. You remember that, Meg Halverson."

At a burst of laughter from down in the living room, Meg lowered her voice and whispered, "If only what's-his-name would get orders to return to the damn Park."

Doris nodded her head. "You're doing fine. Trust your instincts, dear. Marc would say, 'Kid, it doesn't have to make sense if it *feels* good.'" She gave Meg a little push toward the door. "Now with everything done up here, let's go downstairs and have a drink. It's your birthday, for heaven's sakes. I'll protect you from Ellis—or is it the other way around?"

Meg giggled then spoke sarcastically, "So you're going to let me keep on wearing this revealing dress, *Mommy*? There's still time for me to change into my jeans."

Doris laughed."Just be sure to tell Ellis that the dress is for Marc's benefit." She gave Meg a little swat on her bottom and asked,"It is for Marc's benefit, isn't it?"

Meg gave her an innocent look and said,"Oh, sure, I'm out to get your husband."Then she flung her arms around Doris and gave her a hug and a kiss."How I've missed you!"At a knock at the back door, Meg said,"Oh, goodie, that's Flint. It's about time he showed up.And just in time to make the salad. I'll let him in."

Doris watched wide-eyed as Meg posed for a fraction of a second after opening the door for Flint; and she caught the slight catch in Flint's breathing when he looked at Meg.The moment passed quickly and he was soon acknowledging Doris and talking affably.Then he and Meg were talking spinach salad and he was scrubbing his hands and lower arms with a brush as if preparing to do surgery, and telling Meg he would need to use some stove space for the dressing if she could spare it.When he told Meg that the smell of the pasties had floated all the way to the cabin, and Meg was complimenting him on his tie and the color of his shirt, Doris decided that as much as the two might bear watching, she wouldn't be missed.

She was just heading out of the kitchen to join Marc down by the fire, when Ellis, who must have heard Flint talking, came pounding up the stairs past her. Hearing the urgent sound of his feet and seeing the look in his eyes, Doris, reminded of just how damned dull her life had been in Seattle, decided that maybe Meg could use her help after all.

Ellis looked incredibly tall and as sharp as the creases in his shirt and slacks when he thrust his hand toward Flint, and said,"My name's Brodie, Ellis Brodie. I'm Forest Service. And you must be Flint. I didn't catch the last name—Flint who?"

"Flint will do fine." Holding his just-washed hands to his chest, he looked apologetically at Ellis's outstretched hand, and said,"Sorry, I just scrubbed for the salad; but I'm glad to meet you." At that, he smiled broadly, then turned away, poured some vinegar into a bowl of previously fried bacon bits, added a couple huge dollops of sour cream, stirred it, and dumped it all into the little skillet Meg placed on the stove for him. Meg reached around Ellis and dug a wire whisk out of a drawer and handed that to Flint, too, widening her eyes at Doris in a silent commentary.

Once Ellis's hand had been rejected, he buried it deep into his pocket. Dodging three cooks now, he spoke a little anxiously. "Meg says you're a carpenter or a builder. Is that right? I know what needs to be done to this place. Meg and I have spent a lot of time together talking about the cabin and the kitchen remodeling. You have experience along these lines?"

Flint, stirring the dressing furiously on the stove, peered at Ellis over his shoulder and shrugged, "Meg's brother-in-law called it a latent talent, but we'll see." He turned to Meg and said, "Could I ask you to get that little dish of diced shallots out of the refrigerator and those two cut lemons? I can't leave this, lest it curdle. That's fine. Thank you. Now in you go." He was speaking to the bubbling sauce as he dumped it over the bowl of torn up spinach. After squeezing the lemons over it, he thrust his hands deep into the bowl and worked the sauce in lightly with his fingers, turning the greens over and over until everything was well coated. Meg and Doris and Ellis watched him, transfixed. "There we go," he said to no one. "Now let me wash up."

Everyone breathed in unison as he washed his hands and forearms at the sink. Meg made a little ceremony of holding a clean towel out to him. He smiled his thanks then looked up at Ellis while drying his hands. "Now then, you were saying?"

Ellis looked confused. "I was saying… What was I saying?"

Flint spoke cordially, "You were asking about the kitchen here and the cabin. We just got word that the kitchen windows arrived and are ready to be picked up. And we're ready to start tearing off the blue wallboard in here. It will be a mess and we decided to wait until after Meg's birthday. We've ordered the new cupboards and a nifty stove Kurt wanted for over in that corner there. Things are moving along nicely." He smiled at him. "You said you're with the Forest Service. So, you cut the trees and build the roads around here?"

Ellis backed away. "Well, not *personally* I don't. I'm more involved with what a forest can produce to make it profitable."

"Profitable?"

"Commercially viable."

"Viable?"

"Productive, worth using, *profitable*. That's a known word, I believe. Make money? Dollars? You know about *dollars* don't you?"

Flint smiled.

Ellis went on,"I decide for the Forest Service what Meg will do for herself here, so she can make a profit from her land. As the manager of this place, she'll have to stop treating her trees like sacred objects."

Meg spoke up, "I'm right here, Ellis. I can speak for myself." She finished spooning beet pickles into the cut glass bowl, put the container in the sink, and went over to where Flint was leaning against the counter. Licking at a spot of beet juice on her finger, she gave Ellis a bland look and said, "My trees *are* sacred objects, Ellis, so the word 'profitable' isn't appropriate in relation to them or any part of my place. Haven't we had this discussion before?"

"Sorry, I didn't mean to talk around you, Meg." He looked at the two of them standing together, but soldiered on. Giving an offhand gesture to Flint, he told her, "Your carpenter here, Flint here, can take care of the kitchen or whatever, but now that I'm back from the Park, you and I need to pick an afternoon and sit down and discuss what you're going to do with the place to make it pay. I have a lot of ideas for it and, considering what I do professionally, I have a lot of suggestions."

Meg laughed. "You're getting ahead of me. I'm still working over your words about making this place pay. If your suggestions require facts and figures on my part, talking about it would be a waste of your time. All along I've been saying exactly what I want to do: just improve the buildings and spruce up the grounds around the house, and then live our lives here."

Ellis gave her an indulgent smile and chose his words carefully. "Don't take me wrong, Meg. As I've said, having you and the kids living here seems right—on top of the world, king of the mountain, that sort of thing—and putting in a lawn and making a little flowerbed here and there will be nice. What I'm talking about concerns our planning for the use you'll put to the other thousand or so acres. I can help you decide how to *develop it*, to make it profitable. While your, while Flint here goes ahead with the remodeling, I can come up and we can start making our plans. Just say the word."

Doris, standing by the refrigerator, had a unique view of the three others in the room, and she wished fervently that her husband was at least listening to what she knew was about to happen. She'd seen that look on Meg's face before: her Mrs. Edward Halverson society face, from which all traces of what was going on inside her head had been removed. Of course it was the word "develop" that she was going to react to. And that fellow, Flint, beside Meg, looked passive—listening coolly, looking down at his shoes, his arms crossed over his chest and his fingers tucked under his elbows—but he was hardly that. At Ellis's last words, he had moved his elbow very gently against Meg's arm.

As for Ellis, he'd taken what Doris termed an *official* stance. It was easy to imagine him in a uniform instead of the slacks and shirt he was wearing. If he wore glasses he would have taken them off at this point and be touching one of the ear pieces to his lower lip, in a manner that said: "I welcome your opinion, but you're talking to someone who knows more than you."

Taking a cue from the silence following his offer, Ellis gave Meg an apologetic look and said, "If I've overstepped my bounds, Meg, forgive me."

Meg gave him her sweetest Halverson smile. "No, no, there's nothing to forgive. It's just that we're not talking about the same thing, Ellis. I'm still trying to understand your offer of help. The very word 'profitable' brings up a whole different picture in my mind, and it has no part in what I'm talking about. I'm talking about loving the land with its beautiful trees and grass and soil and rocks and sky and wildness; and none of those, in the way I understand it, has any commercial value. I bought this place because the kids and I simply fell in love with it, and want to live our lives *with it.* So I can't figure out what you could advise me on."

Ellis's neck reddened above his collar, and he seemed to have forgotten the others in the room. "All that talk of loving the land and living with it sounds pretty naive, Meg. What I'm asking is that you start using your head and consider what you have here. You've got more than a thousand acres of prime land. I've never seen such a sweet setup as you have. You're only fourteen miles from town, but your land is surrounded and protected by federal land, across which you have the right-of-way. You have water and a good road. About three hundred acres of the land closest to the canyon road levels off, so we could use that for a housing development and even raise Christmas trees on part of it. Don't pass up the opportunity to develop this place. Think of the money we can make. But we have to act soon. A lot of the trees are too old. When trees get pithy they're useless for lumber and only a paper mill wants them. And you might not know it, but the mineral rights go with this place—I already checked that. Gold was discovered in this canyon a long time ago, and there might be other minerals as well."

Before replying, Meg was silent for long moments. Then she turned to Doris, and gave her a what-did-I-tell-you look, and softly spoke the word "coyote." Then turning to Ellis she sighed and spoke in a clear, sad tone. "I'm going to assume that your use of the word 'we' was a slip of your tongue, for there is no 'we' in my thinking, Ellis. About the rest, how could a man who grew up in a Forest Service cabin near a wilderness say what you just said? You grew up knowing what it takes to keep animals and birds wild. With your working for the Forest Service, I assumed...I *hoped*...that you saw unspoiled land like I do. I think of all the things you've taught us about the wildlife here—the hawks and ground squirrels and bears— " she lowered her voice, but it shook anyway "—how could you even use the words "mineral rights" when speaking of this beautiful piece of land? Logging and mining and housing developments destroy wild land. Where are your principles? Where is your sense of responsibility toward the land?"

Ellis scoffed and was going to say something, but Meg turned on him, saying, "I have this picture in my mind of a great ugly machine moving over the land. For its first meal it chews off the trees, digesting them and leaving behind ugly stumps and droppings of slash. For its next meal it bites down lower, removing the topsoil all the way down to bedrock, and this time its droppings are mine tailings. While it's chewing, it cares not a whit that it's destroying the wonderful niches in the land that hold unexpected springs and the sounds of birds and all the things wild animals need to exist. After there is nothing more for the giant machine to eat, all that's left—" she turned to Flint "—all that's left is then buried under concrete and asphalt, with people living in the cracks under highways, amid noise and ground-up tires and cigarette butts and wrappers and oil! Isn't that right, Flint?"

Flint nodded and touched her hand and spoke softly, "You forgot the dumpsters."

Her eyes held on Flint's face, knowing she should be calm, but her anger was still there. She turned back to Ellis, barely able to contain herself. "Perhaps I can answer the question I just asked about your—your waning sense of responsibility to the land. You are employed by the organization heralded as 'The Steward of the Land.' Is it you that has changed? Or is it that organization that's changed? What were the words you just used regarding your tree research: Commercial viability? Productivity? Profitability? And now you speak the words 'mineral rights'? I certainly hope that your employer—our steward—isn't only thinking about the land's *profitability*. For a long time, to my mind at least, that steward has allowed itself to be manipulated and swayed by political expediency. And when that happens, our public lands end up being anything but *cared for*. I think our very survival is tied up with how we treat Mother Nature. We have to stop selling our land to the highest bidder. We have to keep it away from politicians. We have to stop seeing it with greedy eyes. We have to stop abusing it. Wild land is so fragile; all it takes is just one careless decision to kill it."

Ellis made a derisive sound, "I used to think things like that. But saving this place from development isn't going to save the world, Meg. You seem to forget that you consume wood products and water, electricity, metal, and cows along with all us other poor saps."

"Yes," Meg said, "I do. But there have to be wild places. I'm going to keep this little patch of mountainside pristine as long as I can. And maybe the kids will fight to keep it that way a little longer, and maybe their kids will, after them. Who knows, maybe we will buy up land just to keep it from those who want to develop it. Maybe we have to be our own stewards."

When Flint touched her again, her arms, which were shooting into the air, dropped down to her sides. She laughed giddily. "Good grief, this is my party and just look at me—I'm shaking. Dinner is probably ruined." She picked up a wine bottle and thrust it at Ellis, "Your wine needs opening."

It was then she noticed that Sara was in the doorway, with a stricken look on her face. Knowing she'd overheard, Meg said, "Sara! Well, maybe you could call everyone to the table and we'll get dinner on."

Sara turned abruptly and left the kitchen. Meg heard her calling everyone to dinner.

40

GIFTS

Meg opened the oven and transferred the flat pocketbook-shaped pasties onto the platter that Flint was holding out to her. She gave them a worried look. Pushing at one with her finger and seeing a little trickle of juice appear from its top hole, she said, "At least they're not ruined."

Flint asked, "Want these on the sideboard?" When she nodded, he left the kitchen, followed by Doris, carrying the beets. Meg followed, smiling to herself and a bit glassy-eyed, and set the bowl of salad next to the pasties and declared, "We can do no more. Let's eat!"

A solemn Sara sat down beside an even more somber Ellis. Kurt and Callie seemed to be the only ones laughing. Each held one of Marc's arms, pretending to drag him up the stairs, while he moaned, "Not the food. Not the food. Your mother can't cook. She'll poison us all." Once everyone was seated, they passed their plates to Meg. She filled them, passed them back, and they began to eat.

The salad was memorable, having somehow survived all the words that had fallen into it. And the pasties were fine, the crust flaky, the pieces of steak still juicy, and the potatoes and onions…well, they were a bit dry for Meg's taste, but delicious all the same. The first coherent words came from Callie, asking for a second pasty, and saying, "Pasties aren't all that bad, as long as it isn't for *my* birthday dinner." The cream puffs were a sensation, filled with sweetened whipped cream and topped with a generous dollop of Meg's famous hot fudge sauce. Because they could be made to hold one candle—as long as the little hole was bored very carefully into the top—Meg felt she might have started a tradition, after all those years of tedious birthday cakes.

. . .

After everything that could be eaten was eaten, Meg, the birthday girl, was exempted from any further work and sent down to sit by the fire. Feeling banished from her favorite domain, she cast longing looks at the noisy kitchen. With no reprieve in sight, she began roaming around the living room like a caged bear, finally flinging herself in the loveseat.

Ellis, looking hopeful, had followed her down. But after repeated compliments on the food—with little response—there seemed to be nothing more to say. He busied himself by adding more wood to the fire then backed up to it, waggling his hands into the heat as though each finger held a marshmallow. He, too, was anxious for the people upstairs to finish and come down and rescue him.

Before the gifts could be presented, Marc made the traditional birthday toast. After pouring a snifter of brandy for the adults and fruit drink for the kids, he worked his way over to the fireplace. Leaning against its stonework, and in his elegant style, he proposed a toast to Meg.

"I seem to remember the last toast this group made. The occasion was the survival of this family after a tragic occurrence. I see that the faces have changed somewhat. Tolly isn't here this time, but Flint, who was so recently with that good family, is, and we welcome him. And Ellis, welcome. My dear wife and I, though weary after our travels to see our Seattle children, are glad to be here, for we love this family. The occasion for this celebration is the birthday of this lovely creature named Meg, who is giving us that old line that she's thirty-nine-years-old. Mark my words: next year you can count on her being thirty-nine years old again! So, we'll never really know, will we? Be that as it may, we'll tell her happy birthday anyway. My dear Meg, you don't look a day over thirty. Let's all drink to her continued health and beauty, and many more thirty-ninth birthdays to come."

The glasses were raised and the toast was drunk. Marc continued, "I think we're ready to bestow on this fair lady the gifts for this occasion. We'll do this in age order. Callie, since you're the youngest, why don't you start."

Callie, who'd been leaning against Flint, scrambled up the stairs and into her room. She came down bearing a cylinder-shaped package and laid it in her mother's lap.

Meg lifted it to her nose and declared, "It isn't perfume, but it's heavy and has liquid in it." Callie, all expectant, with her eyes big and anxious and her hands clasped together, watched Meg undo the tape and paper very slowly. With everyone groaning impatiently, Meg finally took out a bottle (that had once held olives) filled with many colored rocks and water. Callie said, "They're the prettiest pebbles in the spring, and that's some spring water. You see, if rocks stay wet like that they're always pretty. They are for your bathroom window, Ma, and because you like our spring so much."

Meg held the bottle up to the light and shook it and gave Callie a hug. Callie scampered back to Flint with a big smile on her face. In passing Kurt, she punched his arm and hissed, "She did too like it!"

Marc gave Sara a beneficent smile and said, "Your turn, Sara."

A somewhat dispirited Sara went over to the bookcase and took a flat envelope from between some books. She brought it over to Meg and just stood looking sad. Meg shook the envelope by her ear and said, "Could this be perfume?" Everyone groaned. Then she peeked inside the envelope and withdrew her gift. She put her arms around Sara and said, "You've drawn me a picture of our Canada lynx. And you remembered every hair on him and all the bushes and the little spring." She held the picture high so everyone could see and said, "That's just the way he looked when Sara and I saw him that day we walked down our road."

Sara looked first at her mother, then at Ellis sitting in a chair next to her, and said, "And right away Ellis came up the road in his big truck and drove us to our car and fixed it. Didn't you, Ellis? And you called me 'Punkin'. And I asked you if you had any kids and you don't have any." She turned to her mother and spoke, her voice strangling, "Don't you remember that, Ma? Don't be mad at him." She stood there waiting, the question an agony on her face.

Meg nodded sadly and reached out to put her arm around her; but Sara twisted away and sat down and picked up Muggins instead.

During this, Ellis had pushed back farther into the chair, his young face reflecting his search for something appropriate to say, but he was only able to lick his lips.

Marc, cleared his throat and said, "Moving right along. Kurt, didn't I see something for your mother downstairs in the workroom?"

Kurt almost ran down the stairs, his voice trailing, "Happy Birthday! Now close your eyes, Ma, until I bring it up. I built it myself and I couldn't wrap it. You'll see why." His words were accompanied by some ominous thumps and bumps and panting. Then there was a clunk on the floor and silence. Before Meg opened her eyes, she said, "I'm betting that's perfume." And everyone groaned. When she opened her eyes she saw a lashed and nailed object in front of her. She said, "You've made me something!" It was somewhat big, and she wondered what exactly it was (perhaps a stool or a small table). She decided to let its inventor identify it. "Thank you, dear. Just looking at it I can think of a thousand uses for it, but you obviously have something particular in mind. So you must tell me yourself."

Kurt smiled his half smile and said, "It's to set your radio on in the bathroom when you take your bubble bath. It's so you can listen to the music in there, too."

Meg reached over and gave him a huge hug. "Oh, you. I was hoping it was for that. I always miss music in there when I'm soaking. And you guessed that, didn't you. I'll treasure it always." Addressing Marc she said, "It's time for Tolly's gift. She sent me something that I want to share with you. She opened a box lying on the coffee table and asked that it get passed around. "This candy arrived yesterday, along with this funny card from her and Charlie. For years, Tolly has been trying to make taffy like our mother used to make. I'd say she finally has the recipe down pat, but you'll have to decide that. And you only get one piece each. On the card Charlie says for the umpteenth time how happy and relieved they both are that Flint found his way up here. And I am, too." She beamed at Flint.

Marc nodded approvingly. "Now let's see. Since we started doing this, youngest to oldest—and assuming the older we get, the more frivolous the gifts—it looks like we've finally gotten to ours. Now, my little Chick-a-dee, you put something behind the couch a while back."

Doris said, "I wish I was next, but to keep the age-order, it's Ellis's turn."

Even though he was sitting close to Meg, Ellis got up and was reaching into his shirt pocket, when, in some small motion, Meg stiffened her arms and shrank back. Seeing her, Ellis moved his hand past his pocket and rubbed his chin instead, saying quietly, "The flowers are my gift, Meg. I thought they were very pretty. They still are." He gestured to the table and everyone's eyes followed his hand, paying respect to his gift. That is, everyone but Sara, who said a small sad, "No!" Ellis turned to her and said, brusquely, "Maybe another time."

Meg swallowed and looked at him and said gamely, "So I got some perfume after all. The flowers smelled wonderful all during dinner. And, yes, aren't they lovely? Thank you very much, Ellis." Relieved and very much subdued, she reached over and gave his hand a small pat. He just stared ahead at the fire.

Doris leaped to her feet. "It's Flint's turn, but let me squeeze in here with Marc's and my gift." She pulled a large, rectangular package from behind the couch and placed it in Meg's lap. "Happy Birthday, dear. We had this made for you in Seattle." She added hastily, "Actually, I can't think of a time you've needed this more."

Meg, using the time to recover—fighting to recover and breathing in big nervous breaths—first moved the package up and down, to show everyone it was heavy. In absolute silence, she picked at the knot in the ribbon until she could undo it, and then picked off each little square of tape, until she was finally able to fold back the paper. She brought out a beautiful rectangular mosaic plaque on which was written, in bright-colored glass tiles: "LOVE SPOKEN HERE."

Meg's eyes held on Doris. "It's perfect! I'll hang it where we can see it every day and I'll treasure it. Thank you so much."

Marc said, "My little bride does it again. And, although the order is broken…Flint?"

But Ellis chose that moment to excuse himself. He said, "I'm afraid I have to go. I have a busy day coming up, after being in the Park for so long, and a lot of catching up to do." Turning to Meg, who was getting up from her chair, he said, "Don't get up. I can find my way out, I know the routine." Giving the room a look of regret, he added, "I've been here often enough." He opened the door, turned and said to the kids, "Be good and take care of your mother," and left.

Once the door shut, Flint quickly stood up and said, "My gift is outside. We'll have to go through the kitchen to see it." Everyone stood up, happy to stretch and get away from all the emotions they had witnessed. They trailed along after Flint and Kurt, who ran ahead up the stairs, through the kitchen, and out the back door.

Even in the gathering dusk Meg knew immediately what the gift was. Leaning against the back outside wall were two big poles with heavy cross pieces bolted to them. And lying nearby was a roll of steel wire. Meg clapped her hands and said, "Oh Flint, a clothesline! I haven't had a clothesline since I was living at home on the farm. And it's just like my mother's. Now our sheets will get all windblown and smell wonderful. It will be so nice to come out and hang sheets up here on top of this mountain." She looked around with her arms opened wide, imagining it. "What a wonderful, thoughtful gift. Oh, Flint, thank you so much."

Flint said, "We wouldn't want this wind and sunshine to go to waste any longer." He placed his hands lightly on Kurt's shoulders. "It's from Kurt, too." Kurt nodded his head and smiled, as Flint added, "I even got an offer to help dig the holes, once you've decided where you want it, Meg. We'll put it where it'll get the biggest sweep of wind. Your sister Tolly explained that a good clothesline has to be located across the prevailing wind. Even to a city boy like me that sounds logical. We'll put it up and, after that, it's your turn, Meg."

Meg said, "What was that you said?"

Flint laughed and said, "Do you want it all, or just the part about 'it's your turn, Meg'?"

"Yes, yes, that's it. I thought that's what you said. Thank you. And I don't have to wonder 'my turn' for what, do I?" She looked at Flint, puzzled, and was still looking at him when Marc said, "Brrrr, it looks like we've got a change of weather. I'd like to go back to the fire and have another taste of that fine brandy of yours, Meg."

. . .

An hour later, because tomorrow was a school day, Meg insisted that the children get to bed, even though they were still buoyed up after their wonderful party. After tucking in Kurt and Callie, Meg knocked on Sara's door and made quite a show of tucking her in and wanting to talk.

Sara would have none of it and turned her face to the wall.

Meg sat on the edge of the bed and laid her hand on Sara's shoulder and caressed it. She said, "Sara dear, I'm sorry about Ellis. Can we talk about it?"

Sara made a sound that was more sob than anything, but finally said, "If you hadn't gotten mad at him, he wouldn't have gone away."

Meg sighed. "Oh, Sara, when you're little things seem so easy, but when you grow up you find out they aren't that way at all. When I choose a daddy for you, the most important thing is he and I will love each other. I don't love him, dear, and he doesn't like me enough. You've got to trust me on this, Sara. You kids are so special and you deserve the best daddy there is."

"Everyone at our new school has one, except us."

"I know, dear. Maybe sometime."

Sara hiccupped then turned and looked up at her mother. "You don't even know what Ellis was going to give you, Ma. It wasn't the flowers. It was a pretty gold chain and a gold heart with a *real diamond* in it. He showed it to Cal and me."

Meg said, "I thought it might be something like that. I didn't want him to give it to me."

Sara sobbed, "If you didn't want it, why couldn't he give it to me-ee?"

Meg smoothed Sara's hair. "But it wasn't for you, dear. You wouldn't want something meant for me. Some gifts are very complicated; sometimes there are things attached to them that a person can't see. When you're older you'll understand, Punkin."

Sara looked surprised. "You just called me Punkin."

"You said you liked that name. Would you like me to call you that?"

Sara nodded happily, then looked doubtful. "I guess not. I like you to call me Sara. You've called me that for the longest time, haven't you?"

"Yep, from the very first. When your father saw you, all wrapped up in a little pink blanket, he said, 'Let's name her after my grandmother.'"

"Really? Was I in a pink blanket?"

"Yep, just a little funny-faced doll with peach-fuzz hair, all wrapped in a pink blanket." She thought a moment then looked lovingly down at Sara and said softly, "Anyway, Sara, you don't need any more diamonds. You already have one."

"Noooo. Do I?"

"I've never told you, because you've been too young to know. Because you were your father's first daughter and were named after his grandmother Sara, he said you were to get her gold ring. It's such a beautiful old ring, with little curlicues of gold and a great big diamond in the middle."

Sara sat up. "Really, for me? Can I see it?

"It's not here. It's locked up in the vault in the bank in town—the bank where your father worked. It's very precious and it's safe there. The next time we go to the library, we'll stop by the bank and I'll show it to you. We will have to put it right back in the vault and keep it there, so when you become a young lady it will be waiting for you. By that time you'll know lots of things that you don't have to even think about now. That includes how we get a daddy." She leaned over and kissed her and tucked the blanket around her. "I love my Sara, and now my Sara has to get to sleep."

Sara said, "I'll make a good dream about my ring, Ma."

Meg sighed deeply, "Yes, that ring needs only *good* dreams; no sad ones, ever again. Goodnight, dear."

Erda had followed them in and Meg told her, "Stay with Sara, Erda." Erda nosed Sara's covers, then lay down close to the bed, settling her long nose on her silver paw with that tired little huff of hers.

Meg was about to turn out the light when Sara said, "Ma, does Flint have any kids?"

Meg's hand hesitated and she looked back at her and said, "Sara..."

Sara sounded perplexed, "Is that the kind of thing I gotta grow up for before I can ask him?" With no answer, but having gotten her mother's full attention, Sara began speaking rapidly. "You never get mad at Flint, Ma. I like his long hair tied back like that, like George Washington. He tells us funny stories when he drives us. He knows a real lot, Ma. The other day he told Kurt he should maybe think about becoming a doctor or a scientist. And he wonders if I'll be an artist, and Callie might be a poet, 'cuz she talks like you do. He really likes you and thinks you're a poet, Ma. My best friend, Lynnie, who sits behind me, thinks Flint's handsome. I do, too. Lynnie asked if he was my daddy."

Meg's hand was still on the light switch and she felt like she hadn't breathed. She swallowed before asking, "What did you tell Lynnie?"

"I didn't say anything. I knew Ellis didn't have kids, but Ellis never drives us to school. And I didn't know if I should ask Flint if he has any."

Meg said, "I don't know what to say, Sara. You better let Flint tell you about that himself. You really have to go to sleep. Are you and I okay with these things now?"

Sara mumbled something into her covers that sounded like, "Yeah, okay." As Meg turned out the light she saw Sara's hand steal from beneath the covers and stroke Erda's neck.

41

THE DOORSTEP

Flint was waiting by the sideboard when Meg closed Sara's door. He came over to her, and spoke quietly, "Is Sara all right?"

"She's fine now. Just a little mother and daughter talk." She looked questioningly at him.

Flint made a slight gesture at Marc and Doris sitting below them by the fire. "I'd like to talk to you before I go back to the cabin. Not here, but outside on the doorstep. I'm afraid you'll need to change out of that beautiful dress and put on some warmer clothes so you don't freeze out there. And could you lend me that big green sweater of yours again? I walked here in my shirtsleeves before dinner. We might be getting a preview of winter."

The look on his face and the way he was talking frightened her. "Oh, Flint, I couldn't bear it if you're thinking of leaving or something. Please don't—"

He smiled and pressed her hand for a moment. "It's just a talk, Meg. I'll never sleep if I can't talk to you." Moving his eyes over her and her dress, he said, "The beautiful girl in blue! Now, go, and don't be long. I'll say goodnight to the Websters and wait for you outside on the doorstep."

Meg hurried to her bedroom, found the sweater Flint wanted then got out of her clothes and into her cords and a heavy sweater. She hurried down the balcony steps, made her excuses to Marc and Doris, telling them she and Flint had something to discuss, and went outside.

It was much colder. She handed Flint the sweater, helping him with one of its sleeves, then moved boldly and leaned against him. For a moment they just shivered quietly, then she said, "Tell me again that everything's all right, Flint. Say the words that you're not leaving or anything like that."

He put his arm around her and gave her a hug. "Everything is fine. I'm not leaving—at least, so far as I know. That's your department. It's about that conversation in the kitchen and Brodie using the word 'we,' and about what Sara said, or at least implied. That was a pretty strange conversation. I don't want to butt in or anything, but where does Brodie fit here?"

"Nowhere. I didn't invite him to my party. He did that all by himself. He was here off and on this summer and came to dinner a few times. We all enjoyed his stories about this place. The Littles were entranced with him. He's quite dashing; I'll give him that. He had a knack of inserting himself into the family without my wanting him there. Before tonight, I wondered if he was using his charm as some kind of pretext; and you heard him, he wants my land and got the idea that if he could get me... well, you know. But poor Sara; she just wants a dad."

She went on, "My husband was a dad in name only. Since he died my kids have put a lot of pressure on me about that. I thought I could fill both roles, but the older they get the more I know I really can't. My Papa was the most important man in my life. No matter what mistakes I've made or poor choices, I've never doubted that I was the good person Papa thought I was. He's my guide: his words come back to me time after time, just when I need them. My convictions about caring for the land and respecting it come from him. Even as I spoke to Ellis tonight I could hear myself using the same words Papa used. When Papa died I was desolate, but he has never left me. When he appears in my dreams, I try to hold on so the dream doesn't stop. When I remember how much I loved my Papa, I can begin to understand what the kids have missed."

Flint was very quiet as she said that—Meg could hear him listening. She went on, "When you talk of the fun you have driving them to school, I've wanted to tell you that the kids enjoy you, too. They tell me everything you've talked about—with a lot of laughter, but with a lot of thoughtfulness, too. They haven't had a man pay attention to them, or care what they think. They have a lot of regard for you, Flint. Like I said before, you're welcome to do more with them. Could you tell them that story about the Brooklyn Bridge that you told me? The kids and I have spent all our lives here in Montana, and, frankly, in many ways, though I don't often admit it, it can be a handicap, not experiencing other people and other places. You've had such a rich, diverse life. With all your know-how and growing up in a different place, you have so much to add to our lives. I want that for my children."

Flint answered her. "You have no idea what your words mean to me. Really, Meg, you have no idea. Thank you."

She went on, "I was appalled at Ellis's assumptions there in the kitchen. He means nothing to me, Flint, if that's what you were asking." She laughed. "I'll take maturity over youth any time."

Chuckling, Flint said, "I believe the saying is 'Age before beauty.' But I prefer that word *maturity*." He thought a moment. "Actually, Brodie put me in an awkward position. As much as I like it up here, I don't have any ulterior motives to possess those thousands of acres you were talking about."

Meg waited then said, "How does that put you in an awkward position?"

"My ulterior motives are only to possess the *landowner*. But after all that talk in the kitchen, if I told the landowner that, mightn't she suspect I'm really after her land?"

Meg laughed then made her voice sound serious. "Hummm, I can see where that might be a problem. Perhaps you're going to have to make your case to the landowner, or at least try."

"Well, let's see. I could tell her that money is no problem with me, that I am and have been a resourceful chap. And I could tell her that my idea of a good life is to enjoy the very same things she and her three character kids seem to enjoy. I could tell her that I am proud of what she stands for and what she said tonight. I could even encourage her to speak out on those things, join an environmental organization like the *Nature Conservancy*, make herself heard, write letters, put a little pressure on some senators and representatives." He thought a little more. "And, if that weren't enough, I could tell her that this sweater is big enough to hold a woman, too."

"This isn't some kind of blasé New York City talk, is it?"

He chuckled,"No, this is 100 percent straight Big Sky Montana truth."

She said,"Well, okay then."

He unbuttoned the sweater and turned her so her back was against him, and deftly wrapped it around them both and tugged it closed. Settling her closer against him, he chuckled into her ear,"Your sweater might not survive this."

"Like I'm worried about it."

"You're shaking."

"Oddly enough, it isn't from the cold. It's from my feeling your body against me, all your wonderful lumps and bumps that I've only imagined about a thousand times."

He laughed quietly into her ear,"Ah, yes, my lumps and bumps." He said, "Look at the town down there. Do you suppose anyone's watching us?"

She said, "Every one of them is. They're asking, 'What's that Halverson woman up to now?'"

They stood like that on the step, shivering in the dark, with their eyes fixed on the last glow of light leaving the sky beyond the town.

He spoke softly,"I met you right here on this doorstep."

"I remember."

He whispered into her hair, "The beautiful birthday girl... I didn't know I'd luck out and get to hold her. I've wanted to give her a birthday kiss."

"Only on birthdays?"

"Well, a birthday does present an excuse."

Meg found herself crying, felt the tears running, unchecked, down her cheeks. She said,"For you, I'd have a birthday many times a day. I've been waiting a long, long time for thi—is." A little sob had gotten in there, but she didn't care if it had and snuggled against him tighter.

"Me, too." He rubbed his nose against her cheek, collecting some of her tears on it. Then, speaking seriously, as if cautioning her, he said, "Right now we're standing close and touching each other, but, Meg, if we kiss like I think we might, it'll change everything."

She laughed contentedly, "Things changed the moment you

walked up that road."

"Ah...yes. But I want more than a little tryst in the woods, Meg. I'm forty-five and I have just so much time on this earth. I'm a greedy bastard."

"I'm greedy, too, Flint."

He moved his hands and put them under her sweater. He said, "What's this? No bra?"

She wanted to make a joke of it, but only the sincere words came out. "I was hoping you'd find out about that. I didn't know what you were going to tell me, and a woman has just so many weapons when she's going for broke. 'Always be Prepared' is a great motto."

His voice was husky, and he whispered, "I love you, Meg." He cupped her breasts in his warm hands and caressed them with his thumbs. He bent down and kissed her ear, then ran his lips down the side of her neck, possessively, breathing in her smell. When he moved his hands lower and slipped them under her waistband, he said, "Hummm, good motto."

She sighed then whispered, "I love you, James Trevor Flint." She put her hands behind her and touched his thighs, running her fingers softly up and down them. Then she touched him and caressed him, closing her eyes tight at his response. Half turning, she said, "Being out here on this doorstep is killing me. I want you so. How are we going to do this?"

He said, "Tomorrow. I'll drive the kids to school. With your friends in the house, could you wait for me at the cabin? I'll build a fire before I leave."

"I'll wait there. But when Marc and Doris leave in a day or two... Oh, Flint, I want you in my bed—it's new, you know, and it's still a virgin."

"I'll come to your bed." He spoke gravely, "It's the only virgin around, I'm afraid."

She said, "No, that's not true." In a bleak voice she said, "In spite of everything, in spite of having three kids, I consider myself a virgin of sorts." She paused. "Ed never considered me; he never took the time to... It's hard to say, but I've never experienced the release that a man must feel when..." She went on, "I'm not certain what making love is between two people. I know *what* it is, the mechanics and all that, but

I've never experienced it. When there wasn't time…and everything was over so fast, and he was done…there wasn't any way for me to give back, or say the things that were inside me. Without my ever expressing that, it's like I've been trapped behind a dam with no way to get out and run free."

"Oh, Meg..." He put his lips against her cheek. "I'm so sorry. What you just told me is you've never been wholly loved. That's what making love means, giving your all to your partner. I believe you to be a natural, generous, loving woman, the earthy kind. That's how I read you. Something in you fairly calls out to me."

After a moment, he went on, "I was just thinking about something, about what you told Ellis about your land. You took the land's part, almost as if you were speaking about a person. I gather that your husband didn't physically abuse you, but it was an abusive relationship nevertheless—his neglect and using you for his own convenience, then leaving you without saying goodbye."

At his words a great tenderness came over Meg. She said, "Here on this doorstep the first thing I said to you—"

Flint interrupted, "I know. I remember. You asked, 'How did you find me?'"

She said, "I don't know why I asked you that. I wasn't wondering how you found the house. I was standing in my bathrobe and it just came to me as the only thing to say to you. That day was so strange: I had been waiting for something, but I didn't know what. And I had no idea you were coming. So how did you find me, Flint? You never answered."

"I'll tell you now." He turned her around to face him, holding her tight and again tucking the sweater around them both. "I found you beautiful. I found you just out of your bath. I found your hair in damp waves that I wanted to lay my face against. I found your eyes grey and deep and full of questions. I found your mouth generous, your lips the kind that will part easily when I kiss you. I found you in a blue bathrobe that I wanted to untie and see if you were naked—but then, I already knew you were. I wanted to look at your whole body. I wanted to cry out…some damned thing that would say, 'This woman is the one I want!' How did I find you, Meg? I found you just in time."

They kissed for a long, long time, still wrapped together. Then, shivering, they said goodnight, their words sounding small and private and full of promise.

When he left her on the step she hugged herself and tried to find the warmth she had gotten used to in just that short time in his arms. He called back to her twice, and she answered him. Finally, there was only the beam of his flashlight. For a moment the light stopped on the road, as though Flint was hesitating. But after a moment it moved on again, bobbing along the road, its beam catching on the occasional ice crystals floating down, breaking up as he went through the trees, and then disappearing altogether.

. . .

Only Marc was there when Meg got back inside. She was still shaking, and to keep from doubling over she stood steadying herself by the fireplace, holding on to its stones for their warmth and looking at the fire. But she was mostly feeling the throbbing of her legs and the tremors radiating from her body, and trying to comprehend how her whole life had changed.

Marc looked at her with concern. "Are you okay?"

"Just cold. The fire feels good."

With that reassurance, Marc told her that Doris had already gone to bed, and he had better get some sleep, too. But, after saying that, he stayed, picking up the fireplace broom and sweeping the scattering of ashes from the hearth, while his face worked with his thoughts.

Meg was impatient to be alone and think, but she leaned back against the fireplace and waited for him to speak.

Marc said, "Sorry about your friend Ellis. For a man, this world can be a brutal place where women are concerned. Frankly, he made a damned decent recovery, pointing to those flowers as his gift." He slapped the broom handle and laughed. "I heard parts of that conversation in the kitchen, with him saying '*we* could mine it.' By God, you trounced the bastard. Good show! He isn't the right man for you, my dear, and you know it." He tipped back his head and looked at her. "It was a good party in spite of that. You enjoyed it, didn't you?" When Meg nodded he said, "What time is breakfast?"

She told him 7:00, and suggested that he and Doris eat breakfast with her and Flint and the kids, before they left for school, or maybe sleep in and find something for themselves, as they knew their way around the kitchen. Once she'd said that, she decided something and said, "Look, Marc, Flint is going to drive the kids to school. After he gets back he wants me to join him at the cabin..." She made a point of adding, "*to be with him, to be together at the cabin*." She gave him a special look when she said that, to make sure he understood. She said, "Tell Doris that, will you? She and I had a long talk earlier. She'll want to know."

Marc nodded and smiled. "Got it. Flint's a good man. I like him. He'll do you right, Meg."

She answered softly, "Your opinion means a lot, dear. I think he will, too."

Marc said, "While you were in with Sara, he was telling me about his working on the farm, and we talked about the work up here and me helping him. But somehow he doesn't seem like a carpenter. What did he do before working for Charlie?"

"He was a triage doctor or nurse. Funny, but I don't know exactly which. I do know he worked for many years in a New York trauma hospital. He suffers occasionally from a kind of burnout, something he calls battle fatigue. That's why he left the city and came west. He doesn't really like to talk about it much, but he's getting better."

Marc interrupted her with his laugh. "Well, I'll be damned! So he's a *refugee*, too!"

Meg, surprised, said, "Why yes, I guess he is. He likes it up here. He's wonderful with the kids. He's a gentle thoughtful person, and we like each other and have a lot to talk about. That's most of what I know about him, Marc, but, actually, I believe I know him very well."

Marc had listened closely, and when she finished, he said, "I could tell, just from talking with him, that he's first-rate. Doris already suspected something was up between you two. Before she turned in she said, 'He loves her.' Women pick up on those things a lot faster than men ever could. That's Doris's opinion, at least." He laughed. "Yes, by God, he's a fine man."

Meg said, "Tolly and Charlie liked him very much, and were really sad that he had to leave now that their son is moving back to help run the farm. Tolly wrote me that she wanted to keep Flint in the family. She's the one I should thank for telling him about us up here."

She stopped talking and, putting her hand on Marc's arm, said, "All of this is new to Flint and me, Marc. We're just at the beginning. It might look like we're rushing things, but he's forty-five and there's no reason to wait. I've been in love with him from the moment I met him, and he tells me he feels the same. With his feelings for the kids, we'll be able to figure things out there, too. If he asks me to marry him, I'll do it in a minute. I'm that sure of him."

Marc studied her face solemnly for a long moment, then nodded and kissed her on her cheek and told her goodnight. Still holding her hand, he said, "Look, if my bride and I get up early and go back to town, just take that as our needing to be in our own home for a while. We really did stay too long in Seattle. Flint expects me to help him on some of the work in your kitchen, and I plan to do that. But for a few days, it would be nice for you two to have this house all to yourselves while you work things out. Tell him that from me, will you?"

Smiling, she said, "That sounds like some sort of a blessing, Marc. Is it?"

"I hadn't thought of it that way, but yes, it is." He released her hand and, grinning widely, said, "By God, it's a hell of a woman he's getting, a hell of a woman!" He was going up the steps and turned around. Winking at her, he said, "Take my advice and set the alarm tomorrow afternoon, so you two won't forget you have to pick up the kids at school." And with that he went up the stairs to bed.

As quickly as that, Meg found herself alone. She wasn't shaking so much now. It had been good to talk to Marc, and she was grateful he'd been there. Telling him about this sudden shift in her life had given her a chance to calm down and look at things more calmly. Even so, it would take her a while to comprehend what had happened, and to think about being with Flint tomorrow. What a wonderful thing it was to find out that he felt the same way as she did.

She pushed the remains of the log to the very back of the hearth, then went about turning off the lights in the room. Peering out the window from the dark room, she saw it was snowing more. It didn't look like it was going to snow for long; but then she had no experience with snow here. Hopefully, this front would give them just a little taste of what was going to come when real, true winter set in. She watched the flakes floating softly by the window a little longer.

She was tired, but her eyes lingered on the place in the trees where the cabin was located. On other nights, when she'd been roaming around, unable to sleep, she'd discovered that at the window's very farthest right side she'd been able to see the littlest twinkle of light through the trees coming from the window located over his bed. Seeing it, she'd been comforted by his being there and been able to go back to her own bed, imagining him reading there. But, tonight, with the snow falling, there was no tiny light; she couldn't even see the trees; and she had only her imagination to think of him being there. She hoped he was asleep and dreaming of tomorrow, just as she would be.

On her way to her bedroom she thought how odd it was that things could change so quickly. Yesterday it was fall and now it was winter. Yesterday she'd been lonely and now there was Flint. For a long time she'd dreaded looking into the mirror and acknowledging those little lines around her eyes and mouth and those strands of silver in her hair. Maybe all those things just looked more ominous when one was alone. Now, in her thirty-ninth year, with Flint in her life, she didn't have to face those getting-older years all by herself.

She undressed slowly, then pulled on her frayed blue robe and cinched it tightly around her middle. Scooping up the clothes and working methodically, she hung her cords on a hook in the closet, put her sweater away in a drawer, hung the blue birthday dress carefully on its padded hanger and brushed her blue shoes before putting them back into their box.

Deciding that it probably wouldn't kill her to look at herself closely, she went into the bathroom, went up to the mirror and studied her face as though she'd never really looked at it before. She saw that it was nice, really very nice indeed. Grey eyes with dark lashes under dark expressive brows, and a well-made nose that turned up a little at the end, like Ma's had. Her cheekbones and chin reminded her of Papa—strange she'd never noticed that before. Her hairline was shaped like his, too, coming down to a soft point in the middle. In a few years what silver hair she had would look like stylish highlights. After all her fears, she saw that the lines around her eyes and mouth probably *were* the result of smiling and laughing a lot. Twice tonight Flint had called her beautiful. Could it be that he was right and she was just a little beautiful? Was that what she needed to see—or only needed to hear from someone who mattered? Coming from his lips, it sounded true.

After washing her face and brushing her teeth furiously, she stood looking at herself. As she did, a sureness came into her mind. She was a woman of deep feelings and powerful emotions and strong convictions. She had made a stand tonight, but then, she'd been making a stand all along, with her commitment to her family and to this mountainside, and now to the man she loved. She just hadn't seen it so clearly before.

With that she took off her robe, climbed into bed, and turned off the bedside light.

. . .

She was just drifting off to sleep when she heard a tapping on her window. She sat up abruptly, reaching over to turn on the light and saw Flint through the glass of the window that faced onto the back porch. He looked embarrassed and shrugged apologetically, even as he gave her a hopeful smile. Meg grabbed her robe and dashed out into the kitchen, turning on lights as she went. Opening the backdoor, she saw him standing, unmoving, just outside the protective roof of the back porch, looking about as forlorn as anyone she'd ever seen.

She said, "Oh, Flint honey!"

He was wearing boots and had his jacket on over his pajamas, and both arms were laden. In one hand he was gripping his flashlight, his toothbrush, and razor. And in the other he was holding a snowy bundle that seemed to be his jeans and a shirt. Snow was piling up on everything, on his hair and his eyelashes. But he made no move to come in.

He blurted out, "I can't sleep. I'm going crazy. I've been crazy before tonight, every time I thought of you alone in your bed. I've imagined you just as you are now." He looked fully at her, at her bare feet, and her robe untied and half open. Even so, he backed up a bit. He said, "Coming here with my stuff, I know I look like I'm assuming a lot. But I have to tell you that after all the things we said on the doorstep, and after feeling your skin and your willingness…and knowing what you want and how we feel about each other…Hell, we were making love out there, Meg. And then we had to stop and just walk away from each other. I nearly came back to you, thinking, if only you could come back to the cabin with me. Then I thought about the kids, that they wouldn't know where you were in the morning and neither would the Websters."

He advanced a step toward her. "The thing is, babe, I can't be without you. It's not possible now. I never told you that I loved Annie. She was everything to me, and when I left New York I determined I would never love a woman again. I didn't want to take that chance and end up disappointed and crushed. At Tolly's farm I thought I was doing fine with my monastic life, out there in the bunkhouse. But that ended and I came up here and found you.

"I've been alone for a long time, too. I know the full bite of being without love. Finding you and your kids has made me realize that I've been given another chance. I'm a decent chap, and I'd be proud to help you raise those kids. But you; you're everything I've ever wanted a woman to be, but never thought possible. I've loved you from the very first time I saw you. Did I tell you that? I feel we were meant to be together."

He closed his eyes a moment. "I want us married, at least that's what I believe we were talking about on the step. You're maybe thinking, 'Who in hell is he?' or 'I haven't known him long enough.' But time doesn't matter in this case, Meg. I think we already know the answer to that. I want you by my side. You and I can be more and be better if we have the person we love in our lives. That's what I believe, Meg.

"Does that sound like I'm just making this up so I can come inside, out of this snow, and make love to you? If it does, then I'm doing this all wrong. What I'm asking is, will you have me? What tormented me back at the cabin was what would the kids think if I came out of your room tomorrow morning—the ethics of our living together and sleeping together for the short while before we're married. The last thing I want is to confuse them. But, on the other hand, I don't think I could stand going back to the cabin without you, and tomorrow is just too far away. So what are your thoughts on this, Meg? I mean, what can we do about this?"

While Meg listened to his cascade of words she was trying not to smile, but laughter was bubbling up and she didn't know if she could stop it. Instead, she pulled him into the warm kitchen and closed the door behind him, then kissed his cold cheek while she brushed the snow out of his hair and off his jacket. She took the bundle of clothes from his one hand, shook them out, and laid them on the counter, along with his flashlight and toothbrush and razor. As she helped him out of his jacket, she told him to take off his boots and leave them by the door. And he did that. Then she just stood in front of him, shaking her head and looking at him with a love and a longing that came up from her toes and gathered every feeling it was possible to show him along their way. She said, "I love you and I want you, dear man." She picked up his hands and examined them, brought them to her mouth and kissed their palms and his fingers. Then, giving him a little push, she pointed him toward her bedroom.

She spoke softly, "Don't worry about the kids, Flint. In the morning we'll just tell them that you're going to be their daddy. That's all they want to hear."

EPILOGUE

He had come around to the back of the house, searching for a favorite hammer he'd left, and he now stood watching her. She was hanging sheets on the clothesline, a lumpy bag of clothespins tied around her waist—the still-new bag she'd sewn herself.

Grinning at him around the clothespin in her mouth, she tilted her face up to the sun for a moment. Then she gestured grandly, with the wet sheet in her hand, toward the view of the clearing and the mountain across from them. No words, just that gesture, and her eyes steady and sweet. When she finished hanging the sheet—all the while holding him with her eyes—she reached up and gave the clothesline a possessive pat and tipped her head to the side and smiled.

He came over to her and kissed her throat. Then he helped her finish hanging up her wash, finding the sheets' corners and shaking them out before handing them to her to pin up.

In all that time they didn't speak in words, but in little murmurs—there was no need for words. Her pleasure in the clothesline, and her sharing her joy, in using the morning and the wind this way, was more of a thank you than he could have imagined.

These little things, he thought, these little precious things. She couldn't know how good she looked; her lovely dark hair, once caught back in that silver clip, but loosened now by the breeze and crossing her face in dark strands, and her joyful eyes. And the sheets, stretching and floating out, filling with wind, looking as though happy lovers still tumbled about inside them. And his camera lying forgotten back in the house. Then again, how could a camera record all this that was before him—and inside his heart.

ABOUT THE AUTHOR

Trudi Carleton Peek was born in the wheat growing part of Central Montana, but spent most of her life in mountainous Western Montana—Helena, Missoula, and Bozeman. She now lives in Port Orchard, WA.

Touching Earth, Touching Sky is her first book. Although her professional career has been as an illustrator and artist, she has always written...and those essays and stories are always about Montana...